Karolinum Press

ABOUT THE AUTHOR

Alfonz Bednár (1914–1989) was a Slovak novelist, screenwriter and translator who used innovative creative methods in depicting the social situation after World War II. His stark, unflinching stories of the Slovak National Uprising were particularly notable. After 1945, he worked at the Information Commission in Bratislava, was a lecturer at the Pravda publishing house and editor of the Slovak Writer publishing house. He went on to work for twenty years as a screenwriter and screenplay editor at Czechoslovak Film in Bratislava. He wrote the screenplay for one of the most acclaimed films of Slovak cinema, *The Sun in a Net* (*Slnko v sieti*).

His entry into the literary world came by way of his translations of English-language prose, including the work of Ernest Hemingway, George Bernard Shaw, Mark Twain and Daniel Defoe. *The Hours and The Minutes* was first published in 1956 and became a vital influence for the Slovak fiction of the more open 1960s as well as writing that burst forth following the fall of Communism in 1989.

MODERN SLOVAK CLASSICS

Alfonz Bednár
The Hours
and The Minutes

Translated from the Slovak by David Short

Afterword by Rajendra Chitnis

KAROLINUM PRESS 2025

KAROLINUM PRESS is a publishing department
of Charles University
Ovocný trh 560/5, 116 36 Prague 1, Czech Republic
www.karolinum.cz, redakcenk@ruk.cuni.cz

The translation and publication of this work was supported
using public funding by Slovak Literature Abroad (SLOLIA).

Slovak
   Literary
Centre

Graphic design based on the original concept by Zdeněk Ziegler
Cover by Karolinum Press
Copyediting by Michael Stein
Set in the Czech Republic by Karolinum Press
First English edition

Cataloging-in Publication Data is available
from the National Library of the Czech Republic

ISBN 978-80-246-5896-4 (pbk)
ISBN 978-80-246-5911-4 (pdf)
ISBN 978-80-246-5912-1 (epub)

Printed and bound by CPI Group (UK) Ltd, Croydon, CRO 4YY

CONTENTS

Štefan Tesár, a small but sturdy man of twenty-five, a labourer at the large mill in Lower Brezany, was short of sleep, physically worn out and, for the first time in his life, starting to have misgivings, not yet about himself, but about the group of partisans who'd stayed with him, and about everything around him.

"What can anyone do here?" Tesar's group kept asking, and having drifted into silence they would apply the question mentally to anything and everything. "It's a lost cause!"

The town, where flags were already flying – red flags with a yellow hammer and sickle and tricolours with a blue triangle, bells were ringing and the municipal public address system was blaring out words long only whispered, "To hell with 'em! Death to the German occupiers!", suddenly saw German troops come charging in. The partisans who'd come pouring in on foot or on wagons, singing as they came, had now fled, leaving only Tesár and four others. Tesár was from Závodie, as were four of the others: Hladík, Lánik, Masňák and Šiška. He'd known them from way back, but sensed that he couldn't entirely rely on them, any more than on the two from Lower Brezany and one from Upper Brezany, who'd linked up with the men from Závodie as they fled ahead of the German troops. By now the town was overrun with Krauts, who'd soon be all over the villages as well. Which way to turn? What can anyone do here? It's all over! This line of thinking had beset Tesár's group back in the town and it was still tormenting them, though the group knew full well that taking up arms wasn't a good idea, and abandoning them an even worse one.

There'd been eight of them, and they had submachine guns, cartridges, hand grenades and, in their kitbags, bread, some tinned army rations and cigarettes.

Tesár was biting the nails on his left hand, Hladík, who'd taken some blankets with him when he deserted from the army, was munching on a bitter-tasting bit of wood snapped off a dead willow twig, Šiška, a young blacksmith from the Lower Brezany estate, was musing on how good it would be to spray the Krauts with submachine gun fire, Masňák, a mechanic from the Lower Brezany brickworks, was thinking of his fiancée, who came from as far away as Nitra, and Láník, a young lad who'd just done his school-leaving exams, wanted to escape back home, fearful of the disservice he'd done his father, having been to grammar school at the latter's expense only to run out on him to join the partisans. Besides these there were the three others.

They were on foot, going nowhere in particular, and having managed, early that morning, to escape from Lower Brezany, where they'd been hiding in barns and sheds for the last three days, here they were, heading along the road to Závodie.

What can anyone do here? Tesár sensed the question coming from the seven sleep-deprived and physically exhausted men, all poorly clad and ill-shod, except Hladík, who'd escaped from his barracks suited and booted well enough. What's barely begun can't possibly be lost. The Soviets are marching towards the Carpathians, they'll attack Warsaw, there are Soviet partisans in the Slovak mountains, and the Uprising is being joined by deserters – how could all this be a lost cause?

"There's nothing for it!" Tesár suddenly called the silent men to order, turned his back on them and trotted a few yards ahead of them. His thick black eyebrows quivered above his black eyes. "We must get off the road, cut across the Závodie fields, get some proper rest in Grabovec, that small wood over there, and then head off to the Poruba forest! And there join the partisans! On the upland meadows of Kopečné Lazy, beyond Little Poruba, there's a partisan brigade. There's nothing for it but to hit the Krauts hard, because everything they do is evil."

It was Saturday morning, before the second Sunday in September.

Following what Tesár had said, the eight men, unspeaking and grumpy, went another two hundred metres or so along the road before turning off across the fields.

The fields of Závodie were black with freshly ploughed-up stubble, green with the clover patches springing up over any unploughed stubble, yellow with maize and millet and brown with potatoes left to dry out. The air was torpid with a silent autumn mist, grey, delicate and light, the pale-blue sky arching above it and the motionless, blue wavy outline of the mountains rearing up in the far distance.

The eight unspeaking partisans kept looking back down the grey-white road as if it were some gigantic snake that might fill up at any moment with the grey-green venom of the Germans.

The road led out from the town through Lower and Upper Brezany, then Závodie, after which it rose gently and, before vanishing among woods and forests, it also took in Great and Little Poruba. Beyond the areas covered in trees it dipped towards the distant valley where the people of Lower and Upper Brezany, Závodie, and Great and Little Poruba knew lay Kopečné Lazy, a wretchedly poor village that straggled out along the valley and up the hillsides. All it produced was some pretty awful barley. At the end of August '44 they knew there were some partisans there.

The road had always been a busy one, but since late August, when the whole of Závodie had shuddered at whispered reports of the slaughtering, in Turčiansky Svätý Martin, of fifteen high-ranking German officers and even two generals, and the declaration in Banská Bystrica of an uprising against the Germans, the traffic had died away – though that Saturday morning, as Tesár and his men were making for the small wood near Závodie, dust began to rise from the road and settle on every tree, bush and field as German soldiers in trucks and on motor bikes drove into Závodie.

Tesár's partisans froze when they spotted the dark-grey vehicles and watched in fear as they disappeared from sight in Závodie. A good thing that they'd listened to what Tesár had said! Tesár meant no ill. He likely knew what he was about. But what was going to happen in Závodie? In fear, they scrambled into the wood called Grabovec, standing there as it did in the middle of Závodie's fields and meadows.

"Things In Závodie," said Hladík, spitting out his bit of bitter willow wood, "are going to get lively."

Lánik the school-leaver gave a little shudder.

Three German motorcycles and eleven trucks, with their slanting front ends and looking from the side like little cottages, came to a halt in the centre of Závodie, in sight of the church, school and rectory, in sight of the large inn, the council offices and the fire brigade's storehouse, and at the foot of the tall black pole up which the firemen, after training sessions or fires, would hang their wet hoses to dry, having hauled them up high on a thin steel cable. Scores of German troops alighted from the trucks, all covered in dust and in a foul mood.

They spread out all over Závodie.

In the larger homes, they made people clear out any rooms that had outer walls against the garden or street, but they had to clear them out completely, leaving nothing at all but the stove. The man seeing to that was Sergeant Franz Eulenau, a burly redhead who accompanied his men through the houses, demanding loudly to know if the rooms were "heizbar". His interpreter, a slim, young private, Joseph Hoffmann, whose mouth was all lop-sided, asked the people: "Ken zis rum be heetit?" The people more or less got what he meant and, as they began clearing a room out, were horrified at the prospect of the Krauts staying a long time, doubtless all winter, since they were asking if the rooms could be heated. Whether silently, under their breath or out loud, they cursed the redhead and wry-mouth, but their fears did nothing to prevent them giving both men nicknames that very first Saturday: Sergeant Eulenau they started calling Heatbag and his interpreter Hoffmann Heetit.

At the Bernadič house, where only the youngest daughter, sixteen-year-old Marka, was at home, they checked out both the front and back rooms, after which Sergeant Eulenau yelled at the bewildered Marka: "Nicht heizbar?", and the interpreter Hoffmann said: "Zis not heatit!", because in Mr Bernadič's new house there was as yet no stove in either room.

Then Eulenau and Hoffmann moved on to Bernadič's neighbours, the Letanovskýs.

Mr Letanovský himself was at home alone, his wife having gone chasing after her geese, which were forever running away, his son Jožo and his bride Brigita having been out in the fields since first thing, and the grandchildren not being back from school yet. He'd been on the point of chopping down a young walnut tree.

He was gripped with fear and followed the soldiers into the front room. In the back room his fears only got worse, because Eulenau said "Nicht ausräumen!" and the interpreter, Hoffmann, wagged a menacing finger at him and announced: "Leaf efferysink heer! Moof nossink! Zis one hess heetink!"

"Sorry?" Letanovský queried, and with one thumb and forefinger he pushed back his old, greasy and faded brown hat slightly. "What am I supposed to do?"

The slim, young private Hoffmann started waving both arms in the direction of the new tile stove and the two wide beds standing by the wall with their pillows and damask-covered blankets strewn about them and said: "Leef so! No tidy avay! Heer iss Herr Kommandant!"

Letanovský got the drift, was horror-stricken and stopped asking questions.

Filled with fear, he watched through the window as the redhead and wry-mouth left the yard, stood awhile alone in the back room, quite still, because it occurred to him that any move could cause trouble, not only to him, but to many others as well, perhaps to the whole of Závodie, but then he took in the whole room, looked at the two coverlets and the two pale-blue floral-patterned oval shapes not covered by damask pillow cases, and then quickly, as quickly as he could muster, he gathered up four pairs of pyjamas from the bed, the scented soap, toothpaste and tooth-brushes from the metal basin, along with the sponge, the posh handtowels and eau de cologne, dashed all round the place with them before finally taking them up to the grain loft, where he buried it all under the wheat. Beneath it he also buried the two leather suitcases into which, in the back room, he had crammed their best clothes. Then he sat down on the bench beneath the young walnut tree, sat there for quite some time before going round to his neighbour, Mr Bernadič, for some advice on what to do for the best. Before his eyes he still had the image of the two pale-blue, floral-patterned ovals. He couldn't rid himself of it, couldn't blot them from his mind in any way, because he knew it was all the coverlets' fault. They were the one thing the redhead had noticed, which was why he'd got the idea that the Kommandant would get his best night's sleep in their back room. Good God!

Next door he found sixteen-year-old Marka Bernadič sitting on the threshold, barefoot, with her new canvas shoes tossed under the bench, and shelling beans.

She gave Letanovský just a hint of a smile, because he looked so very scared and wan, looked at him with the puzzled green eyes that were almost hidden behind her relaxed eyelids, and began to speak in her perpetually slightly mocking tone.

"What's wrong, neighbour?" she asked, addressing him the way her mother and father always did. "What's happened?"

"Nothing much, Marka. Where's your mum and dad?"

"They're stacking the clover for seed."

"My lot are out there too, it's a nice day for it – and, tell me, did they come here as well, the redhead and wry-mouth?"

"You mean Heatbag and Heetit?"

"What?"

"Heatbag and Heetit."

"The redhead and the one with the twisty gob?"

"They did."

"And?"

"Nothing. They looked round the house and left. The thin one, the one with the twisted mug, he was funny. He could only open one half of his mouth. Said our place had no heet-ink."

"And did they say anything else?"

"Not sure. All the first one said was 'heatbag' and the one with the twisted gob 'heetit'. They did say something else, but who on earth could make any sense of it!" Marka grabbed another fistful of dry bean pods in her left hand. "But why should we be bothered! There've been Krauts in Lower Brezany for some days now and nothing's come of it. Fear not, neighbour! Nothing's going to happen to you."

"Marka!" Letanovský began scratching his right arm above the elbow from under his rolled-up sleeve, pondering as he let his gaze roam over the fine figure of Bernadič's daughter, who was wearing a light, red, printed-cotton dress. He stroked his moustache, which he always kept trimmed so that it wouldn't poke out beyond the edges of his straight nose. He'd always trimmed it like that in imitation of a lieutenant-colonel he'd seen in Russia during the Great War and still frequently recalled. "Marka, listen. You've got a fine pair of legs. Would you mind trotting over to Grabovec? Mr Schnitzer's there, and his wife, and the kids with them. For a fortnight now they've been spending their days in the wood so as not to be caught by the Germans if they happened to show up. And now the Germans are here. Go on, run over there and tell them not to come back to Závodie. And you can also tell them that the Kommandant will be sleeping in our back room! And that no beds were to be moved! He'll be sleeping in their bedding. God preserve us!"

Marka Bernadič stopped shelling her beans.

"The Kommandant, Marka," Mr Letanovský repeated. "You won't forget that, will you?"

"Kommandant?" Marka asked. "And what's that mean?"

"Nothing, a commander, a man who gives out orders. Just tell Mr Schnitzer."

"As you wish, neighbour. I'm on my way. I'm honestly not as scared as you are. I'll be right back."

She took her new black canvas shoes from under the bench and put them on, smoothed her bright red dress down over her burgeoning young frame, pulled her white headscarf tighter over her fair hair and ran off towards Grabovec, the little wood amid Závodie's fields and meadows.

The German soldiers showed no regard for anyone or anything and put down their noxious green-grey roots in Závodie.

Wherever no men were at home to remove any beds, tables, cupboards and holy pictures from a room they removed them themselves, then brought in straw and hammered hooked nails into the walls on which to hang their caps and any lighter bits of equipment. At the rectory, in the village priest's office, they set up their command post and fixed a sign on the front wall of the building bearing the legend *Ortskommandantur*, while in the village school they set up their kitchens. In the large school playground they parked those great trucks with their slanting noses, their artillery pieces, trench mortars and motor bikes, and from Upper Brezany to Závodie and all about Závodie itself they installed telephone lines. Their commanding officer, a tall, lanky, forty-five-year-old infantryman, Captain Johann Iffland, a man with blond hair, trimmed right back above his forehead, had had himself welcomed by Father Stachovič right there in front of the rectory, and told him: "Gut, gut, mein Herr!", Stachovič having sought to assure him that the German troops would find Závodie to their satisfaction and, with Hoffman, interrogated the mayor, Janderla, as to the presence of partisans in Závodie. "I don't know, Herr Kommandant," Janderla kept repeating, a thin young man with sunken cheeks, he was. "So far they haven't been here – and I'm sure they won't show up now because they steer clear of anywhere where there's German troops, Herr Kommandant." In his turn, Captain Johann Iffland believed him and ordered Janderla to have it proclaimed that the front door of every house must carry a sign listing all its residents! Anyone leaving the house to work in field or forest must have their citizen's identity card with them. On pain of being otherwise shot, along with their entire family, everyone had to ensure that their house was blacked out, there would be a six o'clock curfew and no one was to leave their premises before six a.m. On all houses where soldiers were billeted Sergeant Eulenau wrote "X 236" in green chalk, and in front of the houses, the rectory and the school and on the road at both ends of Závodie, from Upper Brezany and from Great Poruba, patrols were instituted, armed with rapid-firing rifles fitted with angled magazines.

Marka Bernadič was running across the fields and meadows to Grabovec as Letanovský had instructed her, running to find Mr Schnitzer, his wife and their two children, running as fast as she could to tell Mr Schnitzer what Letanovský had told her to say. She kept repeating to herself that the Kommandant would be sleeping in Letanovský's back room under the Schnitzers' bedclothes. Running, not along cart tracks or footpaths, but across ploughland, across clover and maize fields, quite unaware of the soil that was getting inside her nice new canvas shoes, just running to get there as fast as possible, because she was fond of both her neighbour, Mr Letanovský, and the Schnitzers. Goodness knows where the latter are now. By the spring, for sure. There they'll also have water to drink. And it's so very hot! Marka wiped her brow with the back of her hand and carried on running.

Mr Letanovský, with heavy boots on his feet and wearing patched trousers, a waistcoat, and a shirt with the sleeves rolled up, and with an old greasy, faded hat on his head, sat there on his garden bench beside the young walnut tree, staring in a state of surly abstraction at the walnut leaves which – yellowed and slightly soggy – had fallen that morning on the dew-covered ground.

He said not a word to his wife as she returned about ten, driving the geese before her, nor she to him, merely fluttering her faded lips inaudibly, and when his son's two lads came running in from school shouting: "Granddad, Granddad, we won't be going to school anymore, it's being turned into a kitchen!" he told them: "Much better if you were!" Then he became even more surly and abstracted.

He stared at the yellowed walnut leaves stuck to the ground. Poor Marka! Why had he sent her there? Really, a chap never knows what he's doing. Goodness, he could have gone to Grabovec himself. God preserve us!

The Letanovský and Bernadič gardens were both humming with bees. Both men were great beekeepers and great neighbours. They had a honey extractor that they shared as well as other beekeeping paraphernalia. And they frequently sought each other's advice.

Mr Letanovský couldn't leave his bench because his son Jožo and his young bride Brigita had come in from the fields lost in thought and grumpy, and they didn't say a word as they passed.

The entire Letanovský household knew things were going to turn nasty, and no one wanted to bring the bad times forward with idle chatter, arguing or even worse things.

Mr Letanovský was thinking not just of Marka Bernadič, but also of the Schnitzers, two adults and two children, who'd been in hiding at his place since the spring. Závodie had mumbled and grumbled about his harbouring Jews, but gradually forgot about them because the Schnitzers kept well out of sight. Also forgotten was the tittle-tattle about Letanovský getting money and gold from them later. On his bench beneath the walnut tree he now felt that the Schnitzers were no longer his affair alone. The whole village was affected. Someone might betray him to the Germans. Betray? Maybe people would be fearful of doing anything so terrible. Then it occurred to him: which was worth more, his life or the lives of the four Schnitzers? But no, people are wicked and devious. Someone's bound to betray him? What will the National Guard chaps do? They've been making themselves scarce because the Germans would very much like to coerce them into tackling the partisans. But he's not the only one who matters here. There's the whole family. God preserve us! What do the Germans care about shooting the odd entire family? Two families – ten families? The entire village? They'd shot up more than one already. His life – the four Schnitzers – his own family, many families, Marka, everybody in Závodie... Why did he do it? Why had he let his son, the student, talk him into taking the Schnitzers in? Because – because he's known the Schnitzers for a long time, he'd known the older generation of Schnitzers as well – and helping others is the proper thing to do. Why has this whole thing hit people. He remembered the men who'd left Závodie to join the partisans. He knew about them. Mr Bernadič had whispered it to him. The Schnitzers, Jews – they'd always been cheats and deceivers, disgusting people, filthy, unless someone right-minded cleaned them up... Inside Letanovský his anger against them was rising because he knew they wouldn't give him anything, wouldn't pay him back as promised – they'd bring him at best to rack and ruin. He sat on his bench beneath the walnut tree, staring at the leaves, tunnelled lengthwise by tiny little maggots, quite dinky with their twisting green and brown lines, those leaves stuck to the ground.

After one o'clock, his neighbour Mr Bernadič came in from the fields along with his wife, his son Ondriš and his wife and the three grandchildren, and with two girls, Marka's sisters.

Mr Letanovský rose from his garden bench and went in after Mr Bernadič to tell him what had happened and why he'd sent Marka to Grabovec wood. And to consult him. Should he, Letanovský, include the Schnitzers on the list of people residing at his house? He ought to. After all, they're good people, do no harm to anyone and the Bernadič's have long known about them. And then no one has had any faith in Hitler for a long time now. Not even the National Guard men. They'd have betrayed him by now. They've particularly lost faith in him since that assassination attempt, and Závodie, always such a quiet spot... A quiet spot unless things were to take a turn for the worse, as long as nothing was going on. But what now –?

"What's this then, neighbour?" Mr Bernadič broke in on Mr Letanovský's ruminating and, filled with rage, he flung his fork down in front of the porch with a clang. His face, pock-marked and with a week's worth of black stubble, filled with rage. "What are you doing here? We've been good neighbours, but don't you darken my door again ever! You're harbouring Jews! Just wait and see, the whole village will pay the price. What got into you, neighbour...? Were you hoping to make some easy money, come by some property...? You'll be getting nothing from Schnitzer now –!"

"Where's your common sense, neighbour?" Mrs Bernadič interrupted her husband as she turned to face Mr Letanovský. "Good God, man! A fine mess you've got us into! And the whole village!"

"Shut it, woman!" her husband snapped under his breath. "Stop waffling!"

She muttered another Dear God and burst into tears.

"Just wait!" said Bernadič, threatening to go for Letanovský, "you'll pay dearly for this if things go bad because of those Jews! I always told you to leave Jews well alone, but you refused to listen."

"You never said any such thing," Letanovský muttered, "not once."

"Since when have you been so clever?" Letanovský's son Jožo shouted across the fence and spat on the ground. "Don't you go threatening people and keep your hands to yourself! There are soldiers around, we just have to keep our mouths shut and it'll all be all right!"

"And where's Marka?" Mrs Bernadič asked weepily, because she'd spotted the bowl on the bench outside the door with a handful of shelled beans in it. "Marka! Maaarkaaa!"

Letanovský turned round. His whole body was numb with fear. His bloodshot eyes were burning with fear. His stomach was gripped with pain.

"Maaarkaaa!"

From a distance the ground boomed as shells fell, it shook, and the window in the Bernadičes' back room rattled.

In vain did Mr Letanovský wait for Marka Bernadič. There was no sign of her returning. Where is she? Where is she? He couldn't stop thinking about her. Whether sitting out on the bench in the garden, or at the kitchen table, whether he was wandering aimlessly around the yard, the byre or the barn, he kept asking himself: Where is she? Where is Marka? And where are the Schnitzers? What's become of them? Are they in the wood, safe, or not? But where else could they be? There's nowhere else to hide in the whole of Závodie. Only in Grabovec. And what if they did return, for God's sake? Christ Almighty! If only Marka came back, one would know what to do –

The troops saw Captain Iffland installed in the Letanovskýs' back room. The whole house reeked of soldiery, eau de Cologne, tobacco, cigarette smoke and clothes, even quite recently mothballed away in a wardrobe, but now stinking of sweat.

Like this, the Letanovskýs could hardly breathe, because with every breath the stench merely magnified their fear.

"Letanoffski?" Iffland inquired, stroking his rugged features and smiling at him. "Alles in Ordnung, alles gut?"

"Gut, gut," Letanovský assured him, "it's fine, Herr Kommandant."

It wasn't at all fine, because Marka still wasn't back, either that afternoon or in the evening.

Night fell, clear, but dark and cold. And silent as the grave.

In Závodie no dogs barked, because people had locked them away in stables and byres. Few slept that night. In the Letanovský house, on whose doorpost hung a sign bearing the names "Ján Letanovský, Anna Letanovský, Jozef Letanovský, Brigita Letanovský, Štefan Letanovský, Benedikt Letanovský", no one slept except Jožo's boys, Štefan and Benedikt, no one, and no one was asleep next door either, except one little girl and two boys, the Bernadič grandchildren. The Bernadičes waited for Marka until nightfall and when she didn't return, no one dared step outside after six pm to report to Janderla, the mayor, or to the German command post that Marka was missing. Where was she? Where had she gone? Had she run off to get away from the Krauts? Was she too scared to come back?

Mr Letanovský lay huddled up in bed in the front room, not sleeping. His left arm hung down, lifeless, over the edge of the bed. He was thinking about the Bernadičes, Marka and the Schnitzers, and about himself.

During the war he'd seen, in Russia, that the German is a ruthless being, unforgiving and remorseless even to his own. The lieutenant colonel whose moustaches Letanovský had modelled his own on had had a 'lad'. The 'lad' had gone home on furlough, killed his parents and, on his return, was eating the bacon he'd brought back with him. The lieutenant colonel's horse had gone for the bacon and scratched his muzzle on the knife... In vain did the lad plead with the lieutenant colonel, there was no help for him, he had to dig his own grave and then the lieutenant colonel shot him. "But nothing happened to him at home," the soldiers said afterwards, one of whom had been Letanovský, "for killing his mother and father, and now this..." – "It's just divine retribution, fellers," Letanovský had told them. "That's all." – "Yeah, that's it!" – "No horse, however handsome, is worth more than a father and mother!" – "After all, nothing happened to it, just a slight scratch." Although Letanovský had believed it to be divine retribution, he also came to believe that a German is unforgiving and remorseless.

But this Kommandant of ours doesn't look that villainous, Letanovský was thinking about Iffland as he lay there in bed. One might perhaps have a word with him, tell him everything, but everything might –.

Bernadič was lying on his bed in his coat and trousers. His boots were the only thing he'd taken off. He was wondering whether to inform on Letanovský to the Kommandant so as to be excused for Marka's absence. But how could he do that? Letanovský's a decent chap and the Schnitzers are decent folk. Not even Krauts spot everything, no matter how they snoop about. Fitfully he stroked his stubbly, gnarled, pock-marked face.

The clear, dark, cold night dragged on, then as Sunday morning dawned around six, Závodie was cloaked in a delicate morning mist. The air was dank, the dusty ground damp with the mist and dew.

Bernadič, booted and wearing his patched trousers and an old coat, which was now too tight about his broad shoulders, and in the hat that had a greasy sheen at the back, was the first to be seen walking through the village.

He had been despatched from home to Upper Brezany, to his brother's place, to check whether Marta hadn't run off there.

But why there? There are Krauts there too. If he doesn't find her there, he'll have to try Great Poruba as well. She might have escaped to her aunt's place. The wet dust clung to his boots. Behind him lay grey footprints of dry dust. Where can she have gone? Have they picked her up? But where, and why?

"Halt!" a soldier barked at him at the edge of the village. "Weg, weg!"

Bernadič stopped.

The soldier, a tall green-grey fellow in jackboots, with a helmet that covered his forehead, indicated by brusque, neg-ative hand gestures that he was to turn back.

That morning was the start of one terrible Sunday for Závodie, that damp morning, misty and dewy, terrible not just for the village itself, but also for the German soldiers, because within an hour, around seven, the German troops knew everything: that at the Letanovskýs in Závodie there were Jews in hiding, two adults and two juveniles, and in addition, five young men, Matej Hladík, Ján Šiška, Anton Masňák, Josef Lánik and Štefan Tesár, had left the village to join the partisans.

"Vere are ze Chews?" the slim young private Hoffmann bawled at Letanovský at the command post. "Heff you got zem?"

Pale, Letanovský trembled.

"I know where they are," he said, "but they're not in Závodie."

Captain Iffland was seated at the priest's desk, nervously twiddling a cigarette. Bits of tobacco fell out of it onto the scrap of paper on which were written out the names of the Schnitzers, the partisans and the latter's fathers. He licked the cigarette along its length, inspected it and pointed it at the pale Letanovský.

"All four Jews," he said to the interpreter, Hoffmann, "are to be brought to the command post! If he fails to bring them –" and he again pointed his cigarette at the quaking Letanovský, "– if he fails to bring them, tell him he'll be shot and his whole family with him! He is to go and bring them in with soldiers in attendance – thirty men!"

Private Hoffmann passed this on in no uncertain terms.

"Solchiers vill go viz you," he added mockingly with one half of his twisted mouth, "in case enysink heppens to you!"

Letanovský set off for Grabovec wood with the thirty men.

Fear descended on Letanovský's wife, whose pale lips were still twitching, on his son Jožo and the latter's young wife Brigita, and on their two sons. It was a leaden fear. It bore down on their breasts grievously, as if their breasts had been driven through by a solid wooden fencepost. Fear descended over the whole of Závodie. Who'd informed on Letanovský for shielding Jews? Who'd given the partisans away? Fear inhibited people's preparations for Sunday, they couldn't eat, and some couldn't even breathe.

Mrs Letanovský kept muttering a prayer with her pale twitching lips, whether she was sitting somewhere or pottering about the house or yard.

"May he be smitten by God!" she said in the hearing of all, with her back to the Bernadič house. "May he be smitten from now till eternity!"

"Do you think," Letanovský's pale-faced son Jožo asked, "that he's the one who betrayed them?"

"Of course it was him!"

In the Bernadič house a row was followed by tears. Mrs Bernadič wept for Marka, for her daughter-in-law and for Marka's sisters, and the children were also crying.

"Why didn't you put Marka's name on the list?" Ondriš Bernadič asked his father. "You should have."

"How so – when she isn't even here!"

"And when she comes back?"

"Then I'll add her!" Then, just to reassure himself, he added: "Nobody's even checked the lists yet."

"But you'll have missed the boat!" said Ondriš mockingly. "By then there'll be no point adding her name."

"Shut up!" Bernadič roared back. "You've no more sense than a tail-flicking cow. Just put a sock in it! I can see that much for myself: not adding names – bad; adding them – even worse!" He went and got a watercolour pencil and laboriously added at the bottom of his sign: "Mária Bernadič." He stared long at his clumsy lettering with the frightened green eyes set in his twitching, pockmarked face.

At the rectory, Captain Iffland had completed his interrogation of the mayor, Janderla, and although Janderla's sunken cheeks had quivered as he repeatedly said: "I couldn't have known, sir, if anyone from here had gone to join the partisans, honest, nor could I have known that Letanovský was hiding some Jews," he did believe him for the time being, looked him up and down, and, having let him go, brooding over the sheer folly of it, over collective responsibility, he ran one hand over his rugged, unshaven face, leaned back against the old armchair behind Stachovič's desk and gazed abstractedly about the rectory office. He should have had it cleared out, he thought, because it struck him that the books, holy pictures, the ancient clock on top of the safe and the brown leather armchairs and long leather sofa sat ill with his soldiers. He should have had the whole lot slung out!

All this old stuff – the priest was also old – it reminded him too much of civvy street. He took a closer look round and the old, hitherto undisturbed cosiness of the place swept over him. Once again he felt that for over a year now his life had been drowning in all things alien: his own soldiers were alien to him, his very nation, so eager for the spoils of war, so eager to make the entire world its own, was alien to him... While here, every quarter of an hour, the ancient clock strikes, quietly, calmly, but now in an alien manner... This parish priest, he lives here, doubtless surrounded by many dear and devoted people – while he, Captain Iffland, has no one, and devotion cannot be exacted at gunpoint.

On the one hand he himself, he mused, around him his men, men alien to him, and even more alien, and more dangerous, the members of the security service, the Sicherheitsdienst, SD... And against all that a defenceless, inferior rabble, defenceless Jews and dangerous partisans. A moment of devotion, any, would mean an awful lot in this life, but... The war desires him to survive it, if he does, amid the alien! So he mused and, resting both arms on Father Stachovič's desk, he perused the names of the Jews and partisans. Hitler's orders were to shoot anyone who so much as glared at a German soldier! No, not that, that only leads to a major action. And major actions have no borders, they just drive the populace to go and join the partisans. War's war, nothing like what goes on inside the heads of the men from the SD. War has its laws, its order, its sense of fair play...

He glanced towards the two pale-eyed, sturdy SD men, Poller and Dosse, who were sitting on the priest's leather sofa.

Poller and Dosse were smoking as they stared in silence out of the windows.

War's war, Iffland was thinking. A soldier commits no crime once he realises that his actions might be criminal, a soldier seeks redress once he has conducted an investigation and caught the actual culprits, a soldier respects human life, the honour and safety of families, private property, freedom of confession, the observance of rituals – a soldier respects everything –

He glanced at Poller and Dosse.

He thought about collective responsibility. Utter rubbish, crazy: one man does something – and fifty or more others pay for it with their lives –

The field telephone jangled. Iffland had had it placed on Father Stachovič's prie-dieu, which was then moved to alongside the desk.

Soldiers were moving about inside the priest's office, bringing in their kitbags, visors, helmets, submachine guns, blankets, plus two small safes, a green field table and two chairs, and crates of ammunition.

Poller and Dosse were staring mutely out of the windows with their pale eyes and smoking.

Iffland hung up and, having glanced pensively towards Poller and Dosse, ordered brought to him, one by one, the five fathers of the five betrayed partisans.

He questioned them only briefly, because he knew they wouldn't tell him the truth and were not to be believed.

The one-eyed roadmender Hladík said he had no idea where his son Matěj had gone, because he'd enlisted in the spring and hadn't come back yet, though several of his mates were now back, the little sapper, Šiška, who as recently as Saturday had still been working at the Poruba lime works, merely shook his head when Hoffmann as interpreter asked him: "Iss yor son wiz ze partizanss?", and Iffland certainly didn't believe the tall, thin brickmaker Masňák, who claimed that his son was getting married and had gone off to see the parents – his future in-laws, who lived a long way off, out towards Nitra.

"We were supposed to go as well –!"

Iffland had Masňák the brickmaker led back out. "Und du, Lanik?"

"I, begging your pardon, sir, I really don't know." Lánik, whom people had begun mockingly to call Fruity, because he'd planted one of his fields with apple trees and started growing apples such as had never before been seen in Závodie, was a good man, but he was shaking, twisting his hands down beside his hips and thinking about the beautiful young trees that were about, that very year, to give him his first crop of apples. "My son's a student – and even colleges are being shut down – I don't know where he is because –"

"Ja, Student!" Iffland waved a dismissive hand at Lánik and turned his attention to Tesár, who'd just been brought in: "Und du?"

Tesár, a diminutive local journeyman, said nothing.

"Iss yor son Stefan viz ze partissanss?"

Journeyman Tesár failed to respond.

Iffland nodded to the pale-eyed Poller and Dosse.

They crossed over to Tesár and pushed him up against Father Stachovič's bookshelf.

"Iss yor son Stefan viz ze partissanss?"

Tesár remained silent.

"Are you goin' to say sumssink, or not?"

Journeyman Tesár remained silent.

Poller punched him in the face. Tesár crashed into the priest's bookshelf, and when Poller punched him in the face a second time, he bounced off towards Dosse. Dosse's huge mitt caught Tesár in the face from behind and sent him lurching back into the priest's books. Blood streamed from Tesár's nose and mouth all over the bulky tomes of *Dogmatica*, *Biblia Sacra* and *Codex iuris canonici*.

"That'll do," said Iffland with distaste. "Enough! Take him away!"

Father Stachovič's office reeked with the smell of soldiery, hummed with activity, men talking and giving orders, sentries, clerks and the medic carrying out their duties, and Iffland's men getting ready to take up residence in Závodie.

Závodie itself was quiet, none of the locals was out and about except the old bellringer, Mr Galbavý, whose whiskers were said by the villagers to resemble the tassels on the church banner; he came out of the rectory, grumbling under his breath the way he'd been grumbling for the last five years: "This war's just never going to end!" He walked through the village with the altar boys in tow.

He'd wanted to ring the bells, but Father Stachovič had said there'd be no bell-ringing. There'd probably be no services. The people of Závodie had forgotten to attend church. No one came from Great or Little Poruba either, and they both fell under the Závodie parish.

People had other things to worry about, because the burly, ginger-haired Sergeant Eulenau, among other NCOs, was carrying out an inspection of the houses. With eleven men he was going from house to house, inspecting the kitchens, sitting rooms, wardrobes, pantries, stables, granaries and barns. He shouted at people, but people didn't understand him, because Private Heetit had stayed behind at the rectory and Sergeant Heatbag left everyone shaking their heads in response to his yelling "Partizan? Partizan?" In four houses, at the Hladíks', Masňáks', Lániks' and Tesárs', he had everything turned upside down and closely scrutinized in a search for weapons.

Old Mrs Šiška, the mother of Ján Šiška, who was with Tesár's group in Grabovec, took fright when she saw the ginger-haired Heatbag and eleven other soldiers come storming into their yard and she fled and hid in the cellar along with her almost two-year-old granddaughter Štefka.

Two grenades went off with a bang. One outside the cellar door and a second, quieter one thrown by Eulenau into the cellar through the window. Then, as if there were nothing to it, he had the Šiška house turned upside down and sacks of beans and flour scattered all over the floor.

The exploding grenades were audible as far away as Grabovec, and throughout its misty surroundings, and Letanovský, who was being hounded towards Grabovec by thirty soldiers, looked back towards the village. All he could see was the thin mist, tinted orange by the sun.

Grabovec was now quite close. The little wood in the middle of Závodie's fields and meadows, grey-blue, veiled in an orange mist. A little wood. In it, English and Turkey oak trees, though not that many. You could have counted them easily. Different oak trees, young and old, growing all over the uneven ground. In the deepest gully there was a spring. A mere trickle, hardly any water to it, and in dry summers it petered out completely. In the distant past, Grabovec had been much larger, spread over many acres, until the locals cut much of it down and grubbed it out. In the dips and ditches that they couldn't have ploughed they left the different oak trees and any thorny undergrowth untouched.

"This is where they should be," Letanovský told the German soldiers, pointing ahead as they reached the edge of the wood. "This is where –"

The soldiers couldn't understand, but they got the drift. The lanky, swarthy sergeant pointed at the wood and spread out the fingers on both his hands. "Zehn minuten!" and shoved him forward. He and the thirty soldiers spread out round the grove, cut off from the fields by a ring of hazels, blackthorn and the barberry bushes known locally as Christ's thornbush.

Letanovský struggled through the thorny undergrowth into the wood.

Within Grabovec, there were four deep gullies running almost in parallel. He proceeded laboriously along the first of them, his legs aching with fear. Where on earth are they? They must have left. God preserve us! He went slowly along the ditch, looking out for Schnitzer, his wife, their two children and Marka Bernadič. He froze. He didn't find them in the first gully. He'd gone its full length and found no one. He walked the length of the second, and no one was there either. But of course they wouldn't have hidden in such ditches with little coverage, he reassured himself before extending his search to the third ditch. They weren't there either. God preserve us! The fourth gully, the deepest, where the spring was, was densely covered in various dogwoods, hazel, blackthorn and barberry, but it was damp, and Letanovský, having finally got through the prickly undergrowth, shuddered and raised his arms above his head. Above the tiny spring, from which dribbled a wretched little streamlet, glinting faintly from the orange sky, was Marka Bernadič and the Schnitzers, but also the five men who'd left Závodie to join the partisans. It was immediately clear to Letanovský why Marka hadn't been able to go home. They wouldn't have let her. Partisans! Matej Hladík, Jožo Lánik the school-leaver, Tono Masňák, Števo Tesár and Jano Šiška! And where had those others sprung from? And Grabovec surrounded by Germans! God preserve us!

Letanovský was quaking with fear. Marka Bernadič, in her flimsy red, printed-cotton dress and new black canvas shoes, was shivering with cold, sitting on the grass and staring at the folds in Letanovský's shirt sleeves and his trousers with their patched knees. His features were pale, partly overgrown with black and greying stubble, and wide streaks of sweat, still clouded with Saturday's dust, were streaming down his cheeks.

Letanovský had five gun-barrels levelled at him.

"What's up, Letanovský?" Tesár asked, in a low tone but quite brusquely, his black eyes twitching beneath the tufts of his dark eyebrows as he stared at Marka's quaking neighbour. "Why are you here?"

Letanovský gave Tesár and the others standing above the spring a forced smile, let his arms dangle by his sides and said in a hoarse voice, but loud enough for all to hear: "Shh! You've been given away."

"What's been given away? Who gave us away?"

"Shh! Everything, Števko," Letanovský replied in a shaky whisper. "Here – all round Grabovec, Germans –" he said, gesticulating in a circle with both arms, "– right here – Germans – thirty of 'em, near enough – they're waiting for me." He turned to Mr Schnitzer and his wife and two small daughters, twelve-year-old Lili and nine-year-old Viola. All the Schnitzers were trembling with fear, cold and fatigue, because they hadn't slept all night. "It troubles me, but I have to say it – Mr Schnitzer – you're to come with me – if you don't they'll shoot me – they'll shoot up my whole house – you must come, Mr Schnitzer! – You, too, Mrs Schnitzer – and the girls – someone's blabbed – Oh, God –!"

Marka Bernadič, wordless, was watching her neighbour, Mr Letanovský, the lids on her green eyes quite still, her always slightly scornful mouth open as if she wished to say something; Schnitzer's hands, clamped to his thighs, twitched, and his wife, who was sitting between Lili and Viola, was trembling as she patted their hands.

"You're going nowhere, Letanovský!" said Tesár. "We won't let you, you'd give us away."

"But I have to, right away!" said Letanovský. He looked into Tesár's angry eyes and turned to the Schnitzers: "I have to go straight back – the wood's surrounded by about thirty soldiers – an' I've got a wife at home – an' a son – an' he's got his wife – an' they've also got kids – two – an' a third any day now – but you know that, Mr Schnitzer – God Almighty! – but then the Kommandant, the one who lives at my place – he seems quite decent – do come, Mr Schnitzer –! It'll be okay. Nothing's going to happen."

"You're going nowhere, Letanovský! You'll give us away – you'll be shot."

"What?"

"They'll shoot you even if you do bring them out of the woods, and they'll shoot them as well, all of 'em." Tesár pointed at the four Schnitzers. "You're staying here!" he said, turning towards the other partisans, who remained stolidly silent as they gripped their levelled submachine guns.

"Even the kids?" Letanovský asked Tesár from behind. "They'd even shoot the kids?"

"Yep!" Tesár replied over his shoulder. "Even the kids!"

The army-clad Hladík spat out the bit of wood he'd been chewing and said: "There's nothing for it, they have to go! This is only going to cost the lives of Letanovský and the Schnitzers. If they stay here, it'll be Letanovský and all of us." He snapped a twig off a blackthorn and stuck it in his mouth.

Tesár looked at Hladík.

"They have to go," said Hladík, removing the twig from his mouth, "and right now!"

Mrs Schnitzer choked back her tears, rose, got the girls up as well, taking them by the hand, kept choking back her tears, but not fast enough, because several teardrops suddenly plopped down her cheeks.

Tesár turned round. "How many Germans are there in Závodie?"

"I don't know," Letanovský replied. "Certainly over a hundred, could be two hundred. There's the captain, the Kommandant who's living at our place, officers, NCOs – they've got trucks, motorbikes, artillery – small cannon – trench mortars."

"Have the Germans also gone to Poruba?"

"No, Števko, they haven't."

"And do they intend to?"

"I don't know." Letanovský shrugged. "I've no means of knowing."

"Have they been looking for us?"

Letanovský shuddered. "You? You? They'll only be looking for people whose names are on the doors."

"On the doors?"

"Every door's got a list of names on it. But –"

"And what was that we heard? Those two explosions?"

"No idea, Števko. I did hear them, but they were already chasing me out here."

"How many did you say there are? Over a hundred, more like two hundred?" Tesár paused for thought, staring Letanovský in the face. "Go, then!" he said. "But the blood of Christ be your protection against letting on that we're here! Got that? You go too, Schnitzer! You can't put Letanovský in a fix by not going. But the blood of Christ be your protection against saying one word!"

Marka Bernadič leapt up from the ground.

"You can't go!" Tesár told her. "You're staying here with us!" He grabbed hold of her, pressing a filthy hand to her mouth

(31)

to stop her crying out. He placed her next to the blankets and kitbags on the ground and held her down firmly. "Marka's staying here," he said to the Schnitzers and Letanovský, "and if you breathe one word – you'll have her on your conscience. She can't go with you, she's not going, but if you say one word, that'll be the end of her!" Tesár then pointed a finger at Marka and brandished a fist towards Letanovský and the Schnitzers.

"Mummy!"

"Come on!"

"I won't go, Mummy, Mummy –"

Mrs Schnitzer dragged Viola by the hand, Viola turned her pale features back to Marka with frightened, reproachful eyes, tripped over a small thorn bush and Marka stared after her, aghast. She was seized with pity as her eyes slipped down to Viola's utterly helpless legs and those feet in their torn white shoes.

Mr Letanovský and the Schnitzers struggled back through the thick undergrowth of dogwoods, hazel, blackthorn and prickly barberry and disappeared from Marka Bernadič's tearful gaze,

With her face jammed against a stinking kitbag, and despite Tesár's firm grip on her, she writhed there, racked by quiet, woeful weeping. With one hand clamped to her mouth, he used the other to keep her firmly on the ground, and he tried to reassure her: "Don't be afraid! Nothing's going to happen to you, Marka. You'll be here with us! You can't go home, you mustn't. Don't be afraid! Your father's sensible enough not to tell the Krauts where you are. He hasn't even put your name on the door! And Letanovský won't split on you either." Then he tossed a blanket over her, still holding her firmly to the ground, and looked in silence at the unspeaking, reproachful faces of his comrades.

Silent moment dragged by after silent moment, with all manner of things banging away inside the heads of the partisans and Marka until Tesár and the rest began talking over her head.

She listened fitfully. Inside her head was a confused mass of all the things she'd heard on Saturday and through the night coming from the partisans and the Schnitzers, and of her dark fury at Hladík and Tesár, who'd driven the Schnitzers out of Grabovec. What was going to happen? To her the future was like a great, grey, windowless wall.

"What can anyone do here?" Tesár said over her head, picking up his group's repeated question. "Can't you think of anything better to ask? Just that? Everywhere's death and destruction, Lánik? You're wasting your breath. It isn't. We might have had to send the Schnitzers back to Závodie, but then we couldn't have taken 'em with us. The Germans would have shot all the Letanovskýs in Závodie. And we couldn't have taken Letanovský with us either. They'd have come here looking for him. I can't imagine what would have become of us if the Germans had attacked us here! Now, with you talking such rubbish! Risk letting ourselves be captured? Shame on you! I know there's a life at stake, but if it's your own, you don't have to risk those of your father, mother, family. How can you say such stupid things?"

"Stupid! Who's said anything stupid?"

Tesár turned to Šiška.

"You, too," he said. "Your mother's at home, your father, wife and child – for their sakes you can't go back, or let yourself be captured!"

"What are they to you?" Šiška yelled back at him. His fear had begun to evaporate and his eyes shone. He was trembling. "Everything was hanging by a thread – do you think that's easy to take? Mother, father, wife, child – stay out of it, leave them to me! I'm not saying stupid things, but you are! Just you wait! If the worst comes to the worst, you'll be the one to cop it! It'll all come out... It was all your idea! I could have got a job in Brezany – but not the way things are! They'll kill us all in turn, then our families –"

"And how old's your little one?" Marka asked Šiška. "I mean Štefka?"

"She'll be two in October."

"I saw her one late afternoon, she can talk already. She told me 'My tatty's a blatsmiff an' he worts in a smiffy.'"

Šiška smiled.

The Grabovec wood smelled of cold, it smelled of those different kinds of oak leaves rotting and moulding on the brown earth. All the oaks were slender and tall, crowded together, and now their crowns were being slowly swathed in mist, pale orange from the sun and bluish from the sky above, because sun and wind had begun to disperse it. The water in the spring was babbling quietly and spilling across the flat brown stones. Some of the stones below the spring looked as if they were shedding tears. From a distance came the rumble of exploding shells.

"– or, or," Marka heard Tesár again. She was surprised to find herself liking his steady tone of voice. "We can't go home now, Lánik. We'd end up giving ourselves away. The Germans would kill your father and your mother and child, Šiška –"

"And won't Letanovský give us away?" Šiška asked."I don't like the look of him."

"Unlikely. I can't believe that."

"And the Schnitzers?"

"Dunno, but I can't believe that either. Why?"

"To improve their chances. They'll be interrogated."

"Do stop all that! It wouldn't do the Schnitzers any good and Letanovský's scared of us – then there's Marka here –"

"Pity she ever left home! The Jews, Marka, Letanovský... Think about it, Števo! No good's going to come of this! Just shut up! You're talking twaddle! Letanovský will give us away, the Jews will give us away... We could have split up yesterday, the day before!"

Šiška's eyes gleamed.

Marka Bernadič pressed her face into the kitbag. Oh, God! What if the Germans spot she isn't at home? She was overwhelmed with a fear that completely dispelled her fatigue.

"… hold on to what we can!" Now she was hearing Tesár's unfaltering voice as if from afar. "That's all! There's nothing else we can do. Think of home! Imagine those Soviet partisans and soldiers – if they kept thinking about home the way you do! They do think about it, but differently…"

Marka sensed that Tesár's grip on her had loosened. Father, mother, brother, sisters, sister-in-law, the kids! Oh, God! If someone did get away from the wood, give them away… She rolled over.

Tesár pressed her back down.

"Let go, Števo!"

The partisans fell silent.

Hladík spat out the bit of twig he'd snapped from a blackthorn.

"Why are you holding me down?" Marka's eyelids started to quiver over her green eyes. "If I'd wanted to, I could have run away – neither you nor the Germans would have caught me – and you don't have to worry I'd give you away – not now, not ever now – and, anyway, how? – if I gave you away, I'd be giving myself away as well – right, Števo? My name won't be on our door, that's for sure – and – and – shame on you, lads! Whining like puppy dogs. How *can* you go home? Where's your common sense? How stupid can you get! All right, go, go get yourselves killed –!"

"You just shut up!" Šiška yelled back at her. "What do you know about anything!"

"All right, go! Go, Jano!" Marka turned to face Tesár. "Let him go! Eh, Števo?"

She fixed her green eyes on Tesár, her eyelids still flickering. After a moment she turned back to the kitbag.

Tesár covered her with a blanket.

"We'll head for Little Poruba towards evening," said Tesár, "then we'll see."

Masňák was staring blankly at the ground, thinking of his fiancée faraway near Nitra. Hladík was munching away at his latest bit of twig, Šiška was mentally spraying the Germans with his submachine gun, Lánik the school-leaver was thinking it would be best to run off home. He shouldn't have done that to his parents, getting himself a grammar-school education then going to join the partisans! Tesár was biting the nail of his left index finger.

"Wouldn't it be better to leave now?" Lánik asked. "I mean go to Little Poruba now?

"Now?" Tesár shook his head. "In daylight?"

Lánik looked down at the little spring, his head filled with the sight of German soldiers as he visualised them herding Letanovský and the Schnitzers from Grabovec back to Závodie. "They had an exemption," he said, "from Tiso."

Marka glanced at Lánik, whose handsome, smooth features appealed to her.

"Exemption!" said Hladík, spitting out his chewed bit of wood. "The Krauts don't give a fig for Tiso's exemptions. Even Krauts have their uses. Like cleansing the world of Jews. If only they'd finished the job before this!"

"Idiot!" said Marka, glancing towards Lánik. "Listen to him, Jožo!"

"What?"

"Have you started shaving?"

"Yep." Jánik smiled. "Of course."

"With a sliver of wood?" Hladík asked. "You should hang a kilogram weight on each whisker, then they'd grow!"

"And that dimple on your chin, how d'you –?"

Lánik smiled at Marka and ran a thin grubby finger over what was quite a deep dimple. "This one?"

"Yes."

"Like this." And he stretched the skin on his chin until the dimple was levelled out. "Aren't you hungry, Marka? Do you fancy a tin of something?"

"No, thanks!" she said. "I hate the smell. Oof, I'd much rather a drop of milk –"

"Have a go," he said, "try milking one of the kitbags, you might get a trickle –!"

"What earthly good is this war?" Masňák mused. "What use is it? We're trying to do for the Krauts, the Krauts will do for us, and the Russians will do for the Krauts. Isn't it daft?"

"It is indeed," said Hladík. "A little war inside a big one."

"Too true," said Marka, "it *is* daft. It's like –"

"No, Marka." Tesár smiled. "It isn't, because we're hitting the Krauts from two sides. The Soviets at Dukla and on one great, long front, and us here. Never fear, Marka, the Krauts will feel the loss of every man, every vehicle, every machine gun, every rifle. Goebbels himself is already alleged to have said the Germans are scraping the barrel."

"And who's he?"

The partisans burst out laughing. Marka was covered in confusion, blushed and fell silent.

"But why are you laughing at me?" she snapped back shortly. "In our house we never talked about such clever people, we only ever talked about cows, horses, pigs and Hitler."

High over Závodie and the surrounding area, and above Grabovec, the pale-orange morning mist was beginning to break up. It was rising and turning into little grey-white clouds, they were then borne by the breeze along the brightening horizon, melting away, reforming and adding a little ornament to a nice autumn Sunday and its play of colours – the grey of the earth, the yellow sun, the blue sky, the yellowing maize, the potatoes turning brown, and the fresh green of the clover growing across the stubble fields. Before long, the whole of Závodie and the surrounding area, including Grabovec, was engulfed in the warm September sun. The air gradually turned warm and then hot. The mountains beyond Great and Little Poruba were like dark, billowing waves.

At the Závodie cemetery, Father Stachovič and the parish organist were burying old Mrs Šiška, mother of the Jáno Šiška who was with Tesár's group in the wood, they buried her along with her granddaughter Štefka, the little girl of whom Šiška had felt that tiny bit proud, having learned from Marka that she could already say "My tatty's a blatsmiff".

For the people of Závodie, life was reduced to what they had to do and what they mustn't do.

The Šiška family had to place their mutilated mother and grandmother and her granddaughter in a large, plain coffin, which the local carpenter had had to produce within an hour, and Father Stachovič had to rush through their funeral above a pit that two men, the sexton and his brother-in-law, had just managed to dig out in two hours. That had been on the orders of the commander of the Závodie unit, Captain Iffland, because he wanted to order to reign in Závodie. He had banned people from attending the funeral with the sole exception of the four men who were to carry old Mrs Šiška and her granddaughter's bier.

He had ordered the five fathers of the five partisans, Hladík the one-eyed roadmender, the little sapper Šiška, the tall, thin brickmaker Masňák, Fruity Lánik and Tesár the journeyman, to be removed to the old barn attached to the rectory, which had neither a barn-door nor a half-decent roof, and placed guards round it, and he'd ordered Letanovský, Schnitzer, Schnitzer's wife and their two little girls, Lili and Viola, to be brought before him.

His elbows rested on Father Stachovič's desk and his hands were clasped in front of his mouth, with his chin resting on his forefingers while his thumbs gripped his jaw. He stared hard at Schnitzer, a scrawny man in a balloon-silk smock and brown breeches, stared into his gaunt face with its growth of black stubble, at his angular spectacles in which the windows of the priest's office glinted, reflecting the walnut trees outside people's houses and the tall pole up which the firemen of Závodie would haul their wet hoses, stared at the tall man, Letanovský, until his eyes skipped across to the two children, the two Schnitzer girls, Lili and Viola, pale and tearful, before running once more over Letanovský and Schnitzer. He scrutinized them closely. He gave a slight smile behind his clamped fists. He had deliberately been keeping his eyes off Mrs Schnitzer since his first sight of her, because she'd come as a surprise. That tall, fine figure, the long neck, bent slightly forward, the smooth head of brown hair, the pale features with just a slight summer tan. Since that moment he'd avoided looking her way. He was keeping her in reserve after the unpleasant sight of the bespectacled Schnitzer and his scrutiny of the tall Letanovský and the lovely little girls, black-haired Lili and brown-haired Viola, dressed in dark-blue slacks. Twelve-year-old Lili had pigtails and a long flat face that seemed not even to have a nose on it, while nine-year-old Viola had a fringe and her face was more round, pensive, with her lips projecting as if she were sucking a sweet. His eyes drifted down to Schnitzer's wife's hips, held fast within a grey skirt, then up slightly towards her bust over which her brown and green coat was parted. Then they skipped to her pretty, pale face and grey eyes, in which he could read supplication, despair, fear and determination, but he also deciphered a willingness to do anything. His eyes slipped back down to her white hands. Their veins were swollen. They were swelling with blood. He looked back at her face. He felt a tremor. His head swam momentarily with a brief passage of faintness. This one was not remotely like the repulsive Jewess he'd left it to Truppenführer Mohn to give the special treatment to. Mohn is a great devotee of race – and he'd had the Jewess, along with her husband and three boys, shot beside a haystack well clear of the town. Such devotees have always gone for murder... But that had been a repulsive Jewess...

Iffland sensed that waging war on partisans would always be difficult and it made his men apprehensive. Which is why – and for no other reason – Iffland approved of Mohn, because he always afforded the men some distraction. "Partisans and Jews," he'd said to Mohn, when he'd come to report that he'd liquidated the Jews, "boost morale as they stand next to a wall, in a quarry, by a haystack or above a pit. They're excellent for that purpose." – "Yes, Herr Hauptmann," Mohn had replied, "and I reckon we shall have plenty of opportunities." – "Just so," Iffland had concurred, if with disgust. It is disgusting, but after each such execution the men do seem better disciplined and more determined. It also disturbed him, because the discipline and determination of his men sprang from the composure of members of the SD, and the SD's composure could only ever be guaranteed if it was given Jews and partisans to process by its own special treatment. It was vile, ill-judged to lock up men, women and children in bulk... It was unbecoming, unworthy of the Reich and the objectives of a Greater Germany, no – it was ghastly treatment, just as ghastly as shooting defenceless partisans and Jews as they stand next to a wall, in a quarry, by a haystack or above a pit – no...! He was disturbed by it, but he could see no other recourse because to him the SD was a snake that could create a stir among the men and give him a nasty bite.

He propped his chin on his left hand, glanced towards the pale-eyed smokers, Poller and Dosse, who were sitting on the priest's sofa, and pointed his left forefinger at Letanovský.

"Dieser kann gehen!" he said, not to the soldiers, just to Letanovský. "Vorläufig, glaube ich."

A soldier opened the door of the rectory office, nodded to Letanovský and let him go home.

Then Captain Iffland ran his left hand over his blond hair, trimmed right back above his forehead, stroked his grim, shaven face and pointed to Schnitzer and his children.

"Mit denen in die Scheune!"

Two soldiers led them off to the rectory barn to join the five fathers of the five Závodie partisans, Hladík, Šiška, Masňák, Lámik and Tesár, who were standing there, their faces to the wall and their hands tied in front of them. The soldiers bound the hands of Schnitzer and his two little girls likewise and stood them faces to the wall.

At the time, Schnitzer's wife was thirty-five and attractive. Captain Iffland had noticed something about her that he hadn't noticed about any other woman who'd crossed his path during this war, or any whose path he had crossed. Although she was terrified, although Iffland could see her quaking before him, he had a sudden sense of the powerlessness and futility of the power by which he compelled the presence and compliance, as he himself put it, of wartime women. Can at least some inclination be won by force from a woman like that? He could tell that Schnitzer's wife couldn't be a war wife. She might succumb, or kill. Then he thought of her pretty children. Might they be of use to him? Suppose he had them taken away ostentatiously, and so paralyse Závodie morally and – and thereby morally paralyse also...? He glanced at Schnitzer's wife. With his chin resting pensively on his hands, he looked at her arching back as she knelt down before him.

This was going to require him to treat her with all the magnanimity he could muster, he thought. By being magnanimous, pressure her into a degree of devotion to him, not by gun-toting!

He glanced sheepishly towards Poller and Dosse, keeping Schnitzer's wife still kneeling before the priest's desk.

"I'll question you and the kids later," he told her, "separately."

She straightened from the waist up, opened her somewhat tearful grey eyes at Iffland and stood up.

"To Letanovský's with her!"

Two soldiers led her off to the Letanovský house.

Iffland reached for the phone.

The pale-eyed Poller and Dosse were smoking away.

"Eight men should be enough," Iffland said into the phone. "If you need more later –"

The soldiers and Schnitzer's wife ran into Father Stachovič, who'd spent a long time standing over the grave of Mrs Šiška and her granddaughter, and a long time with the weeping Šiška family in their cottage, thinking of the thirty years he'd spent in Závodie. He had returned to the rectory courtyard still dressed as he had been at the cemetery, in a black cassock and white surplice. In the shed he spotted not just the five men, but also Schnitzer and his two children.

He knocked on his office door.

It was opened by a soldier and at a nod from Iffland he went in. His face flushed red and his lips began to quiver because he had spotted, on the shelf that held his large volumes, the letters in gold of his DOGMATICA, BIBLIA SACRA and CODEX IURIS CANONICI bathed in streaks of blood. Bathed in blood, the dogma and canon are binding on no one! He stiffened at the very thought. He tightened his grip on the black book in his hand. It was hard for him to take the plunge, but he did decide he'd tell Captain Iffland what he'd been thinking about during the funeral of old Mrs Šiška and her granddaughter Štefka.

"What can I do for you, mein Herr?"

"Herr Hauptmann," Father Stachovič began, gripping firmly before him the black book in his white hands. He stood there in front of his desk as if rooted to the spot and looked up at Iffland. "Craving your indulgence –"

"Funeral over then?" Iffland asked with a sneer before licking his cigarette and lighting it with his lighter. "The German armed services are not best pleased with your village, mein Herr. Jews, partisans, bandits, workshy people, so many who are plain antisocial! Well?"

"Craving your indulgence, Herr Hauptmann," the priest began, pausing to glance round the soldiers in his office, taking in also the pale-eyed Poller and Dosse, "there's something I'd like to say –"

The two clerks at the field table set up opposite Father Stachovič's desk bent over their paperwork, having a quiet laugh.

"You can speak quite freely, mein Herr," said Iffland. "It'll be worth your while to trust my men."

"Craving your indulgence," the priest began once more, "let me just say how sorry I am for the innocent living and the innocent dead. I've lived among these people for a long time now, something over thirty years – and please don't mind my saying that the deaths of the old woman and the little girl were both misjudged and damaging. Surely there can be little doubt that these are two terrible things. Simple misjudgement on the one hand and the damage caused on the other. Those people in the shed aren't partisans, nor are their sons with the partisans. They've long worked elsewhere. They don't live here in Závodie. There must have been some mistake or a false denunciation. There are instances of culpability that can be punished by God and men. Sometimes the two may punish them jointly, at other times separately – but one person acting alone cannot punish anyone – not even a guilty party – and the innocent cannot be punished by either God or men… And, craving your indulgence, jurisdiction over any life is the preserve of God –"

"Come, come, mein Herr!"

Iffland held his cigarette to his lips with the fingers of his left hand, puffed casually away at it and, with a grin on his face, watched the village priest standing motionless before him, his arms drooping and his hands still gripping the black book. Father Stachovič's words struck him as antediluvian, to all intents and purposes dead.

"Can you vouch for that," he asked the other, still standing there motionless, after a pause, and stroked his rugged features, "that someone in Závodie has been guilty of a mistake or a false denunciation?"

"I can vouch for the fact that these are innocent people. I know the local people well – and in the case of the innocent, neither God nor man may –"

"And the other thing?"

"The other thing, Herr Hauptmann," said Stachovič, "is about the harm done. Punishing the innocent, weak and harmless? I've always thought, craving your indulgence, that German armed forces came here to free us from bandits and not to wreak vengeance on the innocent, weak and harmless for the gruesomeness of the age we live in. Such information as I have is that German armed forces do not make mistakes or commit acts that cause harm. Think about it if you will, as regards those people –" Stachovič raised his black book and pointed it towards the barn, "– and those two children –"

"Children, children," said Iffland, stopping short. A long slug of grey ash fell from his cigarette onto his sleeve. "That's –"

The priest regretted noticing it, because Captain Iffland's rugged features became slightly flushed.

"Children, that's a different matter – but trust me, mein Herr," said Iffland irritably, "Germany's armed forces are a mighty power –" He fell silent for a moment at the recollection that by this stage they were a mighty power only on paper and the radio, and that Goebbels himself had conceded that the Germans were now scraping the barrel – "a mighty power whose might will continue to grow – new weapons – the V1, V2, V3 and so on. If Germany is to come out of this war victorious, then until this new weaponry becomes available, mein Herr, we have to keep seeking our enemies out, seeking them even where there are none. Even among the innocent, weak and harmless. Seeking them out and trying to render them harmless. Both for myself and as a representative of Germany's armed forces I sorely doubt that our armed forces are capable making mistakes and causing harm. Trust me, mein Herr! Any action that I take is taken in the belief that it is in the best interest of Germany's armed forces."

He wagged his sleekly plastered head at Father Stachovič to indicate that he would hear no more of the latter's pointless fine words.

"But craving your indulgence, Herr Hauptmann, are you not, personally and as a representative of Germany's armed forces, concerned about innocence and guilt?"

"No!" Captain Iffland raised his long face, now animated by anger, and looked straight at this old priest, whose pale features were furrowed with wrinkles. "That's not my concern, mein Herr. Such talk of guilt and innocence, it's all claptrap. You, sir, have probably never been a soldier, not even in wartime – you don't have a clue what war's about. You've no clue about the spirit of the age we live in. You're wasting your breath, mein Herr – you'd be better off seeing to it that I'm not put out by your village!"

Iffland wagged his sleekly plastered head again.

"Herr Hauptmann, craving your indulgence, Germany's armed forces are unlikely to breed heroes if they lack people who are righteous –"

"That, mein Herr, is rubbish!"

"But, still craving your indulgence, Herr Hauptmann," said Father Stachovič, "there is one thing I would beg of you. If something else were to happen – Heaven forbid! – do, please, permit me to prepare the condemned for eternal life – under the watchful eyes of your men, obviously."

"Rubbish, mein Herr," came Captain Iffland's caustic reply. "Anyone needing to be got rid of by Germany's armed forces is not even deserving of your goodwill. They'll be going to Hell even without your assistance." He wagged his head at the priest again.

"But craving your indulgence, Herr Hauptmann –"

On the prayer desk next to the office desk the phone jangled.

"Please – out!"

Stachovič, his lower jaw hanging, made a move, glanced one last time at the words DOGMATICA and BIBLIA SACRA, in gold letters and streaked with blood, and left the office.

Outside the Závodie rectory a vehicle drew up.

The bright-eyed Poller and Dosse rose from the priest's leather couch, glanced out into the street and left to join their eight comrades who'd come to Závodie from Lower Brezany to receive Iffland's orders and carry out their major action.

Shortly after, Captain Iffland – with a large tray, his lunch and a bottle of Father Stachovič's wine in front of him – put out his cigarette, sent for the Scharführer and the men from the SD, explained what they were to do with the Schnitzer children – to make a show of taking them away, then not to execute them, but to bring them to the command post! – and had ten men take the five fathers of the five partisans, Schnitzer and his two children to the wood he'd found on the ordnance map of Závodie and the surrounding area, Grabovec.

The men set off through Závodie with the condemned men, carrying not just rapid-fire guns, but also picks and shovels.

In Závodie silence reigned. Nobody did anything, the women did no cooking, nobody ate, the men didn't bother shaving, children didn't scream, nobody spoke to anyone, unless in a whisper. Can people do such things? Kill for the sake of killing? Why had they let Letanovský go? It's all his fault! If he hadn't had those Jews... But who told on him, and who betrayed the partisans? It's all his fault. People were horror-stricken not only by the German troops, but at their own venom. It was midday, between twelve and one, the sky was blue, just the odd white cloud here and there, the warm September sun shone, in Závodie a heavy silence reigned except for the occasional honk of a goose or quack of a duck. The Letanovský and Bernadič courtyards were abuzz with bees.

Letanovský's wife, muttering away through her blood-drained lips, went into the back room and, wringing her hands, she stood before Schnitzer's wife, who was sitting on the bed. "They've taken the poor things off."

"Who? What are you saying – taken? Who?"

"Try not to be afraid, Mrs Schnitzer –"

Schnitzer's wife stiffened where she sat, fixing her tearful grey eyes on Mrs Letanovský, whose features twisted out of shape as she began to weep.

" – try not to be afraid – they've also taken those men, and your husband – and the little girls, poor dears, so pretty. Oh dear –," Mrs Letanovský, dressed in grubby clothes, a cotton-print skirt, smock and apron, mumbled through her blood-drained lips before bursting into tears, "– what point is there in people living on earth? If at least they'd kill them straight off and not torment them for ages first! Oh, God, oh, God!"

Mr Letanovský was sitting under his young walnut tree, staring into the ground.

Mr Bernadič was gazing pensively, from the bench where Marka had been shelling beans on Saturday, at the well, its moss-covered surround and green bucket, and as Mr Letanovský's son Jožo, a tall lad with his sleeves rolled up, crossed their yard towards the dividing fence, Mr Bernadič's pockmarked face winced and he watched in alarm as Jožo grabbed hold of the angular stakes.

"Neighbour!"

"What's up?" Mr Bernadič asked. "What d'you want?"

"Come over here, neighbour!"

Mr Bernadič got slowly to his feet, took a sip of water at the well and walked over towards Jožo Letanovský.

"You shouldn't have done it!"

"Done what?"

"Inform on them."

Mr Bernadič's pockmarked face went red, his lips parted first on one side then on the other. He took fright and couldn't bring himself to tell Jožo to his pale, elongated, bony face he must be crazy.

"No, Jožo," he said after a pause, in a whisper, I haven't informed on anyone, no one in this house has informed on anyone. It was someone else, not me."

"So if it wasn't you," young Letanovský replied, "it must have been your Marka. They say she's out somewhere. Maybe the Germans have picked her up and have been torturing her –"

Mr Bernadič stepped back from the fence, took a sip of water from the bucket by the well and sat down on the bench by the porch, crushed.

At the rectory, Captain Iffland had had his lunch – beef soup, roast chicken, rice and bell pepper salad, with wine as an accompaniment. He'd pushed the slice of walnut cake to one side. He lit a cigarette and set off for the Letanovskýs' to find Schnitzer's wife.

He walked contemptuously past where Letanovský was sitting on his bench beneath the young walnut tree, staring down at the fallen leaves and at two walnuts that had been missed by everyone and were now smirking back up at him as he sat there, dressed and unshaven, just like on Saturday.

Iffland entered the back room.

Mrs Letanovský fled, pressing her filthy apron to her eyes, and Schnitzer's wife leapt to her feet.

"What have you done?" she screamed at Captain Iffland. "Where have you had them take my children? I'm no Jew – and I can easily prove it!"

"Why didn't you...?" Iffland's rugged features, clean-shaven, flushed slightly. "I didn't know –"

"So you're not bothered about my children, only about whether I'm Jewish or not. I'm not Jewish, I'm not – only my husband. I'd left with him for his sake and for the sake of the children because living in fear had got so hard, especially since the spring – what have you done with my children? Why didn't you have me taken away with them? Why did you keep me here?"

She became convulsed with tears. She sat down on one of the beds, Iffland on the other. A faint scornful smile played about his rugged features, clean-shaven. Schnitzer's wife wept into the fists that she had pressed firmly to her eyes. Her fingers glistened with teardrops.

"The children," he began, glancing through the window towards the Letanovskýs' yard, which was deserted. "I just had them brought osten- –"

Schnitzer's wife leapt to her feet.

"What have you done with my children?" she shrieked. "How could you have the gall to take my children and keep me here and –"

"I merely had them ostentatiously removed," he replied all too gamely and stridently. "I'll let you have them if you'll –"

"Ostentatiously!" she shrieked, choking on the word. Twitches distorted her tear-soaked fingers. "Ostentatiously you had my children taken from me, ostentatiously you've had them killed – you coward! Ostentatiously is how cowards commit murder! Why did you have them taken away? Tell me, why...?"

A single spasm ran through her body, causing her neck, which had been slightly bent forward, to straighten. She sank to the floor next to the bed.

Iffland watched her briefly, picked her up off the floor and laid her on the bed. He stood over her, ashamed of himself, because he'd been expecting entreaty, despair, humility, a readiness to do anything, he'd also been expecting Schnitzer's wife to be a little yielding in exchange for her children. He looked down at her face, the white complexion, slightly tanned in summer, the faintest hint of down showing white against her cheeks, her tiny nostrils. He undid her blouse and began to loosen her tight clothing. Pausing briefly, he ran over and opened the window before returning to the bed.

He felt a thrill as she opened her grey eyes wide.

"What – have you done – with my children?"

Her eyes clouded over and her head abruptly detached itself from the pillow.

"You'll get your children back," he said, "I'll take care of them for you –"

"What a sorry wretch you are, Hauptmann," said Schnitzer's wife in an alien, surprisingly deep tone, "a wretch and a coward! You've had my husband led away, and my children, to be shot and killed – and you have the gall to come after me –!"

Iffland stared at Schnitzer's wife, confounded at his own self, at his having been capable, in the sight of the men from the SD, of just that much generosity of spirit, that much magnanimity. Can even so little count as magnanimity – having her husband killed, her children threatened with death, and offering her their lives in exchange for her yielding? He was amazed at himself as he gazed on Schnitzer's wife lying there. She was fading from his sight, which had grown cloudy with such ruminations.

All was quiet in Závodie and the surrounding area. The sun shone down on Grabovec, filling it with the fragrance of those different kinds of oak leaves, with the smell of the drying earth and the dying grass as it turned to brown. All was quiet in the wood that was Grabovec, all quiet in the hollows and among the tall oak trees.

Flying low over the bounds of Závodie and the Grabovec wood came a huge, dark-grey Soviet plane, the roar and clatter of which woke Marka, who'd been asleep on the ground under a blanket.

She raised herself up slightly on her knees and elbows, looked about her for some sight of the partisans, and young Lánik the school-leaver, his handsome, smooth face all pale and his eyes wide open and filled with fear, began gesticulating to her to stay flat on the ground. He put a finger to his lips.

Then she caught a confusion of German voices, all shouting and laughing.

Oh, God! flashed through her mind. She lay back down, drew the blanket over her head and with one eye, the one closer to the ground, she peered through the grass at the partisans. They were crawling across the ground, crawling their way along the streamlet trickling feebly from the spring, crawling up and along the gully. Oh, God –!

Marka lay quite still lest Tesár spring towards her and stop up her mouth with his filthy paw. His hand had reeked of oil, yuck! She clenched her teeth, but immediately had to open her mouth, opened it as wide as it would go, couldn't help herself, she had to open it. She grabbed hold of the wilted drab-coloured grass and lay flat on the ground, as flat as she could, with her ears, her head and her entire body riven by crackling, a squeaking sound, men shouting and general clamour. Her eyes glazed over and caught only vaguely the sight of Lánik the school-leaver, the one who'd signalled her to lie still, toppling down into the streamlet that flowed from the spring.

She wiped away the saliva that was still trickling out after she'd thrown up.

Tesár sprang across to her. "Come on!"

She grabbed her blanket, skipped across the gully, took hold of the two Schnitzer children and set off from Grabovec at a run.

In the Letanovskýs' back room, Captain Iffland, who wasn't keen on the ever increasing sound of ever louder gunfire, stood inert over Schnitzer's wife, who was staring ahead of her in tears. Suddenly he turned, ran from the room and made a dash for the rectory. As he ran, he skirted past Mr Letanovský, who was sitting on the bench beneath the walnut tree and staring into the ground.

Mr Letanovský gripped the seat of his bench as Captain Iffland hurried past, and from the whiff of the army about him sensed what was coming. He hadn't said there were partisans in Grabovec, how could he have? Marka was there... Great God in Heaven! He stood up and looked along the deserted street.

If Bernadič... He sat down again. If Bernadič already had Marka back home, he'd go and seek his advice... But Marka was in Grabovec – poor thing, poor thing, dear Marka –

He sank, crushed, on the bench and stared down at the light-brown shells and white kernels of the walnuts that had been trampled by Captain Iffland's boots as he dashed past.

After all the shooting Grabovec had fallen silent. On the ground, steeped in the smell of gunfire, nothing now moved. The slain included the ten German soldiers, also the pale-eyed Poller and Dosse; scattered about the gully, on the freshly dug earth, were picks and shovels and the lengths of rope with which the hands of the condemned were to have been bound, and face-up in the stream lay Lánik the school-leaver. The water flowing from the spring washed over his bloodstained head and made his curly hair wave gently. Only the dead were still there, the living having fled, although it was still broad daylight. The tall, slender English oaks and Turkey oaks stood guard over the gullies and above the thorny undergrowth, gently waving their leaves and twigs in the lightest of breezes. Despite the great death that had passed through the wood, Grabovec was still a lovely spot. It shielded the earth as it always had done whenever reapers and mowers had sharpened their scythes in its shade or old peasant women had paused to rest in its shade on their way back from the fields with their great sacks of green grass, dried hay or the weeds that had infested their potato crops. Lovely indeed was Grabovec.

Twelve minutes after the shooting, the army showed up with trench mortars and let Grabovec have it. All that remained of it were the slender trunks of the English oaks and Turkey oaks, now all smashed, split and jagged. The smell of this second round of shooting at Grabovec clung to the ground, all quiet was the wood, now open to the afternoon sun, a profound daytime quiet, with the only the rumble of bombs landing in the far distance.

Marka Bernadič kept running with the Schnitzer children, and when the children could run no more, she let go of them, one of them to be picked up off the ground by Šiška, the other by Masňák, she ran on and on and behind her the others, lumbering and trudging awkwardly, having gathered up the rapid-fire guns dropped by the Germans, but they ran as they might, taking brief rests, hidden among the tall stalks of seed clover, maize or millet, in order to get their breath back, then across ploughland they crawled, everyone was making haste – Schnitzer, Marka, Hladík the one-eyed roadmender, his son Matej, Lánik the fruit-grower, now on his own, without his school-leaver son, Masňák with Lili Schnitzer in his arms, and his father, too, the tall, thin brickmaker, and Tesár, dragging his battered father along by one arm, and the little sapper Šiška with his son Jano and Viola Schnitzer, running with them were also the three men from Upper and Lower Brezany, but having almost reached the edge of the fields and meadowland of Závodie, by a field of abandoned bean poles, the Závodie journeyman, Tesár, who'd been given such a beating at the rectory by Poller and Dosse, could go no further and fell, exhausted, to the ground. They all stopped and those who were already far ahead came rushing back.

"I can't go on, Števo." Old Tesár could scarcely breathe. "I – I can't go on."

"Stay here," his son said. "Marka, you stay here as well, with the kids. Hide somewhere – anywhere – just hide – and in due course, as soon as you can, come and find us in Little Poruba. That's where we'll be. And what'll you do with the kids, Marka?"

"Never you mind, I know what to do," said Marka Bernadič to the panic-stricken Tesár. "You just leave it to me, Števo!"

"Marka –"

That was all Schnitzer could get out before Tesár yanked him by the shoulder and made him turn round.

Without more ado they carried on running, without Marka, without the children and the battered Tesár, and once among the fields and meadows of Poruba, they finally dropped down into a deep-bedded stream hidden among carrs of willow and alder and had a good laugh, at themselves and at the Germans, and began consoling poor Lánik the fruit-grower, who'd suddenly broken into tears at the loss of his school-leaver son.

They got their breath back, calmed down somewhat and stayed there in the stream.

"What can anyone do here?" the partisan Tesár asked yet again, laughing. "The same as we've just done! That's all! Hit 'em hard wherever we can! Hit every one of the fiends!"

Schnitzer was sitting quietly on a rotten willow trunk as he began poking a handkerchief under his angular spectacles to wipe his eyes.

"Why did he come after you?" the weepy fruit-grower Lánik asked regarding his dead school-leaver son. "Who put him up to it? You – you – Števo – you, was it?"

"Not me, Lánik. He came of his own accord. Here, have this."

Lánik looked through his tears at the rifle Tesár was holding out to him.

"Take this."

Lánik's ears blanched.

"Take it!"

Lánik took the rifle from Tesár and laid it slowly across his knees. "The poor boy – just a lad!" he said, taking time to wipe his eyes once more, then suddenly he shouted: "Not even Almighty God will save whoever gave us away!"

At the rectory back in Závodie, Captain Iffland was sitting at the desk in the parish priest's office, looking at the thin lieutenant who'd come back from Grabovec, thinking of Father Stachovič and what he had said: "… craving your indulgence, do, please, permit me to prepare the condemned for eternal life…", and licking the length of a freshly rolled cigarette. "A partisan?" he asked the thin, stiff lieutenant, who'd just reported what he'd found in the shot-up wood called Grabovec. "One?"

"Yes, Herr Hauptmann, just the one!"

"Dead?"

"Yes, Herr Hauptmann, dead!" The lieutenant was smiling secretly at Iffland's stupid question and thinking back to the partisan who, untouched by any shell fragments, had been lying there facing the sky, and to how the water was playing with his hair.

"No one else?"

"Sorry, Herr Hauptmann?"

"No one else? No children?"

"No, Herr Hauptmann, no one else, not even any children."

Iffland clenched his fists where they lay on the desk.

"How's that possible, you shitbag? Where are those bandits, the partisans, and the kids?"

The lieutenant's neck reddened. "I had my orders, Herr Hauptmann, to blast the wood out of existence. I did as commanded. The remains –"

"The remains," Iffland began in a low, caustic tone, "of our fallen are to be brought away discreetly!"

"Yes, sir!"

"The partisan – who is it, where's he from? What's his name?"

(54)

"He had no papers on him –"

"Any weapon?"

"A Russian submachine gun."

"Get everything ready for a major action!"

"Yessir, Herr Hauptmann, sir!"

Then from behind Father Stachovič's desk Captain Iffland really lashed out at Závodie, which was paralysed with fear. He ordered all relatives of the partisans and their fathers to be moved out of their homes and into the village hall, then he gave the command for each of their empty houses to be ransacked and burned to the ground.

Over Závodie and beneath the grey sky, the silent air was filled with red-brown smoke from the burning cottages, and in due course the dust from the fires settled on the road leading to Upper and Lower Brezany to be sent swirling as the men aboard a truck with its slanting front end bore away such remains as they'd managed to gather up in Grabovec.

That night, before eleven, Iffland gave yet more orders.

"At two a.m.," he said, "check the lists on the doors against the actual residents! Start in five different places at once. At four-thirty a sortie to Great Poruba! Any resistance to be suppressed by all available means! No one trying to flee is to be spared! Stock up on any victuals!"

Then he turned to Truppenführer Mohn who, in his extremely thick-soled jackboots, riding breeches with buckskin inserts, a green-grey tunic and a peaked cap, had been walking up and down the priest's office, turning by the door and the safe that held the church register, as he rolled and gathered up the priest's flimsy, threadbare carpet.

"Well, Herr Hauptmann?"

Truppenführer Mohn paused and turned his thin, spotty-cheeked face towards Captain Iffland.

"I have only been acting in terms of collective responsibility," Iffland said. "I've had one woman and one child shot, and one Jew with two children, and five fathers of bandits, and I've had the bandits' other relations brought to the village hall, that's twenty-seven people, three old men, four old women, seven younger women and thirteen children, and I've had five houses burned down – let's see now what the evening check-up will tell us –"

"You call that reprisals?"

Truppenführer Mohn sucked his cheeks in, opened his mouth wide and clicked his tongue.

"And you've kept the Jewess for yourself?"

Iffland made no reply.

Mohn started ambling up and down.

"My advice, Herr Hauptmann, would be – bearing in mind the priest's wine that'd be left – hang the priest and the Jewess on a single rope, prepare a sign to go with it, something like 'A priest and a Jewess on the way ... to heaven!', interrogate all the hostages in the village hall, along with the mayor, then douse the whole lot in petrol – now that really would amount to reprisals in terms of collective responsibility, Herr Hauptmann!"

"That would be a major action, Truppenführer!"

"Our commitments to our race, the party and the government of the Reich oblige us to undertake major actions."

"But I'm not sure of the justice of it – in this instance. It strikes me that the information we were given was not true and that the partisans who did for your men aren't from this community."

"An enquiry will clear that up."

Truppenführer Mohn stopped wandering up and down, halted in front of Iffland and smiled at him out of his thin, spotty face.

"How come?"

"So far, Herr Hauptmann, I've always discovered just the truths I needed – but – but now you're getting impatient, me too. Interrogate the Jewess, the priest and anyone else –"

"My object is," Iffland retorted, "to deal with the tactical side of things. I leave the political side up to you, Truppenführer, just as long as it fits in with the tactical side."

"That's the point of our collaboration."

"And that's how I see it, too."

"Good then."

Truppenführer Mohn clicked his tongue.

"You question the Jewess!" he said. "On my own plate I've got a pretty young partisan girl, though I'm afraid her looks won't last too long."

He clicked his tongue again, took leave of Iffland and the latter having said to the Oberleutnant: "Make sure everything's okay", headed for the Letanovskýs'. The house wasn't far from the rectory, about four minutes' walk, but before he reached it Iffland determined there was no going back and this was the only way he could proceed after the unfulfilled promise he'd given to Schnitzer's wife. This was the only way he could proceed. There was no other way.

The evening was quiet. Závodie, reeking of the burned-out houses, seemed to have died. Military background noises, the clumping of German jackbooted feet, the rasping of camouflage masks and rifles as soldiers saluted him, all reminded Captain Iffland that his men were rather too buoyant. He'd lost ten men – and he'd lost the Jews and partisans. Somebody was going to have to pay –

He stopped.

The priest and the Jewess? he wondered. He also remembered the four SD men Mohn had brought in by car. The priest – that would lead to a major action – and a major action would drive the locals into joining the partisans. Letanovský and the Jewess – Letanovský had been hiding Jews –

He made a move and strode off to Letanovsky's house. He ignored the guard outside, entered the yard and drowned out the ideas going round inside his head. Rubbish! Ridiculous! Generosity of spirit, nobility – he can dispose of her husband, promise her her children... War allows him only that much generosity of spirit. Did she know about the partisans in the woods? She couldn't have not known! The bitch! What can he offer her? Ten men fell in the wood. Bitch! One last thing

(57)

then – take her to bed for as long as it's fun, interrogate her, torture her and then have her publicly hanged with Leta-novský! He thought of the tall pole on which the Závodie firemen would dry their hoses. That would be interesting. Hang her and Letanovský from a steel cable and haul them up high! Mohn would be delighted. Iffland crossed through the kitchen, ignored the two soldiers saluting him, and entered Letanovský's back room.

The room was in total darkness, not a hint of the gloom of night, and there was a smell of fresh bed linen and some faint perfume.

Iffland was momentarily paralysed, then he closed the door, stood there awhile but without switching the light on, then he crossed the room silently and sat down on the bed. Fatigue had got the better of him. He rose awkwardly to his feet, thought about opening the window, but then sat down again.

Schnitzer's wife was lying on the bed by the wall opposite, breathing quietly and staring wide-eyed into the total dark-ness. Suppose he was telling the truth, she thought. Suppose he had wanted to save the children. But in exchange for what? For her! She shuddered. Then she lay there in silence, breath-ing quietly and following by ear every move that Iffland made.

Iffland quietly set aside his cap and pistol, quietly removed his tunic and quietly lay down on the bed. He tossed a quilt across his chest.

What's stopping him? Schnitzer's wife turned her face towards the dark where his bed stood. Why isn't he coming over?

Iffland was quite aware that Schnitzer's wife wasn't asleep, but was scared to make a move.

Use force? Sleep with her? Interrogate her? Torture her? Have her publicly hanged, high up on that pole? He stared into the darkness. Hasn't there been violence enough? The kids are gone. No need for them. How he'd been ready to use them to exact a little devotion! What had he to offer in place of her kids, whether they'd been murdered or hauled off somewhere, by what means might he get her to yield a little to him? By frightening her to death then offering her life? Life on those terms is of no worth to anyone. Rubbish! It's not fair play.

He was startled by the words that he might let slip. A cold shiver ran through his body. His breast was sweating.

"There was only one partisan left in the wood," he said. "The others all got away, just one got left behind – your children weren't there –!"

Schnitzer's wife didn't respond, though one question did flash through her mind: Can I have sunk so low as to have to give myself up for the sake of my own self only? To a murderer? A miserable wretch? Her head was shot through by a dull pain.

Captain Iffland wanted to rise, but he hadn't the guts. He was quite disconcerted by Schnitzer's wife, who was lying quietly and breathing quietly on the other bed, disconcerted also by his own self and by how his body was shaking in nasty, chilling waves of cold. In the total darkness of the back room at the Letanovskýs' silence reigned, a silence like a huge solid block of black matter, crammed inside the room from floor to ceiling and from wall to wall. Inside that solid, seemingly material silence he didn't dare so much as to stir even, to rise and go across to Schnitzer's wife because he knew she'd offered herself up to him in order to save not her children, but her own self.

At two o'clock, soldiers began checking the lists of names on the doors of all the houses against the actual situation, to see if anyone was missing or supernumerary. Except for the rectory and the Letanovský house they checked every last one.

At the Bernadič house they drove everyone out into the yard and made them line up, an NCO shining his torch in each sleepy, frightened face in turn: he counted nine people before shining his torch back on the sign attached to the doorframe and doing a re-count.

This time he counted ten.

Then he read all the household out by name. Bernadič responded with "Here!" – "He's here," – "She's here," and pointed to his family members.

"Wo ist Maria Bernardic?" the NCO yelled as Bernadič made no response to the last name. "Wo?"

Bernadič didn't understand him, but he knew what he was asking, and he said: "M-marka left us on S-Saturday, we don't know where she's gone, but she must have gone either t-to Brezany, to her brother's place, or to P-poruba, to her sister-in-law's –"

"Aha, Poruba," the NCO yelped, "zu den Partisanen! Anziehen! Und mit uns!"

Bernadič knew what the man's yelp meant. He put on his shoes and coat and departed with the soldiers.

The night was dark and dank. Závodie was shrouded in an ever denser mist.

Captain Iffland was not asleep, just lying there on the bed, staring into the darkness and keeping his ear tuned to whatever movements Schnitzer's wife might make.

She rose and began to dress.

Iffland listened. She was taking her time dressing. Perhaps she might make a run for it. She was no war woman and one surely had to show some magnanimity. He wasn't even in the habit of having war women executed. He would keep them for himself, pass them on to his fellow officers, then they were despatched to brothels for use by the rank and file, but what became of them after that, well, he couldn't care less. He remained motionless, lying there motionless as if asleep. She'd known about the partisans in the wood and had said nothing. Iffland could tell by ear how Schnitzer's wife was proceeding with her clothes and shoes. He mulled coldly over the concession he shouldn't have made. The Jews are gone, the partisans are gone, he's lost ten men. The troops might actually enjoy the sight of her hanging from the column, which could be a good thing. She's not a war woman, but she will be, she'd already been ready to give herself up just to save her own skin, just like all war women – and how disgusting is that! Iffland lay there, motionless.

Shortly, Schnitzer's wife crossed to the window, opened it and climbed silently through it into the yard.

The prone Iffland was once more caught in a current of cool September air, which bore with it from the Bernadič house the sound of weeping over Bernadič himself, who'd been marched off to the command post.

If a patrol or sentry stops her, he thought, he'll tell them to let her pass... But no, no patrol's going to stop her. It's bound to be just some idiot patrolling the street outside, the type who sees no further than the few metres assigned to him to walk up and down.

Iffland lay there and ruminated about collective responsibility. The idea of the collective responsibility of the members of families whose menfolk had gone off to join the partisans struck him as ridiculous. Slaughtering families and entire communities, torturing and killing defenceless people – it makes no sense and just slows down any advance or retreat; such reprisals carried out by the Gestapo, the SD, SiPo or SS might be good for morale, but how would his own men respond if they had to do likewise...? Truppenführer Mohn is all for major actions, he's tried the lot: murder, rape, setting up brothels for officers and men, cutting off women's breasts and nailing their mutilated bodies to wooden fences, throwing babies up in the air and catching them on bayonets before tossing them onto a fire..., but that is no proper way to proceed, it's got nothing to do with tactics, it drives people to join the partisans... No, no, mein Truppenführer... Deep inside, Iffland caught the echo of a sense long buried beneath the dust and ashes of war, the sense of having done right by yielding and letting Schnitzer's wife go. A priest and Jewess to Heaven? The men would just laugh at that – but Mohn will have to be appeased – somehow, somehow or other... There's those relations of the men who'd been named being held in the village hall – then there's still Letanovský – there'll be tears being shed for someone here or there, that could point to something –

The weeping from the Bernadič house rippled through the silence of the night.

Suddenly, Captain Iffland realised that he and his entire troop were like a war woman, who only yields in order to stay alive a little while longer. V1, V2, V3 and so on – V20 – and so on, it's all rubbish! Everything's rubbish, there's only one thing that isn't: the troop of which his company is a part has to fight its way through to Banská Bystrica, clear all the obstacles to rearguard action and save its own bacon. Base objectives. The objectives of a war woman. Ugh! He rose with the memory of what Father Stachovič had said: "… craving your indulgence, do, please, permit me to prepare the condemned for eternal life…," donned his tunic, set his cap on his head, belted his pistol and headed for the command post.

"Franz!" he bellowed at the burly, ginger-haired Sergeant Eulenau lounging in the parish priest's office, "Shitbag!"

"Yessir, Herr Hauptmann, sir!"

Iffland looked in disgust at the stupefied Eulenau.

"You shitbag! What a crappy dump you've housed me in! All Jews and bandits! Search Letanovský's house and bring the Jew woman and Letanovský here!"

"Yessir, Herr Hauptmann, sir!" Sergeant Eulenau clicked his heels and left, taking six other men with him.

Iffland sat down at Father Stachovič's desk, grinning to himself at the vision of the shit-scared Eulenau, who would be unable to bring Schnitzer's wife to him.

Závodie was sunk in a darkness that was pierced only here and there by the thin blue beam of a German torch. No one slept, bar the odd German trooper. People lay half-undressed or dressed and spoke in whispers.

"Come in," said Father Stachovič, who was lying on his bed, fully dressed, but without his dog collar and shoes, and thinking about hapless Závodie. "Come on in!"

"Were you asleep?"

"No."

"Come with me."

"Where to?" he asked his housekeeper. "Where am I to go? Who's asking for me?"

"Come to my room – right away! Please!"

The priest struggled to his feet, put on his slippers, and followed his housekeeper to the back room next to the kitchen. "Good gracious!" he said when he reached the small candle-lit room. "Where did you spring from, how...?"

Marta Bernadič, who was standing in the middle of the room with the Schnitzer girls, with just black canvas shoes on her feet and wearing a flimsy red dress and a white headscarf, was shaking with fear and cold. She was panting.

"Where in God's name did you spring from? What's wrong with you, Marka?"

After a brief pause Marka smiled back at the pale-faced priest. She half-closed her eyes.

"We had this idea," she began in a whisper, "that no one would be snooping round the rectory, that not even Krauts would be that cheeky, so we got into the yard from the back, from the garden. We spent a while in the barn, then in the stable, then we made it across to the woodshed and from the woodshed into the lumber room and from there through the window using this board." She pointed to an ironing board. "The housekeeper passed the board out to us. We were lucky her window was open."

"Oh, dear me! What was I supposed to – ?"

"Sh!" Father Stachovič hissed at his housekeeper, whose dark, chubby features were a picture of loathing mixed with fear. "You're shaking like a jelly! Keep your voice down!"

"We're okay – but Tesár's beneath the tower –" said Marka, pointing towards the church, "by that old iron door. He didn't make it to join the partisans. I could have, but Tesár and the children couldn't."

"Goodness gracious!"

Father Stachovič stood there, white as a sheet, and stared at the exhausted Schnitzer girls.

"Stay here!" he told Viola, Lili and Marka and then turned to his housekeeper: "You keep quiet, not one word! Get them something to eat."

"What though?"

"Whatever's left over from lunch."

Then he went off to his bedroom and sat on the bed. After a moment he went back. He stood in the middle of the room and watched the hungry Marka and the hungry Schnitzer girls. They were gobbling down some cold, oily rice and bits of meat, the remnants of his lunch. He plied Marka with questions and she replied with her rice-filled mouth.

"So much rice got used up today, dear God," said the house-keeper, "we've hit rock-bottom – rock-bottom. There's been none to be had for ages now, not for ages –"

"Keep your voice down!"

The sound of footsteps came from the kitchen and someone knocked on the door.

"Not a word!" All tensed-up, Father Stachovič turned and left the room for the kitchen.

"To Herr Hauptmann!" the soldier in the kitchen command-ed. "Herr Hauptmann wishes to see you –"

"Really!" said Father Stachovič. "I'll be right there."

In his office, the clock that had been placed on the safe that held the church register struck four times in a deep tone then thrice more at a higher pitch.

Captain Iffland, leaning back in the priest's old armchair, lapsed briefly into thought because an odd memory had borne him off to Augsburg, where once, in a moment of boredom, he'd discovered that nothing takes eleven minutes. Three o'clock, that's the zero point, nothingness, utter nothingness, he got to thinking, and the clocks took a full eleven minutes to strike that nothing. The reason was that Iffland had been living within earshot of five clock towers, each of their clocks telling a different time so it used to take fully eleven minutes before they'd all struck three. Where have those wonderful times gone? he mused, sunk deep in such fond memories in the priest's office, back then even nothing took eleven minutes, but now – what can happen in a mere second –?

"Franz!" he shouted at Eulenau, rose and linked his hands behind his back. "Where's the Jewess?"

The burly, ginger-haired sergeant stiffened.

Then Iffland took out a cigarette, ran his tongue along it, lit it with his lighter, then removed it from his lips with his left hand, keeping his right hand behind his back, and stepped up to Eulenau. He rose on tiptoe, then dropped back onto his heels, his toe tips pointing upwards, as he swayed back and forth from the waist.

Eulenau quaked, and the six soldiers behind him stood there like so many figures of wood.

"Franz," he shouted, "Copperknob! You didn't catch the Jewess! She gave you the slip! Ha ha ha!" For a brief moment he said nothing, then let fly at Eulenau with all the bile by which he judged himself: "You shitbag –"

"Yessir, Herr Hauptmann, sir!"

"– you want to be charitable towards women, you came over all chivalrous, but you're forgetting that this is a modern war, not some mediaeval tournament! Let that be the last time, you ginger git –"

"Yessir, Herr Hauptmann, sir!"

"– and mind we don't give you a knighthood –"

"But the men on watch, Herr Hauptmann –"

"Go to hell, and take 'em with you! We might yet string the lot of you up very high, you shitbag –!

Father Stachovič had been listening from behind the door, and when Iffland stopped shouting he knocked.

"Good evening, Herr Hauptmann."

"Take a seat, mein Herr."

The priest sat down at his own desk.

"At times like the present, enormous things can happen in the tiniest instants," Captain Iffland began, adding caustically:

"At times like the present, mein Herr, the German military has demands to make of you, too. Even of you, mein Herr! You shall interrogate Letanovský and Bernadič, because I have your word that you'd like to prepare the condemned for eternal life, and you will get out of them everything that might be of assistance to us! I think you know what I'm getting at."

Father Stachovič sat there in front of Iffland and his own desk, hugely distraught, wearing a suit, a black overcoat and slippers. And a grey scarf round his neck. He stared towards the gold letters on his CODEX IURIS CANONICI, which still shone where they weren't spattered with blood. His jaw sagged. His eyes remained fixed on the blood-spattered book. Marka's here at the rectory. God have mercy! She wants to go to Little Poruba to join the partisans. To be with young Tesár, someone said. She can't go home and she can't stay at the rectory. The blood-stained books were shining bright before Father Stachovič's eyes. No confessor may ask questions about a confessant's accomplices. Certainly not, Herr Hauptmann! The seal of confession is inviolable. So saith canon law. But today, what is a sin and what a virtue? What is guilt and what is innocence? What is evil and what is good? And what is the canon today? Marka, the children... This is all so dreadful, Herr Hauptmann! Even the children crawled along the ironing board. Merciful God! And Tesár's standing there, waiting at the foot of the tower by the door. That iron door –

"Well, mein Herr?"

Father Stachovič turned to face Iffland.

"If you wouldn't mind, Herr Hauptmann," he said. "If you wouldn't mind, look at that book."

Exasperation puckered Iffland's leathery forehead.

"It's a compendium of canon law. There's blood on it. Blood-spattered canon law is binding on no one. Not even me. What I hear of in the confessional I'll let you know, Herr Hauptmann. You have my word of honour. I shall require military protection, if you'd be so kind. I shall hold confession in the church. But, craving your indulgence, why am I to hear the confession of Mr Letanovský and Mr Bernadič? Why just them and not all of those in the village hall?"

"I've questioned them both and don't believe either of them. Let's be frank, mein Herr. We shan't be in your village for much longer. Two days. Three at the most. We're waiting for reinforcements, then we'll move on. I want to find out as much as possible. Letanovský and Bernadič have been condemned to death by hanging. In a case like this much also depends on you. There are no men in the village hall, just old folk and some kids – just worthless trash. I don't believe Letanovský – and for now that trash really is of no account. It's of no use to me right now."

Father Stachovič shifted and the chair beneath him creaked.

"Is there no other recourse worth considering, Herr Hauptmann?"

"No. Don't you worry, mein Herr! Forget about recourses – in your own best interests as well! Certain things even I've told you, and if you're a man of honour you'll recognise that I also have a moral right to apply force to make you forget. It's in the interest of Germany's armed forces and of your village."

Father Stachovič went off to the church, behind him four soldiers leading Letanovský and Bernadič, he lit a candle, fearing to switch the lights on lest it be seen through the large church windows, which hadn't been blacked out, passed through the church to the vestry and there concealed his stole beneath his overcoat. Taking hold of the key of the iron side door to the tower from its hook in the vestry, he went to the base of the tower, unlocked the door and, having let Tesár through, and with his stole now round his shoulders, made his way back to the confessional, where the four soldiers were waiting with Bernadič and Letanovský.

Letanovský and Bernadič had their hands bound in front of them.

Father Stachovič turned to the soldiers, pointed at Mr Letanovský and said: "Untie his hands!" He took fright at his own loud voice, which resonated through the empty, darkened church. "Untie his hands, please, so he can cross himself before and after making his confession." Then, beside the confessional, he used his small candle to light the long one set in a tall candle-holder that he'd taken from the side altar of St Augustine before blowing the small one out.

The soldiers untied Letanovský's hands.

"Come, Mr Letanovský."

Mr Letanovský knelt before the latticed window and Father Stachovič began hearing his confession.

The soldiers re-bound Letanovský's hands.

"Untie his hands," the priest said to the soldiers, pointing at Mr Bernadič, "so he can cross himself."

Mr Bernadič knelt before the latticed window and Father Stachovič began to hear his confession.

The Závodie church was large. The long candle set in the tall candle-holder cast its light only on the confessional, Mr Letanovský and the four soldiers, of whom now one, now another, punctured the mass of darkness with a bluish ray of torchlight as they pointed it at this picture or that statue. Close to the confessional was the St Augustine side altar with its wooden statue of the bareheaded and bearded saint holding a huge book. The dim, poorly lit saint was gazing down past his book at the ground with his dark, contemplative eyes. His right index finger and the ring and little fingers of his left hand had been snapped off.

"Since my last confession," the kneeling Mr Bernadič told Father Stachovič through the latticed window, "I have committed the following sins –"

The priest developed a sudden headache.

"– the following sins –" Mr Bernadič recalled the words from when he had been a child, words that he'd repeated on numerous occasions throughout his life, but at this instant they struck him as ludicrous and degrading.

"When did you last come to confession?" the priest asked him. "Wasn't it at Easter?"

"Yes."

"And since then, what sins have you –?"

The priest broke off. He shuddered as, once more, just as when he'd been hearing Mr Letanovský's confession, he had an urge to leave the confessional and the church and hear no more confessions. Through the little window with its wooden latticework he was inhaling Mr Bernadič's tremulous, foul, warm breath.

For over thirty years Father Stachovič had been inhaling, in his confessional, the breath issuing from lungs, throats and mouths young and old. Through the voices of his parishioners, carried on their breath, he had extracted and learned, following a list of biblical and ecclesiastical commandments, following a list of vices and virtues, their secret lives; he had learned a great deal, but by no means everything, being constrained by the rules of the confessional and by common courtesy, and his parishioners never told him everything about themselves. He had never broken the seal of confession, though he could have used much that he learned from confessants to his own advantage. More than once had he been tempted, but had stood fast and not abused their confidences. He knew of priests, past and present, who were guilty of such an abuse, but he had no such desire.

The case of these two men affected so many others, he mused in the confessional inside the dark church. Both were facing death – and nothing obliged him to deny them the benefit of confession, if not for their lives, then at least for the hope of life eternal. This is all so dreadful, Herr Hauptmann. This is no way to treat people. And to break the seal of confession? For the sake of some German army captain... To what end?

He was shaking with the cold night air inside the church, suffused as it was with the smell of long extinguished candles, and the whiff of wild thyme that had long dwindled away, he shook with the terror to which he'd let himself be driven by Captain Iffland.

The soldiers were getting impatient and marking time in their hobnailed boots. In the dark, silent church their boots clunked metallically and grated noisily across the coloured stone floor tiles.

Mr Letanovský, since Saturday still wearing his work clothes and an old, short overcoat, had his hands tied in front of him. At his feet lay his hat. In the knapsack on his back he had a loaf of bread and a one-litre pot of lard. That's how the burly, ginger-haired sergeant Eulenau and his men had come upon him in the stable. He was shaking because he'd told the priest everything about himself, which he now thought a terrible mistake. One shouldn't tell even the best priest everything, he kept thinking, one mustn't... Mr Letanovský felt sorry for himself and all the people imprisoned in the village hall.

One German soldier shone his torch on St Augustine. The large wooden book cast a shadow across the saint's face up to his eyes.

Mr Letanovský looked into the saint's dark, contemplative eyes. God in Heaven! Why hadn't he made his escape? Why had he trusted the Germans and their Kommandant? His eyes hurt when the soldier switched the torch off.

The soldiers were still clunking and grating with their hobnailed boots.

Father Stachovič listened to them.

Mr Letanovský's whole body was in the painful grip of fatigue, his eyes were burning and his heart was beating painfully. He'd told Feather Stachovič everything, but he hadn't told the Germans. Should he have said there were partisans in Grabovec wood? Why hadn't he told the Kommandant? What had he been afraid of? The priest's going to tell the Kommandant – but then he knows anyway. No, he doesn't. The partisans could have entered the wood only after he and the Schnitzers left it. "Don't be afraid, Mr Letanovský," the priest's words kept coming back to him, as they often had before when he'd been to confession, "don't be afraid! I'm obliged to question you, they said, and try and get something out of you. But I won't tell on you." Mr Letanovský shifted the burden of his heavy, aching frame onto his left foot. Maybe the Germans won't do anything. He shifted his aching frame onto his shaking right foot and suddenly recalled the merciless lieutenant colonel who'd shot his 'lad' because his horse scratched its muzzle on his knife. God Almighty, how could he have escaped? Shooting everyone in his house would be as nothing to the Germans. Oh, God Almighty! Those poor blighters – Mrs Šiška, her granddaughter Štefka, five houses burned to the ground, I wonder, what did happen in the Grabovec wood? Marka, the two Hladíks, the two Masňáks, the Šiškas, Lániks, Tesárs – Bernadič from next door – what happened to the Schnitzers? And the people held in the village hall? He shifted his anguished frame onto his shaking left foot. Maybe it won't matter that he's told the priest everything, but – no... He decided that if the Kommandant asked him again about the things he wanted to know he'd not say a word, however much he threatened him. He looked up from the ground to the confessional, at Mr Bernadič, he looked at him, but saw nothing.

The priest heard Mr Bernadič's confession in the same manner in which he heard the confessions of all his parishioners. First he asked after any sins against the Ten Commandments. He wasn't even thinking about what he was asking, because it struck him as ever more pointless to ask about such trifles in the face of the death now looming over Mr Letanovský and Mr Bernadič. He was thinking of Tesár, whom he'd let into the church through the rusted old iron door; he'd had trouble getting it open because no one had opened it in years. He was thinking of the Schnitzers and their children, of Marka Bernadič, and mentally he repeated: "This is all so dreadful, Herr Hauptmann! You can't do this to people! " Poor Mr Letanovský! Always so right and proper. He inhaled Mr Bernadič's warm, foul breath with its fear-induced quiver.

"In what way have you sinned against our Lord's Eighth Commandment?" he asked him. "Thou shalt not bear false witness against thy neighbour –?"

Mr Bernadič remained silent.

What is all this as against the death that awaits him? Father Stachovič pondered. What are his sins as against such an ignominious punishment and the fear of such a terrible death?

"– in all sorts of ways – sometimes one does say a bad word about someone – lose one's temper –"

"That'll do, Mr Bernadič," said Father Stachovič through the latticed window. "I grant you absolution. Just tell me: did you tell them Mr Letanovský was hiding the Schnitzers?"

"No."

"Did you betray the partisans?"

"No, I betrayed no one. How could I have told on Letanovský? I never split on anyone. Good God! Nobody in my household has let on about anything. My daughter Marka possibly, if they caught her and have been torturing her somewhere –"

"Don't be afraid. You can tell me everything. I won't say a bad word about you to the Germans, though the Kommandant wants me to. And don't worry about Marka. She's at the rectory, with me she is – and so are the Schnitzer children. Nothing's going to happen to her."

"At the rectory – with you?"

"Yes."

Mr Bernadič began to weep.

"Deinde ego te absolvo," said Father Stachovič in his strong, husky voice through the little latticed window out into the darkened church, "I absolve thee of thy sins in the name of the Father, and of the Son, and of the Holy Spirit. Amen."

He blessed Mr Bernadič, stepped slowly out of the confessional and touched the confessant's lips with his stole.

Mr Bernadič got to his feet and turned to face the four German soldiers and Mr Letanovský. Now he wept even more violently.

The soldiers took a piece of rope and rebound his hands, as they had Letanovský's, went over with them to the main altar, and, after the men had received the sacrament from the

(72)

priest's trembling hands, they put Bernadič's greasy cap back on his head, Letanovský's hat on his and then headed out of the church, two in front and two behind, lighting their way with torches.

Father Stachovič replaced the tall candle-holder at the foot of the altar of Saint Augustine, glanced up at the saint and into his dark, severe eyes, lit a short candle from the long one, blew the long one out and went over to the base of the tower.

"Tesár," he said in a low voice, "stay where you are. Hang on till morning! The bell-ringer, our Mr Galbavý, will bring you something first thing because you'll be hungry, then he'll find you a proper hiding-place."

Father Stachovič locked the church, which now sank back into darkness, and went slowly back to rejoin Hauptmann Iffland in the rectory.

Four men, members of the SD, were sitting on Father Stachovič's couch, Truppenführer Mohn having fetched them by car at Iffland's behest. Their faces were covered in black smears as if they'd just escaped from a burning building.

They grinned as the priest entered his office.

"Be so kind as to recognize, Herr Hauptmann," he began, "that a priest can only hear at confession things that count as sins, and nothing about what might be qualified as virtues. I have done my duty. I have heard the confessions of Mr Letanovský and Mr Bernadič. People whose lives are at stake see sins or virtues differently from people who only come to me because they've got nothing better to do."

Iffland burst out laughing and said: "All right, all right, mein Herr!" He carried on laughing.

Father Stachovič, his chair creaking beneath him, forced a smile and slowly looked away from Iffland.

"A confessant will admit to his sins, but not to his virtues," he said. "A priest probing a confessant's virtues would raise suspicions."

Iffland's tired eyes began to hurt. As more than once already that night, fury at Schnitzer's wife surged up inside him.

His left arm was propped from the elbow on the desk and the ring and little fingers on his hand began to twitch.

"You have to convince people," he responded brusquely, "to see sin as virtue and virtue as sin, mein Herr. That was also down to you. I thought that much was obvious. It goes with the spirit of the new times. I understand the seal of confession much as you do, mein Herr! Now, to business, if you wouldn't mind!"

"Well, for example, Mr Bernadič is deeply troubled and regrets," the priest steeled himself, "not taking his daughter, Mária, to the field with him. If he'd had her with him, she wouldn't have got lost. He treats that as a sin. In other circumstances, he'd have treated it as a sin if –"

"Hold it there!" Iffland snapped. "General terms first! Then any details! If there's time!"

"Do you have a map, please?"

From a pile a papers Iffland extracted the ordnance map of the area round Závodie and spread it out on the desk. Rubbish! he snapped mentally, meaning Truppenführer Mohn's crackpot notion that Bernadič's daughter might be the partisan girl he'd mentioned.

Father Stachovič rose from his chair and leaned across his desk and the grey-green area on Iffland's map. He stared at it for a moment, seeking... Merciful God! Herr Hauptmann! Marka! Where to hide the children! Marka wants to leave. To join young Tesár and the partisans. She doesn't want to remain at the rectory. The children need to be entrusted to Mr Galbavý, he can take charge of them, as well as seeing to Tesár... This is all so dreadful, Herr Hauptmann! The priest's eyes went on scouring Iffland's map.

"Here's Závodie, mein Herr!"

"Yes, yes, that's Závodie." Father Stachovič placed a finger on the map. "Here's the road, Herr Hauptmann, these are the settlements of Great and Little Poruba. Then the road leads through the mountains, with dense forests coming right down to its edge. I think this is a most dangerous spot for advancing troops. And this, all the way over here, is the first community in the next valley. It covers a large area and is actually made up of several different hamlets. Lower Kopečné Lazy, Upper Lazy, Little, Great, Long and New Kopečné Lazy. It's ideally suited to partisans and right now it's probably occupied by a major company of them. You may be certain that Great and Little Poruba are so far quite free of any groups of partisans because –"

"So I've been informed," Iffland interrupted Father Stachovič, staring sneeringly at the latter's faltering jaw with its growth of grey stubble. "I know that much myself, mein Herr! I'm perfectly capable of ascertaining which village does have partisans in it and which one doesn't! I'm after something else!"

Father Stachovič straightened up and stood erect facing Iffland.

"All of that's perfectly familiar," he went on in a sarcastic tone of voice. "Where is Maria Bernadič?"

"No idea."

"Were there any bandits from Závodie in that wood?"

Father Stachovič sat down again. "All I got from hearing Mr Letanovský's confession was that –"

"Think twice about what you say, Mein Herr, it's their relatives we've got locked up in the village hall!"

"All I got from hearing Mr Letanovský's confession was that there was nobody in the wood apart from the Schnitzers. Craving your indulgence –"

"Think twice about what you say, Mein Herr! I'm still going to question Letanovský myself. "

Father Stachovič's chair creaked beneath him.

"Was there any truth in his denunciation?"

"No –" said the priest, spreading his large white hands before him, "– no, Herr Hauptmann."

"Here in Závodie, is there an illegal national committee? Who's on it?" Iffland's voice had begun to falter choppily. "Does Závodie have any Communists? Is anyone in contact with Great and Little Poruba and Kopečné Lazy, and if so, who?"

"Craving your indulgence, Herr Hauptmann, please bear in mind," said the priest slowly, mindful that a confessor must not enquire after a penitent's confederates, "that only a grasp of the overall situation allows for any appreciation of the details. The concentration of partisans at Kopečné Lazy, which is a fair distance from both Závodie and Poruba, puts such things as you are pleased to be contemplating quite out of the question."

Iffland lit a cigarette.

"And of the things you are pleased to be contemplating I know nothing. I don't think they apply to Závodie."

"No?"

"No, Herr Hauptmann. As I heard those two men's confessions, I tried to winkle such things out, but neither Mr Bernadič, nor Mr Letanovský –"

Iffland ran his finger over the map. "On the road to Little Poruba, are there," he asked, "any obstacles? I mean natural or man-made?"

"No. It's a good road, wide and pretty undemanding."

Silence descended on the rectory office. Iffland could see that the priest was not minded to assist him and was preparing to resort to threats. The priest just stared at the blood-spattered books. Merciful God! Those young men with the partisans, Marka, the children at the rectory, Tesár under the church tower, Mr Letanovský, Mr Bernadič... Where are the partisans from Závodie, where's Mr Schnitzer, the partisans' fathers? What's going to happen to the people being held at the village hall? Poor Mr Letanovský, poor... Merciful God! This is all so dreadful, Herr Hauptmann! Iffland stared at the priest and at the four soldiers sitting and waiting on the former's leather couch. The silence was shattered by the jangling of the telephone.

"Has anyone from Závodie," Iffland began again, "left to join the bandits, the partisans?"

"No."

"No?"

The phone jangled a third time.

"X 236," Iffland said into it, "X 236, Captain Iffland –"

Father Stachovič listened but without understanding a word. He let his gaze roam round his office. The prie-dieu, which used to stand before a white relief of Golgotha, had been pushed up to the writing desk, on it the phone, a grey metal box with wires leading from it through the blacked-out window, at the far end of the office a table that the troops had brought with them, beneath it, on the floor, two men sleeping, in their clothes, their boots unlaced, beyond their heads their helmets, masks, shovels, kitbags, automatic rifles, and not far from the table two small safes. Father Stachovič listened to Iffland, but couldn't understand what he was saying.

He stared at the blood-spattered books.

Iffland hung up. "So, mein Herr!"

"Yes, Herr Hauptmann," Father Stachovič began. "Mária Bernadič –"

Iffland came to life.

"Mária Bernadič's whereabouts are unknown," the priest said calmly. "Her father has no idea where she might be. She's a young lass, not yet seventeen. She might be in touch with the partisans, she might have joined them, or she might not. She might be hiding out with some relations. She might have been captured by your men. I don't know. As for Mr Bernadič, in your place – craving your indulgence – I'd let him go and have him followed. Daughters can be used as bait. She's a frail lass and won't survive long if she's hiding out somewhere. She'll come back home. You should follow all the Bernadič's. It's bound to be worth your while. Searches, surveillance, just keep track of them. Mária Bernadič could well have precious information that might be of use to you… And as for Mr Letanovský –"

"That's a different matter, mein Herr." Iffland had remembered Truppenführer Mohn and the pretty partisan girl: "It's rubbish."

"That's the very point, Herr Hauptmann," said the priest. "Craving your indulgence, sir, you suspect him of knowing about the partisans in the wood and not telling you. He didn't know. The partisans only entered the wood after Mr Letanovský had left with the Schnitzers. He hadn't known about them. Be so good as to check out what I've just said – please – Schnitzer's widow is still here – I think –"

"It's still a different matter, mein Herr," Captain Iffland shouted at the trembling priest, then he fell silent for a moment before shouting again: "I don't believe Letanovský. Anyone who shelters Jews is capable of anything. I don't believe him and I'd be glad if you stopped believing him as well. You wouldn't wish – you wouldn't want –" Iffland continued in his caustic tone, "you wouldn't want me to stop believing you as well! Now would you? Please!"

"But if, Herr Hauptmann –"

"Stop there!"

Had there been any truth as to his denunciation or not? Iffland looked at Father Stachovič as he sat calmly on his chair. If there had been –

"Mein Herr!"

The priest raised his broad, pale visage somewhat.

"Was there any truth as to his denunciation?"

"No, Herr Hauptmann."

"You're quite convinced?"

"Yes, I am."

Worn out and sleep-deprived, Iffland looked sharply at Father Stachovič as if from that broad, pale visage he might read the truth he'd made his own and the extent of his own power. If the old man is right, then it had all been pointless, the execution, ten men lost, the houses burned down, the prisoners being held in the village hall... If he is not telling the truth, if he is lying... Iffland paused briefly to ponder what that would mean. Questioning the women and children in the village hall, then the mayor and perhaps some others – and driving half of Závodie into joining the partisans. If it had all been pointless, the execution, ten men lost, the houses burned down, the prisoners being held in the village hall, ordering a sortie to Great Poruba, a tough lot to answer for – conversely, a special action by men of the SD, their progress held up, the name of the German people tarnished... Collective responsibility is rubbish, it goes against the conventions of war and only fits in with the thinking of the latter-day butchers who'd become infected with an Idea. Idea, idea, ideological warfare! Rubbish! Truppenführer Mohn's having fun with a pretty partisan girl, possibly Bernadič's daughter. That's fair play, but according to Mohn –

"Mein Herr!"

"Yes, Herr Hauptmann."

"Don't wish me to stop believing you as well! I don't believe Letanovský and I still have to interrogate him myself. Don't wish the same upon yourself, mein Herr!"

"Yes, Herr Hauptmann. Craving your indulgence," Father Stachovič went on calmly, "the justice I seek is for your own sake and that of Germany's armed forces."

"I have always been just, and so have Germany's armed forces," Iffland snapped, wondering briefly whether his troops might not get something out of seeing a priest dangling from a rope. In the absence of the Jewess... I bet she was lying when she said she wasn't Jewish. Iffland had a brief sense of satisfaction. A good thing he hadn't forced her into submission. She might not be Jewish, but that only makes her worse – being infused with Jewish sperm and the Jewish spirit... "Now, if you don't mind, mein Herr!"

Father Stachovič didn't budge.

Iffland signalled to the four grimy soldiers sitting on the couch.

They sprang up and dashed across to the priest.

"Now!" He signalled them to hold back. "Now!"

"Craving your indulgence, Herr Hauptmann," the priest said calmly, the grimy soldiers standing at his back, "I should merely like to say that the only way you can do justice to yourself and to Germany's armed forces, Herr Hauptmann, is by doing justice to Závodie."

Iffland smirked.

"Remember this, mein Herr," he said, "Germany's armed forces are just, they respect the rights and honour of the family, human life, private property, freedom of confession and the performance of ritual – do not doubt that for one second! Please leave now! I'd advise you to stop. I still have to re-interrogate Letanovský – and you'd better hope it won't turn to your detriment. You wouldn't want me to interrogate you as well!"

Father Stachovič rose.

"And I could at any moment!"

The priest turned slowly to face the four begrimed soldiers, walked shakily away from them and left the office, his mind on Mr Letanovský. Perhaps he could have saved himself if he'd revealed the presence of partisans in Grabovec. Why hadn't he done so? Had he been too scared? This is all so dreadful, Herr Hauptmann. I expect you need Mr Letanovský. Závodie has to take fright at the death of one of its once most decent citizens and your men need to be kept amused. That's why you don't yet need the trash in the village hall. The trash might tell you more than you desire to know, and Mr Letanovský is telling you little or nothing. Or – maybe you know nothing at all, Herr Hauptmann. Poor Mr Letanovský! You'll have to make him out to be a partisan, because the real ones have slipped through your fingers. Father Stachovič went to his little back room to join his housekeeper, Marka and the Schnitzer children and began to pray with them for Mr Bernadič and Mr Letanovský, for Mr Schnitzer and his wife, for the people in the village hall, and for Lili and Viola, who listened mutely to the quiet prayer. Father Stachovič was also praying for himself because he knew that that night he had ceased to be a priest.

Captain Iffland sent for Sergeant Eulenau and Private Hoffmann and then had Letanovský and Bernadič brought before them from the priest's cellar, where they'd been held.

Eulenau and Hoffmann came and stood to attention.

"This one," said Iffland, pointing at Letanovský, "is going to need a way out. Get a plank of wood and think of a suitable inscription!"

"Yessir, Herr Hauptmann, sir!"

Then, with the aid of the four men with grimy faces and of Private Hoffmann, he spent almost an hour interrogating Letanovský and Bernadič – or hearing their confession, as he'd put it to the priest – but all he got out of them was that Bernadič had no idea where his daughter Mária was. Iffland stood with his back to Letanovský, Bernadič, Hoffmann and the four soldiers and stared at the white relief of Golgotha, old and dead, as he listened to the groans and stifled cries of the new, and living, Golgotha. A major action, he mused, of the kind Mohn wants, will drive Závodie to join the partisans – this kind of major action will so terrify Závodie that no one will move... This kind of major action will satisfy even Mohn and his men... This actually is a major, a very major action. Mohn has his pretty young partisan girl.

After an hour Iffland let the living Bernadič go.

"What do we do with this one?" he asked, pointing to Letanovský as he lay on the floor. "Is he dead?"

"Not yet!"

The night passed, the night in which Father Stachovič had prayed for Letanovský and Bernadič, for the people imprisoned in the village hall, for Tesár, Marka, for Lili and Viola and for himself, and after the night came a misty Monday morning, when, beneath the pole used for drying hosepipes and facing towards it, the relations of the partisans and their fathers stood in four lines.

At around nine o'clock the soldiers came back from Great Poruba with their loot of hogs, calves, heifers, clothing, pots, two sewing machines and some flat-irons. They came to a halt beneath the pole and chatted among themselves.

"That wouldn't be my choice of a road to heaven!"

"The road to heaven is a thorny one!"

"Yes – interesting, that –!"

"Absolutely right!"

Guards stood by the twenty-seven old men, old and young women and children, and the soldiers who had come to a halt beneath the black pole looked up and at the white plank of wood that Eulenau and Hoffmann had nailed to it. It bore the inscription that Eulenau and Hoffmann had concocted: "Zu Partisanen gelaufen – jetzt muss er an die Himmelspforte schlagen! – He ran off to join the partisans and now he has to knock on Heaven's door –"

Here and there, weeping sprang from the twenty-seven captives.

The soldiers chatted and laughed.

"Ha ha!"

"Ran off to join the partisans and now he's knocking on Heaven's door –"

"Yes, but how? His hands are tied!"

"Poor chap!"

About twenty metres above ground, hanging from the pole by a thin steel cable, was Letanovský. He was warmly dressed, in an old, short overcoat, at his back he had a knapsack containing a loaf of bread and a one-litre pot of lard. A nail had been driven into the pole and on it hung the automatic rifle that the soldiers had brought back from Grabovec, the one which had been that of the dead school-leaver, Lánik.

Around nine-thirty, Iffland ordered back to the village hall the captives who'd been forced to watch Letanovský's execution and stand there beneath him since five o'clock in the morning.

Now he was walking up and down Father Stachovič's office, from the door to the safe and back, as he dictated to his clerks the actions of his men and the SD men assigned to him. He was out of sorts, because he had woken that morning with the bitter thought that Germany's armed forces did not rule over life and death. Such rule did not belong to those that take lives, but to those who also give and so must resist the idea of collective responsibility. Iffland sensed that his heart and mind were in tatters. He says one thing and thinks another, and with every passing moment he says and thinks something different... Rubbish!

"Reprisals," he dictated with a horrible sense that Germany's armed forces had been transformed into a crazed murderer who deliberately left tracks behind him, "...reprisals: killed during searches: one woman, one child; executed: one Jew, two Jewish children, the five fathers of five partisans; burned down: five houses; ten men, members of the SD, died fighting bandits –"

The clerks stared at Iffland open-mouthed.

What madman had given such orders? Iffland crossed from the door to the safe on which the ancient clock stood. What – what madman – could want to photograph, identify and announce the victims of his reprisals?

So much for Saturday and Sunday in Závodie. Then Monday began.

Fight, hit back at 'em, wherever possible! Hit every one of the fiends. There's nothing else for it, just this! And just this was all that remained inside Tesár, who'd fled from Grabovec and from the deep-bedded stream by Great Poruba, and just this remained inside all those who'd escaped with him to Little Poruba. Hit them hard for having sought to shoot eight people, hit them for having killed Tesár's father, for the Schnitzers and for all the things they've done in Závodie and will yet do. What was it that he'd seen ablaze in Závodie? Hit them back for the school-leaver Lánik!

"That poor boy," said the fruit-grower Lánik in the school at Little Poruba, adding tearfully: "My poor boy – just a lad –"

"Don't cry now, my friend!" Šiška, whose wife and daughter, Štefka, had been buried in Závodie, tried to console him. "Don't cry now! We'll give 'em, those damn' Krauts, what for! Never you fear!"

The Little Poruba school, which was the command centre of the company of partisans, was full of men and a noisy confusion of excited Slovak and Russian voices. The men from Great Poruba, who'd fled when the soldiers came to loot the village, were explaining what had happened. One of them was lying on a bed of straw, having been badly beaten and kicked because he'd faced up to the soldiers who'd come to plunder his father's stables. The school was filled with cigarette smoke and the smell of sweating human flesh, while much was going on outside.

"Števo!"

Tesár looked round for Jakubec, the tall, swarthy lieutenant and commander of the unit, and crossed to the teacher's desk.

"Števo!" Jakubec began in his croaky, now failing voice. "These men will go with you: Hladík, Masňák, Šiška..." He read out the names of a further three men from Lower and Upper Brezany and then the names of fifteen young men who'd come over from Great Poruba. "Occupy Klin and wait there in case the Germans start retreating that way! Attack them as they retreat along the road beneath the hill."

Amid the pandemonium, the thick smoke, the strong background smell, the clatter of automatics, rifles and grenades being assembled and distributed, Tesár took on board the tasks he and his group were being set by Jakubec. He gazed at the freshly wiped blackboard and the writing in large, white letters: A PLAGUE UPON 'EM! DEATH TO THE GERMAN OCCUPIERS! In the event of protracted fighting the other side of Little Poruba or within the village, or in the event of an orderly German retreat, they were to fight a way through to link up with the rest. Not easy, that! As they needed to appreciate. Tesár stood over Lieutenant Jakubec and listened.

"Take good care of yourself, Števo!" Jakubec's spent voice sounded hoarse. "Take good care!" He tapped the table with his knuckles. "May Christ and the Virgin Mary protect you so you only shoot when the Germans are in retreat, when they're right beneath you."

"Yes, Comrade Lieutenant, sir!"

Tesár rejoined his group who, at Little Poruba, had donned uniforms, taken up their arms and become a unit. It was given the name Dawn.

"They'll be digging trenches," Jakubec's hoarse, spent voice was heard to say as he spoke to the fathers of the partisans from Závodie. "Hladík, Lánik, Masňák, Šiška..." Then he named the other men, the ones who'd come from Great Poruba. "Schnitzer, you go to Kopečné Lazy to the brigade headquarters. You can register there."

The fruit-grower Lánik left Šiška's side and went over to Lieutenant Jakubec. He stood in front of the desk and waited a moment, clenching and unclenching his fists as his arms hung loose.

"Comrade Lieutenant!"

"What is it?"

"I'm Lánik," he said slowly, "I'm supposed to go with the trench-diggers – but they killed my boy – I'd rather go with Tesár –"

"Eh?"

"With Števo Tesár."

"Will you take him with you, Števo?"

Lieutenant Jakubec looked down from the platform at Lánik's pale, sad face, furrowed with bitterness about the mouth. "Števo!"

"Yes, sir, Comrade Lieutenant, sir!"

"Will you take this man, Lánik, with you? He wants to go with you."

"Happy to, Comrade Lieutenant!"

"How old are you, Lánik?" asked Lieutenant Jakubec.

"Sixty come Thursday."

"Come on then, Lánik," Tesár called. "Let's be having you!"

Fight, hit back at 'em! Tesár was resolute as he took charge of his unit. What else might the Germans do in Závodie? What had that fire in Závodie been? Hit 'em hard, and any who assist them! Who'd informed on Letanovský? Who'd betrayed the

Schnitzers and who'd let on that some Závodie men had gone to join the partisans?

By Monday evening so many men had gathered at Little Poruba that some had to go on to Kopečné Lazy, because Little Poruba didn't have enough boots or guns for them. They'd come as they were when the Germans from Závodie began looting Great Poruba. Some had at least managed to pull on some trousers and unlaced shoes, others had just had time to leap out of bed.

The houses, farms, Poruba forest and the road were all one hive of activity.

The road leading from Upper and Lower Brezany, Závodie and Great Poruba rose quite steeply beyond Great Poruba and about half-way between the two Porubas it was bisected by the side slope of Klin, a hill covered with a scattering of hazels and dogwoods and carved up with huge grey boulders. The hazels and dogwoods were quite sparse and there were no proper trees at all. The pine forest that had once been there had been cut down by the locals long before, the soil had been washed away by rain, and all that was left was rocks and sand.

During the day Klin had to be occupied from first thing, because it was likely that if the Germans were to raid Little Poruba, it would be in the daytime, likewise if they were to try to break through Little Poruba to Kopečné Lazy. From Klin, Tesár's unit was to block the road and attack the Germans from the rear, while from the front – held up in the forest beyond Little Poruba on a road that had been mined – they'd be attacked by the Soviet partisans hiding in the woods alongside the road and in Little Poruba, which had otherwise been largely vacated. The only remaining residents were mostly young men. The many older men, the women and children had left on wagons for Kopečné Lazy, five or six hours on foot from Little Poruba.

On Tuesday morning with a cool breeze blowing, Tesár, wearing new army boots, new army trousers, a shirt with the sleeves rolled up, a belt with a gun and some shells, and an army cap, was leading his unit towards the treeless, rock-covered Klin when they suddenly came to a halt, because below the hill a woman in a brown tracksuit was running towards them. In her hands she held the two ends of the brown and green scarf tossed loosely over her head.

"Halt!"

She stopped.

"Who are you? Where've you come from?"

"Great Poruba, I've been walking and walk-..."

"Good God!" Tesár exclaimed. "Is that you? I hardly recognized you, looking like that –"

"Are you here? Everybody? And – the children?"

"Your husband's at brigade HQ."

"And...?" Tesár looked in silence at Schnitzer's wife, the muscles of whose face had started to twitch. A spasm ran up her arms. She opened her grey eyes wide and drew back slightly, as if having noticed something. "And the children?"

"Marka's taken them."

"Where – taken where...?" Schnitzer's wife clenched her fists. "What have you done with my children?"

"Stop shouting! I don't know where she's taken them. What's the latest from Závodie?"

"They've taken Mr Bernadič. And where – where –?"

Tesár went red in the face, his thick, dark eyebrows twitched above his nose and for a moment he just stared into nothingness. They must have picked up Bernadič because of Marka. They must have caught Marka with the children, and with his own father. Tesár quivered with uncertainty and rage at Letanovský and the Schnitzers. He looked sharply back at Schnitzer's wife.

"But they haven't taken Letanovský?"

"No."

"No?"

"Where – what have you done with my children?" she yelped in a hoarse, faltering and stifled voice. "Where – are –?"

"I don't know," said Tesár and was about to let her have it because it was actually the Schnitzers who were to blame for everything, including the Germans' taking Marka, the children, his father and Bernadič, but shrank back when a gust of wind blew the scarf from her grey hair. "What was that fire in Závodie?"

"Where are – what have you done – with my children –?"

"Don't you know?"

"What?"

"What the fire in Závodie was. On Sunday?"

"What have you done – with my children?"

"Go and report to the battalion in Little Poruba!"

"What – have you," she was screaming now, "where have you taken my children?"

Tesár had had enough, so he took his unit off to occupy Klin at a point above the Poruba road. They duly did occupy it; having deployed his men behind rocks and bushes, he sat down and stared blankly at the road in his frustration. Thoughts were spinning round inside his head, playing havoc, bad ones driving out the good, and worse ones the bad. How had Schnitzer's wife got away? What had happened to her? And Marka? Had she been caught? And his father? And the children? Tesár fell prey to a harrowing stupor. He couldn't get out of his head how brusquely he'd sent the Schnitzers from Grabovec back to Závodie, how the Schnitzer kids had sat motionless in the wood, their hands tied in front of them and their legs embedded up to the waist in the soil dug out of a pit by the condemned men. The Germans were shouting over their heads, laughing and gurgling. Tesár looked blankly down at the road, his mind's eye seeing Schnitzer in tears, and the children, too, as he handed them to Marka. What *was* going on in Závodie? Marka wouldn't be coming now they'd taken Bernadič. And what would become of his own father? Poor man. Tesár looked blankly ahead, sitting there on his rock and glancing just now and again at the grey deserted road. After three or four hours the sun began to shine feebly on him through the morning mist drifting about the Poruba hilltops. A weasel ran past along the road.

There was silence, only from faraway came the boom of mortar-fire and shells landing.

How ludicrous is this little war, going on within the big war. Ludicrous and stupid. Tesár was overwhelmed by a deep sense of sorrow. What's it all for? Schnitzer's wife must be out of her mind now, she's turned grey and her children are gone, and Marka, and my father. He glanced to left and right. Šiška's hat had a little bunch of wild thyme poking out of it.

And so the painful days passed, in the town, in Upper Brezany, in Grabovec and in Little Poruba, days long and arduous – Saturday, Sunday, Monday, Tuesday – and Tesár had a sense that it was not mere days, but entire long years that had been hitting him with distress.

Wednesday came, and on Wednesday afternoon the troops in Závodie were reinforced by three more platoons, three armoured vehicles and four trucks, and on Thursday morning the commander of the Závodie troops, Captain Johann Iffland, wearing a long, shiny, rubber cape and high, shiny top boots, stroked his swarthy, freshly shaved face and bade farewell to Father Stachovič. "Very well, mein Herr," he said, "I'm sorry not to have been better pleased with your village. In Lower Brezany I was much happier, even with the priest!"

The priest merely looked down. This is all so dreadful, Herr Hauptmann. He clasped his hands before him.

"So now you can get on with burying Letanovský," Iffland said. "We have discharged our duties, so now you can. We have only achieved so much, but others will follow us, mein Herr, so I suggest you act in a manner that will leave them more satisfied with you than I have been!"

Father Stachovič looked back up. "Craving your indulgence, Herr Hauptmann," he said, "about those people held captive in the parish hall –?"

Iffland smiled.

"No, mein Herr," he said, "don't force me to destroy everything that I might! And we're not the last to show up in your village. So, mein Herr..."

Iffland offered the priest his hand, which was concealed within a tough leather glove.

"God be with you, Herr Hauptmann!"

The warming sun had dispersed the mist and Klin, damp with the mist and dew, grew fragrant with the tufts of wild thyme that were still growing in the measly soil; even the old grass, now brown and drooping, added a fragrance of its own.

Father, Marka, the Schnitzer children? Mrs Schnitzer – maybe she's lost her mind, she's certainly turned grey. Lost in thought, Tesár was fixing some wild thyme to his cap. He placed the cap back on his head and at that moment the wind filled his ear with the faint rumble of a column on the move.

Klin received some reinforcements, a squad of Russian partisans bearing light machine guns with drum magazines, and their commander, known in Little Poruba only as Scarface, having posted his young men behind boulders and the denser hazel and dogwood bushes, began looking for a position for himself, one which would afford him a good view of his men and of the road. In some agitation he strolled passed Tesár's men. The young twenty-three-year-old, small of stature and lithesome, had a broad, brown scar on his left cheek. He halted beside Lánik, looked him over and shook his head.

"Old man," he said, "*idi*, you go!"

"What?"

Scarface pointed towards Little Poruba, and as Lánik looked blankly back at him he said that he was old and he himself young, so he should go to Little Poruba, and he, Scarface, would take his place.

"Oh, no!" Lánik replied, "I'm going nowhere, I'm staying right here – the Krauts murdered my son – a mere schoolboy!"

"Son?" Scarface queried, smiling. "Schoolboy?"

Lánik nodded sadly and stuck firmly by his boulder.

"In my case," Scarface told him, "They kill whole town – *idi*!"

Tesár came running across to Lánik.

"It's true, Lánik," he said, "you really should go to Little Poruba and beyond. I know you could take it here, but if we had to make a run for it – what then?"

"And haven't I run off with you before this, and didn't I keep up?"

"Be reasonable! Yes, you ran, but – that time nobody was shooting at us – and anyway, it was a bit of a miracle that we did run and escape."

Scarface swayed at the hip.

"I'm not going!"

"*Idi!*"

"Listen, Lánik," said Tesár sharply, "do as we say – stop dithering – while there's still time!"

The rumbling had ceased.

The next gust of wind brought it back.

Lánik, his pale features creased with anger, stepped aside from his boulder, looked back at it, took the measure of Scarface and Tesár, glanced once more at the rock and left for the far side of Klin. There, full of resentment, he took cover in a thick hazel bush.

Tesár went back behind his own boulder.

The rumbling ceased.

The next gust of wind brought it back. Could it be the Krauts from Závodie? Behind his boulder Tesár was on edge. Even that faint rumble seemed too much for three motorcycles and eleven trucks.

"May Jesus bleeding on his cross protect you, men!" Tesár stepped out from behind his boulder and took a quick turn round his unit. "May Jesus bleeding on his cross and heaven knows who else protect you, now will be the time to start shooting, if they do happen along! Once they're in retreat. But only start shooting once they're directly below Klin!"

Then he returned to his boulder. The rumble of the column fell silent, only to become slightly more audible each time the wind gusted.

"Števo, here!"

Tesár looked round after the voice that had suddenly chimed up behind his back, but now all he could see was some black canvas shoes, a pair of pretty legs covered in scratches, and a red dress. Marka vanished from sight. She was running towards Little Poruba, which she'd only left to come to find Tesár. The sound of men laughing came from behind several boulders.

"3 armoured cars, 15 trucks, around 220 men, 4 infantry support guns, trench mortars, machine guns –" Tesár read, holding in his right hand the stone Marka had tossed at his feet with a piece of paper wrapped round it, "your father, Lili, Viola all safe, hello from all of us, they hanged Mr Letanovský, our father's back home, they killed Mrs Šiška and Štefka, your house, the Hladíks', Šiškas' and Lániks' have all been burned down, stick to your guns."

Tesár stared at Marka's note. He was still holding the stone. He felt sorry for Šiška. He looked across in his direction. All he could see was his hat and behind it a fresh posy of wild thyme. Should he tell him – or not? If he does... No, he mustn't tell him yet... Who did Marka get all this from? She'd heard all sorts of stuff over the course of that day and night in Grabovec. But how could she, she, Marka, possibly know what infantry support guns are? Who told her? Good lord, Marka! She must have copied it from some other note, some other, then come running here with it, on her way to the battalion HQ. Or had she been there already? And where's she been till now? Poor Šiška –!

The rumble of the column was getting louder.

Tesár rose to his feet and did a round of his men behind their boulders and bushes. He felt so good about Marka as he told the men: "Three armoured cars, fifteen trucks, around two hundred men, four infantry support guns, trench mortars, machine guns – my father's safe, so are the Schnitzer girls, they've hanged Letanovský...", felt so good about her mouth, always with that slight sneer, the green eyes always veiled by her eyelids, and about her red dress and black canvas shoes.

The rumble of the column was getting louder.

"Letanovský?" Hladík asked, popping into his mouth a bit of wood snapped off a hazel twig. "Serve him right – for harbouring those Jews."

"And what else has been going on in Závodie?" Šiška asked. "Where was the fire?"

"I don't know –"

Scarface began waving to Tesár, to get him back behind his boulder, waving angrily.

Back in Závodie, Father Stachovič, wearing a black cope, his special funeral vestment, was burying Mr Letanovský, who'd been seen by the whole of Závodie and everywhere round about as an inoffensive and thoroughly decent man.

Why had they hanged him? people asked themselves. It can only have been because of the Schnitzers! Who'd informed on him? Who'd given the Schnitzers away, and the partisans? In the Letanovský yard people stood quietly while the funeral rites were played out; the Letanovskýs and many others were in tears. How dare people do such things?

As Mr Galbavý, the old bell-ringer, whose long, white whiskers were like the tassels on the church banner, was leaving the yard to go and ring Letanovský off on his final journey, he paused to speak to the organist.

"This war," he grumbled, "is it never going to end...?"

At that very instant a shrill voice rang out. It came flying out of the Letanovskýs' front room. People just had to smile: Brigita, Jožo's wife, had given birth to a baby boy.

As the funeral procession made its way towards the cemetery, everyone froze at the cemetery gateway, because an artillery barrage had begun to thunder, crackle and bang from the direction of Poruba. A faintness seized the crowd and Father Stachovič felt as if he'd lost all command of his arms and legs and that he was walking only by means of some alien force. The Hauptmann had received information that the partisans were way over at Kopečné Lazy. Merciful God! How badly he'd been informed! Had Marka had time to reach

Little Poruba? To pass on her message? This is all so dreadful, Herr Hauptmann!

The barrage crashed and banged.

Father Stachovič, his head full of the terrible fate of the man, brought the funeral ritual to a speedy end here at the cemetery, because he wanted people to be able to disperse and not risk being so crowded together.

"... by Thy grace bless this grave," he prayed in Latin, his voice shaking, over Letanovský's deep grave, which had been dug out next to the shallow, shared grave of old Mrs Šiška and her granddaughter Štefka, "and grant unto him Thy holy angel for a guardian – forgive also all the sins of those whom we bury so that they, with all Thy saints, may rejoice in Thee without end –"

From the direction of Poruba the barrage still crackled and banged.

"Kyrie eleison!"

"Christe eleison!" the organist responded to the priest's tremulous singing. "Kyrie eleison!"

"Pater noster –"

"Our Father, which art in Heaven," prayed the people of Zavodie, men, women and children, praying in a muffled tone steeped in sheer fear, "hallowed be Thy name –"

The barrage crackled and banged.

"– and forgive us our trespasses, as we forgive those who trespass against us –"

From the direction of Poruba the barrage rumbled and crackled and the Germans' infantry support guns banged and banged away, mines went bang, rapid-firing rifles crackled and Soviet submachine guns chattered – Little Poruba was on fire in three places.

On the horizon Tesár could see smoke in three places.

The unit on Klin was tingling with fear and impatience. Tesár chewed the nail on his left ring finger right off, he still had Marka's stone in one hand, Šiška was picking one by one some wretched stalks of grass that had sprung from the paltry soil cover on the rocks, Hladík had in his mouth the bit of hazel twig, all shredded at one end because he kept gnawing at it nervously, Masňák was rubbing his knee against a sharp projection on his rock, and the barrage kept on thundering, crackling and banging.

Tesár couldn't see as far as Little Poruba, nor could any of the men in his unit. Where was the fighting? On the road? On farms? Inside houses? Beyond the village in the woods?

Twenty minutes passed.

A shiver shot through Tesár's breast. He tossed Marka's stone aside.

A motorbike appeared on the road beneath Klin. Four soldiers on it: the young, slim Private Hoffmann, the burly, ginger-haired Sergeant Eulenau in the sidecar, behind Hoffmann on the back seat the slim lieutenant in the shiny rubber cape, and behind Eulenau a soldier who was actually hanging on between the machine and the sidecar. Grenades exploded, submachine guns chattered, the bike was still moving, the hanging soldier slipped off, the thin lieutenant fell off his seat, Eulenau's head flopped, as did Hoffmann's, and still the bike travelled on a short way. It was followed by two trucks with their slanting front ends. Grenades going off, submachine guns rat-tat-tatting. The trucks came to a halt at right-angles across the road. Tesár wiped the sweat from his brow. Fight! Fight! Hladík spat out his bit of twig and blazed away at the cabin of the first lorry, Masňák pressed his knee against his rock's sharp projection and blazed away at the soldiers jumping off the second lorry. Tesár looked along his gunbarrel at the shattering windscreen of the second lorry and Šiška took aim with his submachine gun and sprayed the men who had jumped from the first. Some flung themselves to the ground, others took to the slope below the road. He threw two grenades after them. He was shaking with rage and proceeded to fire away even at the trucks' grey tarpaulins. The motorbike and two soldiers in the ditch, two trucks standing across the roadway, from Little Poruba a great din and the crackle and clatter of gunfire – fight, fight back, hit back and hard! – Klin reeked of gunfire, reeked with such intensity as to be stifling, a stifling silence down on the road, nothing moving.

A mine shell.

Exploding on Klin among the rocks.

Two Great Poruba men fell and rolled down onto the roadway.

A second exploded.

Hladík fell and slid about five paces down the slope.

"Follow me!" Tesár screamed and shouted. He wiped the sweat from his eyes. "Follow me! Follow me!"

A shell exploded, two men from Great Poruba and three from Brezany stopped crawling up the hillside. They lay silent on the ground.

Another shell.

Tesár felt a warm and wet sensation inside his rolled-up left sleeve. As he crawled up the rough sandy ground he glanced back. Šiška – Masňák – four men from Great Poruba. Behind them on all fours the nimble Scarface, he glanced back and gesticulated to his squad.

A shell.

Another shell.

Scarface, having turned to face his squad, coiled up like a snake on the sand and the faded grass with its odd clumps of wild thyme, rolled onto his back and stopped moving.

A shell.

Where Masňák – his mind forever on his fiancée from near Nitra – had been, all there was now was a shallow depression in the stony, gritty earth.

Away from the shells! Away! Away! Don't get yourselves killed! Or captured! Tesár spat out a mouthful of sand and soil. Away! Away!

"Šiška!"

Tesár passed Marka's note to him.

"Hit back hard, Šiška," he said, "They've killed your Štefka –!"

"What?"

"– and your mother, possibly your wife, too – hit 'em!"

Šiška grabbed the screwed-up paper and crawled away from the motionless Tesár. Crawled away from the shelling, clutching Marka's note in a fit of rage at Tesár.

Tesár spat out some soil, fine sand and grass and wiped the sweat from his eyes with his right hand, beneath a stripped hazel bush he rolled onto his back and ran his hand over the blood streaming from his rolled-up left sleeve. There was a sharp pain beneath his left shoulder, sharp and deep, his whole arm hurt as if someone had whacked it with a chunk of wood. He looked up at the stripped hazel bush and the sky beyond, which was scarred by long, grey-brown smears of smoke coming from Little Poruba as it burned. Fight, hit every one of the fiends! Štefan Tesár, his bushy back eyebrows twitching with pain, stared up into the grey-and-white smoke-smeared sky, stared, motionless. The sky paled, he lost sight of the smears, his eyes stinging with sweat, in his ears the gunfire fell silent and in his eyes the light went out. The air above him rang and clattered with gunfire and the stripped hazel bush rustled in a gentle breeze. From Klin, its rocks and dismal hazel and dogwood bushes it bore away the stifling stench of gunfire.

Before long the pain restored Tesár to consciousness.

The shooting had stopped, and when Lánik, hiding in a hazel bush, heard someone shouting from further round the hill, he crawled all the way across and, aghast at the sight of his fallen comrades, dragged Tesár away: he it was who'd been calling for help.

* * *

"Young Letanovský, as I'm sure you all know," said Father Stachovič four years later in Tesár's office at the regional national committee, "Jozef Letanovský, son of the late Mr Letanovský, is chairman of our local natonal committee, in Závodie. He's very pushy, as dangerous as all who hold office on the basis of 'merit', and, naturally, he can be influential in so many regards. I don't know why people keep turning to me, but I've already had lots of letters, even from Mrs Schnitzer – she's better now, bless her – and from her children – and the day before yesterday I had another one from Marka Bernadič. Please, take a look."

Tesár, who was more than surprised at Father Stachovič's coming to see him, was agitated by what he'd just heard and pained at the mention of Marka. He shifted in his plain, green armchair, held the letter in his right hand and read. The thick, dark tufts of his eyebrows became animated and his now podgy face gleamed as his eyes settled on the lines: "Someone keeps following me. I've done nothing bad. I'm afraid it's more about my father than me. For a long time now, Chairman Letanovský has been blaming my father for informing on his late father, who was executed by the Germans, and that he gave away the Schnitzers and the Závodie partisans. I'm quite certain my father gave no one away. After all, he and the late Mr Letanovský had always been good neighbours. Forgive me, but please let me ask you a favour..." Tesár read Marka's letter. A dull pain passed in waves from his head to his breast, a dull pain, not new, but distinct.

Štefan Tesár, deputy chairman of the regional national committee, stared pensively at Marka's letter. He read it very slowly, taking his time, returning constantly to lines already read, because their content kept eluding him. His mind took him back to Závodie, to Marka Bernadič and what she did, what she did for him, Štefan Tesár.

In April 1945, one Sunday, and the people of Závodie forgot to go to church as they had on the second Sunday in September. No one came from Great or Little Poruba either, they'd had other things to worry about. In the centre of Závodie, outside the church and the rectory, outside the school, the huge inn, the parish hall, and at the foot of the tall pole on which the village firemen used to hang their hoses to dry after a practice or a fire, and on which Iffland had had the tortured Letanovský hanged, people were standing about in groups to welcome some Soviet soldiers. Tesár the partisan was also there to greet them, raising only his right hand high, because he now lacked his left one, Marka Bernadič was there, standing next to him, wearing heavy boots and a tracksuit, and Hladík and Lánik and Masňák, all three now without their sons, and others were there, too, including the Šiškas. Old sapper Šiška was in tears. The church bells stopped ringing. Old Mr Galbavý, Závodie's bellringer, came out of the church with the altar boys. "Three times we've rung the bells," he grumbled behind his white whiskers, those tassels from the church banner, "and nobody's come into the church. What's wrong with you? Is this war never going to end?" – "But it's over, old man!" Marka called across to him. "Come on, stop being silly! Come on now!" – "What?" – "I said come along now!" She left Tesár's side and ran over to the bell-ringer – and at that moment Tesár felt that she'd taken half his joy from him – she took the bell-ringer, old Mr Galbavý, by the arm, turned him round, she herself then turned and made to enter the church with him. Men, women, everyone was watching them. "You mean the war really is over?" Mr Galbavý asked Marka in the church doorway. – "Indeed it is!" – "What?" – "Indeed it is, I'm telling you, come on now!" – "What?" – "I said come on!" She was laughing. The sun was shining and her fair hair glistened, while her green eyes travelled up and down the doubting bell-ringer, her eyelids resting serenely over them. "Come on now!" Tesár watched her sadly. Old Mr Galbavý turned slowly, nodded to her and approached the side door, old and rusty. He unlocked it and a moment later many of the people swarmed together in front of the church, because first to come out of the old side door at the base of the tower was old Mr Galbavý the bell-ringer with his arms full of blankets, Father Stachovič's fur coat, some old overcoats, woollen shawls, a large wrap, and he was followed out by the Schnitzer children, dishevelled and filthy, and Marka bringing an electric fire and portable cooker and behind her two young American pilots, much in need of a shave, and finally old Tesár, Števo's father, gaunt, pale, his dark face also in need of a shave. His father looked at the crowd and at the whole breadth of sun-drenched Závodie, which since the second Sunday in September he'd only seen through a narrow window in the tower. He came over to him. "You've lost an arm?" he asked Števa, his son. "How are you going to work? Earn a living? Better if you'd lost your legs. Without an arm a man's only half a man." His son merely nodded, fuming at his father, at Marka, at all those people. Old Mr Galbavý smiled at the Schnitzer children, at the Soviet soldiers, who'd stopped in front of the church. He turned and went to the rectory. "What – what have you done with my children?" a voice shrieked from behind the crowd that was surrounding the Tesárs, father and son, Lili and Viola and the American pilots. "What – what have you done with my children?" The Soviet soldiers stepped aside as did the people of Závodie, men, women and children, the American pilots stepped back, foolish people laughed and the sensitive froze, the cry had come from Schnitzer's wife, dishevelled, grey-haired, and she ran towards her children. They took fright and backed away from her. She bent down to them, looked closely at thirteen-year-old Lili, at her long flat face that seemed not even to have a nose on it, stroked her unsightly black plaits, then she looked at ten-year-old Viola, the one with the rounder face and furrowed cheeks, stroked her hair with its long fringe that now hung down as far as her eyes, and her lips that projected slightly as if she were sucking a sweet – and suddenly she stood up straight, turned to face the crowd and screamed: "Where – where's the Hauptmann? What… what have you done with my children? Where…?" Schnitzer's wife ran off, away from the people, who looked stunned and bewildered. Marka put the electric fire and stove down on the ground, grabbed Lili and Viola by the hands and ran after her with them. She took her by the arm and led her home, to the Bernadič house, where she'd been in hiding since Christmas. Not long after, just a few days, the

Závodie partisans, Tesár and Šiška, and young Letanovský, who had been made Závodie's local national committee chairman only because the Germans had hanged his father, began to persecute Mr Bernadič, charging him with having betrayed the partisans, Letanovský and the Schnitzers. If it weren't for Marka, he'd surely have been put away, convicted, but she managed to ensure that didn't happen, though even so, Bernadič had to spend some time in hiding, in his brother's loft at Upper Brezany. "I'm not staying, I'm leaving Závodie," Marka told Tesár early in the summer following the war. "I don't want to stay at home. And you, Števo? You shouldn't pander to Jožo Letanovský. He's wrong, the way he keeps attacking my father, because my father never gave anyone away, not Jožo's father, not the Schnitzers, nor the partisans. He'd never have done any such thing. He's lucky that I was with you during the uprising. Otherwise he might be dead by now. I'm angry with you – and – take care!" Marka Bernadič did leave Závodie to be near the Schnitzer children in Bratislava. Tesár was angry with her too. From that time on he began to hate her, because he thought she didn't want him like that, without one arm. He was also left pining for her, and after her departure something nasty began to brew between Tesár and Šiška, because Šiška held him to blame for the death of his little daughter Štefka and his mother, and he had to fight back against his conscience for having abandoned Tesár on Klin under shellfire.

"Right, so –!"

Father Stachovič was sitting quietly in a green armchair at the local national committee, watching the pensive Tesár, noting his brown left sleeve, empty and tucked into his left-hand pocket, and his heavy lower jaw drooped as he brooded. He was thinking of the books that had once been in his office, stained with streaks of blood, and of Marka, who had been to see him during the night after that terrible September Sunday and told him: "They won't go poking about at the rectory – but Tesár's at the foot of the church tower – in the old iron doorway…" His whole frame was shot through by a wave of uncertainty as to whether he wasn't meddling quite improperly in matters even though they affected him too.

Father Stachovič waited.

"Well –?" Tesár folded the letter and handed it back. "What's this really about?"

The priest's eyes ran over the mottled chipboard desk top and the chipboard cupboards and shelves.

"I –"

"Do you think Marka's right?"

"I don't just think so, I know so." The priest lapsed into a brief silence. "And I took the liberty of coming to see you to tell you something you may not know. Something you ought to know."

Tesár smiled dubiously at Father Stachovič with his shiny, increasingly fleshy face.

"Look here," said the priest. "The Bernadič family suffered endless trouble right after the war, and, but for Marka, I don't know how they'd have survived it all. Now it's happening all over again, and troubles of her own – and very serious ones at that – have overtaken Marka herself. Yesterday I received a telegram to say that she'd been expelled from college. That would be a crying shame, because these last few years she's become quite a different girl from the one we knew in Závodie, she's taken courses, got herself an education...! So I told myself that I won't have it – I'm assuming you're more fair-minded than the Germans – I won't have someone cashing in on the memory of a man who was rightfully condemned and rightfully executed, albeit he's the man's son, and going about doing wrong by others."

"Rightfully? Letanovský was executed rightfully?" Tesár smirked angrily at Father Stachovič. "That's nonsense. Stop talking such utter rubbish, Father!"

The priest's pale face, pleated with wrinkles, went red. His large white hands twitched.

"Look here!" he said, then lapsed into silence before continuing angrily. "I'm not long for this world, so I really don't have time for talking rubbish. Never in my life have I talked rubbish, though for all I know you think I've done nothing else my entire life. But this isn't about people talking rubbish. It's about Letanovský, because the remarkable thing about this whole affair is that Letanovský was condemned and executed rightfully, and not only from the Germans' perspective, but from yours, too." Father Stachovič's jaw sank. "I know that to be the case. I spoke to him before his execution, that's to say I had to hear his confession. He it was who betrayed himself and the Schnitzers to the German captain and in order to save his own bacon he told on you as well, except that –"

Tesár flinched. His coat pocket lost its hold on his empty left sleeve.

"– by then that did him little good. The Hauptmann took a different view of matters. He blamed Mr Letanovský for the loss of his men who, in Grabovec, you'd succeeded in... He may have given you away, but having seen you in Grabovec, he didn't let on who you were."

"And this is all true?"

"It is the truth," said the priest with a nod. "Evil sometimes destroys those sustain it. Practically always. Mr Letanovský had given away himself, the Schnitzers, you – and he knew you were marked out to die – all that just to save himself, and you can see how –"

Tesár fixed his gaze firmly on Father Stachovič, his right arm resting on the arm of his chair and his mouth half-agape. The thick tufts of his dark eyebrows puckered above his nose. In his office silence reigned. Father Stachovič was thinking. He was shaking a bit, partly now from age, but also because of what he had just revealed to Tesár.

"Would you mind taking it upon yourself to stop young Letanovský treating the Bernadič family so badly? The only thing that matters is for him to stop treating them badly. That's all that matters. I think you could well help Marka. Times like the present call not for half-persons, but for whole persons – but then you know that well enough, all kinds of things have gone before this and – craving your indulgence, I have every respect for you as a hero, though I'm not too sure if someone can be a hero if he flies in the face of justice."

Tesár, who was fighting back hard against the dull, stabbing, but long familiar pain, was slightly embarrassed, he rose, picked up the phone with his right hand, lay it on the desk, dialled with his right hand, placed the receiver to his ear and waited.

"Janko, is that you?"

Father Stachovič rose.

"I'm coming round. It's about Letanovský and Bernadič again. This has to be brought to a close once and for all...! I'll be right round to explain certain things to you." – "Who's it about, Letanovský, the Bernadič girl?" Tesár heard Šiška ask. "The Bernadič college girl? No, no, Števo, leave well alone! For the sake of the cause. Even in our colleges we need good, solid, reliable cadres – and it's right that we look back to the parental generation. I don't trust Bernadič... And who's been digging this up again?" – "I've got Father Stachovič with me and..." – "Stachovič? And you suppose that our policy with regard to cadres is to be influenced by priests? Come on, Števo..." Šiška, chairman of the regional people's committee, hung up. Tesár turned to face Father Stachovič and spoke into the phone: "Good, I'll be right there, I'll explain a couple of things to you and that'll be the end of it."

The priest thanked him.

Together they went out into the corridor, where he thanked him once again.

With his right hand, Tesár tucked his left sleeve back in his pocket and made as if to go to see Šiška, chairman of the regional people's committee, whose mother and little girl, Štefka, had been killed by the burly, ginger-haired Sergeant Eulenau. The priest's eyes followed him. Tesár took to the stairs and his left sleeve slipped from his pocket. For a moment he stood on the stairs, waiting for Father Stachovič to leave. He heard his slow footsteps receding and eventually went back into his office. Exhausted, he sat down in his green armchair, stared at the chipboard desk top and drifted into the thoughts that had been tormenting him of late: What was there to be done? There was nothing that could be done now. For the first time in his life he felt misgivings about himself. He sat and waited for the phone to ring, in case Šiška rang back having perhaps had second thoughts, but the telephone was silent.

It was July, during the harvest, early evening, after a brief storm.

Lieskov, a tiny village in the foothills, was all-pervaded by the pleasantly fragrant cool of summer, the chirring trill of crickets and the gurgle of the unusually high water in the stream. The air, cooled by a short, sharp shower, quivered with a weak northerly breeze, but without flinching, and only slowly, very slowly, did the heat that had come upon Lieskov first thing begin to fall away, having warmed up the roadway, the tiny yards and outside walls of the cottages as well as having quite discomposed the people.

In the next to last cottage at the upper end of the village, Zita Černek had the radio on.

She had opened wide the kitchen door, which led out into their little yard and to the concrete footbridge over the stream that gave them access to the wide main road. The heat in the kitchen was tempered by the pleasant coolness wafting in from outside.

The kitchen radio sat on a solid wooden bracket.

After the Černeks bought the radio, Zita's husband made a wall-mounted shelf of beech wood and fixed it in place with huge nails above a large, grey bracket fungus from which straggled quite far downwards the brownish-purple stalks and grey-green foliage of a thing they called 'old maid', a rather ludicrous and humble house-plant that never flowered.

The children were already in bed and Černek wasn't at home.

Zita was listening to the evening broadcast, a recording of the trial that had taken place in their town that afternoon.

"Prisoner at the bar, Majerský," she heard the prosecutor's resolute voice coming over the radio, "according to the testimony of witnesses, you are a subversive and saboteur, you have tried to subvert and sabotage the local collective, you have expressed yourself with disdain on the subject of

Soviet combine harvesters, and you have abetted the cell of the rich people in the village whose object is to thwart the transition from individual husbandry to collective farming in Temešany. How do you plead?"

"I have not tried to subvert the collective and I've never carried out any acts of sabotage," Zita Černek heard Majerský's familiar, somehow timid voice, "I've never even seen a Soviet combine harvester, nor have I abetted any cell of rich people."

"You're lying!" Zita shuddered at the sound of the prosecutor's sneery tone of voice. "The witnesses have proved beyond all doubt that you have attempted to subvert and sabotage the collective, that you have expressed yourself with disdain on the subject of Soviet combine harvesters, and that you have abetted the cells of the rich people of Temešany. Do you confess?"

"Yes – Comrade Prosecutor –"

"You see, prisoner at the bar Majerský! I advise you not to argue back and tell untruths! Remember, this is a court of law! It is clear beyond all doubt that all the things which you have committed of late stem from your past. You were in the glorious Slovak National Uprising and even back then you abandoned your unit with a view to betraying it and delivering it into the hands of the enemy –"

"I betrayed no one," Majerský replied in a low, strangled voice, "Comrade Prosecutor –"

Zita Černek sat down on the bench below the old maid, propped up by her arms on the table top.

"It would be better, prisoner at the bar, if you said nothing," came the resolute and sneery voice of the prosecutor. "As witness, Comrade Černek, tell us how matters stood with the defendant, Majerský, in the glorious Slovak National Uprising, or, as the case may be, after the Uprising had been pushed back into the mountains."

Zita was breathing fast, the radio without a voice still whirred quietly beside her head as, mortified, she waited to hear what her husband would say about Majerský.

A moment passed.

The radio whirred voiceless, giving out a sound like grain being tipped onto a metal sheet.

Zita waited.

"Comrade chairman of this tribunal," the prosecutor began, "kindly read out the statement given by the witness Černek."

On the radio the man chairing the tribunal cleared his throat twice.

"During our glorious Slovak National Uprising," the chairman began, "I was with the defendant Jozef Majerský and till roughly the middle of February I was with him in the mountains, after the Slovak National Uprising had been driven up into the mountains by the fascist occupiers. At the time, mid-February, the defendant Jozef Majerský ran off from our unit with a view to betraying it and delivering it into the hands of the fascist occupiers –" Zita listened, horrified, to the unrelieved monotone of the chairman's voice and stared into the corner between the kitchen door and the door to the sitting room, trembling in sheer anguish on behalf of Majerský and rage against her husband, rage that was turning into utter loathing.

Outside, on the road the other side of the footbridge, two lights crossed as two cars drove past.

* * *

Almost seven years previously, in February 1945, Lieskov at night had been silent, as always during the blackout. The cottages stood dim above the dirty snow and within the dim walls the windows showed black.

Hans Moeller, a German soldier whose mother had died on the day he was born, was on guard duty at the top end, outside Hanka's cottage, the last one in Lieskov, shuffling his feet and, in his drowsy state, he kept coming back to the idea that he wasn't the most unfortunate man in the world. The war surely can't go on for much longer and Lieutenant Hals isn't a bad chap – and if I do get killed, there'll be nobody to weep over me. Moeller shifted his weight onto his other foot and thought about the greater misfortune of a soldier who does have a mother to weep over him. He had his back to Lieskov and was staring into the night that shone white with its covering of old snow, into the dark beech and fir woods beyond the village and into the dark, overcast skyscape.

Below Hanka's cottage, inside the Černeks' new one, the last but one cottage in Lieskov, Černek's wife Zita was rocking the cradle of her ailing seven-month-old baby boy.

Her wavy brown hair, from which she'd removed her warm, green, floral scarf, glinted in the sharp light of the bulb hanging over the table, and having sat down on the bench and bent over the cradle – ready for bed, so no longer wearing her heavy jumper, red apron and thick brown dress, and with just dark-blue slippers on her feet – and having straightened up ready to rise, move the cradle next to her bed and lie down, in came, into her unlocked kitchen, Majerský, a tall, slim man. He quietly closed the door behind him, then, stunned at the sight of her supple shoulders and supple figure, he stayed by the door and made no further move.

"What...?" he managed to exclaim after a pause. "Is that you, Zita?"

"It's me – and –"

"Do you live here?"

"Yes."

"Are there any Germans in the village?"

"There are."

"Here as well – at your place?"

"No, no – but – leave now, Jožo, go for God's sake! There are Germans in the village – hang on though –" Černek's wife Zita's eyes darkened with anger, "– what is this? Where did you spr-...? Why have you come? Here? To me? Dear God, what now?"

"Zita –!"

"No, Jožo – but wait – no, leave, get out of my house, go somewhere else –!"

"Zita," Majerský said, "I'm starving and – my eyes are terribly sore –"

Their loud whispering having reached a pause, they said nothing for a while, simply looking at each other. Majerský looked at Zita with his eyes streaming, at her smooth features, broad at the cheeks, broader at the forehead, her whole face starting to swell with anger, her long, smooth neck, the deep curve of her white chemise, drawn tight with the thread running through it, and Zita looked at him, her eyes filled with terror and acrimony. Both became acutely aware of their own heartbeats, the eyes of both shone in the light of the bulb above, which was reinforced by the white, partly floral-patterned shade, each had been startled at the sight of the other, and Zita was overcome by fear of the German troops who'd arrived in Lieskov in late January and had now been there for three weeks, uncommunicative, silent as the grey-green mould that takes over any bit of bread that's gone off. The backs and breasts of both of them came out in a sweat.

It was very warm in Zita's tiny kitchen and the snow clinging to Majerský's brown boots began to melt, slowly forming a dirty puddle round his feet on the fir-wood flooring.

"You as well...?" she asked Majerský in a clearly audible whisper. "And –?"

"Me as well," Majerský said, gesturing slightly with the fiercely tingling arms in which he was holding a rifle now bedewed with heavy condensation. "And you, Zita, how...? I came in because I could hear the cradle being rocked – at least someone's still up here, I says to myself – real people –"

Zita hopped up from the cradle. Her white chemise billowed across her breasts. The cradle rocked two or three more times.

"Follow me."

She opened the door into the unlit back room, which had a cold damp smell, because Zita didn't heat it.

After the pleasant, warm air in the kitchen, Majerský was hit hard in the face and his sore eyes by the stale, dank air.

He paused in the doorway. Cakes of filthy snow parted from his brown boots right there on the threshold to melt into a filthy puddle.

"Come on," she said in a loud, sharp whisper. "Get in here! We have to keep the door shut so no light reaches the windows. We've got no blackout curtains in this room."

"But what...?" Majerský began in a whisper. "Is it just you here like this, and –?"

Zita silently closed the door, offering no reply, and Majerský stopped asking questions as well, merely listening in the darkened room as she made up a bed that had been buried beneath two huge quilts and three pillows.

First she tossed the heavy bedspread onto the other bed, then the quilts and on top of them the pillows.

"Lie down here," she said, pointing at the whitely glimmering sheet, "as you are – then I'll fetch you something warm, you need to get warm, then you can tell me if you... At the top of the street, outside the Hankas' cottage, there's a German on guard. Did he spot you?"

"But, Zita, I – no, he didn't spot me, but I'd better go. He'd have started shooting."

"Lie down!"

Majerský lay down on Zita's bed in his sodden boots, puttees and filthy, shabby, sweat-soaked uniform, he set his cap on his chest and lay his bedewed rifle alongside him.

Zita placed the three pillows across him and both quilts over them, putting the bed back as it had been, then she straightened the quilts, smoothed them down and finally added the heavy bedspread. Then she straightened and tidied the other bed. She edged the kitchen door open just enough so that she could tell by the shaft of light from the kitchen if the two beds were looking the same.

They were as like as two peas in a pod, exactly the same, side by side beneath the same kind of heavy, red bedspread.

She opened the door a mite more for one last check on the beds, slipped through into the kitchen and closed the door behind her. Fearful and frantic, she pulled on her thick white jumper, grabbed her jumper from the bed, tossed it aside, quickly donned her blue flannel petticoat and started to shiver, because her neck, the top half of her back and chest and her bare shoulders had been struck by the cold and damp of the back room, then she glanced at her little boy as he slept. He lay there peacefully, taking in short, audible breaths and letting out the occasional moan. His face was red and feverish. She tied a wide hemp cloth round the light bulb above the table so that the bright light wouldn't wake the lad, then she turned and glanced at the stove with its red-hot coals.

"God in Heaven!" she whispered. "What now?"

She quietly fed some more coal into the stove.

She turned and looked helplessly ahead of her, her mind full of all the things that had happened in Lieskov since early October, when a troop of Germans had driven the partisans from the village and burned down seventeen cottages. She thought of the men the Germans had hauled off, and the women and children burned to death. People had informed on one another, for God's sake...! Men of the National Guard had given people away, and then one another. Any excuse was good enough for that kind of perfidy. They would think back to age-old grievances, differences, arguments, lawsuits and scores to settle... Good God, what now? If anyone were to find out there's a partisan here! How can one person inform on another? She should have booted him out like a stray dog, told him to go back to wherever he'd come from, find somewhere else. She ought, for God's sake, to have told him – but then she had – what now? The local Germans aren't the worst, but they do stop by at houses, to buy milk, or fruit – they take nothing by force, pay for everything, even bread. With her eyes aglow, Zita glanced helplessly at her baby boy, feverish and flu-ridden.

In her agitation she wandered aimlessly about the kitchen, in her blue slippers, her thin white chemise, her thick white jumper and her blue skirt.

Zita Černek had first been Zita Furka, then Zita Ragala. She'd been given her Christian name by a priest who'd christened a number of girls in his parish with the same name, both under the monarchy and later. Her second marriage had been to Mišo Černek, a seasonal labourer, with whom she'd spent several seasons in Bohemia.

The cottage – one room, the kitchen and pantry, which you entered from a tiny yard – had been built by Černek in the spring and summer of 1938. He'd had no option but to build it on a damp patch of land beside the stream, which was why the cottage was immediately damp as well. The porous stone compounded into the foundations had drawn moisture up out of the ground and into the walls. Access to the Černeks' cottage from the main road through Lieskov was by the long concrete footbridge overarching the stream.

In October forty-four the Černeks' cottage had not been burned to the ground. It took the German troops who had come storming into Lieskov a whole day's fighting to drive out the partisans. Although their commander, a Major Schwind, had received from the local National Guard a list of the names of nine men who'd gone off to join the partisans, Černek, Zita's husband, wasn't on the list, and although Major Schwind had had all males aged between sixteen and sixty brought to what had been the squire's residence, where they were interrogated, he still didn't discover that Černek was also a partisan. He had the assembled men taken away and then ordered seventeen of Lieskov's cottages to be burned down. "Our holy war must not be paused on any account!" Schwind constantly reminded himself and others, which was why he'd had the women and children shot at as they fled from the cottages set ablaze with platelets of white phosphorus, and why he'd had the four fleeing children the soldiers had caught tossed into the flames of the Turčoks' blazing cottage. Seventeen cottages had burned down, Schwind's soldiers had left and people grieved, choking with rage as they buried their dear ones. "It was a miracle this cottage survived along with me and the baby," Zita would tell herself, though she feared that her punishment might yet catch up with her.

The German troops who'd entered Lieskov at the end of January had been accommodated in the village school and what had been the squire's residence, now partially converted into offices of the Lieskov sawmill.

"Herr Oberleutnant," Staff Sergeant Obmann, commander of the unit with which he had come to Lieskov by road, bellowed at Lieutenant Paul Hals, commander of the Lieskov garrison, at the squire's residence, where the local command post had been set up, "it strikes me you're a bit late getting up!"

"Yes, sir, Herr Oberscharführer," said Lieutenant Hals, beginning to get dressed. "There now, Herr Oberscharführer – good to see you, welcome –"

"Sleeping for so long is a waste," Obmann told him, "you'll get plenty of sleep-time in the grave. Just hang on and wait for your grave!"

"Yes sir, Herr Oberscharführer!"

"Wait for your grave. The partisans'll dig a hole for you and you'll lie there all comfy – ha, ha – like on top of some seventeen-year-old girl...!"

"Yes sir, Herr Oberscharführer!"

"Idiot!" Staff Sergeant Obmann bawled. "Cretin! If only the war were over – that would be quite something, eh?"

He left the command post with his eight men in tow and Lieutenant Hals finished getting dressed.

He'd been embarrassed before the men and Corporal Köhl and right then he'd have enjoyed nothing more than to kill Staff Sergeant Obmann personally!

Lieutenant Hals had long loathed people like Obmann and if nobody was listening he would curse: "SS, SD, SiPo, Orpo, Gestapo – thieves and murderers the lot of 'em! It was them who taught the nation not to work and fight, but to steal and kill! All those *Blockwarts* – Nazi house-wardens, those spies and informers in every housing block; there's not a beast alive as wouldn't be offended by such bestiality as theirs – and this whole war's going to the dogs!" Lieutenant Hals hated *Block-warts*, who, even before the war, in peacetime, had kept an eye on every person in Germany, so Hitler would know what even his subjects' dreams were about. "House-wardens, bastards," Hals would mutter to himself, "they should keep their eye on party members among the populace, find practical ways for party members living in the same block to cooperate – mean-while the war's going to the dogs!" Hals was distressed that the Germans were losing the war, for which he blamed the *Blockwarts*, those snoops.

"The army has no need of snoops!" he told himself as he was dressing. "In the army there won't be any! The Ober-scharführer would like the men to be out catching partisans, to keep him amused. No, in the army there won't be any *Blockwarts*!"

"Unteroffizier Köhl!"

"Yes, sir, Herr Oberleutnant!"

"Set up a six-man patrol and patrol the village!"

"Yes, sir, Herr Oberleutnant!"

God in Heaven, what now? Zita was thinking about Ma-jerský, lying there in her room under a pile of bedding. What shall I give him to eat? He's hungry.

Under all Zita's bedding Majerský shivered from the damp and cold. The quilts were cold for not having been dried and aired in the sun in ages. To well above the height of his boots his legs had been soaked by the deep snow through which he'd waded all the way down from the mountains to Lieskov. He raised a hand, cold and stiff, towards his face, levered the pillow up slightly off his head and ran his hand over the bed-spread, all to ease his breathing a little.

The pillow dropped back onto his face and outstretched arm and again he began to suffocate. He got hold of the wet rifle with his left hand, used it as a prop to prise himself up off the cold, stiff straw mattress and, carefully, so as not to move the quilts above him, eased himself towards the edge of the bed, his face to the bedspread. From there he took five deep breaths, in and out. He shook with cold, while his face began to burn with fever.

Zita's baby boy started to cry. He calmed down a little when she began rocking his cradle. Even from inside Zita's bed, Majerský could easily make out the thudding of the cradle's battered rockers on the fir-wood floorboards. Thudding and rumbling.

As he lay there Majerský's fear began to evaporate and with it the agitation with which he'd been overcome having realised it was Zita's cottage that he'd entered, but his face, neck and chest began to tingle with dismay at having intruded on Zita, stayed on in her place instead of making himself scarce the moment he saw her, and having let himself be hidden away like this. But escape? How? He recalled how close the German patrol was.

He could hear the thudding and rumbling of the battered rockers coming from the kitchen.

Zita's baby boy started to cry again.

Majerský slowly ran his right hand across his face and rubbed his sore, closed eyes, rubbing them as if trying to rub darkness into them, the only treatment he knew for sore eyes.

In the forests of fir trees way beyond Lieskov, at the foot of White Crag, where, following the smashing of the partisan troop, he and eight of his comrades had remained hidden in a bunker, a solid bunker well lined with logs of fir, he'd noticed, a fortnight before, that he couldn't look at snow. There'd been a fresh fall of snow in January, white as sugar, and the sky then cleared, leaving not a single wisp of cloud. In the frosty sunlight the snow, which covered the ground, the fir trees and any broken branches on the ground, had warmed into countless tiny crystals that glittered as vibrantly orange, green and blue sparklets. The sun shone out of the clear sky down into the forests, tossing blankets of snow from the trees, the sky shining with a blue glare, glinting down through the green branches of the fir trees, and the forest around the bunker grew warmer during daylight – but Majerský could tell that his eyes were getting worse and worse, that the blue sky and white snow held an unseen toxin that was going to leave him blind. "There's nothing but poison in the light," he'd begun telling his comrades, "some terrible poison!" His eyes had begun to sting, hurt, water terribly, and when, two days later, he'd gone with his friend Baďo, in bright sunlight, to fetch some water from the nearby spring, he'd yelped at him in a whisper: "Oh, my God, Jano!" – "What's up?" Jano Baďo asked in a whisper – short, dark and hunch-backed he was. "Why the oh my God?" – "I can't see, Jano!" Majerský was pressing at his weepy eyes with his filthy hands and Jano Baďo guided him back to the bunker. Two weeks passed and in those two weeks Majerský had begun thinking: If he could stand to see daylight and snow at least a little bit, he'd run off. Leave them all to it, let them all die in the bunker if it came to it, let them eat one another from sheer hunger, just make a run for it, so what if the Germans were to catch him immediately and hang him! "Get away, away!" something kept shouting inside him, and in the course of that terrible fortnight he'd wiped his sore and streaming eyes with the filthy sleeve of his scruffy army great coat. More than once he'd told his comrades in the bunker during those terrible two weeks: "I'm peeing with my eyes! With my eyes, guys...!" – "True enough," the dark hunch-back Jano Baďo had responded, "more with your eyes than with your... ...!" The men had a good laugh at that. Majerský went right off them, they'd begun to disgust him – all except the young Frenchman: he hadn't laughed at him, because he hadn't understood them – and then Majerský had begun thinking even more about getting away.

In Zita's bed, whose pillows were slowly starting to warm up, he kept wiping his eyes with a corner of the heavy cotton pillow case that had been pressing into his face. His eyes were hurting again, burning almost as badly as in January because of all the deep, white snow he'd had to look at as he ploughed through it to reach Lieskov.

In the fir forests beyond Lieskov, there had also been, besides himself and the hunchbacked Baďo, Černek. He would often say: "I've got a wife and baby boy in Lieskov," but not once did he go there, nor would he let any of their comrades venture down to the village. "It's a dangerous village, on the main road. There are always Germans around. I don't want to do anything that might put my wife and son in danger. I shan't be going there till the war's over. And don't any of you try either!" One day the toxic blue light of the sky and the white light of the snow were just too much for Majerský because his eyes had given him an unbearable headache, so he'd come off his watch back to the bunker. "You don't fancy it out there anymore, eh?" Černek asked him in a tone creepy with malice. "But if there was a bit of skirt in it, you'd stick it out, right?" – "I just can't be out there," said Majerský, "or I'll just snuff it." – "So snuff it!" Černek snapped back at him. "Why are you being so mean, Mišo?" – "Because any of us could get sore eyes, surely?" It was then that Majerský began seriously considering whether to clear out, and if he had to, he was minded to escape to Lieskov.

From the kitchen to the room he was in came the sound of the worn rockers of Zita's cradle, the wailing of Zita's baby boy and the roar of the fire blazing away in the stove.

She's heating something up or cooking something, thought Majerský and his whole body, except for his cold, wet feet, flushed hot with shame. His face began to burn even more. His breathing quickened.

He heard an empty pan strike the stove.

He couldn't see anything, but from the sounds coming from the kitchen – the cradle thudding, the fire in the stove roaring, and a pan striking the stove – he had a clear vision of Zita standing by the stove, one leg extended, her foot on the rocker, as she rocked the baby in the cradle.

Hunger had filled Majerský's mouth with saliva.

In 1945, Zita married a second time. In 1933, when she was eighteen, she and her mother had found work in Bohemia, on an estate at Radotín, under Majerský's stewardship. That was the first time he'd been both working-class and a steward, and from that first spring he had carried on exactly as the older stewards had advised him: "Jožo, fear nothing! Just be canny!" – "You'll be getting plenty of flour, lard and all that, even bacon!" – "And you'll be getting all sorts of goodies if you shape up well!" Majerský had acknowledged that the older stewards' advice wasn't bad, and at the Radotín estate he appreciated the folly of not acting accordingly. Canny I am, he thought, that being what everyone said. He had Mrs Furka and her eighteen-year-old daughter Zita, slender as a reed and with brown curly hair, brought to him, and it was the daughter, more than Mrs Furka, the mother, he was addressing when he said: "You two won't be going out into the fields; you'll do the cooking, but make sure it's good and there's plenty of it, we need everyone well-fed, perhaps even to bursting." Majerský then laughed and gave Zita a wink. Mrs Furka and her Zita were alone in the world. Mr Furka was dead and Zita's elder sisters had married the kind of people her mother was not inclined to go visiting. She used to say she'd rather carry on working, alongside Zita, for as long as she could, and when Zita got married, she'd move in with them, because among all her five daughters Zita was her favourite. They both, mother and daughter, were delighted at what Majerský had just said and so stayed in the kitchen, along with two other lasses, to feed the hundred and twenty workmen for whom Majerský was responsible. For a time, all had gone well for the workmen, Mrs Furka and her Zita, there, at the Radotín estate.

From inside Zita's bed Majerský could hear her scrambling on the kitchen stove the five eggs that he'd heard her crack into the pan. He uncurled, stretching his aching legs and spine as he choked back his saliva.

A February night descended over Lieskov, all white where the snow lay undisturbed, while elsewhere it was trampled down and grimy. The cottages, burned out or not, jutted up towards the overcast sky like great silent headstones. The trampled areas of snow, lit up for around two daylight hours by a feeble sun, froze as evening fell and, on the wide road, crunched beneath the jackboots of Staff Sergeant Obmann and eight men, all wearing long white hooded capes, as they walked through Lieskov, stopping at each cottage and keeping their ears pricked.

Their truck, two dogs and two more men had remained on guard at the edge of the village, outside the sawmill.

Lieskov was dark and silent.

One private, Hans Moeller, who was on guard at the upper end, outside the Hankas' cottage, kept shifting his feet wearily as he stared out into the night, whitened by the snow and darkened by the forests of beech and fir and the overcast sky. "Moderleiwe üöver alle Leiwe," he whispered in his Münster dialect, then stopped before whispering on in a different vein: "There's no greater love than mother love – no, not that. If a person's got no mother, he can cause her no grief. Any such person is just lucky." Moeller looked at Lieskov as he held his ice-cold rapid-fire rifle in his freezing-cold hands.

Lieskov was silent.

Staff Sergeant Ernst Obmann distrusted the silence and kept proceeding from one homestead to the next.

He'd check through the whole village several times over, he decided, that would kill some of the time, oh, that long, long time that remained until the next daytime action. You never know, some night-time action might even happen along. If not, the men can at least get some rest in the warmth of the command post, perhaps even some sleep – and he was going to have to advise the lieutenant of this other thing: the guards posted about the village for the night are idle and inattentive! Paul Hals, the lieutenant – who is he? He looks like a retired Saint Bernard dog! What a slouch! He'd have to borrow him once in a while, prod his idle mind into life, whip it into action so as to – to –

Obmann strode through silent Lieskov from one homestead to the next.

In her kitchen, Zita was scrambling the five eggs on the stove, which was taking time to heat up, and with one leg stretched out to the cradle she was rocking her whining baby boy.

Since the moment when Majerský had walked into the kitchen she'd managed to overcome her fear for the boy, herself and for Majerský, too, though she was still trying to stifle her qualms at not having driven Majerský out of her house and into the night.

He deserved nothing better! I should have kicked him out, something inside her kept saying. What now? Oh, my God! The Germans could show up at any time. Exterior doors mustn't be locked. That was their order. I should have kicked him out, I should have –!

Her qualms had begun to wane and fall silent, but now they'd come back and were lashing out at her flustered mind and quaking frame.

The eggs in the pan were beginning to thicken. Zita slid the pan towards the edge of the stove.

Oh, my God! What now?

She slid the pan even further towards the edge of the stove. She'd give Majerský something to eat, she'd thought. Maybe someone somewhere will also give her husband Mišo something to eat, keep him in hiding if he's alive... Who knows where he is! Many women now know about their menfolk, she knows nothing about Mišo, Majerský will go back to the partisans. She'll pack something for him to take to them, some bread... She'll ask him if he knows anything about Mišo. Zita turned the pan slightly and stirred the scrambling eggs with a sticky spoon. Slowly and silently she opened the door of the stove, added three more logs and quietly closed it again. She suppressed her anger at Majerský. Great God, she couldn't possibly drive him out – you can't treat a human being like a dog – only Germans had been doing that sort of thing, driving people from their cottages, their villages, driving them into fires, tossing their children into the flames –

She stepped back from the stove to slice some bread for Majerský. But how was he going to eat? In bed? The bed would get jumbled up. As she turned towards the dresser her baby boy began to cry. She came back to the cradle.

At Radotín, at the estate, she'd quite fancied Majerský from first setting eyes on him. He was slim, tall, thin-featured, quite strapping and slender at the waist. He was wearing new breeches and highly polished boots with soft leg portions. She'd looked at his sharp, close-shaven features, bluish-black where he'd shaved, at his thin black pointy moustaches, and his dark, smoothly combed hair. A warm spring came to Radotín. Zita and her mother cooked for the workers and one day, after supper, when there was no one else in the kitchen, Majerský had boldly asked: "Dear Mrs Furka, what would you say if I took your Zita as my wife? Married her?" Zita's mother had looked up at Majerský in surprise and, hands on hips, she had turned with a smile to the blushing Zita. "But, steward Majerský, what makes you ask that?" she had asked. "Because I've grown fond of Zita, I like her, no, I love her!" Majerský had said with such vigour and resolution that Zita had let him put an arm round her. He had drawn her to him by her delicate forearm and stroked her brown curly hair with his left hand. "Now, now, steward Majerský!" Zita had said after a brief pause, drawing away from him. For three weeks Mrs Furka was over the moon, as was her daughter Zita, and indeed Majerský, because Mrs Furka, who'd always been wont to say: "Only a real man can bring a little cheer to a poor girl!", had entrusted Zita to Majerský and was oblivious to everything, even to the fact that if Zita was out of sight, so too was Majerský. Except that after those three weeks – Zita recalled that it had been a Thursday in May – Zita's mother had suddenly shouted at her: "You have to stop seeing that steward!" – "Whatever for, why?" – "Because he's married! He's got a wife and two kids somewhere in Temešany!" Zita blanched, then turned bright red. "And who," she asked after a long pause, "who told you that, Mum?" – "Who? Never you mind!" The following day Zita had plucked up the courage to ask Majerský while they were alone: "Is it true, Jožko, that you've got a wife and children? I'm thinking, we too, I could be pregnant." Majerský hadn't replied and just avoided Zita and her mother for the next two days. Many of the workforce reported seeing him lost in thought. On the third day he entered the kitchen and bawled at Zita's mother: "Your cooking has to improve, woman! Right now it's just pigswill!" – "And what am I meant to be cooking with? You don't give us the things we need!" – "What's that? I don't give you stuff? You've been stealing it, woman, taking it for your own use! Sugar, lard, bacon...!" – "Well just look at him now!" Mrs Furka had screamed back. "And what do you do, sir? You're the number one thief round here!" A huge red patch spread across Majerský's cheeks and pointy nose, just like any other time when he fell into a rage. "Right – all right then, woman, but you'll pay dearly for that – and – we'll have the rest out in court!" Majerský, in a fine old rage, had left the kitchen and the next day sued Mrs Furka and Zita.

Zita's baby boy was crying quietly and plaintively. Zita rolled him over onto his other side and went back to rocking.

The worn rockers of the cradle thudded and bumped.

All about the Černek cottage the night was very quiet; even the crunch-crunch of the snow under the jackboots of Obmann's men had ceased

The whole of the upper end of Lieskov was silent, as if immersed in dirty oil.

"Don't just stand there daydreaming!" Obmann's German bellow sliced through the deep silence outside the Hankas' cottage, where the German private, Moeller, was on guard duty. "You lice-ridden cur, you! The Führer should have had lice-ridden curs like you boiled down to make soap long before this! Doing thirty paces this way, thirty paces that! Shut it, you lice-ridden dog! Lice were munching on you even in your mother's womb! Pity they didn't gobble you up completely instead of – instead of – doing thirty paces this way, thirty paces that!"

Obmann turned and led his men to the front of the Černek cottage. There he came to a halt again.

He pulled up short and listened. "What's that?" he asked Sergeant Kniewald, who was standing beside him. "What's that banging noise?"

"Dunno."

"And what *do* you know?" Obmann glanced at his illuminated watch.

It was near on ten-thirty.

The cradle's rockers were thudding and bumping regularly.

Staff Sergeant Ernst Obmann hadn't heard any sound remotely like it in ages and he was reminded of the huge diesel engine located in the concrete basement of the mill that his father had bought in Ahlen when Ernst was three. That engine had thudded in exactly the same way when they used to play at the back of the mill, Obmann mused outside the Černeks' cottage. What's an engine like that doing here? An engine? Or a dynamo? For a secret transmitter? And where is it? Underground? Obmann nudged Sergeant Kniewald: "Scharführer, with me!"

The nine Germans, in white capes and hoods and gripping their rapid-fire rifles, burst into Zita's kitchen.

"Oh, God, help –!" Zita grabbed the hot cross-bar on the oven and rocked her baby with her right hand.

"Heigh-ho!" Staff Sergeant Obmann turned to Sergeant Kniewald and the others, pointed at the cradle and said: "Here's something I've never seen before and I thought it was – ha-ha-ha! – and it's just a puppy-dog – ha-ha! – and standing over the puppy a bitch – ha-ha! – and a pretty white one at that, just right for bed! She's getting ready for the night! She thinks the war's over – that there is no war – that there never was a war – or maybe she's expecting a partisan to call –"

Zita was paralysed by a sudden sensation of cold, then shot through by a sudden fever because she'd never seen the Germans of Lieskov in white capes.

Obmann's men, who were relishing the agreeable warmth of Zita's kitchen, the smell of scrambled eggs and the white of Zita's chemise, jumper and complexion, waited for a sign from Obmann, then they sat down, one after the other, on the benches round the table. Obmann sat down on a chair, looked in turn at Zita and the two doors and stretched his legs out in front of him. With cold curiosity he surveyed Zita, her heaving breasts, her hips.

Still holding the hot cross-bar of the stove with her left hand, she went on rocking the baby with her right, even though he had now dropped off, and with her huge, frightened brown eyes she watched Obmann, watched him as if unable to move.

Obmann's face was smooth, pale and thin. His aquiline nose gave way conspicuously to his eyes and mouth. His sunken cheeks were drawn backwards. This was a face you just couldn't get a grip on, as if anything said to the man would have just trickled off it without response.

He shifted his gaze from Zita to the men.

Suddenly, it struck Zita that his face was like the steel cone on which they split timber at the sawmill.

He looked back at Zita, clamping his lips together and causing the corners of his mouth to be drawn backwards.

Zita stopped rocking the cradle, dashed across to her waiting bed and took hold of her clothes.

"Aber nein!" said Obmann, pointing to the cradle. "Aber nein!"

She went red in the face.

"Leave me alone –!"

"Nein, nein!"

"But for God's sake, please, be reasonable, let me get dressed!" Zita cried, terror-stricken, and began to shake all over. "You must realise it's –!"

"Nein," Obmann said calmly, "nein!"

He surveyed his grinning men until his gaze settled on Otto Drossel, who had two bits of sticking plaster pasted crosswise beneath his right cheekbone. "Otto, you tell her!"

"Do vot he say, voman!" Otto Drossel, he of the sticking-plastered face, told her brusquely. "Ton't be seely, get beck to your stofe ent ze cradle! Ent stay zere!"

Zita was beside herself with fear at the things she might have to do just to keep the soldiers relaxed. Majerský, oh, God –!

Her legs shaking, she crossed to the dresser, got a loaf of bread and cut herself a slice. She recalled the partisans who'd got hold of some wheat flour for her, and with the slice of white bread in her hand she walked back over to the stove and began to eat the scrambled eggs she'd cooked for Majerský. First she gnawed the bits off the messy aluminium spoon and licked it clean, then with the end of the spoon she took small bits of the thickened eggs, nibbled at the bread and ate, for all that her stomach was in revolt, she ate so that the Germans wouldn't register the pan and eggs and start asking who they were for. She forced the scrambled eggs on herself, unsalted and unappetising. During the day she'd forgotten to bring some salt in from the outside larder, and after Majerský had arrived she'd been afraid, because the people of Lieskov were not allowed out into their yards after six in the evening.

Obmann's section, his *Schar*, sat on the benches at the table in Zita's kitchen, four men in white on one and four on the other. In the warmth, they soon began to peel the fur gloves off their left hands and the white hoods covering their grey-green field service caps.

Zita's eyes twitched, as did the skin of her brow when she spotted on Obmann's peaked cap a little square of black cloth with a metal skull and crossbones fixed to it.

Slowly she chewed her bread and thick, unsalted scrambled eggs. Soldiers sporting death's heads had put half of Lieskov to the torch, shot at children and women, dragged off the men and tossed children into fires – Milan Turčok a second time, after he'd managed to escape through a window – oh, God, oh, God, help me –!

"There's been a spot of fighting hereabouts," said Obmann, "some of the houses have been burned down. There'll have been partisans involved, and since they've been here, they're still around. The blight of partisans is like – like – and Oberleutnant Hals is a useless shitbag!" He took his cap off. His forehead receded sharply.

"Partisans," said Sergeant Kniewald, "are like fleas – indestructible."

"Fleas are *not* indestructible, Scharführer."

"Maybe not," said Kniewald to Obmann, "but, Herr Oberscharführer, they do come back time and time again."

"You just don't understand this war, Scharführer," said Obmann. "It's a war of ideologies and a war of ideologies has everything: an idea, fleas, partisans – and – things that you can't shake off however much you try."

Zita, her head full of everything – she herself, like this, in front of so many men, her sick baby boy, Majerský in the other room, oh, God, oh, God, if only she'd sent him packing! – she stared hard at the yellowy-white scrambled eggs, shaking with cold, stifled by the heat, staring at the eggs so as not to have to look at the men, staring into the pan and pressing hard against the stove because that way she found it easier to breathe and her fear began to dissipate.

Obmann's section was a good one, in the view of its commander, because in the last three days – in the course of daytime actions – it had successfully razed four bunkers. In three of them it had shot some starving partisans, and into the fourth it had packed a seven-member Jewish family that had been kneeling before Obmann in the snow, and set fire to it. With these four daylight actions Obmann was pleased, as he also was with their night-time actions.

Zita ate slowly, her eyes fixed on the pan.

"How come she's stuffing her guts this late?" Sergeant Kniewald asked. "What's she been up to till now? She's a pretty one. Pity we folk have taste – and how tasteless it is for blokes to have to wait and watch one another getting down to business. Ha ha ha ha!"

Obmann glanced round at the laughing men. They were all under twenty-five, and all good-looking except for Sergeant Kniewald, who had a seriously projecting lower jaw with protruding yellow teeth and permanently drooling chops.

Zita fought back hard against the sudden onrushes of shame and fear that left her weak at the knees, turned her hands to wood and made her mind foggy. By turns they got the better of her, then she of them. And she fought back the tears that stung so.

Obmann calmly looked over Zita's kitchen, the stove and oven, faced with off-white tiles, the dresser, the iron bed ready and waiting for her, the walls painted with a pattern of geese walking across some grass, each with seven goslings in tow, and the floor made of planks of fir, left wet and grimy by their boots over by the door. His eyes rested on the image of a naked crucified Christ and on the large, grey bracket fungus nailed to the wall beneath it. From the bracket fungus, as from a plant-pot, dangled an 'old maid', a plant with large grey-green leaves. Then his gaze slid across to the sitting-room door.

He pointed a thin finger at it. "Wer," he asked Zita, "wer wohnt dort?"

"Who liffs zere?" Drossel asked. "In zet room zere?" He pointed to the door to the sitting-room.

"Sorry?" Zita queried, though she'd understood immediately. "I didn't get what you said."

"In zet room," Drossel repeated more sharply, frustration getting the better of him.

"Nobody." Zita shook her head, despite the stiffening of her exposed neck. "Nobody lives in there. There's only me and the boy –" she said, pointing, spoon in hand, at the cradle and the baby sleeping in it – "I never have a fire on in there, I don't have enough firewood, and we sleep in here because we can keep it warm."

She pointed to the oven and tiled stove.

"What's she saying?"

Drossel translated what she'd told him to Obmann.

"Wo ist dein Mann?" Obmann asked Zita. "Nicht – nicht zu Haus?"

"Vere iss your husspant zen?" the pink stripe on Drossel's face contracted. "He's not vit ze partisans, no?"

"Oh, no." Zita steeled herself and smiled. "He's is Germany, he works there, in the mines. There are very few men here in Lieskov, only the old ones are left. Many of the others were picked up by the German army in October."

"I see," said Obmann with a contented shake of his head after Drossel had translated for him. "This is a village of partisans. Let's hope our men have sorted at least some of the partisan canker out. Not, let's hope, like with Lieutenant Hals. That old Saint Bernard who should have been pensioned off!"

Zita turned to face Obmann, steeled herself once more and smiled at him.

For a while Obmann listened to what she had to say.

"What did she say?" he asked Drossel. "What a vile language this is! Not even the Russians are going to understand it."

"She says," Drossel translated, "that she was hungry and so scrambled her last eggs. She doesn't have any more, but if we wouldn't take it amiss, she could offer us some bread, or if we cared to wait, she'd cook something up for us."

"She needn't bother," said Obmann, "we've got plenty of food in the truck. "Just ask her, Otto, if all's quiet in the village, if she happens to know anything about any partisans, if any come into the village – and so on and so forth, you know – and why she isn't in bed yet, what's she doing up so late."

"Why on earth," Drossel began, "why –?"

Zita removed her jumper, crossed to the bed and gathered up her clothes.

"Ach, nein," said Obmann, whose gaze had been captivated by Zita's white and smooth, supple shoulders, "nein."

"Ass you are!" Drossel advised her. "No put cloze on!"

"Please, for God's sake," she whispered with a catch in her voice, "let me get dressed."

"Nein!" said Obmann, smiling and shaking his head, "nein, du –"

Zita's eyes glistened with tears. She grabbed her jumper.

"No put cloze on! To ze stofe!"

Lying in Zita's bed and with one ear on the bedspread, Majerský then heard Zita open the cupboard and take out a loaf of bread and a knife that she then placed on the table.

"Have some bread at least," he heard, "it's all I've got right now."

He was breathing in short bursts, not moving, scared that his breathing might be heard in the kitchen, breathing in short bursts, and perspiring all over, body, face and hands. The palm of the hand that held his rifle was wet. Sweat was pouring into his eyes, making them sting and once again, as back in January, they began to feel very sore. In his mind's eye he could see the toxic glare of the snow and the blue sky. He listened with one ear on the coverlet, but he couldn't understand everything. Why had he done it? Why hadn't Zita sent him packing? Goodness, oh, Christ...! Zita, with almost no clothes on – and those blokes! He started, thinking he'd heard Zita cry out. The humming in his ears fell silent. No, no – dear God! – why hadn't she sent him packing, how could she be doing this, she of all persons. Zita Furka? Majerský started to shake, and his wet fingers, resting on the bed frame, began to stick fast to the smooth wooden edge.

In the kitchen, the German hubbub had gone quiet.

Obmann had allowed his men to cut themselves slices of Zita's white bread. They'd stopped talking and were eating in silence. It tasted good after the various kinds of shop bread and army bread, though it did go slightly dry in their mouths and throats. Obmann cut himself a small slice, bit into it and was carried back to Ahlen, to his childhood. A shadow of rage swept across his smooth features because back at the Ahlen mill there'd been good bread and good times.

Slowly Zita ate her unsalted eggs. She had to force herself because for dinner she'd had plenty of bread and the green bean soup left over from her lunch. She kept her smooth white arms pressed to her sides, and her breasts added lift to her white chemise.

Oh, God... And she'd have given eggs scrambled like these to Majerský. At which point her eyes flashed with fear. Dear God...!

She glanced at the floor by the kitchen door, where Majerský's boots had left a dirty puddle, at the four damp patches leading to the sitting-room door, and at the actual puddle by the threshold of the sitting-room door.

What if one of them spotted it! The damp patches carry on right up to the bed.

She looked down into the pan. She'd eaten barely a third of the unsalted scrambled eggs.

"You not hengry?" asked Otto Drossel. "Vie you eat so slow?"

"Sorry?"

"Vie you eat so slow?"

Zita glanced involuntarily at the puddles by the kitchen door and the door to the sitting room. "I can't really be bothered," she told him, "I don't like eating alone. And it doesn't seem right to be eating when I don't have anything to offer you."

"What did she say?" Obmann looked at Drossel. "Why's she smiling?"

Drossel translated.

"Aha," said Obmann as he noted her tiny, healthy teeth and the pink outlines of her gums, "how very polite of her! Not at all what one might have expected!" He took a bite of his thin slice of bread. "And why's she smiling?"

"Vie you smilink?"

"I'm glad," Zita began, "really glad you've come – because I don't have to be afraid – take it from me, you spend every night in fear as you lie there awake, in a village like this – and I don't get much sleep right now, what with the baby being poorly... And now you've come, thank God, you've come – "Prickly tears began to drip from Zita's eyes, adding a sheen to her cheeks "– I'm so glad you're here – I really ought to offer you something, but I've got nothing – " Zita was speaking through her tears "– I should cook something up for you, but I've got nothing in the house, we're not allowed out, not even to the larder outside – but please, in God's name, let me get dressed – don't keep me looking like this!"

She burst loudly into tears, put the pan to one side on the stove and looked at Obmann and his crew with an expression distorted by crying, then smiling and then crying again.

"Please, in God's name, let me –!"

"She's asking for something," said Obmann, "Otto –!"

Drossel opened his mouth to speak.

"There's nothing more precious," said Kniewald, "than what a person gets by having begged for it. Hah ha ha ha!"

Next door, Majerský had managed to catch what Zita was saying and that she was crying, and he heard the Germans guffawing. He hadn't understood everything, but the short-lived satisfaction of knowing that the Germans suspected nothing became submerged in fear and self-pity. They were going to search this room... Poor Zita! She didn't deserve any of this from anyone – great God in Heaven... Fear left him momentarily gasping for breath. He was bathed in a cold sweat. His filthy underwear was clinging to him, to his back, front and legs.

In Bohemia, at the estate in Radotín, back in 1933, he'd had a hundred and twenty workers under him and he'd kept them on short-commons. At first he'd supplied Mrs Furka and Zita generously with provisions, but then gradually cut back on them. He cut down on one lunch a week, then two, then after three lacklustre lunches he'd have a decent one done with more of everything, ever acting in accordance with what the older stewards advised him. "You can cash in on the canteen, Jožo, just go for it!" had been their advice. "You won't make much out of anything else. You can take a bit of this and fail to hand over a bit of that – and no one will notice a thing! Men who are that knackered will eat even dog entrails! All you have to do is cook them! Where dining's communal, stuff can just trickle or come pouring your way." After he'd broken off with Zita and her mother had told him: "It's you who's the number one thief round here!", he sued them both for defamation of character. At the Radotín district court he'd won the case, because his master, Jan Pospíchal, owner of the estate, was also keen to bring an end to the trouble in the canteen as soon as possible, and Mrs Furka and Zita were made to pay the legal costs. "Get out of my kitchens," he'd bawled at them, "and you can count your blessings that this is how it's ended. Things could have been worse!" Mrs Furka and Zita began having their wages cut, because they couldn't afford what the trial was to cost them. Josef Majerský as steward took on some new girls and one older woman and began looking among his workforce for some more personable young men. He came upon Jano Ragala, a ruddy-featured, strapping lad. One time he took him to the pub, treated him to a drink or two and turned their talk to the pretty girls back at the estate. With the boozing came just the right frame of mind and when Majerský had satisfied himself that Ragala did have some interest in girls, he said: "You're a poor sod, you are!" – "Why so?" Ragala asked. "What makes you say that, Mr Majerský?" – "Because you haven't been to bed with any of them. Now Zita Furka, the one that used to be in the canteen kitchen, there's a pretty girl! A bit light-fingered, a bit prone to pilfering, but pretty she is! If I weren't married, believe me, man, I wouldn't hang about!" – "She's quite something, I agree, and that barn where she works, hm, if I put my mind to it..." – "Get away with you, you poor fool! She wouldn't let you near her!" – "Oh yeah? I'll tell you this, sir, give it three days and the deed's done!" Jano Ragala smacked his palms together: "Care to bet on it?" Majerský had looked at the ruddy-featured Ragala and said: "One hundred!" – "Hm..." Ragala began to waver. "All right, but how shall I prove it to you, sir?" – "Don't be daft," Majerský said, brushing that aside, "why should I need you to prove anything? You'll just tell me and that'll be good enough! You're a decent chap, aren't you? The best is my guess!" – "All right, sir, let's shake on it!" They shook hands and their table having been approached by Levý, the chief engineer on the Pospíchal estate, in his oil-soaked dungarees, Majerský got him to act as witness. Levý sundered their joined hands with a single blow, merely asking how much the bet was for. "A hundred," Majerský told him. "It's all about," he added, "whether or not Ragala here's gonna get a certain girl." – "Okay!" said Levý, who showed no further interest in the bet. He didn't have to, because Zita's mother, who was convinced that only a real man could bring a poor girl a bit of joy, told her: "Listen, Zita: that Jano Ragala keeps hovering round you. If I were your age..." – "Oh, mum, you said that once before, when the steward started his hovering." – "He's a bad lot," her mother had said, "but this Jano seems thoroughly decent." Jano Ragala won his bet, and when he came to collect his hundred crowns from Majerský, Majerský handed them over. "Was it good, Jano?" he asked. "It was, sir!" Ragala was slightly surprised about the hundred crowns, but among the workforce he insisted that he'd never known anyone as decent and trustworthy as Majerský. Then Ragala began seeing Zita regularly and after a time Zita stopped caring. She thought things would turn out all right anyway and that she would forget Majerský, but she couldn't forget him. Nor could he forget her.

"Ach," said Obmann drily and testily to Sergeant Kniewald in Zita's kitchen. His receding lips barely even began to part. "Not me. I just don't fancy her. She's filthy, unwashed and she stinks."

He turned his smooth, white, thin features, where everything seemed to recede, towards Zita.

"Filthy," he repeated with his eyes on Zita's white shoulders and rough brown hands, "filthy and she stinks. Her hands are so hard and scratchy I'd not want 'em messing about inside my pants."

"Ha ha ha ha!" Sergeant Kniewald guffawed, thrusting out his jaw with its yellow protruding teeth. "Her hands aren't smooth, I'll give you that, but she's got other bits that are smooth. Ha ha ha ha!"

The SS men laughed.

Zita's kitchen was filling with cigarette fumes because the SS men were smoking, and with that odour that soldiers carry with them: the smell of mothballs, eau de Cologne, sweat and everything else Obmann's section had picked up on their way to Lieskov.

Zita got a griping pain in her gut. She did her best to resist the surge of fear that hit her whenever she saw the Germans' grey-green uniforms or got a whiff of that military odour. She clung fast to her oven.

"Ach," said Obmann once the mirth had subsided, pausing for thought and glancing up at the naked Christ on the Cross, then at the 'old maid' dangling from the big grey bracket fungus almost onto Kniewald's head. "Scrawny women have no appeal to me."

Zita was not scrawny. Obmann could see that, but he wanted to deflect any interest his crew may have had in her away because of the daytime action that lay ahead.

"Night-time actions," he said, "need to be prepared for, just like daytime ones!"

The men began chattering among themselves.

By this stage Obmann believed nothing and believed in nothing, only in daytime and night-time actions. He had been reduced to this by the events of late January and February. Nobody could have detected this from his smooth, receding face, but mentally Obmann had begun to sneer at The Cretin. That was his name for Hitler. Memel, Pomerania, Brandenburg – full of Russians now and The Cretin was still assuring the world that the war wouldn't be won by Inner Asia, but by Europe. Inner Asia was heading into Europe, bringing with it all the crap the human animal is capable of. The Cretin was sending his emergency reserves into battle, the conference in the Crimea was over, Stalin, Churchill and Roosevelt had been the ones conferring – a fine bunch! – the Americans were in Prüm, the Russians in Breslau, and The Cretin was drooling, spluttering and telling the world that an epoch-making change was just round the corner. Such a change had already happened inside him, Ernst Obmann, because what was an Obmann today? Just someone clearing some place called Slovakia of some partisan garbage. Someone carrying out daytime actions. A German soldier was a great soldier, but guilty of one grave error: that of not believing in race and the party and not carrying out exterminations in full, but only in part. Hals? Could that retired Saint Bernard exterminate anything? Shit-scared of firing! Except for firing the odd fart into his pants! But the partisan garbage had to be exterminated – and that was part of Obmann's mission, because in that garbage he saw a plague in embryo. He had to clear out anything that had even a hint of the partisan about it. That's what daytime actions were for. The troop of SS that had arrived in early January to relieve the previous troop in the town had carried on with the good work of its predecessors. In a young birch grove outside the town it had executed up to thirty pieces of partisan garbage, as Obmann put it, by means of a special technique invented by Otto Drossel, the SS man with a plaster on his face, the man who had interpreted for Obmann and Zita. The partisans who weren't partisans, but only relatives of partisans, and who'd been picked up around the villages in the foothills, had hand grenades tied under their chins. With grenades under their chins the condemned men had dug a common grave. Then over the grave, one at a time, they'd been shot from the side, shot in the grenades. Not a single trace of the head of any one of the victims had remained. "That's great," Obmann had told Drossel. "I agree with this special technique of yours, because garbage that's headless is no longer a threat, and it can improve the soil for the future, headless garbage is like – like – you're so imaginative, Otto!" Obmann saw himself as the Staff Sergeant of a justice that cleanses, and administering a justice that cleanses gave Obmann's day-time actions their meaning. He saw such people as a threat and would complain that the army was failing to keep him supplied with politically undesirable elements. Which was why he acted on his own initiative, along with his men and dogs. "Our Party's policy," he used to say, "is a tremendous thing! It embraces a new, superlative morality – under it you can eliminate whoever you like, because no one can ever meet the requirements of such a superlative morality – and it would a sheer waste of time trying to work out whether this partisan garbage meets any such requirements or not. If only the army was politically educated – if – if – then we wouldn't need to bother with these daytime actions!" Night-time actions were different. They involved alcohol and women. "The ideal terrain for night-time actions are women with smooth hands and a rough soul," was Obmann's watchword on the subject.

"What's interesting," said Obmann to Kniewald, "is that everywhere here I've found nice food and awful houses. With us it's the opposite: nice houses and awful food."

"I've noticed that, too."

"Otto," Obmann said to Drossel, "ask her what they bake their bread with."

"Vot you use," Drossel duly asked, "to pake pret?"

"Rye or wheat flour," she replied, taking half a spoonful of the cold, unsalted scrambled eggs, which she'd begun eating again. "And even barley."

Obmann heard Zita and Drossel out, nodding as he recalled his father's huge mill at Ahlen. With a thin finger, conspicuous for the black half-moon of grime on it, he pointed at the cradle.

Zita shuddered with shame and cold. Although it was very hot in her little kitchen and the surface of her body had begun to smart all over, she was shaking inside. Once more, prickly tears began to force their way into her eyes.

"Here the food is good," Obmann said to Kniewald, "and the people are hospitable. Ha-ha! That mayor of theirs, and the bigwigs around him...! Naive vermin! The timorous are always hospitable."

"And feeble."

Obmann glanced at Kniewald.

"Timorous," he repeated, "and feeble." He pointed to the cradle. "This thing I only know from fairy-tales," he said, "and books."

"Cradle and grave, cradle and grave," Kniewald remarked in turn. "Best two places for a good sleep."

"Scharführer," said Obmann to Kniewald, "we shall be giving you a new title – you – you really ought to be more a Scharphilosoph than Scharführer."

"Yes, Herr Oberscharführer," Kniewald replied. "I should be delighted! Without wisdom the world is a pretty dreary place."

"Ha-ha!" Obmann laughed and looked towards Drossel: "Tell her to start giving the pup a rock. I find the sound quite affecting."

"Mr Oberscharführer iss eskink," Drossel told Zita, "zet you rock ze puppy."

Zita shot a glance at Drossel and Obmann.

"Rock!" Drossel snapped after a short pause, then barked: "Rock ze puppy, vill you!"

"I'm really sorry," Zita said imploringly, her lips trembling, "but I'd rather not. He sleeps so little as it is, he's poorly and keeps waking up –"

"Rock!"

Zita put her bread and the pan with the unfinished scrambled eggs down on the stove and began to rock her little boy. She was shaking, though you couldn't tell because with one hand she was holding the metal bar on the stove and with the other the cradle.

Obmann – the Staff Sergeant with a white stripe and star on his collar, from which he had turned back his white cape, that smooth, pale, thin face, the aquiline nose that gave way so conspicuously to his eyes and mouth, his sunken and receding cheeks, a face like the steel cone with which they split timber at the sawmill, the receding forehead with smooth black hair combed back, the clamped, indrawn lips – Ernst Obmann, Staff Sergeant, sat at his ease, his back resting against the back of Zita's chair, lost in memories of his childhood, his lovely childhood.

Zita was shaking, rocking away, fearful for her little boy, for herself and for Majerský, who was lying in the sitting-room in the unmade bed. Out of the corner of her left eye she looked at the puddles of water by the two doors and at the drying and shrinking foot marks between them. Will they notice them? Or had they noticed them already? Oh, God...! She'd do whatever they demanded of her, just as long as they didn't find Majerský. Her white chemise quivered across her breasts.

In the bed, Majerský was shaking hot and cold, fearing for himself, Zita and her little boy, fearing that the bedding piled over him was quivering. In its turbulence his blood filled his head with an unbearable pain and one single thought: He shouldn't have done it! He should have stayed where he was...! He gripped his rifle with one damp hand.

Far away in the mountains, there above Lieskov at the foot of White Crag, his comrades had remained, remnants of his platoon, which in September had attacked a German depot, for two weeks they'd defended, against the Germans, the valley in which lay the village of Melichava, for ten days they'd held on to Melichava and then, out of ammunition, the platoon had scattered under the German onslaught, leaving behind their dead and wounded, and retreated piecemeal up into the mountains. Eight of Majerský's comrades were left in a bunker. The short, dark, hunch-backed Jan Baďo, besides him two students, Štefan Cipko and Michal Martinec, who'd come from Bratislava and were much given to debating whether the spirit of the twentieth century was political freedom or political slavery, or to observing a stony silence, then the taciturn Jean Panais, a very young French lad who'd escaped from the Dubnica ammunition factory, two Jews in their thirties, brothers, both tall, Ernest and Julius Waagmann, the one a commercial engineer, the other a doctor of laws, and two more men, Juraj Haško, a lieutenant, slim to the point of being skinny, and a hulky individual with shoulders and upper arms like the beech branches in the forest, and with grizzled features and grizzled hair, Mišo Černek from Lieskov, Zita's husband. The men in the bunker knew that Černek was from Lieskov and that he wouldn't let them go anywhere near it out of concern for his wife and baby son, and if Majerský had had even an inkling that he'd find Zita there, he'd never have given the place a second thought. Zita wasn't from Lieskov. Černek had brought her there to their new cottage. Majerský's comrades had remained in the mountains way above Lieskov and latterly had lived off the cow and calf that the students, Cipko and Martinec, along with the Frenchman Panais, had driven up there during a terrible blizzard from a gamekeeper after he'd had to move a third time, by order of the Germans, from Melichava to a remote gamekeeper's lodge. "Adieu, veau, vache, cochon, couvée!" the Frenchman Panais had kept repeating to the gamekeeper's tearful wife and the cursing gamekeeper himself, and Cipko, Martinec and the Waagmanns translated for the others: "Farewell, calf, farewell, cow, farewell, pig…!" They'd all had a good laugh at this, more than once, and when Panais tried to explain to them what "couvée" meant and no one could grasp it, they laughed even more. They'd remained in the mountains way above Lieskov, all except Majerský, who couldn't because his eyes had grown so painful. He wasn't like the rest of his comrades anyway. Even back in Radotín, in Bohemia, he'd been a different sort of person, and although all manner of things had happened there, he had never changed. At Radotín, Zita, a pretty lass of eighteen, couldn't get Majerský out of her mind, not even when she started going out with Jano Ragala, and Majerský couldn't get her out of his mind either, though it had been he who had offered her to Ragala and let him keep her. Jano Ragala loved Zita dearly and he loved her all the more the more his mates, young and old, made fun of him. "You're a silly idiot, Jano!" they used to say. "How stupid can you get? She used to bed the steward behind your back, still does and always will!" Jano Ragala did and didn't believe them, but one night he did, having sat beneath Majerský's sitting-room window, eavesdropping. For a long time he'd heard nothing, but eventually, as dawn was about to break, he caught the sound of Majerský's voice and words that for long thereafter he associated with the wide, foul-smelling yard, the great barns and stables, the green reapers and weeders, the huge grey threshers and the bright early-morning sky giving promise of a hot July day. "Come now, Zitka," he'd heard Majerský say, "do what I'm saying!" – "All right, for your sake I'll do it," Zita had said, "But the baby will be yours..." – "Maybe it will, maybe it won't, but does that matter, Zitka? The main thing is that it's on the way. Jano's a dimwit, you can use it to catch him." Jano Ragala could hear Zita crying and moved away from beneath Majerský's window.

In Zita's kitchen the cradle thudded and bumped with its worn rockers on the fir-wood floor.

Majerský gave a sudden shudder in Zita's bed.

In the bunker above Lieskov he hadn't wanted to be completely useless. He'd stayed inside it because of the bright light of the snow and the blue light of the sky, sometimes he would tidy away the blankets on the hard fir-wood bunks, sweeping away any dross, he'd done the cooking, and when once the taciturn student, Martinec, had said: "I wonder what my Dana's getting up to in Bratislava," Majerský, who happened to be shovelling water out of the bunker onto the glaring white snow outside, said: "My Zita, some girl she was, man! Zita...! Kind, meek, ate everything I cooked for her. And suddenly, hm... " – "Jožo," Černek, a man of surly, ample, grizzled features, addressed him "save your breath – and – by the way, what was your Zita's surname?" – "Why?" – "Just asking. Listen, Jožo, did you know a chap called Ragala? He used to go off to Bohemia..." That made Majerský jump, he blenched and carried on shovelling water out of the bunker.

He shook his head. "No, I didn't..." – "Come off it, Jožo! Stop lying! You knew him well. He and I have talked about you. He said you fixed him up with some girl. Do you know what became of Ragala?" – "No idea. What?" – "You know perfectly well what. I don't believe a word you say. Up to now I've quite liked you, Jožo. Not anymore! Save your breath or you'll get a taste of lead!" – "Why, Míšo?" – "You talk too much and you keep going on about your eyes – you can die for all I care, you bloody malingerer!" – "If *your* eyes did to you what mine are doing to me, Míšo!" Majerský retorted, "then you could talk!" Saying no more, Majerský carried on slopping away the dirty water from the warm bunker, keeping his eyes closed against the white snow and the blue sky. By this stage he was determined to escape and when, that same day, four Soviet partisans showed up on horseback with orders for them to make ready to fight their way through to link up with the advancing Soviet troops, Majerský just looked at them in silence, looked at their scrawny horses, listened and kept his thoughts to himself. He hadn't fully understood them, but he did grasp that Hitler was losing on all fronts and beating a hasty retreat. "Gitler kak retivaya loshad," said one of the partisans, a podgy, sheepskin-clad little chap with young, angular features. He was sitting on one of the bunks, tapping one boot tip against the other to get the snow and mud off them. "Kak retivaya loshad – da, no Gitleru i knut i vozhdi!" – "Eh?" Majerský asked Lieutenant Haško, "What's that about Hitler?" – "He says Hitler," Haško explained, "is like a runaway horse, he needs reining in and his hide whipped!" – "Well," said Majerský, "he's spot-on there!" He listened to the Soviet partisans and his own comrades discussing the need to make ready for a getaway any day soon. By the time the mounted partisans had left, Majerský's mind was made up. He made his escape, first along the footpath that led to the stream, then along the stream all the way to the remote gamekeeper's cottage above the village of Melichava, from where he turned off through clearings and dense forests towards Lieskov, because he knew that was the last place his comrades would go look for him.

Zita, her body on fire, shot through with waves of cold, rocked her ailing infant.

Staff Sergeant Ernst Obmann sat there, leaning right back in Zita's chair and dreaming of his childhood, his lovely childhood, not far from Ahlen. Ahlen, my Ahlen! A city of black, the coal, the mines, the black factories – but then his father's white mill, white on the outside, new, inside even whiter from the flour. Ernst is playing behind the mill with his pals, with his elder brother Pauli, and from below ground comes the rumble of the massive, gigantic diesel engine. Its slow strokes rumble on. The engine is massive, gigantic, it powers the mill and the short-lived, precarious prosperity of the Obmanns: Paul Obmann, his wife Ilsa and the two boys, Pauli and Ernst. Ahlen, my Ahlen, what will be left of you? Obmann had already passed through any number of towns where you could see from one end to the other because the wrecked buildings, almost razed to the ground, were beyond blocking the view of the mass destruction that had been wrought.

"Otto," he said, turning to Drossel, the SS man with the plastered face "tell her to rock faster."

"Rock!" Drossel told Zita. "Rock fester!"

Zita complied.

"Gut, ja, ja," said Obmann, "ja, ja, gut!"

Zita's little boy watched his mother with his inflamed face and feeble, dark eyes. His fair, wavy hair shone in the gloom cast by the lamp beneath the hempen towel.

Zita was still holding on to the bar on the stove and to the cradle and, slightly bent over the child, her back now ached as, trembling with fear, she was too scared to stand up straight or even move. Despite wearing only her chemise and a flimsy blue skirt, she had begun to sweat all over from the heat of the stove.

Obmann sat there and stared at the cradle, at the strips of wood it was made of, old now and smoothed by hand contact, at the heart shape carved out of the one above the little lad's head. "Ja, ja," he assured Zita, now her rocking had reached the right rhythm, a rhythm to match that of his father's diesel engine not far from Ahlen, "ja, das ist gut!"

Obmann's men sat there and watched their Staff Sergeant in astonishment. Sergeant Kniewald and Drossel were smirking. They knew their man and knew what was to come. The Staff Sergeant had a faraway look and although he'd said it wasn't good to have a daytime action preceded by one at night, he was getting ready for one. They waited.

Pensive and distant, Obmann lit a cigarette.

Obmann and his section felt good in the warmth of Zita's kitchen, warm, cosy and pleasant, because the kitchen was small and the grey-white stove with the tiled oven was a good source of warmth even though, by now, the last logs had almost burned away.

Obmann was breathing slowly and gently so that his nose could capture the warmth of Zita's body as it spread across the kitchen.

In Lieskov, a village in the foothills, darkness and silence reigned, its houses and cottages dimly grey above the grimy snow, with blackened windows set in the grey walls. A wintry February night lay over Lieskov, all white where the snow remained undisturbed, while elsewhere it was trampled down and grimy. The cottages, burned out or not, stood against the grey, gloomy night like silent headstones. The trampled areas of snow, lit up for around two daylight hours by a feeble sun, froze as evening fell and, on the wide road, it crunched beneath the jackboots of the men whom the incensed and resentful commander of the utterly exhausted Lieskov garrison, Lieutenant Hals, had, out of fear of Obmann and his group, sent out with Corporal Köhl to patrol Lieskov.

Lieutenant Paul Hals, in his grey-green uniform and a grey-green cape, and wearing a helmet, had been wandering from room to room in what had been the squire's residence, waiting for the Staff Sergeant to show up. He's bound to be up to his usual tricks somewhere, he thought, and the war's going to the dogs! Then Hals was struck by a frightening idea: how about grabbing the Staff Sergeant and tossing him to the partisans! He removed his outsize spectacles, withdrew a grey-green glove from his cape and gave them a wipe.

The patrol walked on through dark, silent Lieskov.

At the upper end, outside the Hankas' cottage, doing his thirty paces this way, thirty paces that, was the German private Hans Moeller, going from beyond the Hankas' place almost as far as the Černeks', counting his steps "– one, two, three, four, five, six –" with his helmet pulled down to his eyes, which were fixed on the grimy snow. In his freezing hands he held his cold rapid-firing rifle as he marched this way and that, turning and counting in order to bear up against the insult he'd had from Obmann: "– you lice-ridden cur! Lice were munching on you even in your mother's womb! Pity they didn't gobble you up completely...!"

To him this was grossly offensive, because he'd actually never set eyes on his mother. After Obmann's insult he'd got to thinking: the kind of mother that you'll never ever see is the dearest kind, because you've nothing to shout at her for and so you can't shout at her. He could find nothing wrong with her. She hadn't been a lice-ridden mother and he's no lice-ridden cur, lice-ridden curs are all those from lance-corporals upwards. Moeller counted, marched and turned, proceeding slowly from the Hankas' almost as far as the Černeks' cottage, seething with rage.

"Gut, gut," Obmann said to Zita, "das ist gut, ja, ja!"

Zita kept rocking, humiliated and embarrassed, because she'd no idea why she had to do it. She had a vague notion that it could be because SS men hadn't seen a cradle before. Maybe Germany didn't have them anymore. Seeing as even here people already have cots and prams. This is an old cradle, from the Hankas', decrepit and bumpy, and the Hankas don't even know where it is. If Mišo had stayed, he'd have made some new rockers. The cradle travels about Lieskov in the wake of new babies. The Kubíks have also said they want it. She ought to pass it on to them. Zita rocked on, feeling humiliated, shuddering hot and cold and fighting back her tears.

Suddenly she began to laugh in a high-pitched, unnatural laugh, a squeaky giggle, as if someone was strangling her, and she shook with cold.

Obmann glanced at her arms, now roughened with goose bumps. "Hm, Otto," he said to Drossel, "ask her what it is that she finds so very funny!"

"Vot you larf at?"

The high-pitched, squeaky giggle carried on tripping from Zita's throat.

"Silly pitch –!"

Obmann's lips drew back slightly as he took in the pink gums above Zita's close-knit, healthy teeth.

"It's you I'm laughing at," she said in that squeaky voice, "haven't you seen a cradle before? So your babies, where –?"

"No!" said Drossel. "Not until now!"

"You've seen so much of the world –" Zita burst out laughing again, still squeakily and seeming to choke, going red in the face, then turning quite pale, "– so many babies you've tossed in fires, so much of the world you've seen –"

"What's she on about?" asked Obmann. "What's she laughing at?"

"Us having never seen a cradle before," said Drossel. "Says we've been all over the world and never seen a cradle!"

"I haven't seen one." Obmann thought he'd much rather be alone in the kitchen. The sergeant was right about it being in poor taste for blokes to have to wait their turn. "This is the first one I've seen and I'd like to slip a little offering in it – because – I've heard that's what you're supposed to do with cradles."

He smiled at Zita, she was silent now, still trying not to cry. In its rigid state her whole body just twitched.

"Sergeant," he said, turning to Kniewald, "you're the philosopher among us. You think of something clever!"

"I did once hear it said –," Kniewald paused, sticking his yellow teeth out over his lower lip, "– that the grave of liberty is the cradle of art – but what could that – no, that's right, Herr Oberscharführer: grave of liberty – cradle of art, it's –"

"That," said Obmann, "is a dangerous saying, a dangerous offering, Scharführer, no, perhaps this instead: the grave of a cradle – the cradle of liberty, eh?"

Obmann was smiling at Zita, watching her through the smoke that he was slowly expelling between his thin lips.

Zita shuddered with shame, cold, heat and revulsion. She was revolted by Obmann's thin lips, drawn back as they were, and his white teeth. She choked back her tears. Poor Mišo! Goodness knows where he is. She was briefly shaken by fear, a different, a new fear, as something suddenly flashed through her mind: how were the men who'd remained up in the mountains going to suffer? What were they going to suffer at the hands of people like these if they were caught? She looked at Obmann. She'd hardly be able to ask Majerský now if he'd heard anything of Mišo Černek. But then – but then, why would she ask him anyway now? Humiliated and degraded, fearing for all her worldly possessions, she began to understand Majerský, the man lying in her bed. She was ready to let bygones be bygones. Poor man! Oh, God, what now? What he did to her at Radotín, that was nothing. Maybe he does know something about Mišo… But what good is that now? She carried on rocking to oblige Obmann.

At Radotín, on the estate, he'd kept an eye on Ragala, Mrs Furka, Zita, and having seen that Ragala and Zita were going out together, he'd laughed venomously and said: "Just you wait, you've got it coming!" then he'd hounded Zita and her mother out. He thought Ragala would leave as well, but he didn't. One time he and three others had lain in wait for him, beaten the living daylights out of him and dumped him behind the huge granary next to the estate. The police didn't even launch an investigation and shortly after Jano Ragala left Radotín for Prague, where he just muddled along, begging and looking for any casual work. Mrs Furka and Zita had gone from one estate to the next, each with a pack on her back, and one night, when they were down to their last seventeen hellers, exhausted and hungry, they'd crept into the cattle shed of the Týnec estate so silently and secretly that the 'security guard' didn't spot them, there they'd got the cows to stand up, knelt down beneath them, sipping a little from one, then from another, then from a third, and so allayed their hunger. In the morning they were found by staff and taken off to the bailiff. Mrs Furka and her Zita managed to talk him into letting them stay on at the estate. His name was Juřena, he had a squint and was forever spitting, but he'd been talked round and kept them on despite some concern that the police would come looking for them. They didn't. A year later, in 1940, late August, Zita married Jano Ragala at an estate near Kolín, in Bohemia. She'd run into him there, and when he asked her where her baby was, she just shrugged indifferently and said: "I should have had one. I don't know if with him or you, but it left me." – "Left?" he queried. "Of its own accord?" – "Just so, Janko." Zita married Ragala and had a bad time of it. He would beat her and shout at her: "I didn't want you and they made me marry you!" Jano Ragala and Zita broke up very soon after their simple wedding. He joined a criminal gang in Bohemia who used to fasten a steel cable between trees on either side of a road to make cars stop at night and then rob their better dressed occupants. Once, during an exchange of fire with the police, he was injured. Jano Ragala subsequently died in Pilsen hospital. In the spring of 1939, Zita herself went back to Bohemia in search of work, with her mother, now sick and weak, and there she married Černek, an ageing bachelor, having told him the full story of her past with Majerský and Ragala. Černek took her away from their casual labours and brought her to Lieskov, to live in his new cottage beside a stream on a wet meadow.

Obmann's men were waiting for a night-time action, watching their Staff Sergeant, who was deep in thought, his mind elsewhere. Kniewald and Drossel exchanged furtive glances.

Obmann's narrow lips were drawn backwards.

Those were good times, he was thinking, at the mill in Ahlen, good times, it had been a wonderful childhood until those creditors showed up and did for his father and the mill. Then came life in black Ahlen, The Cretin, Hitlerjugend, Streifendienst, the young Ernst Obmann had had to learn how to hold a rifle as naturally as a pen, then those jackboots, riding breeches – and you didn't even register how you'd let yourself be gnawed away at by race, The Party, The Idea, The Cretin – and then Russia, Russia, hospital in Königsberg, Russia again, a vast, awful, dreary land... Ah, Russia, there there'd been so many opportunities for special treatment, he had specialised in *politruk*s, he'd hang them up by their feet and use a red-hot iron rod to brand their chests with stars, hammers and sickles – to comply with the demands of The Idea, the Party, the government, The Cretin – and now these daytime and night-time actions in some place called Slovakia, which to this day still bakes white bread, lives in fear, but not in such fear as to be afraid to be hospitable, daytime and night-time actions, and the bounden duty, even here, to rid Europe of the plague and canker of partisans.

"Du –!"

Zita looked at Obmann, a darkness of fear and fury erupting from her gleaming eyes towards Obmann's narrow lips, drawn backwards as they were, because in that single, short word, spat out with a discharge of venom, she sensed the fate of Majerský, her own fate – and her little boy? Ferko? The hand gripping the bar on the stove began to go numb. Zita looked at Obmann, listened to the incomprehensible speech borne on his noxious breath and carried on rocking.

The little boy seized hold of the lathed sides of his cradle with his tiny hands and hauled himself into a sitting position. He looked round at Obmann's men. And whined.

Zita slowed down her rocking lest he bang his head on the topmost lath.

"Otto," Obmann turned to Drossel, pointing to the cradle, "tell her to rock faster!"

"Rock fester!" Drossel told Zita. "Ze Oberscharführer say you're a pitch – a schwein – a hole, an zet ve hev not com here to safe you from ze partisans – you are tresh, stinkink garbitch, you hev turnt Oiropa into picksty!" Drossel had begun adding his own invectives to whatever Obmann chose to say. "Ve shell search ze ozzer rum – en if ve fine enny sign off your hassbant, zen you vill see – it vill be ze screpheep for you! Got it? Rock fester! Ze Oberscharführer insist! So rock!"

"He's poorly," said Zita, "have some consideration!"

"Lay ze puppy down and rock fester!"

Zita stopped rocking, bent down to the little boy, put her arms round him and made to pick him up.

"Nein, nein!" said Obmann calmly, indicating that she should leave the boy in the cradle. "Aber nein!"

"My poor little boy," said Zita, choking back her tears, "lie there nicely now, there you are!" She lay him back down, turning his face away from Obmann's men and the light. "Time for beddy-byes, hush now, rock-a-bye baby, sh, sh!"

She began rocking.

The little boy obeyed and was still.

"Ha ha ha ha!" Sergeant Kniewald roared with laughter and turned to Drossel: "Say, Otto, what's the difference between a fish and a woman? You don't know? A fish stinks from the head and a woman smells from her... Hah ha ha ha!"

Obmann glanced at the two doors and at the red pots lined up on top of the tiled stove.

Zita rocked away with that evil darkness in her gleaming eyes. Majerský in that bed, footprints left by him in front of both the doors and running from one to the other, footprints leading to the bed, and she underclad in front of so many men – all this filled Zita's entire being with a burdensome, dull pain. By this stage she didn't know if he really had come, if it wasn't all just a bad dream. She couldn't get out of her head all the things of Míšo's that she had in an old chest in the loft, clothes, two sets of his Sunday best, two hats, a short grey overcoat, shoes. And his underwear. A razor, some blades, shaving soap and a shaving brush. His papers in a drawer, identity cards bearing his photo. She'd put them all together in one drawer. She'd tossed some hay over the chest, but what if... She rocked the little boy fast and he kept wearily opening his burning eyes. He doesn't sleep much now, the poor little mite.

Obmann, his lips drawn backwards, his face like the kind of steel cone used for splitting timber, was dreaming of Ahlen, the beautiful region in which it lay, southern Westphalia. The whole of Westphalia is like Ahlen, everywhere the flying dust of white flour settles on the black soot and black soot on the white flour. Ahlen, my Ahlen, what will be left of you? In his mind's eye he could see the effect of the cataclysm on so many towns and villages, Russian and German. Talk of "Das Ende von Krementschug!" was all very well, he thought. The end of Krementchuk! But das Ende von Ahlen, too! Ahlen, my Ahlen! Maybe now just heaps of concrete blasted to bits, heaps of bricks with mortar stuck to them, holes exposing cellars, basements collapsed – and somewhere in among all that lived his father and mother, those human lice who'd had the gall to bring him into a world like this. Obmann stared coldly into Zita's perspiring face, smooth, bedewed, broad in the cheek, even wider at the forehead, his eyes roamed her brown curly hair, her long white neck, her white chemise billowing over her breasts, her blue skirt, wide at the hips.

Zita kept rocking with an insuperable rage inside her and with no thought as to what might be going to happen, having begun to have every respect for all those the Germans had it in for, even Majerský. Poor man, let's hope it turns out all right, that they don't find him, that nothing happens to him!

Majerský could hear the bumping and thudding of the worn rockers coming from the kitchen and although he hoped that they'd do nothing bad to Zita as long as she kept rocking, the rockers banged and rumbled inside his ears, striking at him as if they were actually hitting him across his throbbing, inflamed head. He was shaking, soaking wet all over, the quilts also shaking above him. Slowly, cautiously, so as not to move anything, with one arm, one leg, he shifted ever so slowly towards the coverlet, the edge of the bed. He'll go, make a run for it! Where to? His head was jarred by the laughter that always gushed up whenever the men in the bunker repeated their "Farewell, calf, farewell, cow, farewell, pig..." The Frenchman would always try to demonstrate what "couvée" meant, but they never knew if it was a wheel, a basket, a bowl. He himself would just laugh, invariably shaking his head in incomprehension. He'll go, but there's not a chance he'll be able to return to that spot at the foot of White Crag. What would Černek say? Would he give him a taste of lead? Why had he threatened him like that? He'll make a getaway! Not past Zita's kitchen. No, that way the Germans might hear him. But what way out of here? Slowly, quietly, as quietly as anyone who's shaking all over can, Majerský slid out of Zita's bed, retrieved from it his army cap and rifle, placed the cap on his head and noiselessly propped the rifle against the wall.

He could hear howls of German laughter coming from the kitchen.

He tidied the inside of Zita's bed. Then the three pillows he'd been lying under, the bottommost first, making a neat pile of them, then he started on the first, bottommost, quilt.

In the kitchen, the rockers were thudding away and the SS men guffawing. One of them was spinning some yarn.

Everything had driven Majerský away. He'd left, not knowing where to.

In 1944 he was forty-one, and when, in his village, because at the time he was still at home, in Temešany, a Czechoslovak and a Soviet flag had flown for two days, he told his wife: "Listen, old thing, it's a nice day, don't say anything to the lads, have the elder one carry on going to work as if nothing's happened, and I'll be on my way. Stop crying and shush! If anyone asks, tell them I went to the ministry in Bratislava and that something happened there – that's it, I got run over by a car and am in hospital there!" Back then, Majerský had had all sorts of ideas: things were going to be exactly like after that other war alongside the Czechoslovak legionaries. Anyone who so much as fired just once into the air against the Germans was going to be valued. There were no Jews anymore, the devil took them, their properties remained and there was going to be a call for dab hands. The Russians were already in Warsaw, in Bucharest, and once they let go, that'd be the end of Hitler, not so much as a greasy stain would be left of him. He'd gone to the partisan brigade's command post, been given hand grenades and a rifle, donned a uniform and then did whatever his company was doing. He was well liked because he wanted everyone to be as one. "It's a poor partisan," he used to say, "who's in it because he has to be, a good one is one who joins up unbidden!" The Germans had put paid to their company and, apart from certain other groups, all that was left was him, two students, two Jews, the Frenchman, the hunchbacked Baďo, lieutenant Haško and Černek, Zita's husband. In the mountains at the foot of White Crag, far from Lieskov, they'd dug out a bunker, lined it with logs of fir, stocked it with whatever they could and waited.

Raucous laughter in Zita's kitchen, the rockers were thudding, and Obmann's men were creating a racket.

In Zita's sitting room Majerský had tidied the bed, set his cap on his head with hands all ashake, drawn the lappets down over his ears, picked up his rifle and now slowly, silently and with great caution he was tiptoeing towards the dim window. He paused, his mind having suddenly been swamped by memories of his room at the Radotín estate. That was where Zita used to come to see him, her pretty young face always animated by laughter and fear as she drew her bare feet under her on the bed.

He moved forward.

He was being driven to leave Zita's sitting room by the raucous German laughter, the pandemonium, and by the friends who'd remained in the bunker, that handful of disparate characters who'd still been able to block out hunger, cold and fear with laughter. The Frenchman Jean Panais, who could find no better way to explain the meaning of *couvée* than by kneading a nest out of snow and putting in it four snow eggs, he'd laughed and said: "Ça, c'est la couvée!", though most of all he was being driven by Zita, though he himself had no idea what was actually driving him away, because his senses told him it was down to his shivering body, his splitting headache, burning eyes and churning stomach. In his right hand he held his rifle, his left holding on to the bed frame, a cold strip of wood, smooth, and he was taking slow, shuffling steps, barely an inch at a time, across the strip of carpet woven out of rags, shuffling, barely inching, trying to stay erect lest his debility made him lose his balance and fall over. God forbid! His mouth filled with a rush of saliva, then suddenly dehydrated right down his throat before another flood of vile saliva filled it up again.

In the kitchen the rockers were thudding away. The German pandemonium, German raucous laughter.

Majerský inched step by tiny step towards the grey of the window. Jean Panais... Ça, c'est la couvée...! Majerský was overtaken by a new wave of fear. The Frenchman, he'd been very fond of him – and if the Germans make for the hills, following his footprints, they might find him... God forbid! Step by tiny step he made for the window. Somewhere here is the foot of that other bed and it's still a good way from the window. Majerský suddenly had an acute sense of the horrific distance to the window, that he'd never make it in this life, he'd fall over – and that would be that. Zita, Zita! With your little lad in his cradle... Ever so slowly he slid his wet, sweaty hand along the smooth, cold wood. The window was gloomily grey, like the gloom that arises when fear and hope merge, suddenly his eyes flickered as if they were about to fragment. That French lad, poor guy, he used to sing such a weird song –

One time, in the bunker at the foot of White Crag, they'd been translating it. "Le vent passé sur les tombes," Jean Panais had said to Ernest Waagmann and Waagmann had translated it: "The wind blows across the graves..." – "la liberté reviendra..." – "freedom shall return..." – "on nous oubliera..." – "On nous oubliera?" Ernest Waagmann had asked. "Pourquoi?" – "Je sais pas. On nous oubliera!" – "We shall be forgotten," Waagmann translated, glancing at Panais. "Nous rentrerons dans l'ombre," Panais ended. "We shall return to the shadows," Waagmann translated. – "Why?" Černek had asked. "Why to the shadows? We shall have our say everywhere." – "Aha," the hunchback Baďo had responded, "We shall return where it's cool, not just dark!"

Majerský heard Zita let out a tear-filled shriek.

Zita's scream reminded him of the green fir forest, the toxic blue sky glimmering through the green, and the white snow glaring toxically in the sunlight, but also of the desire to be in that snow, beneath that sky, in the green forest, to be standing guard, whether by night or day, to having his eyes filled with searing tears, yet having to guard the bunker from the long, deep chine that gave easiest access to it. He would go back there, to the foot of White Crag, he thought, he'd go even if it cost him his sight, even if Černek gave him a taste of lead – why had Černek said that? – he'd apologise to his comrades, begging each in turn to let him stay, and then as the need arose, he'd go to the gamekeeper's cottage, to Melichava... Oh, my God – Zita, Zita... He'd go back, link up with the Russian partisans, fight his way through to the army with them as soon as need be... Zita – Zita, forgive me for everything, Zita...

Once more he caught the sound of her tear-filled shriek.

Zita, Zita... Majerský's rifle slid from his grip, hitting the floor with a dull thud, because just then it had dawned on him, what if Zita were married to Černek? He gasped in horror. No, he can't go back there now, to the bunker at the foot of White Crag –

In the kitchen, Staff Sergeant Obmann, his head bursting with thoughts, reminiscences and his entire lucky childhood and his later life, as it were riddled long before with bullet-holes, was chatting to Sergeant Kniewald. He was charmed by both his own words and Kniewald's comments because the men were laughing at them as they both, but he especially, felt able to utter endless profanities at the expense of the perspiring, vilified and humiliated young mother and her sick child.

He sat there, smoking, leaning comfortably back in his chair and opening just the middle bit of his mouth with its thin lips clamped tight and its corners drawn backwards. His entire face seemed in retreat, everything trickled off it, nothing got caught on it, either through his half-closed eyes or through his ears pinned tight to his skull, because the whole was like the kind of steel cone used for splitting timber.

In her confusion and fear, hope and rancour, humiliation and rage, it occurred to Zita that not even a bullet would snag that face.

"She's sweating," said Obmann. "She's giving up, so far gone that she'll be grateful if we put a bit of life back in her – and when she starts to stink, we'll have her boil some water, then we can give her a wash. Hals – that retired Saint Bernard! What's he up to? Instead of firing at partisans, he's farting in his pants."

The men burst out laughing.

"Herr Oberscharführer," Kniewald began, his jaw and its yellow teeth jutting forward, "when I was little, they taught me that there's no greater blessing than the curse of paradise: In the sweat of thy face shalt thou eat bread!"

"You had some very clever teachers, Scharführer."

"It's taken me till now to realise just how clever."

"Extremely. You *are* our philosopher."

"Do you know what would give me the greatest pleasure right now?"

"No. What? What would, Scharführer?"

"If she had to keep rocking until she and the little shit were awash in sweat –"

Obmann parted his lips in the middle. The laughter subsided. "You've got no imagination, Scharführer," he said, "you never did have. Philosophers never do, but if they do, it's not up to much. The only one with any imagination here is Otto, and his is pretty feeble. What I'd like is to sit out the war right here, with her having to keep rocking till she and the little shit changed into skeletons. The bones would rattle and ringing out over the putrefaction there'd by fanfares, fanfares and drumrolls –" Obmann crossed one leg over the other and began rocking his jackboot, "– fanfares and drumrolls – ha-ha – ha-ha!"

"Ha ha ha ha!" Kniewald guffawed, as he wiped his drooling chops with his sleeve. "Ha ha ha ha!"

Obmann glanced at the wall and the image of the naked Christ on the Cross, and at the large, grey bracket fungus, out of which brownish-purple stalks and grey-green foliage of a thing they called 'old maid' straggled, as from a flower-pot, almost as far down as Kniewald's head, a rather ludicrous and humble house-plant that never flowered.

The SS men laughed.

Obmann parted his lips in the middle.

"These folk would appear to be Christians," he said after the laughter died down, "they have baptisms, they pray – personally, I never prayed, it's too awkward – here they pray and hope to go to Heaven. We help them on the way – we can help this one too! It'll be easy to find something left behind by her husband – maybe even the partisans have left something... Every one I've ever interrogated to date has confessed – those who remained silent, well, that was their admission – ha-ha! But there's one thing we're forgetting. We should do the baptising first, and only then send them to heaven. What do you reckon, Scharführer?"

Kniewald thrust his jaw forward, parted his drooling chops and protruded his yellow teeth.

"Be sparing with your holy water, don't piss all over yourself!"

"Ha ha ha ha!"

"Once we've all had our go at being sparing," said Obmann through pursed lips, "we can go ahead and baptise the little shit." He pointed his foot at the cradle and rammed his boot into the heart carved in the board above the little lad's head. "In churches, baptism is done with cold liquid, we'll be doing it with warm. Scharphilosoph, don't piss all over yourself, don't shit yourself, and be sparing with your holy water!"

"Ha ha ha ha!" Obmann withdrew his boot from the heart.

Zita was overcome with the shakes, her eyes burned with pent-up tears and the sweat that was trickling down from her forehead. Her body had gone rigid because, half-bending, she hadn't dared let go of the oven and look away from the two doors by which the puddles left by Majerský were still drying. Inside her inflamed mind she screamed: Majerský, come out, Majerský, come in here for God's sake and kill at least one of them! Her bare neck and shoulders were suffused with icy fear, which then passed through her whole frame.

Obmann opened his mouth.

"Then we'll ask her where her husband is, in what town and what things he writes to her," he said. "If she says he's in Berlin, we'll take it he's with the partisans. We'll wash her down, give her a helping hand and then we shall see. Ha-ha!"

Zita was rocking away, perspiring and screaming mentally for Majerský to come and kill at least one of them.

Lieskov was gloomy beneath the overcast sky, silence reigned on every side, only on the wide road did the frozen snow crunch beneath the jackboots of the German patrol. Lieskov was a small village, thirty-four cottages it had, seventeen burned out, a winding brook ran through it and crossing it there were fifteen wooden and concrete footbridges leading from the highway to the tiny homesteads. Each pathetic little yard was home to heaps of snow-covered manure, piles of beech logs that had been brought in and, close to the houses, the spindly, spiky broomsticks of pear and apple trees. Not one yard had a gate, all being quite open and easy to size up from the road. The school and the nearby former squire's residence, which housed the offices of the Lieskov sawmill, had been taken over to accommodate the German garrison. That was headed by Lieutenant Hals, who couldn't abide *Blockwarts*. He wasn't that bothered about partisans because Lieskov lay on a main road along which German soldiers passed, whether on foot, horseback or by vehicle, as did the Slovak home guard and troops from Hungary. Germans stood guard at the top end, by the Hankas' cottage, outside the school and the former squire's residence, and down by the sawmill. Lieskov lay in darkness, the German guards and patrols catching just the odd glint from the partly grimy, partly clean snow.

A breeze began to gust. It blew two large gobbets of snow into Private Moeller's face beneath his helmet. "It's snowing," Moeller muttered, "winter's not over yet... seventeen, eighteen, nineteen, twenty, twenty-one..." More snow flew under his helmet into his face, which was still sizzling with rage against Obmann. I've been a soldier seven years now – and one lice-ridden cur is all he's become. They're all lice-ridden curs, SS, SD, Gestapo, the army – all of 'em vile from lance-corporal upwards! The bastards! "... ten, eleven, twelve..." He counted his paces, turning where he had to. From above the Hankas' cottage almost to Černeks' cottage. Gobbets of snow brought some relief to the hot sweaty hands that gripped his cold rapid-fire rifle.

Night-time Lieskov had turned Zita's kitchen window grey.

Majerský's hand was trembling, shaking in agitation as it made contact with the slightly loose brass handle. The handle grated, the noise magnified inside Majerský's ears, and the window thundered in his ears like when tanks go trundling over a wooden bridge, but Obmann's lot didn't hear it because they were roaring with laughter and Zita's cradle was thudding away on the kitchen floor. Again there was a thud inside Majerský's ears and again he heard Zita shrieking and screeching. Zita's voice, as she screeched inside his ears, was ghastly, as if someone were slowly strangling her. Zita's shrieking sliced through his whole body like a great, red-hot blade. Suddenly everything went quiet. The sweat-drenched Majerský opened the inner casements, quietly, all the way, placed one hand on the handle of the outer casements. They squeaked, rattled and the window rumbled. Majerský's aching head rang with every beat of the rockers, the raucous German laughter and with his own blood rushing. He opened the window, pushing the casements as far back as they would go, and leaned out; the ground was quite close, he straightened up and listened. Silence. Slowly, with care, he slid his rifle out and crawled out himself into the tiny yard and towards a pile of beech logs with a dusting of snow. The wind cast large, wet gobbets of snow onto his hands and into his face. From the wood pile he slowly crossed the little yard, out onto the little concrete footbridge over the stream that gave access to the road from the Černek cottage, paused and listened to the soldier, Moeller, counting his paces aloud, "… one, two, three, four…", as he moved away from the cottage. Majerský stepped off the bridge into the stream. His breathing came in short, fast bursts as he waited to see if Moeller would come back.

"Ja, ja, das ist gut," Obmann told Zita through pursed lips, "das ist das richtige Tempo!"

Zita was rocking away, her whole body and face soaked in perspiration. Her eyes, fixed on a point beneath the table, were darkened with sheer venom. Suddenly her composure returned briefly, because she'd remembered that Števo Kubík, who'd spent time in Germany, had worked down the mines somewhere near Hamm. Hamm, Hamm – but where exactly? His father was forever going on about it. If they ask her where her husband is, she thought, she can say in Hamm, working down the mines. But are there mines in Hamm – and if not? But all right, she will say he's in Hamm –

Zita was briefly seized with joy, followed at once by regret that the idea had even occurred to her. It's a morning in September, her little boy still a baby – Zita's singing *Hush-a-Bye Baby*, rocking the cradle out in the yard, "when the bough breaks, the cradle will fall… Hush-a-bye baby…" Mišo still at home, partisans outside… Zita was crushed with self-pity.

"Ha ha ha ha!"

Sergeant Kniewald was laughing his head off because Otto Dressel, the SS man with the plasters across one cheek, had just told him he'd got a good litre of holy water stored up and that they could start baptising Zita's little boy. "Ha ha ha ha!" Kniewald wiped his drooling chops with his sleeve. "How shall we go about it? One at a time or all together – into a pot? Then give it to her to drink. She'll think it's mulled wine. Ha ha ha ha!" Kniewald turned to Zita and said: "Guter Wein – ein gutes g'selliges Ding! Ha ha ha ha! Zu rechtem Gebrauch gab Gott uns den Wein! Ha ha ha ha! Gott mit uns!" He slapped himself across his old-fashioned waist band with its inscription "Gott mit uns", and then once more. "Ha ha ha ha!"

Against the tumult of the Germans' merriment Zita clung tight to the oven. By now she was in a state of shock worse than anything that had gone before because they suddenly seemed inebriated – or was it she who was inebriated and losing her grip? No, they were terribly drunk on something and she was losing her senses, her mind, everything... She tightened her left hand round the warm bar.

"Rock!" said Drossel, the SS man with the plastered face. "Lent us a cookink pot!"

"A pot?" Zita queried, taken aback, dismayed at having offered them nothing more than the dry bread. "What for? What are you going to cook? I could –"

"Vine!" said Drossel. "Zere are nine off us, each von vit half litre at least – so, a pot to holt seven litres! Ve vill boil some holy vater!"

Zita stopped rocking. She reached up to the shelf above the stove and took down an eight-litre pot. She passed it to Drossel, who grinned, making the filthy strips of sticking plaster stuck crosswise on his cheek wrinkle up.

"So then," he said, "who wants to go first?"

Leaning for support against the oven, Zita had stopped rocking her little boy, who was feverish and all red in the face, listless and blinking his tired eyes. She watched Obmann, who was sitting there with his lips drawn back, his cold eyes half-closed and his face like a steel beak. Please God, don't do anything bad to me! her eyes called out to Obmann, though she'd no idea what these men were about to do to her.

"Du –!"

"Keep rockink!" Drossel bellowed. "Rock ze puppy dok!"

Zita slowly set the cradle rocking.

"I can't wait," said Kniewald, "my holy water's about to burst. Ha ha ha ha!"

He got to his feet. His cap collected a web of the brown-ish-purple stalks and grey-green foliage of the old maid dangling down from the huge bracket fungus beneath the naked crucified Christ. He shook them aside, picked up the pot and stood it on the floor in the middle of the kitchen.

"... dreiundzwanzig, vierundzwanzig," Majerský listened to the approaching Moeller from his spot in the stream, "sie-benundzwanzig –"

Obmann was considering whether he shouldn't send some-one out for the booze they had in their truck. The men with the truck might as well come along, too, and their dogs. He looked at Kniewald.

"Come on then, Scharführer," he said, "show her what you're worth!"

"Ha ha ha ha!"

Sergeant Joseph Kniewald stood over Zita's pot, shifted his rapid-fire rifle onto his left hip and started to unbutton his white cape. "Ha ha ha ha!"

Zita screamed, leapt to the cradle and grabbed her feverish little boy, she was screaming without any words for Majerský to hear, when suddenly her scream did form itself into the words "Help, Majerský help!", she fled across the kitchen and rammed her back against the door to the sitting room. Behind her back the door opened. She froze.

Obmann gave her a light grin.

"Scharführer," he said to Kniewald, "get on with it! Have you got holy water down to your knees?"

"Ha ha ha ha!"

Outside a gunshot rang out.

Obmann leapt to his feet, set his peaked cap with its metal skull and crossbones on his head and looked at his men.

Kniewald's jaw dropped, exposing his protruding yellow teeth.

Zita clasped her feverish baby to her breast, propping his head against one shoulder, and burst into tears. Through her tears she saw the six men in white dash from the kitchen clutching their rapid-fire rifles.

She ran into the sitting room, let out a silent yelp and with a new flood of tears closed the window through which Majerský had escaped. She stepped back from the grey window having glanced out at Lieskov in its veil of darkness, stood briefly by the made bed in which she'd hidden Majerský. She stepped back to the door into the warm kitchen. She was brought up short by the crackle of a rapid-fire rifle, first one, then several. She waited a moment, got her breath back and entered the kitchen. She straightened out the cradle and lay her little boy back down in it. Her aching legs were buckling. She took hold of a thick brown dress, sat down on the bench where Otto Drossel had been sitting, and put it on. Her little boy was blinking, feeble and feverish as she rocked him, gently, so gently that the worn rockers weren't even audible. She wept, wept silently for the feverish little boy, for herself, for Majerský. Her hands and face began to quiver the way the leaves of an aspen quiver whenever a breeze wafts through an aspen grove, her whole body was trembling and although she was watching the open door, although soldiers were running and tramping this way and that outside, shouting, and although there were three more bursts of rapid rifle fire, she heard nothing. She clasped her hands above the boy, half-bending, with her clasped hands she rocked him gently, just a little. As she rocked she began yielding to self-pity for having married Černek, for having given him a little boy. For these people kill little boys, toss them into fires –

The kitchen door flew open with a bang.

In ran Otto Drossel, the SS man with the plastered face, he kicked the red metal pot on the floor aside and ran to open the other leaf of the door. "In here!" he shouted to the white SS men. "In here!"

Two of Obmann's white-clad men entered carrying a wet, mud-spattered and bloodied Kniewald, placed him on the floor and ran back out.

Zita sat there motionless.

The two men came back at once, this time with Obmann, the wet and bloodied Staff Sergeant, and they set him down next to Kniewald.

Zita sat there motionless, Drossel looked at her, at the cradle, which was no longer banging like a diesel engine, while Zita's little boy stared up at his mother through now open, now half-closed, burning eyes.

The men in white returned, pausing in the doorway.

"Schurz as well?" one of them asked Drossel. "Though he's already –"

"Him too?" said Drossel. "Why do you ask?"

"Dead!"

"Him too. And the rest!"

The men in white lay the dead and cooling body next to Obmann.

Zita watch with eyes aflame as the men in white ran out and back twice more fetching another two wet, mud-spattered and bloodied corpses and laying them on the floor. She rocked the cradle quietly. She turned her flaming eyes towards Obmann and Knievald, who lay groaning on the floor. Traces left by Majerský in the other room, her husband's clothes in the trunk in the loft, hidden under the hay, the stomping and shouting of the soldiers out on the road – everything came pounding at her and her aching frame like heavy rocks, everything was stifling her. They'll search the cottage, the idea pounded away inside her head, they'll kill me, burn the house down... They'll toss my boy into a fire... She bent over the cradle, picked him up, quilt and all, wrapped him tight in it, then wrapped him in a thick white jumper of hers as well before squeezing into the gap between the warm oven and the wall.

Some vehicle came to a halt outside the Černeks' cottage.

From the yard came the sound of lots of German voices.

Dash outside, occurred to her, jump with the boy into the stream and smother him in the stream –

The kitchen suddenly filled with soldiers wearing helmets and mottled capes, the grey-green soldiers without capes, and Obmann's men in white – and faced with this avalanche of vindictive, alarm-filled eyes, Zita squeezed into the corner, shivering, because cold air had come streaming in through the open door and the gusting wind was driving the falling snow inside and any warmth out.

Lieutenant Hals appeared.

"Ja," he said from the doorway as he turned towards Zita, "ja –"

"The bitch can't understand you," Drossel informed Hals. "I can interpret for you, Herr Oberleutnant."

Hals, a burly fellow, turned his broad, exasperated, ageing, deeply creased face sporting a huge pair of spectacles towards the scrawny Drossel. He tossed his head and his huge glasses glinted.

"Would you – if you don't mind?" he asked. "Her –" he said pointing at the pale, shivering Zita, "– I'll deal with her alone. Interrogations via an interpreter take too long – before you know it, the injured could die and the dead begin to putrefy! Help see to them instead. I'll see to my fallen sentry myself!"

He pointed to the floor at the groaning Kniewald and at Obmann, who was still moving his legs, but with the death rattle upon him. *Blockwarts*, the bastards – and the war's gone to the dogs! The five men's white capes, partly covered in mud, were starting to seep bright-red blood. Hals glanced at Obmann with utter loathing.

From outside, the wind drove more falling snow into the kitchen.

Hals's glasses glinted.

Zita, immobile and frozen stiff, huddled into her corner as if wishing to merge into the wall so as not to be seen, and her immobile, gaping eyes watched as the men in white capes carried the corpses and the groaning injured from the kitchen out into the waiting truck.

A moment passed and the truck bearing Obmann and his section left and passed out of earshot, after a short pause, though for Zita it was extremely long and terrible, because Lieutenant Hals was staring at her, tearful, compressed into her corner and clutching her feverish little boy, through his huge, glinting spectacles, after a pause during which Zita's features could pale no more and her terror-stricken eyes could fill no more with dread, Köhl's patrol brought Majerský in. His knees and waist were limp, his cap was gone, as was his rifle, his face was blood-stained and practically from top to toe he was soaking wet and covered in mud. His mud-coated head hung loose and his dark hair hung over his pale face. The soldiers shoved him into the corner between the kitchen door and the door to the sitting room.

Hals flashed his spectacles and turned to Köhl.

"Unteroffizier!"

"Yessir, Herr Oberleutnant, sir!" The stooping Corporal Köhl tried to stand up straight, but his stoop held.

"Our captive is *not* to be mistreated!" he said. "We shall need him during the enquiry! Was he unarmed when he surrendered?"

"Yessir, Herr Oberleutnant, unarmed!"

"Did the man they killed, Moeller, have a weapon?"

"A rifle, Herr Oberleutnant!"

Hals turned towards Zita, crammed with her little boy between the oven and the wall, pale and trembling, and advanced to the middle of the kitchen. "Ist der da Ihr Mann?"

Zita peered through her tears at Hals, who was pointing to Majerský, propped up in the corner and broken. "I don't understand what you're saying," she said.

She had an inkling of what the bespectacled soldier was saying but didn't know what to do. Confess, or not? "I don't know, honest to God, I don't know what you're saying, I don't know what you mean to do with him –"

"Ja – oder nein?"

"Yes," she said, "please, for God's sake – don't kill him, for my sake, don't kill him –!"

"Ja – oder nein?" Hals watched Zita. If only they'd killed Hitler that time... crossed his mind. Hitler – Oberblockwart! In order to put paid to one ideology he invented another, deluding Germany's soldiery – even had it pre-printed on servicemen's identity cards that they were not to kill any enemy who surrendered voluntarily. Hals kept watching Zita, crammed into her corner. How – how is it possible to protect anyone from an Idea? Kill them – or let them live? "Ja," he bawled at Zita, "oder nein?"

Zita shook her head.

Lieutenant Hals had Majerský removed, he then left and Zita stared long at the pools of blood remaining there on the floor then out through the open door at the yard and the densely falling snow. She placed the boy back in his cradle and, having closed the door, stood in expectation of a ghastly night and of ghastly nights and days to come.

* * *

"The defendants are sentenced as follows..." The voice on the radio, that of the chairman of the tribunal, went quiet, a monotonous voice, quite unperturbed, and the radio crackled like the sound of grain tumbling onto a sheet of metal. Zita was sitting beneath the old maid, the large grey bracket fungus and the solid shelf on which the Černeks had positioned their radio, she just sat and waited, her eyes fixed on her husband, who was sitting on the bench across the table, his broad, wan face, all sweaty about the nose, and staring into the table top, the chairman of the tribunal cleared his throat, then he cleared it again, and the radio crackled like tumbling

(167)

grain. "Jozef Majerský, born seventh of September nineteen hundred and three in the village of Temešany... a smallholder by profession, permanent abode Temešany... is sentenced to... twelve years in prison, all his possessions to be confiscated. His wife, Mára Majerský, née Szabó, born... his son František Majerský... and his son František Majerský to be evicted from the district –"

Zita let out a yelp.

Černek placed one large white hand on the table, its flabby, podgy palm upwards. His broad, wan face, all sweaty about the nose, wore a grim smile.

The radio above the bracket fungus emitted the verdicts being doled out to Majerský's seven co-defendants. Zita listened to the radio only fitfully, her eye on her husband, but gradually the voice of the chairman of the tribunal passed from her hearing, passed and was lost amid the hum of her seething blood.

"Well, what of it, what's he to us?" was Černek's response to the verdict, "one Majerský here or there – he'd have been in for it, in for it, even without my testimony – he's a subversive and saboteur – people at the collective farm blamed him for everything – after the war, after the war he got a farm, the landed estate at Temešany having been broken up, and he worked on his portion with his wife, and his sons – those in the collective, they are what they are – they didn't put in the effort, didn't work, just bellyached along the lines that if Majerský could do all right privately, why shouldn't they be doing just as well collectively? – and they started leaving the collective farm – a subversive and a saboteur – and he, wouldn't you just know it, he met all the quotas required of him! – if only the collective had done likewise – all would be just fine – " Černek started opening and closing the fat fingers of his huge, broad hand, "– it would be just fine – he was a good farmer – but good farmers aren't what we need, what we need are..."

He raised his head slightly along with his new, brown hat that hadn't yet moulded itself to its wearer.

Zita's brown eyes began to turn dark and menacing.

The radio up there above the 'old maid' wound up its transmission of the trial of the kulaks and those who would subvert and sabotage the Temešany collective.

Zita shifted in her seat.

Following a brief pause, a bright, young male voice announced: "Today the harvest is a joy to behold." And it went on: "Because almost everywhere where, until quite recently, all the work involved was done manually, now we have every kind of harvester to do all the heavy work once demanded of our peasants. And at this year's harvest there are more such machines than ever before. Harvest-time places increased demands on the organs and organisations, indeed on every member of our Party –"

Černek glanced at Zita, at her still young face, though her brow was now sundered by two sharp wrinkles, a face darkened and menacing thanks to the fury raging in her brown, wide-open eyes.

"– and also by restricting any losses that may occur during transportation to the absolute minimum," the bright young voice on the radio went on, "we may expect high, even record high yields per hectare –"

"There you have it," said Černek jabbing a big fat finger at the scowling Zita. "Record high yields per hectare, record yields per hectare – and that's the reason, that's why I testified against him –" Černek began tapping his finger against his chest, – "so that, so there'd be record, record yields per hectare – because I'm, d'you know what I am? – I'm the district coordinator for agriculture – and it's up to me, me, to see to it that our collective farms run like clockwork –"

"– we mustn't lose sight of this," the radio on the shelf above the bracket fungus declaimed, "especially because the view has spread within some organisations that harvest time is not a time for sitting about holding meetings, and that has led ultimately to some party bodies actually ceasing to function at such a critical time as harvest, because in our villages –"

"That's why I testified," said Černek, "because at harvest time meetings still have to be held, tribunals to sit – so why don't you ask me why I testified? Why I leaned one way first time round, and the second time I couldn't? Because after I heard –"

Zita shifted in her seat, her head setting in motion the brownish-purple stalks and grey-green foliage of the 'old maid' that she was still keeping going.

"Why don't you ask me why I testified?"

"All right, so you testified..." Fury was making Zita's restrained voice quaver. "But you didn't have to take the line you did. In thinking of yourself you forget about others! All you think about is you, as if you were the only person in the world! Majerský never did anything to you... So why did you testify against him –?"

"Because," Černek replied, "they wanted *you* to testify, you too! You're supposed to know him better, you could have said more about him than I could – and I didn't want you to testify against him, so I did, me, so you wouldn't have to lie about him, they wanted –"

"They? Who?"

"The work we are putting into this year's harvest," the radio ground on from above the bracket fungus, "is enormous, but gratifying beyond all bounds –"

Zita got up, pushed aside the stalks and leaves of the 'old maid' and switched off the report on the year's gratifying harvest.

The kitchen lapsed into silence. The open door admitted into the warm kitchen the pleasant cool of a summer's evening, the chirring trill of crickets and the gurgling of the stream.

"I wouldn't have testified!"

"You reckon?"

"Keep your voice down, Mišo!" Zita, wearing a floral linen dress, ran across to the door and was about to close it.

Černek took a good look at her, at her white trainers, tanned calves, broad hips and her breasts undulating with linen flowers. "Don't shut it, it's hot in here!"

"You're so loud and –"

A car passed along the road the other side of the stream.

"What of it!" said Černek, "let them hear, let them hear even inside the flashy cars they come driving past in! They came to find me, took me away and said that if –"

"You just shouldn't have done it to him, Mišo –" Zita was breathing fast as she stared scornfully at her husband who was now all atremble, "– it's just not done! You –"

"– do you mean, d'you mean to say, Zita, my Zita," Černek replied in a jerky and slightly choking voice, "do you mean to say your testimony would have been different from mine? Your testimony wouldn't – wouldn't – it really wouldn't have been any different from mine – and there were many in that court-room whose testimonies were far worse – they took me in and said: 'Sign here!' – they knew full well I'd been with Majerský in the Uprising – they know about everything, they've got their eyes on everybody – and I was scared – for you, the children – everyone's scared – so I testified –" Černek began pounding his broad chest with his fists, "– because I, because I didn't want you to have to testify against him – everybody's scared, but when I heard what others were saying against him –"

Zita shuddered.

"Next time," he said, looking straight at Zita, "next time, I wouldn't either – no, I wouldn't – I'm sorry how it turned out – getting twelve years for nothing – that's a lot, not even Majerský deserved that – and me a coordinator for agricul-ture! – I have tried, Zita, I've tried to ensure that cooperatives go like clockwork, but not anymore – not anymore, up to now I have been – but not anymore, because I told them how it was with Majerský –" Černek clenched his huge fists on the tabletop and raised them so tightly clenched that his knuckles turned white, "– I have been, but not anymore – make no mistake, I do have the guts where Majerský is concerned, despite how he treated you, your late mother and the late Ragala, despite the time he came down from the mountains to you! I told them how it was with Majerský, there – on the radio there, and then they told me that people like me were of no use to them... All right, but I did tell them about the Majerský business! It did matter to me..." He lapsed into silence.

"When did you tell them?"

"At the tribunal, as broadcast on the radio!"

Zita sat up straight, spluttering scornfully.

"When?" she asked. "I listened to the trial on the radio and I didn't hear you."

"What?" Černek turned to face her. "I told them what Majerský was like with us in the mountains, what happened to him and what he did when he came to you, I said –"

Zita stood erect and curled her lips scornfully.

"Everybody heard it. Majerský and his wife and children, his family – and it didn't get broadcast!"

Zita's cheeks began to burn.

She crossed the kitchen, stood outside the door to get a deep breath of the pleasant cool of a summer evening following a storm. Lieskov was fragrant, alive with the chirring trill of crickets and the murmur of the dwindling water in the stream.

Hot tears streamed down Zita's cheeks.

The road and trees outside the Černeks' cottage suddenly lit up. Two posh Tatraplans drove past followed a moment later by a Tatra 8. Behind them they left the unpleasant smell of burnt petrol.

The plane had sailed up and away from Košice airport and it was then that they began to look about them, each spotted the other and both were filled with alarm at the realisation that they were who they were and that they were there.

Jozef Mitúch, an engineer, shuddered with a sense of foreboding such as he had never before felt, not particularly concerning, but unfamiliar, and as he looked through the porthole at the ground below, at an angle and sliding away into the depths, it suddenly struck him as like some recent past that people are loath to look back to and of which they no longer have any clear perception. As he watched the earth slipping away he kept asking himself: Is she here? Isn't she in Germany, or America? She'd been ready to make her escape. Even boasting about it. She'd failed to escape with the Germans, but why hadn't she left before this? What's she doing here? Mitúch's alarm, not particularly concerning, but new and unfamiliar, applying not just to his own person, but to many other people, kept nudging him to look her way.

The ground stopped slipping away into the depths and levelled out. The plane buzzed and hummed with a steady, sonorous voice, now and again listing just slightly to left or right. Little white clouds scuttled back behind them, delicate and dainty.

Mitúch watched Gizela Gábor. She was sitting across the aisle, three seats ahead of him. She kept her head turned towards the porthole.

Gizela Gábor had been very surprised to see Mitúch, but suppressed her surprise and alarm, falling back on the detachment that had always been her great defence against herself and others. The pleasant view of the ground from the plane afforded her only very brief moments of relief from the questions that were piling up inside her head: He's here? The Germans failed to pick him up. He'd slipped from their clutches. How come he hadn't died from that injury and the blood-poisoning? He'd been pale and by that stage couldn't even speak. It is him. No one else. Gizela Gábor fixed her gaze on a tiny train passing below.

The plane's passengers began reading the papers, smoking, dozing, chatting together and a group of four young people began passing round an already open wine bottle.

Mitúch and Gizela Gábor spent almost the entire time between Košice and Bratislava looking down to the ground far, far below.

In Bratislava they alighted, lost in thought, and when they boarded the Prague plane, they found themselves sitting quite near each other. Gizela Gábor just in front of Mitúch, the engineer. He gazed at the mass of fuzz on her yellow fox fur. He couldn't wait for the moment when he'd leave the plane and go to his meeting of geological researchers. He'd wanted to be well clear of Gizela Gábor, never to see or bump into her. Gizela Gábor, whose back could sense the unpleasant pressure of Mitúch's close proximity, was wondering how to address him, because she wanted to know what he would tell her and hoped his first words would give her an inkling of what he thought of her. She didn't yet know why, but she was increasingly curious to hear what Mitúch's first words would be. She hoped they were going to help her as a drowning man is helped ashore by a random surge, or that they would at least offer her a straw to grasp.

Away from her! Mitúch had resolved, because in Gizela Gábor he sensed a danger to himself, his interesting work, his wife, the children and everything else that made up his life. See nothing of her! Hear nothing of her!

I have to get to him. Gizela Gábor had made up her mind to stop Mitúch in Prague and speak to him. I have to!

It was seven years since they'd last met.

They'd last seen each other at the beginning of April in 1945 and that was also the last time they'd spoken. That meeting had boded nothing good for either of them, because it was one outcome of events in Molčany, where both had been living, and a product of the relationship that had sprung up between them.

Aboard both the Bratislava plane and the Prague plane, alike buzzing and humming with a steady, sonorous voice through the clear air that offered a good view of the ground far below, the thoughts of both kept turning, at shorter or longer intervals, to Molčany.

* * *

In forty-five, Molčany had enjoyed the first Wednesday in April in peace and quiet, though from the south – from Račany, Adamovce, Borovce and Mlynská – had come the ceaseless sound of gunfire, and louder than at other times.

All around Molčany, its fields lay quietly, crisscrossed by circular, arcing or right-angled trenches, their beds glinting with mud and water as they stared mutely up into the early-evening sky, fields churned up by jackboots, hooves and wheels ever since the last exercises carried out by the men of Molčany's first two German garrisons commanded by Hauptmann Borek and Major Dietbert. Between Molčany and Račany, which lay seven kilometres to the south, a straight, deep, anti-tank trench lay desolate. Its bed glinted with water and around its edges was a thin, brown layer of the dead earth that had been scattered far and wide so as not to form any kind of mound or hump. The road to Račany crossed it quietly and without fuss. Along both sides of the road some tall concrete blocks stood menacingly, their spiky iron rods poking out into the air. The ground around the blocks was burdened with heaps of gravel, bags of cement stored in wooden sheds, and huge round concrete objects, hollow and resembling curvy bottles. The spiky iron rods poking out into the roadway from the concrete blocks were alive with flitting, twittering shrikes.

All peace and quiet was the road to Čermanská Lehota, five kilometres to the west of Molčany, brightened by the new white concrete bridge that stood three kilometres from

Molčany over a fairly wide stream that had been regulated. In a ditch not far from the bridge lay the rusting remnants of iron and sheet metal of a burned-out Mercedes. Two German soldiers were walking up and down the two sides of the bridge, staring grimly ahead from beneath the helmets that shaded their eyes.

In Molčany, eleven burned-out houses stood in peace and quiet. The Mitúchs' stray dog Caesar had been chasing a grey tom-cat in and out of their windows and doors. At the eleventh house, the widow Plátenička's cottage, the cat now sat on a soot-coated wall, licking its lips and watching Caesar. Caesar was sitting on the ground and barking.

From a little way beyond the burned-out houses, in the school yard, came the loud, heart-rending lowing of twenty head of cattle, hungry and increasingly lean bullocks and heifers that German soldiers had driven in from the foothills, from the partisan villages of Greater and Lesser Hámre and Lipník. They were tethered to the wire fence and just stared down at the ground, drooling copiously into the straw trampled down beneath their feet and mixed with sand, soil and manure.

A German trooper, Kurt Kalkbrenner, paused next to them, cast them a pitying glance, swore and entered the school, which housed the local command post.

It was late afternoon and the constant rumble of gunfire could still be heard coming from the south, from Račany, Adamovce, Borovce and Mlynská.

In a silent, darkening bunker dug into the earth in the young, unthinned beech wood on Úplazy, an elongated elevation about two hours' walk from Molčany, sat the partisan Porubský, son of Molčany's parish odd-job man, slicing the bottom crust off a loaf of bread. He'd set the loaf on a wooden block and used his knife to measure it into equal parts for six other partisans and himself.

It cost him some effort to choke back his saliva. He looked round at the men in civilian clothes and army capes, the remnants of a partisan unit that Dietbert's men had smashed up in October forty-four by the brickworks on the far side of Molčany. Misty-eyed, he saw the men as but shadows. He looked away from their shining eyes to the dull glimmer of the water seeping between the thin beech logs with which the bunker was lined, then let his gaze drop back to the bread and he cut one slice. He cut another.

"Dad's hardly likely to show up now," he said huskily, his voice coming in jerks from his sore throat, "because..."

A long stream of saliva shot from his mouth and dribbled onto his muddy boot.

The men gulped back their own saliva.

"He's hardly likely to show up now," he said. "The Krauts must surely be getting ready to clear off, Dad's going to be scared, those guns aren't going to let up at this stage –"

The partisans began chatting together.

"Gosh, I'm gonna to be spending a whole day and night washing myself from top to toe!"

"I'm gonna eat and eat – I could just murder a nice bowl of soup!"

"I'd go for a glass of milk, sweet or sour! Or stuff myself with oranges!"

"Oranges?"

"Yeah – a whole kilo, two even! Right now I don't even know what they look like. One Easter I bought myself heaps of them – and just ate and ate them – if only that could be right here and now! Every time spring comes around I get this huge hankering after them!"

"Dad's not likely to show up now," Porubský broke in on the partisans' chatter, "he'll be scared, because once a German starts to run he'll shoot at anything that moves even the slightest –"

"Give us the bread!"

"Haven't smelt that smell in ages."

"No, not recently – 'cept when there's a breeze from that direction."

It was getting dark.

(177)

A grey truck drove through Molčany, stopped outside the command post and then left with six SS-men under the command of Rottenführer Kolping, heading for Greater and Lesser Hámre and Lipník. At the approaches to Lipník and Greater Hámre Kolping's men were to destroy three bridges and block the road to Molčany before returning to the command post there.

Darkness fell.

It was night, and that night was when the full complement of years, months and days began to be supplemented with the final hours and minutes.

Molčany, quite a long village, strung out along either side of the main road, quaked that night in fear while seeking comfort in hope, because the times had begun to offer people that moment through which they had to pass into a new life. When would it all end? How? The moment was approaching, recoiled from and expected, and people were taking to their beds with their shoes and clothes on, or merely sitting on their beds.

"I've made up my mind," said Gizela Gábor, the twenty-seven-year-old widow of Martin Gábor, who'd been in charge of Aryanizing the Stahl estate and brickworks in Molčany and who in October had been killed during the Uprising by the partisans Porubský and Zubák. "I'm leaving with you."

"Of course, naturally," Oberleutnant Walter Schrimm assured her as he had previously. He was seated opposite her on the green sofa in the drawing room of the Stahl villa and wearing a new forage cap. His voice had a slightly impatient ring to it. "Gizela! A sweet name! As ever, a sweet, pretty name, a good name."

Gizela Gábor leaned gently back in her deep, green armchair, rubbing one leg against the other, and after her black satin dressing-gown, smooth and glossy and decked with tiny, gaily coloured parrots, slipped from her shapely knees she waited a moment before bending down to wrap it back round them.

"Of course, naturally," Schrimm told her after he'd had a mental flash of the text on a porcelain vase they had at home in Stargard: *Geld ist Geld, Welt ist Welt, ein schöner Nam' alles behält*. "Perfectly natural, Gizela. Money is money, the world is the world, but in your pretty name is everything. Gizela-gazelle-gazella!"

"Will you stay a little while longer?" The gaily coloured parrots slipped from her breasts. "A little longer?"

Oberleutnant Schrimm, commander of the German garrison in Molčany, self-consciously raised one hand to his head, let it fall back, raised it again and removed his large new forage cap.

The wide windows of the Stahl drawing room shook slightly as the gunfire rumbled on.

It was going up to twelve,

"Let's put time on hold awhile, Gizela," he said, having glanced at the brass clock with its shiny spheres spinning remorselessly this way and that. He turned off the lamp above the sofa, already dimmed by its shade, on which ancient sailing ships, brigs and cogs, seesawed amid the blue of waves. "Let's not look at the clock."

"Good, Walter," she said. "Shall we leave?"

"Of course, naturally."

"Is there still time?"

"Still! But we've stopped it – my gazelle!"

"Walter, my Walter – aah...!"

Walter was the commander of the fifth and last German garrison in Molčany. The first garrison, which had been in Molčany for only one week in early September, had been commanded by Hauptmann Borek, the second, made up of German soldiers, Vlasovites and a troop of SS-men, had been commanded by Major Dietbert. The second garrison had swooped on the partisans in Molčany, torched eleven houses and launched an attack on the partisan villages in the foothills: Greater and Lesser Hámre and Lipník. The third, fourth and fifth garrisons came to Molčany to rest and relax after their encounters with partisans and had been commanded by Oberleutnants Vogel, Bürster and Schrimm. Major Dietbert had expedited the death of the Aryanizer of the Stahl estate and brickworks, who'd cosied up to him. The Aryanizer, Martin Gábor, had handed the hidden Stahls over to him and he himself had shown Dietbert's men the way through the woods to the track that led to the Stahls' brickworks. He knew there was a concentration of partisans at the brickworks and that they could be easily caught on the hop by an approach from the forest. He was angry with them for a variety of reasons, including depriving him of the estate's horses. At the brickworks, Dietbert's men fell on the partisans, killing many of them and driving those captured, along with some of their kinsfolk, into the forest beyond Molčany, where they shot them in a steep clearing known as Dead Fallow, about half an hour's trek from Úplazy. Two days later Gábor paid for his assistance with his life: he burned to death in the Stahls' Mercedes, which the partisans Porubský and Zubák had attacked with hand grenades by the bridge between Molčany and Čermanská Lehota. All the officers except Borek, that is Dietbert, Vogel, Bürster and Schrimm, had lived at the Stahls' villa. Gábor's young widow, Gizela, wined and dined them and their subordinates and whenever there was no feasting and boozing she spent her nights alone with the commanding officers. She took no account of anything, not even of herself, because after Hitler had uttered his despairing "If I go, everything goes!", Gizela had realised the awful fix she was in, which she had sensed ever since her husband, previously the estate manager at Račany, had become the Aryanizer of the Stahl estate and brickworks. By this stage, the commander of the last garrison at Molčany, Oberleutnant Walter Schrimm, was tired of the war, retreat and flight, and at Molčany, where he and his men had been sent to draw breath and to act as a warning to the partisans operating in the foothill villages of Lipník and Greater and Lesser Hámre, he had soon fallen in love with Gizela Gábor and succumbed to his longstanding conviction that war was stupid – because while you can do anything in wartime, you can't use a gun to make a life. "You can't achieve that," he told Gizela, "even if you believe in racial superiority, a grand Idea and all the other garbage invented by modern times, even if you shrink in fear of Hitler's keen-edged sword and become a professional criminal and murderer." Walter Schrimm now sensed the approaching end of the war and wanted nothing more than to flee into peacetime with Gizela Gábor and all her items of value and live. To flee into peacetime, abandon himself to living, and never, never again to believe in an Idea because, once you do believe in it, even killing becomes just grinding drudgery whose sheer monotony you need to relieve.

"Gazelle!"

"Yes, Walter?"

"Are you afraid of being on the move with us? In retreat?"

"I can't say I wouldn't be afraid, but I have to go."

"Don't be afraid, with me nothing's going to happen to you! We shall flee together and make it successfully into peacetime."

"You put it so nicely, Walter!"

At half past twelve there was a phone call from the command post.

Schrimm got dressed. "Good-bye, Gizela, sweet name of mine!" he said to Gizela Gábor as he was leaving. "I'll be back just as soon as possible. If I can't make it, I'll send a car. I'll have you taken to Rakytovce. Wait there for us at the regimental HQ. Everything's been taken care of there."

Gizela Gábor rubbed one leg against the other, rolled over onto her left side and stared vacantly. The windows were shaking with explosions, but that passed her by. She stretched out on the sofa enjoying the warmth coming from the huge tiled stove in the corner, which supplied heat to two other rooms as well.

She gazed at the gaudy mess of colours on the Stahls' carpet. She wondered if Jozef Mitúch had been pleased she'd sent the maid to him with that message on Tuesday morning: "The Germans will be leaving any day now." Maybe. She smiled. Maybe he was more pleased at that than if she hadn't had Dietbert, Vogel, Bürster and Schrimm. Mitúch's an ass. Let's put time on hold! Let's escape together into peacetime! Schrimm – a good bloke, perhaps, but he's also an ass. A sentimental old bull! Dietbert had been the best of them. Handsome, strapping and elegant. An aristocrat! Escape into peacetime with Schrimm, yes, but in order to find Dietbert! "I'll take you with me, Gizela, sweet name of mine!" Schrimm's words came back to her, "we'll go to Stargard, nothing must happen to you on the way there. You can't stay here, here you'd either perish or certainly not live like a human being! Stargard is a quiet little town, but my parents have a factory there, a distillery – and we could live and live! Escape into peacetime!" At twelve forty-five Gizela rose and began putting on some warm clothes.

Beneath the overcast sky the night was silent and dark, further darkened in the village by the blacked-out windows, and very dark up on Úplazy, in the dense young beech wood where the partisans' bunker was.

"Right," said the partisan Porubský in his hoarse voice, still issuing jerkily from his sore throat, "shall we get going?"

The partisans remained silent.

"Since we've succeeded in doing away with Gábor," he said, "and successfully derailed that railway engine before Christmas, blowing up a bridge should be child's play, shouldn't it?"

"We're in, Števo," Zubák responded. "Let's get going!"

"What a way to make a living," said Mezej, "Jeeze! But life after the war's over has got to be worth living!"

"But hell!" said Hriška. "I shan't have a job in either Stahl's or Gábor's stables!"

"Certainly not with either of them now!" Porubský laughed huskily. "They've copped it, silly!"

"So I'll have nowhere!"

"Is this a stupid thing to be doing or not?" Mikuláš asked. "I just don't know anymore."

"Even if it is stupid," Porubský broke in hoarsely, "we have to get on and do it! We have to go! Otherwise what are we here for? What for, eh? We have to destroy the Krauts wherever we can. The fewer of them left in the world the better. We have to help the Soviets!"

"Let's get going!" said Stanko. "Though I honestly don't know if this'll help 'em."

"It will," said Porubský, "and it'll help Molčany as well. So let's get cracking!"

"You three go," said Porubský, the parish odd-job man, to Zubák, Mezej and his own son. He'd brought with him to Úplazy a sack containing a loaf of bread, a chunk of bacon, two blocks of curd cheese, five packets of German tobacco and some explosive charges. "You go, you three. And you three as well," he said to Hriška, Stanko and Mikuláš. "You, Ondriš, you stay here. Go and get some sleep. You were up all night, like you said. I shan't be going home now. Hand me a rifle. I'll stay up the rest of the night. Get going, since you're so set on it, though I honestly wouldn't advise it, 'cos the Krauts are definitely edgy –!"

"Where did you get the charges?" Porubský's son Mišo asked. "Who gave them to you?"

"Skittle."

"And where did he get them from?"

"No idea. Why all the questions? Skittle never tells me anything, which is why I never ask him things. Just don't mess up! You really oughtn't to be doing this. Skittle suggests you cut the railway line. Pass me a rifle, Ondriš."

Pavela, whose feet were frostbitten, could walk, but not run, handed Porubský a rifle and went to lie down inside the damp bunker.

"I say, Pops," Mikuláš asked old Porubský, "why didn't you bring any oranges?"

"Cheeky! Good grief –!"

"Let's get going!"

"And while we're gone, you stay quiet, Pops, and don't frighten the thrushes! Today they were singing so beautifully, a joy to listen to them."

"Get along with you, you...!" Porubský, the parish odd-job man, sat down in front of some dense bushes, lay his rifle across his knees and stared into the darkness, in which the quiet footsteps of his son Mišo and with him those of Zubák, Mezej, Hriška, Stanko and Mikuláš, were soon lost.

A nocturnal breeze caused the young, dense beech wood to rustle. The breeze brought with it a whiff of the earth as it opened up with spring-time, and of the damp, sticky, pale-green buds with which the wood was coming back to life. The fragrance of the beech wood in bud and the tobacco smoke issuing from his stubby, curly pipe bore Porubský away to those distant moments when he'd sat resting like this during the Great War, when the beech woods on Úplazy had been felled, and when beneath Úplazy, from Dead Fallow to beyond Molčany, there'd been a tiny mountain railway. He'd been sixteen at the time. The older men had sat around smoking and having a hard time trying to converse with the Romanians who'd come to Molčany, erected wooden huts on Dead Fallow, and joined numbers of Molčany's own men in clearing Úplazy of its trees, also constructing timber chutes and sliding the beech logs down them. Shortly after that he'd joined up. After the war, he'd been in the woods like this on more than one occasion, without a pipe, waiting up all night for a stag. Into these memories flashed a Romanian woman, one of the young ones who'd come to join their menfolk in the wooden huts on Dead Fallow.

"White as white butter," he had remembered her more than once after the Romanians had left Molčany, "raven-haired and her clothes all embroidered top to toe! But a chap could do no more than look at her because she'd been here with some fellow who never let go of his axe, day or night." Old Porubský smiled as he stared out into the darkness.

Gunfire was rumbling away to the south.

To his right Porubský caught the sound of solid timbers cracking and the groaning of a locomotive. Aha! They're already wrecking the track. Mišo was right when he said they wouldn't have made it in time with the charges. He slightly raised the fingers holding his short pipe up over its hot lid. The bastards! They're buggering off at last! They'd be raiding the village for horses and carts to load up with livestock and anything else to take away with 'em. That mayor Šimko's a right idiot! Instead of making himself scarce he's been toadying to 'em! But even with horses and carts the Germans aren't going anywhere. Porubský touched the breast pocket of his old overcoat. Inside it rustled the order listing the forty owners of a horse and cart. They were *not* going to be got ready as the order required! The mayor needn't have bothered bringing it to him. The order's here! No one's going to go round telling the horses' owners! At that point a wave of cold passed through him. Had Mišo and his pals taken leave of their senses, embarking on something like this? Blowing up a bridge, blocking the main road! That wasn't why Skittle had sent them those explosive charges. They were to cut the railway line with them, in a way so the Krauts couldn't relay it. It might have been better not to bother with the charges and just take the order round and get the homesteaders to give up their horses. Just as long as nothing happens to the lads! The Germans are going to have to scarper on foot. They won't be able to grab any horses or men. That would be a waste of horses – they'd have just shot them somewhere anyway. Old Porubský was seized with regret and rage, because he'd started listening again to the sound of solid sleepers being shattered in the far distance.

The shattering of the sleepers went on and on.

Porubský began shivering with cold and fear for his son. He wasn't greatly fond of him, but having heard he was in the bunker up on Úplazy he'd begun going there to see him. He would take food for him and his comrades, going the long way round to Úplazy so as to tramp up the stream and not leave any footprints in the snow. Even after the snow thawed, he would still make the same detour along the stream.

He would sit there, calmly breathing in the fragrant spring air borne along on the breeze and untainted by the distant stench he'd smelt at other times when visiting his son at Úplazy. The Germans aren't likely to grab the old girl, he thought, meaning his wife. What use would she be to them? He tamped down the tobacco burning away in his pipe.

The dark night dragged on and on beneath the overcast sky, suffused with the damp cold of spring, washed through with waves of warm air, dragging slowly on like black smoke in a diminishing breeze.

Through the dark beech wood the six partisans were heading towards Molčany to destroy the bridge on the road to Čermanská Lehota and block the road to Račany to prevent the Germans getting away on carts and in trucks, though Porubský had brought the explosives and a message from Skittle, Mayor Šimko's errand boy, that the charges were to be used – if it were still possible – to rip up the rail tracks somewhere the other side of Rakytovce.

They were making their way down through the beech wood, six men of the forty-five that Dietbert's men had attacked by the Stahl brickworks. They were driven forward by a determination not to let people like Gábor get away with anything, not to let the Germans get away with anything, driven also by a determination to test, in their own eyes and the eyes of one another, whether they were still as they had once been, whether they were the same even after a long winter spent in the bunker on Úplazy and after moments of fear, cold, hunger and profound depression, hopelessness, feuding and rage, moments when they'd had to make fun of each other, needing to test if they were still the same as they'd been in August and September, when, blithesome and singing songs, they'd taken up arms as yet undaunted by the Germans' numerical superiority. They'd been overjoyed when old Porubský brought them those explosives. Now they were moving forward with silent tread, not talking and with caution. They were also being driven forward, as in the past, by a determination to assist the Soviet troops, having come to believe that only Soviet soldiers could stop the Germans turning people into cattle.

And they were being driven forward by something else.

In October forty-four, when Dietbert's men had attacked the partisans at the Stahl brickworks, two Soviet partisans had also fallen and three others had been seized by Dietbert's soldiers. Porubský's men were driven by a determination to seek retribution for them on anyone who so much as resembled a German soldier.

They moved on with silent tread and not talking through the dark beech wood.

The sunken lane leading down from the mountains to the fields and meadows of Molčany was still wet, muddy and slippery. Here and there the deep ruts left by heavy wagons were full of sludge. The air quivered with the damp fragrance of the forest in bud. To the south they could hear the distant pounding of gunfire and the noise of solid railway sleepers being shattered as German soldiers blasted the line to pieces.

Mišo Porubský, the son of Molčany's parish odd-job man, was in the lead, his entire being infused with an intense, soaring elation. Any time now it could all be over! This was the one single idea that his elation brought to him. It was a powerful elation that had grown slowly but surely because he'd been the one who, throughout the long winter in the bunker, had alone kept the six men together and prevented them from running off. He was feeling good as he made his way down through the forest, heading towards an action that could be his last, feeling good that he and his men still had enough guts left over from the euphoria of August and September that in countless other men and units had completely evaporated. He walked on in silence, treading quietly and with caution.

In Molčany, the night passed slowly for some, quickly for others.

As three o'clock approached, the agitated commander of the Molčany garrison, Oberleutnant Walter Schrimm, rushed to the Stahls' villa and, heatedly and in a foul mood, shouted to Gizela Gábor: "Listen Gizela, I won't be able to have you taken from here by car... It's become too dangerous – you can't leave with the men – and – and our explosives have gone missing, for destroying a bridge, blocking the main road – that's Kolping's job, but he's not back yet and he'd have been able to get all kinds of stuff away, his truck's plenty big enough –"

Gizela didn't grasp what Schrimm was telling her.

"– Kolping had specific tasks to carry out in the partisan villages – and explosives, we don't have any – where did they go?"

Schrimm fell silent, breathing fast, his mind on Rotten-führer Kolping, who was meant to have blocked the road from Greater Hámre and returned to Molčany, but he wasn't back yet. Schrimm was terror-stricken because he couldn't fathom what might have happened to Kolping and his group, and now he was too scared to send out a search party.

Gizela stared at Schrimm in bewilderment.

"It'll be too dangerous now –"

"Why, Walter?" she asked. "Why dangerous? Has something happened?"

"No, Gizela, nothing's happened, but I'm afraid for your safety."

"Afraid? What of? Your car will come back, and its driver, if that's such a concern."

Gizela Gábor felt the chill wind of fear at not getting away by car and affected an even greater lack of concern than at other times.

"All right, Gizela, but –"

Gizela Gábor looked at Schrimm, puzzled and offended, and sat down on the green sofa.

"Do you happen to know? Have you heard?" Schrimm fixed his dark eyes searchingly on Gizela. "Are there any partisans here in Molčany or round about?"

"I don't know anything! Come off it! How could *I* know anything of the kind? How could I be remotely interested? Maybe there are, maybe there aren't. My husband was killed by partisans –"

"I know, Gizela, but that's your fault!"

"What is?" Gizela burst out laughing, exposing both rows of her pretty white teeth. "What's my fault, Walter?"

Schrimm found himself able to look unwaveringly into Gizela Gábor's oval face and blue eyes merely because he was saying unpleasant things to her. "It's your fault," he said, "because it was only thanks to you that I neglected my most natural duty: I failed to have the inhabitants of Molčany checked out properly."

"So have them checked now!" she said. "Start with the Mitúchs!" She stopped short. "Not that that will help you much, because Jozef Mitúch was taken away by Dietbert's men who were here during September and October. They'll have killed him somewhere for sure."

Gizela Gábor was suddenly as shocked at her casual pronouncement regarding Jozef Mitúch, as at the realisation that lying about Mitúch and Dietbert's men could scarcely be of any help to her with Schrimm. Her oval face reddened slightly and her blue eyes half-closed. She suppressed the alarm that stirred inside her at the thought of Jozef Mitúch. He, a former lieutenant, had been in contact with the partisans. He'd told her that much himself. If she gave him away, no one on God's earth would know as much about her as he did. What if he decided to get his own back...? She pulled herself together.

"There's no danger, Walter," she said and stood up. "And if there's no danger to me, then nor is there any to your car and your soldier. And if you've neglected something, then that's down to you. Not me. A great deal is demanded of a German officer," she said, recalling Schrimm's own words, which she repeated: "More is demanded of a German officer than a body can take."

"That's perfectly natural, Gizela." Walter Schrimm watched her searchingly through his half-closed eyes. After a moment he said: "All right, Gizela. I'll send a car for you. Wait for me at the regimental HQ in Rakytovce. Put some warm clothes on and take some items of value with you!" Schrimm paused for thought. "Don't worry about the driver. I'll pick someone reliable."

"Thank you, Walter," she said, placing her hands on his broad shoulders then stroking his cheeks and neck. On his head she straightened his big new forage cap of thick grey-green cloth. "I thank you for so many things –"

"Gizela mine –"

She stroked his cheeks again.

"– do you think," he began, "that that Mitúch –?"

"Hardly," Gizela Gábor replied, "because he was taken away by Dietbert's men in the autumn. He definitely won't have come back. Not one of those taken has come back."

"So – till we meet in Rakytovce."

"All right, Walter."

In the dingy surroundings of Molčany, on Monk's Lea, at the point where two deep, sunken field tracks meet, Porubský's partisans halted, because that was where they had to split up, one group to head for the bridge on the road to Čermanská Lehota, the other for the anti-tank trench and concrete blocks on the road to Račany. They formed two groups. Four of them, Porubský, Zubák, Mezej and Stanko, made up one group, and two, Hriška and Mikuláš the other.

"Right," Porubský whispered hoarsely, his voice rising up from his sore throat, "we four will blow up the bridge and you two will make the road impassable. This is where we split up, go our separate ways... We may not meet again... No shooting – we don't want to draw attention to ourselves!"

Porubský was quaking with fear, but he was trying to speak slowly and with resolution.

They began shaking hands. That helped quell their fears.

"Count slowly to two thousand," said Porubský, "then light the fuses! Mind how you go! Start counting!"

They split up.

Porubský, Zubák, Mezej and Stanko headed fearfully, noiselessly, without speaking and with caution, for the bridge, and Hriška and Mikuláš for the concrete blocks.

The night was dark, the air fragrant with spring.

At three o'clock Schrimm's man, Private Karl Gemert, arrived with the car at the Stahl villa.

"Please, ma'am," he addressed Gizela in the drawing room, "shall we?"

Gizela Gábor glanced at the scrawny soldier, whose nose was twitching with glee at the prospect of an easy escape from Molčany, and, wearing boots, warm trousers and a long fox-fur coat, she picked up her small, but solid leather suitcase.

"Let's!"

She was quite phlegmatic about leaving the villa, previously the property of the Stahls, former owners of the Molčany landed estate and brickworks, for all it was a fine, large villa. Through its five wide double windows it looked out on the huge flower garden, which burgeoned with forsythias from spring onwards and wound down in the autumn with the last of the Michael roses, and it had a wide, block-paved patio. The whole area of the villa and gardens was surrounded by orchards, planted with dwarf and half-standard pear and apple trees. The villa itself had nine spacious rooms. At the far end of the courtyard was a garage. Gizela's husband, Martin Gábor, had taken everything over from the Stahls, the land, the garden, the villa, the garage, the Mercedes, the estate grounds, the courtyard, the steward, the office staff, the farmhands and general labourers, the machines, horses and livestock, nothing of which had been his to start with. He'd never felt good at the Stahl villa, and his young wife, Gizela, had always felt bad there. "There's an evil spirit here!" she would often say. "It's everywhere, in every corner." And that was why she tried to drive it away, with carousals, fun and games and crowds of visitors, and why she felt indifferent about abandoning it. She said nothing to the maids, left everything open and all the lights on, including the lamp in the sitting room with its shade covered in seesawing brown sailing ships.

Nothing bothered her as she sat in the car with Karl Gemert, just that last conversation with Oberleutnant Schrimm and the reference to Jozef Mitúch.

Walter, she sought to reassure herself in the car, was hardly going to find time to catch Mitúch and interrogate him – and Mitúch was not so dumb as to let himself be caught. He'd escape, all the Mitúchs would escape and go into hiding somewhere.

The car, its headlights dimmed, set off from Molčany, stopped before the new concrete bridge, and, the surly sentries Follen and Willich having let it through, it took the road to Čermanská Lehota, Dubrovník, Great and Little Tomkovice and Rakytovce.

Gizela Gábor held on to her little suitcase, constantly running her right hand over her person to check she still had everything – five watches, rings, earrings, necklaces and bracelets.

"You know, ma'am," said Karl Gemert gaily, "Running away with you would be great... If only I could take you all the way home with me!"

"Where are you from?" Gizela asked, to put his mind more on home than on her. "Far from here?"

"Roßwein. I'm a bookseller. If I get back home... I should need money. After the war I'd like to move... Dresden, Leipzig, Halle!"

Gizela took fright. If he managed to take to Roßwein everything she had on her, five silver Schaffhausen watches, twelve gold and fifteen platinum rings set with gems, gold earrings, chains, bracelets and pearl necklaces, then Halle, Dresden or Leipzig might well be the outcome. She patted her fur coat, into which she'd stitched a leather pouch containing three diamonds.

"Dresden, Leipzig, Halle," said Gemert, and after they'd passed Čermanská Lehota, he added pensively: "For over ten years they've been spinning us lies in Germany. The Slavs are a lower race, Jews – they're the kind of race that – that's – only fit for turning into mattresses, soap, artificial fertilisers – or sending up the chimney. Have you any idea, ma'am, how many books such lie-spinning sold? After the war's over, plenty of books will still get sold because the lying will just go on. Like before, there'll be those down below and those at the top. The ones on top will get to thinking that the ones down below are only good for making mattresses, soap and artificial fertilisers. Lies will still be spun. And for more than ten years, that's for sure. Do you know the fairy-tale about lying?"

"No," Gizela replied rather at a loss. "I've never heard it."

The road, lit by the dimmed headlights, rolled on nicely by. The car blew the night air of spring into Gizela's hot face.

"One day, Lady Lie was walking across the world," said Gemert, "she walked on and on, pushing forward, and having crossed the whole world, she wanted to return home, but now she couldn't."

Gizela waited for what happened next. "And is," she asked after a moment, "is that it?"

"Yes, that's it. That's the whole tale."

By the light of the speedometer Gemert looked at his watch. It was quarter past three.

"Pretty short."

"A short tale, but one that will last a long time yet."

"Is Roßwein a nice town?" Gizela asked, her mind more on the possessions that – as her reward for concealing them – had been left behind by the Stahls and that she now had stitched inside her coat. "I've never heard of the place."

"There are plenty of places around the world that a person never hears about – and my birthplace is the most wonderful of them. Books never sold well there. But Halle, Dresden, Leipzig! That was something that my father before me always hankered after."

Gizela Gábor had begun to worry whether the bookseller beside her was entirely reliable, whether he might not rob her. But Walter, she reassured herself, was such an oaf that he might well have actually chosen someone reliable. She stared ahead into the darkness.

Karl Gemert, Gizela's driver, was under orders to be back in Molčany by four o'clock, but he had a feeling that he wouldn't be going back, and that put him in a good mood. His excuse would be, he mused, that he'd had to protect the lady from... But from whom? Gemert assured himself that he'd think of something before they arrived.

The regulated watercourse that ran through Molčany splashed and gurgled, from south of Molčany came the pounding of shellfire, and ahead, on the railway line, solid oak sleepers were getting smashed up.

"Here's where we split up," Porubský whispered, "Mezej and I will cross to the other side, you two go along this side. There's said to be two soldiers on the bridge. So quiet all the way – no shooting...! Jump them!"

The partisans counted in silence and shook hands.

They split up.

Porubský and Mezej dropped down towards the river and having reached its splashing and gurgling water, they plunged into it to half-way up their thighs and waded through water and mud across to the other bank. The water was cold, chilling their thighs. They were shaking with fear and cold.

In Molčany, the lowing of the starving cattle in the school yard was heart-rending.

"Sir!" the German trooper Kurt Kalkbrenner called in a whisper as he ran into the Mitúchs' small back room, where Jozef Mitúch and his eighty-five-year-old mother usually slept. "Sir!"

Jozef Mitúch awoke from a brief sleep, switched the light on and spotted at once the wild-eyed look, the fear written across trooper Kalkbrenner's face and that his grey-green hempen tunic was heaving.

Alarmed, he looked straight at Kalkbrenner and sat up in bed. Old Mrs Mitúch, his mother, also began to stir, groaning.

"Sir," said Kalkbrenner, and as he spoke his lips trembled and his voice was cracking, "there are Russian tanks only forty kilometres away...! Sir –!"

Jozef Mitúch the engineer listened briefly to Kalkbrenner, noting his shining eyes, trembling lips and heaving tunic, then he leapt out of bed wearing a tracksuit. He pulled on the brown jerkin that he'd left tossed across the foot of the bed, then ran through the kitchen to the front room where his brother Adam, his wife Beta and their four children slept. "Adam, get up!" he said to his brother, and when his brother opened his eyes and blinked into the light, Jozef said, speaking quickly and in a very loud whisper: "Adam! There are Russian tanks only forty kilometres away...! – The Germans are on the move – they'll be taking any horses and wagons – and this German of ours says you should hitch up the best wagon you've got and head out into the fields – towards the spinney – or into the forest –"

Adam Mitúch, the engineer Jozef's brother, wriggled in his bed, raised himself slightly, then lay more comfortably on his broad back. He ran a sturdy hand across his face, somewhat clammy with its night-time sweat.

"And where would that put them right now?" he asked. "Forty kilometres?"

"Forty kilometres? That'll be somewhere around –"

Adam leapt from his bed. His wife Beta raised herself slightly, her frightened eyes flashing white across the room before briefly resting, filled with loathing, on Jozef. Then the four children also began to stir.

Jozef Mitúch left the room, pulled on his socks and boots in the kitchen and began speaking in a low tone to Kurt Kalkbrenner, who was tossing his entire kit and caboodle into a pile on the floor.

"Come with me to the stable."

"Will you be staying?" Jozef Mitúch asked Kalkbrenner. "Have you decided?"

"Yes."

The German trooper, Kurt Kalkbrenner, was forty-five. At home, not far from Hartan beneath the Katzen-Gebirge, he had a twenty-two-acre farm, a father, mother, wife and six children. He'd spent most of the war with horses and for over two years now, ever since the fall of Kotelnikovo, he'd been fleeing homeward with all kinds of horses. "In this war, I think I've managed not to kill anyone," he would tell Jozef Mitúch, "and I don't think I'll kill anyone from now on. Others have done all the killing – terrible!" At the end of February 1945, he'd reached Molčany with the company of soldiers commanded by Oberleutnant Schrimm. There he'd been billeted with the Mitúchs. The Mitúchs were ordinary folk who'd looked on Kalkbrenner as a hapless individual. They'd set up a disused old bed for him in the kitchen and put some straw on it. Kalkbrenner's job was to look after the six Styrian horses that he'd tied up – half-hairless and lean – in the Mitúchs' shed. Besides the horses, he was also in charge of the company stores. With the help of Jozef Mitúch, who at first could hardly understand him, he'd explained to the family where Hartan was, what the Katzen-Gebirge was like and that Hitler's war was basically over. "It was a vile business all round, really vile, did so much harm to the whole world, and to my own neck of the woods, and there's more to come," he said, smiling with his pale-green eyes. "A human is only human. Believe me! He can't carry on doing vile things forever, no matter how good it makes him feel. Believe me – it's been ghastly!" This made the Mitúchs laugh and they quite took to Kalkbrenner. They began offering him food, and, although he was quite hesitant at first, he began taking lunch and dinner with them, and whatever he brought in from the army kitchen he tipped straight into the Mitúchs' pigs' trough, offering his army bread to his half-hairless horses. "Things might still all go to the dogs," Adam's wife Beta was in the habit of saying, "but at least let's eat!" and she'd set about slitting a chicken's throat. At the Mitúchs' there was plenty of meat: smoked pork and fresh chicken, and after meals like that Kurt Kalkbrenner started to feel good for the first time in years. He put on weight and acquired a rosy complexion, his spirits rose and he suddenly caught himself having strange ideas. He felt grateful to the Mitúchs, a condition long forgotten and one he hadn't experienced in years, having for so long had no one to be grateful to. He offered Jozef Mitúch some money, and, the latter having declined to accept it, he began bringing things that, at the time, counted for a lot with the brother, Adam: new leather headstalls, new bridles, new halters, harness trappings, pieces of leather for soles, packs of army tobacco, and the more he brought, the greater his sense of gratitude to the Mitúchs, because he felt he was bringing too little and that his gifts were an insult to them. So he opened his heart to them, showed them photos of his parents, his wife and six children, and began to hope that he would end the war in Molčany, maybe even at the Mitúchs'. The Mitúchs had a smallish but well-kept farm, a pretty orchard, some nice livestock and two nice horses, and that of itself revived Kalkbrenner's fury at the war for having dislodged him from the very kind of life being led by the Mitúchs and having cost him several years of that life. He often gave the Mitúchs advice, helped them with their work and introduced them to rational management. Added to that, through March and April, he talked increasingly often to Jozef Mitúch about how he might end his war in Molčany. "I wouldn't if I were you," Jozef told him one time. "It would be dangerous for you. And you wouldn't see your Katzen-Gebirge again." – "I know what you mean." Kalkbrenner's broad features grew sad. "Where there's guilt there are worries. We Germans are both guilty and worried – it's terrible! But I'd have the fewest worries here. I shall stay here. Not at your place. I'll end the war here. Listen. I'll do something that'll make even the Russians leave me alone. They won't take me captive. And they'll even take me back to Hartan themselves!" – "How do you mean?" – "Will you help me?" – "Me help you?" – "Yes," Kalkbrenner replied, smiling good-naturedly. "You have to help me because I know you send victuals off somewhere. I think to some partisans. You have to help me. All I want from you is some mufti. Nothing else. I'll help put something in your way as well, because I want to end the war here…" Kalkbrenner had thought everything through and was all set on doing things his way. From Jozef Mitúch he got some old white trousers, a soiled, white linen shirt, a shabby twill coat and a hat with holes in it, and he kept them all hanging on nails in the Mitúchs' stable. On the first Wednesday in April he repaid Jozef Mitúch for his civilian outfit with some stolen explosive charges.

The war in Molčany was not ending quite as Kalkbrenner had anticipated.

Adam Mitúch, Jozef Mitúch's brother, wearing dark-blue trousers, a dark-blue shirt, his old brown coat and a cap, with his old overcoat and some horse blankets under his arm, dashed out of the room, ran to the stable, and the Mitúchs started wandering aimlessly about the house. Adam hitched the horses to his wagon, drove across the garden, and having taken an axe to prise up and knock down their new fence, he took the long sunken lane along past the chase they called Petrová, slowly and quietly, out into the fields.

The sunken lane, in paces already dry, in other places still soggy after the recent rain, deadened the rumbling of the wagon. Only from the jangling of the hooks and rings on the harrow might anyone have known someone was heading out into the fields.

Now and again Adam checked with a foot, a hand or his riding crop that he had everything on the cart. He had. A harrow with which to work over even any unploughed areas if things got tough, and he had a bag containing some bread and bacon, and on the cart itself some dried clover, chopped straw and oats for the horses, also a metal water bucket and the blankets. And under his left foot an axe.

The people of Molčany were shaking with cold and fear that early April morning. They ran from house to house and Adam Mitúch and his fine horses hadn't gone that far when the whole of Molčany was chattering in low tones about what was happening and what was coming next.

"The Russians will be here any time now!"

"There are already tanks in Mlynská, Borovce and Adamovce!"

"Oh, God!"

"There's already cannon fire in the area! The Germans will be taking whatever's the easiest way out!"

"Horses and wagons need to be taken out to the fields and hidden somewhere, or the Germans will grab everything they can! They're meant not to leave a single team behind. But then how can they possibly flee on their own sorry nags and in those three small trucks?"

"They're bound to grab whatever men and livestock they can! They won't get far, they'll slaughter everything and shoot men and horses. Nothing must be left for the Russians!"

"Oh, God! Oh, my God –!"

"Perhaps we should bury some stuff in the ground –!"

"Hm, too late for that now, oh my God –!"

Anyone who could was sneaking away from Molčany out into the fields.

Not far from the abandoned Stahl villa, where the lights were still on following Gizela Gábor's departure, was the German troops' command post, in the new school building.

Behind the teacher's table on the platform, once polished with oil, but now scuffed by top boots and jackboots, stood Oberleutnant Schrimm. He was very tall and held his large head, covered in sleek black hair and crowned with his new forage cap, very high. He had an ordnance map of the Molčany area on the table, along with some paperwork and lists of the people who possessed teams of horses.

"Fetch me the mayor!" he bellowed at the two soldiers standing in front of the table.

"Immediately!"

The lights went out.

The soldiers lit some candles.

Schrimm glanced at his watch, which he kept on the underside of his left wrist. It was going up to four.

The soldiers led in the mayor, Štefan Šimko, and when the terror-stricken Šimko couldn't make head or tail of what Schrimm was hollering at him, Schrimm sat down and thumped the desk hard with his fist. The table juddered and with it the platform beneath, and Schrimm's ineffectual shouting having fallen silent, a small, thin soldier with a stoop, who had some white ointment smeared around his eyes, said that Kalkbrenner knew some engineer in Molčany who spoke German.

"What?" Schrimm froze. "What engineer? What's he doing here?"

"I don't know, Herr Oberleutnant," said the soldier with cream round his eyes, "but Kalkbrenner said –"

"Where does he live?" Schrimm asked. He was seized with rage at Gizela Gábor. Long before this, she had refused to interpret between him and the mayor and other members of the populace, and contact between the garrison and the locals had been limited to the sale and purchase of straw and hay for the horses. The bitch! He'd neglected so many things because of her! Now because of her he wouldn't be able to destroy the bridge and block the road from Račany. "Where does that engineer live?"

"It's Mitúch," said Mayor Šimko, eager to please because he was scared stiff and wanted to help Schrimm. "He lives that way –"

"Was?" Oberleutnant Schrimm asked quietly. "Ingenieur Midach?"

"Gut," said Mayor Šimko. "Mitúch, gut. That's your man!"

"Fetch him here!" said Schrimm to two of the soldiers. "Engineer Mitúch!"

Ever since Adam had led his team out across the garden into the fields, the Mitúch household had been filled with a resentful silence. Adam's wife Beta had kept skirting round her brother-in-law, the engineer, in silence, but after he'd come back from the stable, where he'd been talking to Kalkbrenner, and was doing up his boots, she went and stood behind him. For a moment she just stood staring at his broad back.

"Why did you send Adam out to the fields?" she asked quietly. "Are you out of your mind?"

"So the Germans wouldn't pick him up and steal our horses and the wagon."

"And what if he gets killed out there? That's heavy guns blazing away out there."

"Don't be afraid, Betka, there's nothing to fear! They're not blazing away at the fields yet. Nothing's going to happen to Adam. I'll give you a hand with the kids. That's why I stayed. We won't leave your mum here either."

"You can't know...," she retorted scornfully, plucking the tips of her warm grey headscarf this way and that beneath her chin. "You can't know whether anything's going to happen to him or not! It's your fault this house is scared to death! Why did you give your old clothes to that German? Back then, with the partisans, you put your life at risk. And now you're giving our stuff away."

"Shut up!" he shouted and turned to face Beta. "Do be quiet!"

The two soldiers came to the door.

Is this," one of them began, "where Mitúch, the engineer, lives?"

"That's me."

"You're coming with us!" said the soldier. "We need an interpreter at our HQ."

Beta looked in alarm at the soldiers, who followed her brother-in-law out of the kitchen.

Jozef Mitúch, Adam's brother and Beta's brother-in-law, had not been a partisan. Only at home did they think of him as one, because there no one drew any distinctions among the men who'd been in the uprising against the Germans. During the uprising, they'd crushed his platoon in the east of the country and only because at that moment in the unfathomable confusion there his commander, Captain Michal Bajzík, had defected to the Germans and handed over his entire regiment. Then at Stakov, Mitúch had begged a frightened housewife for some clothes, white trousers, a white linen shirt, a shabby twill coat and a hat with holes in it, then without knowing who for, he'd taken down a long-handled weeding knife hanging from an apple tree and made his way across almost the whole length of Slovakia, on foot and carrying the weeding knife, all the way to Molčany. Whenever he'd spotted any Germans, he'd set to work in some field or other, hacking away at anything that had roots, be that potatoes or hemp. The people of Molčany thought he must be quite clever, since he'd managed to dodge the Germans and get away from an army that, betrayed and thrown into chaos, had fallen apart. Nobody held his presence in Molčany against him, many fended for him, though many had no idea of his existence, because he never went outside in daylight. He thought the Uprising had been pointless and done more harm than good, he'd wanted nothing to do with it and lived for himself only. Few people knew about him. People who did know him well were Gizela Gábor, whom he'd started visiting in January, Mayor Šimko and Šimko's errand boy Skittle, the son of the widow Pláteníčka, whose nickname had come about because since childhood he'd been the pinsetter at the village skittle alley. Even before January was out he'd started coming to Jozef Mitúch to get victuals for the artisans up on Úplazy.

"What are you doing here?" Oberleutnant Schrimm asked him at the school. "How long have you been here?"

"Ages. This is where I evacuated to."

"Oh really? Where from?"

"From eastern Slovakia, Michalovce."

"Michalovce, eh?" Which of them's lying. Gizela or this bastard? Probably Gizela, so she could get away by car. This bastard should have been shot long ago! "Well –"

"Michalovce's already –"

"Of course, naturally! So –" Schrimm pointed a grimy finger at the mayor, Šimko: "– tell him why –!"

Jozef Mitúch, engineer, filled with as much loathing for Gizela Gábor, whom he'd no longer been able to visit after Lieutenant Schrimm took up residence in the Stahl villa, as for Schrimm himself, calmly did as bidden and asked Mayor Šimko, who was standing in front of the teacher's table and quaking somewhat in his boots, his good-as-new brown trousers and coat, and clutching his hat in his hands, why he had not advised owners of any horses and wagons to have them all on stand-by by four o'clock at the latest.

"I received no such order, sir." Mayor Šimko, paralysed by his own deceit, because he *had* received the order and taken it round in person to the parish odd-job man, Porubský. He raised his right hand slightly, the one holding his hat, and began to tremble. "If I had received it –"

"What's he saying?" Schrimm asked Mitúch. "What's the mayor saying?"

"That he received no orders from you."

"What?" Oberleutnant Schrimm paled slightly. "What? My orders?"

Silence descended on the school. The candle flames flickered. All over the walls and in the corners the huge shadows of the soldiers moved this way and that. – The school echoed to the heart-rending outpourings of the starving livestock.

Two explosions made the windows rattle and the doors shuddered slightly.

How can this be? It took Schrimm a moment to recover his wits. Did Kalkbrenner fail to deliver to the mayor the order that he was to go house to house and advise owners of any horses and wagons to have them all on stand-by by four o'clock at the latest? Kalkbrenner and Mitúch? Had Gizela been telling the truth even though she'd lied about Mitúch? Schrimm stared blankly ahead. The order had been typed quite clearly. By Gizela still. How could Kalkbrenner not have delivered it?

Lieutenant Walter Schrimm had had clear orders from the regimental HQ in Rakytovce: Assemble all the teams available in Molčany, load them up with arms and equipment and be in Rakytovce by eleven! Kolping's unit was to destroy the bridges on the roads to Greater Hámre, Lipník and Čermanská Lehota and block the road to Račany! The rest of the men were to withdraw on trucks, or the one attached to Kolping's unit!

The orders were clear, but for Schrimm in Molčany the war was ending otherwise than how he'd imagined it.

"Get me Kalkbrenner!" he bellowed at a subordinate. "I want him here, right now!"

"Yessir, Herr Oberleutnant, sir!"

Jozef Mitúch cowered somewhat beneath a surge of fear, buckling somewhat at the knees, but then drew himself up. Blood was pounding in his ears. He was weighed down by a terrible sense of guilt. He'd gone about it the wrong way. In exchange for the stolen explosives he'd given Kalkbrenner the old clothes in which he'd fled from his demolished unit in Stakov all the way to Molčany. He'd sent Skittle with the explosives to the partisans so they could sever the railway track. The Germans wouldn't be able to destroy the line, they wouldn't be able to retreat and they'd be put to flight in confusion. But the soldiers were going to find Kalkbrenner as he was changing, or maybe they'd find him already changed. Where was he going to leave his uniform, his rifle and accessories? Where would he hide? In the cowshed under the decking, as he'd said? That's not a good place to hide. The pit's full of liquid manure. What if the soldiers do find him, or the stuff he's left behind...? Mum, poor thing, Beta, the kids, Adam out in the fields... Inside his head, heart and blood Mitúch began to quake with the sheer might of the moment, when things kept coming and going not just in Molčany, but inside his very own self. Maybe that's how it has to be! Probably there is no other way! Mitúch felt a slight tightening in his throat. Shake off the Germans effortlessly along with everything they'd brought with them, effortlessly shake off the fear – with no victims, now that would be simply... That would be ghastly... To live in some donated, gifted freedom, with no respect for oneself... He now had to make up for the months of negligence and idleness spent with Gizela in Molčany! The mighty moment was hurling him down into trepidation and he lent only half an ear to Oberleutnant Schrimm, who was prone to shouting savagely to veil his own fear, as if hearing him against a background of gushing torrents.

"The Mayor is to let it be known, without fuss and unobtrusively – but immediately," Schrimm bellowed, "that all owners of teams of horses and wagons should proceed, with their teams, to the front of the command post! They themselves can then return home!"

Mitúch set his face against a sudden surge of stupor, in which he sensed a danger of his becoming indifferent to all things, he turned to Mayor Šimko and glanced at his gleaming forehead and neck, where the arteries made the man's skin bulge as if under it he had plump, bloated leeches, skin that was ageing and crinkled. Only confusion will help here, confusion alone will put paid to Schrimm and, with him, to Gizela, he thought as he stared at Mayor Šimko's fat, pulsating arteries and reproachful eyes.

"Mr Mayor," he began, as brusquely and insistently as Schrimm had spoken to him, "go round with your drum and put it about that all owners of a team of horses should hitch up and head for the fields or forest!"

Mayor Šimko gawped and raised his right hand, still holding his hat.

"Das ist mein Befehl!" Schrimm bawled at him, and to Jozef Mitúch he said: "Thank you, Herr Ingenieur. Kindly stay here a moment. I shall be needing you again."

"Gut!" said the mayor as he turned away. "Gut!"

Mitúch was sweating all over. From Schrimm's mocking tone he sensed that he wouldn't be leaving the school building any time soon.

Mayor Šimko sent his errand boy, Skittle, to get Porubský, but because Porubský had stayed up on Úplazy with the partisan Pavela and was squatting on guard outside the bunker, it was his wife who came with the drum. It wasn't the first time she'd acted as town crier at Molčany. She'd done it quite often, whenever her husband wasn't at home.

This can't be right! Mayor Šimko was thinking, even though Mrs Porubský was already standing there before him with the drum. Surely the Germans need every team, every cart they can lay their hands on to get away from here. They'll get nowhere with their own scraggy jades. How far would they get them? The sooner they're out of here the better. But what would people say? Mitúch, what an idiot! Paying court to Gizela Gábor, sure, he's good at that. But he will keep poking his nose in everywhere and doesn't understand a thing. Once the Germans have scarpered I shall have to have words with him!

Shortly, Mrs Porubský, mad at her husband, son and at Šimko, began drumming at the lower end, but there was no one there and no one was listening. "Oyez, oyez, oyez. The citizenry be advised that all owners of horses and wagons are to hitch up with a will and drive to the front of the school! There they will be loaded up with military materiel! The owners of the horses and wagons shall then accompany the German troops to ensure nothing happens to them in Molčany." She beat the drum and proceeded to the front of the pub.

At the Mitúchs', the small, thin soldier with a stoop, with white ointment round his eyes and wearing a grey-green cape, asked Beta, Adam's wife, "Wo ist Kalkbrenner?" And again: "Kalkbrenner ist hier?"

"What?"

"Wo ist Kalkbrenner? Kurt Kalkbrenner! Er ist mein Kamarad. Wir beide sind von Hartan... Kurt Kalkbrenner!"

"I don't know what you're saying," said Beta, because she didn't know the name of the German who'd been living with them, and she shook her head. "I can't understand a word of what you're saying." She looked into his eyes, smeared round with white ointment. Dear God, what happened to you?"

"Kurt Kalkbrenner!"

Beta shook her head.

"I don't know," she said. "I don't know what that is."

The soldier shrugged and left.

Beta went back to the children, who'd run squealing from the front room into the kitchen and hopped onto Kalkbrenner's empty bed.

"Shush!"

Adam Mitúch and his wife Beta had four children, two boys and two girls

Beta began putting their best shoes on them and dressing them in their warmest clothes. They looked in surprise at her dressing them so nice and warm and wondered why she was looking so worried, nor did they know why all this so happening so fast and in the dark. There was no electric light, only candles. And where was the German? The Kraut? They were standing on Kalkbrenner's bed.

Oh, God! She popped into the other room and came back at once with two large woollen shawls, one dark-grey, the other pale-green. She tossed them onto Kalkbrenner's bed. Soldiers were on the move, they were after something, looking for something – oh, God!

"Mummy, what do we need woollen shawls for?" asked the youngest, Amalka.

"Quiet, kids!" the eldest, Janko, chided her, a chubby lad of solid, rubicund features. "Quiet. Kreeg kaput! Mummy," he asked "where's the Kraut?".

"He's left," said Beta, bursting into tears. "Do be quiet, all of you!"

"What's wrong, Mummy?" Janko asked. "Is this the front thing?"

"Where's Daddy?"

"The cowshed," said Beta. "Wait here, I need to go and tell him something." She dashed out of the kitchen, hurried across the dark yard and entered the cowshed. Oh, my God! The soldiers are still out and about, maybe they're looking for the German. It's all his fault, that engineer's. If only the Germans would get him! He's a horrible man. Went chatting up the Gábor woman and took stuff to the partisans. In the shed, the cows stood quietly, staring towards the greyish entrance and waiting for their morning feed.

Beta Mitúch turned round in the entrance to the cowshed, looking back into the dark yard. Her ears and cheeks were warmed by the air drifting from inside the shed, enriched with the night's ordure. Then her face was struck by the morning cold from the yard. The German had been bumbling around here in the shed! Oh my God, if the soldiers – I do hope they don't find him! Had he had time to change his clothes? She wanted to call out to him, but didn't know how. Something made her jump. She turned round and looked back inside the darkened cowshed.

"Herr Ingenieur?" She heard the crisp, loud whisper coming from inside the shed. "Herr Ingenieur?"

"Gut, gut," said Beta. "Where are you?"

"Ja, ja, Frau Midach?" came from the bin for chopped straw. "Ja?"

Beta went up to the bin.

The bin swayed as Kalkbrenner clambered out of it. He looked whitish about his trousers and shirt, the clothes in which Jozef Mitúch had come back to Molčany from Stakov. Kalkbrenner dusted some of the straw off and reached back down inside the container to retrieve the satchel containing his uniform.

"Ja, ja, ich gehe schon." He went on speaking for a while, pointing at the satchel and at the decking beneath the cows, but Beta couldn't understand a word he said. She didn't know Kalkbrenner had his uniform in the satchel. His uniform might still come in handy, he told her, because a front line is a tricky thing. It moves this way and that. Everything he'd had was down there, under the decking. That's where he'd tossed everything. Any soldiers who showed up would find no trace of him. Beta listened, but without understanding a word. All she noticed was the way he kept pointing underneath the cows.

"Wo ist Herr Ingenieur?"

"Inžinier? That swine?"

"Ja, ja. Das ist ein sehr guter Mensch."

"Some soldiers took him to the command post."

"Ja? Zur Ortskommandatur?"

"Gut," said Beta, "gut!"

Kalkbrenner, prostrate with fear for himself and for Jozef Mitúch, began patting her hands in the dark, gave her wrist a squeeze, said something or other more, and then ran out of the cowshed, after which Beta caught just a flicker of his white trousers crossing the yard to the barn and round past the barn into the garden.

She heaved a sigh and hurried back to the children in the kitchen.

Molčany was surrounded by darkness, a soft darkness that thudded with the distant gunfire.

The partisans, Porubský and Mezej on one side of the stream, Zubák and Stanko on the other, were lying on the ground near the bridge, listening to the heavy footsteps of the two German sentries, Follen and Willich, tramping up and down the bridge.

Follen and Willich met in the middle of the bridge, skirted past each other, paused briefly at the ends of the bridge, turned back onto the bridge and skirted past each other again in the middle of the bridge.

The partisans counted in silence.

Lying on the ground next to the road to Račany were Hriška and Mikuláš, counting, listening and watching the huge blocks of concrete jutting black against the grey sky.

Porubský was lying in a damp, waterlogged field, trembling with cold and fear, his hands shaking on the cold clods of earth.

Follen and Willich met in the middle of the bridge and stopped.

The stream gurgled and gushed.

"Nee," Porubský heard one of the guards say. "Nee!"

Follen and Willich started chatting.

"Changeover at four."

"Who's coming?"

"Muttek and Pauer."

Porubský and Mezej were crawling towards the burned-out wreck of Stahl's Mercedes.

Follen and Willich parted and went to their respective ends of the bridge.

Porubský's throat had gone dry and began to feel sore. He reached out one grimy hand and touched Mezej.

The sentries had paused each at his own end of the bridge and turned. Follen took one step and stopped.

"Wer da? Halt!"

That was the only shout on the bridge, after which no one shouted anything, it was quiet except for the sounds of six men fighting and six sets of lungs breathing. The stream gurgled and gushed, sleepers were being shattered in the far distance along the line, the air thudded with the sound of distant gunfire.

Adam Mitúch was driving along the sunken lane. Looking before him at the horses. They were black, handsome and even in the dark their backs had a sheen, they went slowly along the lane, gently plodding and their bodies swaying from side to side. Adam was hugely fond of his horses, and because Kalkbrenner was forever saying "Ach schöne Pferde! Herrlich!" he'd grown quite fond of Kalkbrenner as well. He'd keep driving around the area, he mused, and, if necessary, he might even start harrowing any unploughed parts, or he might hide away in Barren Grove. If only the Germans would clear off! What's going on at home, he wondered, suddenly thinking of his brother, the engineer, who'd promised him, in the stable, that he'd take care of everyone, meaning their mother and Adam's wife and kids. Adam's calm was restored somewhat.

Far away, seeming to extend round the entire southern horizon, the front rumbled and boomed.

Those had been the words Kalkbrenner had used one time at the Mituchs' as he listened to the distant booming of cannon-fire and shells. "That's the front rumbling, booming away!" he would say. "Those bangs, it's bombs going off!" – "Carpet bombing!" – "Things are flying everywhere, there's no telling who's going to get killed where." One time he'd said to dear old deaf Mrs Mitúch, Adam's mother: "Ja, ja, das ist Bombenteppich!" – "Just you wait," she'd replied: "the Russians are coming!" "Ja, ja, Rus!" Kalkbrenner had agreed, laughing. Adam Mitúch slowly carried on along the sunken lane and listened in horror at the cracking of those solid sleepers, the heavy panting of a locomotive, he listened in horror to the ever louder explosions coming from the bridges and points that the Germans were destroying along the line, but the horror was relieved by tiny quivers of joy at the prospect of an imminent end to it all. The stable, cowshed and grain loft would no longer be invaded by random prowlers who didn't even know whether wheat grows with its roots up or down. The Germans would be gone and with them all ills; liars and cheats would go to blazes, and a person could breathe again. There'd be no more spying on people to check what they're saying or thinking – phew, what horrible times these had been. His good humour was restored.

The wagon drove on, the hooks and rings on the harrow jangling away.

The air was suddenly shaken by an explosion nearby, Adam's ears were set buzzing, the horses went berserk and reared up, the poler struck a spark from a stone with its hoof, and two more explosions shook the air again.

The arteries on Adam's neck were throbbing. Shells! No, no, that wasn't shells. He gulped.

A shell whizzed through the air.

Adam reined his horses in.

The shell exploded on the far side of Molčany.

It didn't take long for Adam's breathing to settle and, having had his calm restored along with that of his horses, he stayed put in the sunken lane. All you could hear then was the shattering of sleepers, explosions further down the line and the booming of distant gunfire.

Came four o'clock.

Darkness all around. Cold filling the air.

Schrimm's men, many of them with their sundry orders, were going from farmstead to farmstead and house to house, acting out Schrimm's orders. Just like Porubský's wife, who was still drumming all round the village. One lot was trying to find Kalkbrenner, others teams of horses, and the third lot any carts and wagons; yet others were looking to see what they might still collar in the way of comestibles. Of the forty teams Oberleutnant Schrimm had got listed on various bits of paper in pencil, pen and ink or typed, four pairs of sorry-looking horses and four sorry-looking carts had gathered outside the school. Only Mayor Šimko had provided a worthwhile wagon and a fine pair of bays. The men of Molčany were nowhere near their stables because they'd run off to the fields and forests. Many men, those who'd had the time, had dismantled their better carts and wagons, removing and hiding the wheels and, from the lighter ones, even the axles, and scattered whatever they could around their lofts, sheds and yards.

"Wo ist Ihr Mann, wo sind Ihre Pferde?" the corporal who'd entered the Mitúchs' kitchen with four troopers demanded of Beta. "Wo ist er?"

Adam's wife stood up straight above Amalka's feet, on which she'd be retying her shoelaces.

"Wo ist er?"

"What?" she asked, despite having gradually gathered that they were looking for Adam. "What do you want?"

"Wo ist Ihr Mann?" the corporal asked again, shouting at her even more loudly than the first time. "Er muss zur Ortskommandatur!"

"Komandatúr?"

"Ja, ja," said the corporal. "Zur Ortskommandatur!"

"It's that way, in the school," said Beta Mitúch, "in the school, in the village it's –" She pointed, her hand trembling slightly, "– it's there – the *komandatúr*'s been there ages, ever since you arrived."

"Ja?" the corporal asked Beta, who had bent back down over Amalka's shoes. "Ja?"

"Ja, ja," said Beta, "it's in the school – how come you didn't know? – even this lot's going mad now, goodness me! – gut gut."

The corporal and his men left, a lance-corporal arrived with three other troopers. They asked nothing of anyone, crossed the yard to the shed and brought out the six big Styrian horses, lean and mangy, with scattered patches of white from the powder Kalkbrenner had sprinkled them with as recently as Wednesday afternoon.

Two helmeted soldiers entered the school. They went and stood to attention in front of the teacher's table.

"What is it?" Schrimm turned away from the telephone. "What is it?"

"The bridge leading to Čermanská Lehota has been destroyed," one of the men said.

"Follen and Willich have been killed, disarmed!"

Jozef Mitúch stiffened, because that wasn't what he'd sent the partisans explosive charges for, and Oberleutnant Walter Schrimm stiffened because he'd had no inkling of any such thing, and in the silence that had now taken over the school the windows were being rattled by explosions in the distance, and the lowing of the starving cattle was heart-rending.

"The road to Račany has been blocked!"

Two minutes flew past.

"Right, Herr Ingenieur," said Schrimm, whose voice had softened thanks to his fury and despair and acquired a nasty hint of scorn. "You will stay here! Muttek and Pauer!" he addressed the two helmeted men and pointed to one corner. "Keep an eye on him! I think we may have to give him special treatment." He could feel his back perspiring. He looked at his map. Molčany, Čermanská Lehota, Dubovník, Great Tomkovice, Little Tomkovice, Rakytovce. Twenty-five kilometres. He knew that much anyway. He stared at the twisting white line. From Molčany to Rakytovce through fields and forests – around ten kilometres! He stood up straight over his map. "Stop collecting horses and wagons! Start grabbing civilians!"

"Yessir, Herr Oberleutnant, sir!"

The little lieutenant, whose glasses were glinting in the candle-light, stood erect. "Women too?"

"No."

The school sprang into life.

"Where's Kalkbrenner?" Schrimm bawled at the lieutenant, who'd been about to step away from the desk. "You have to fetch him for me, even if he – you have to! – I need him –" Schrimm was shaking with rage, "– you have to find him! – alive, killed, doesn't matter...!"

Schrimm turned to the telephone fixed to the blackboard, which was covered in scribbled numbers and straight and wiggly lines and smudged with grey and white patches where things written in chalk had been rubbed out by hand. Behind the confusion of numbers, lines, scrawlings and smudges Schrimm could see, even by candlelight, the five parallel lines of a stave, a treble clef and some notes.

"... for each man killed," Schrimm was phoning the regimental HQ in Rakytovce, "at the very least..."

As he listened, he stared at the Horst-Wessel-Lied, that ancient, now forgotten song.

"Two killed, one missing! Kolping isn't back yet... Probably partisan units –" Schrimm listened, staring at the Horst-Wessel-Lied. The ancient party hymn about fighting and freedom. Horst Wessel, the lunatic! Got himself killed by a communist. Where there's fighting there is no freedom. "... thirty hostages for each of them? Follen, Willich, Kalkbrenner... Yes... Yes sir, Herr Major, sir!"

The whole of the Molčany parish was in darkness.

Kalkbrenner was standing rigid, still stupefied by the explosions that had shattered the bridge and toppled both tall concrete blocks, leaving their sharp iron rods digging into the roadway, he was standing not far from the Stahl brickworks, both feet rooted in the soil of an anti-tank trench above a muddy puddle that glinted faintly in the bed of the trench.

He was shaking with fear born of the alien nature of the world of Molčany and with stirrings of rage against those who'd toppled the blocks onto the road. He tried to kid himself he'd be safest anywhere where no German soldiers would show up. He knew for sure they'd go nowhere near the fat bottle-shaped concrete objects because they'd been abandoned as undefendable against Soviet tanks and troops. He'd been an alien in uniform, and now he was...? Get rid of the uniform? Not get rid of it? Go back to Molčany? Make a run for somewhere else? But where? At that instant Kalkbrenner felt alone, terribly alone. He stood in the anti-tank trench, unable to move, because any step he took could spell disaster.

Hřiška and Stanko, who had toppled the concrete blocks, were slowly making their way back up to Úplazy, treading silently and not speaking, along a long anti-tank trench because it led to the Stahl brickworks and from there a sunken lane led on into the forest. Now and again they paused, waiting in case they might hear something. It was dark, with not a sound anywhere, just the gunfire thudding away to the south.

Because of the fear-driven rush of blood in his ears, Kalkbrenner could hear nothing apart from explosions near and far and the sound of sleepers being shattered. His legs ached and he was shaking with exertion. He made a move in the direction of the road, where he would hide inside one of the concrete spheres. The loose soil gave way beneath his feet and he slid back down to the bottom of the trench.

The partisans stopped.

"What's that?" Hriška asked in a whisper. "Over there."

They could hear footsteps squelching towards them. Both, Hriška and Stanko, got a glimpse of a pale figure in the anti-tank trench. It seemed to be trying to climb out of the trench.

"Who's that?" Hriška demanded in a whisper. "Halt!"

Kalkbrenner froze. The satchel containing his uniform slipped from under his arm. Just as Hriška and Stanko reached him, rifles at the ready, his courage deserted him and he noted that, once more, he was drowning in a terrible fit of nostalgia. The dark surroundings of Molčany again struck him as terribly alien, so alien the place, so alien the people.

"Who are you?" Stanko asked him, poking his rifle close to his right groin. "What are you doing here?"

Kalkbrenner felt an icy tickling sensation run up his right leg and across his belly.

Hriška stepped up close to Kalkbrenner. He tripped over the satchel. He picked it up and looked at it.

"What's this?" he asked Kalkbrenner, poking him with his left leg. "How did you get here? What are you doing here? And what's that stuff you're wearing?"

"Yes, da, I pattizan," said Kalkbrenner, "ich hab' dem Ingenieur Midach den Sprengstoff gegeben –"

"Come!"

Kalkbrenner tripped, stayed stuck where he was in the mud and turned. "Ich bin Kurt Kalkbrenner," he told Hriška and Stanko, "hab' ich dem Ingenieur Midach den Sprengstoff gegeben –"

"What?"

"Dynamit, Ekrasit," said Kalkbrenner, "hab' ich dem Ingenieur Midach gegeben –"

"What's he got?" Hriška asked Stanko. "Dynamite, ekrasite?"

Hriška opened the satchel and began pulling out the uniform, piece by piece – cap, tunic, trousers, shaking out each piece in turn. "He's got nothing here," he said, "just some odd bits of clothing. In the light we'll have a look what it is."

"Ja, ja," said Kalkbrenner, "ich hab' dem Ingenieur Midach –"

"What?" said Stanko to the blenching Kalkbrenner. "You, an engineer? You bastard! A German partisan! Let's get moving!"

He gave Kalkbrenner a shove.

The water and slime squelched beneath Kalkbrenner's feet. He walked ahead of the partisans and they directly behind him. They held their rifles aimed at his oddly white outfit.

A quarter of an hour passed, then ten minutes more.

The final hours and minutes had begun to supplement the complement of years, months, weeks and days.

Inside the school at Molčany, which housed Schrimm's command post, Jozef Mitúch, the engineer, was standing in one corner, his face to the wall. Behind him stood the two helmeted soldiers, Muttek and Pauer, thinking about the road that had been blocked, the bridge that had been destroyed and about Follen and Willich, who had been killed. Mitúch's arms and legs ached and his whole frame was rigid with fatigue. His brown tracksuit was flapping, as was the handkerchief poking from his tracksuit pocket.

Schrimm, his mind on Rottenführer Kolping, his man and the car, on Gizela Gábor and her driver, Karl Gemert, kept looking at his watch, which he wore beneath his wrist, at its pointed hour and minute hands and the quickly rotating second hand, and because he already sensed what was coming – Kolping wouldn't be coming back, he could have been captured, or killed, though who by? Gemert couldn't now get back with the car – he was giving in to rage directed at Gizela Gábor and to fear for his and his men's safe withdrawal from Molčany, fear lest the troops failed to seize enough hostages to cover their retreat.

And what if Gizela came back? Schrimm sat down and lit a cigarette. Gizela's got those valuables with her – and what about Gemert?

The command post was filled with a subdued bustle. Schrimm looked on at, listened to, saw and heard the comings and goings of the troopers as they got ready to flee.

"Herr Oberleutnant!"

Schrimm turned to face the blackboard and the signaller.

"The regiment's not responding, regimental HQ isn't responding –"

"Stop calling!" Schrimm glanced at his watch.

Four hours and eleven, twelve minutes gone –

Then he glanced at Mitúch's broad back. His head was throbbing, his arms shaking all the way up to his shoulders. He was breathing in short breaths, oblivious to what was going on around him – the hustle and bustle in the school, where the clerks, the medic, signaller and the detachment of guards were all packing up, or the bustle in the school yard, where cattle were lowing and soldiers were hitching mangy horses to wagons with huge thin wheels and loading their equipment onto them – his mind was elsewhere: Must wait for Gemert and Gizela! They're bound to come back. HQ could hardly be interested in them... He'd wait here for them... Gizela can't stay here, she mustn't! Molčany has to be defended from the south, from the direction of Račany – and take off with Gizela and the rest of the men. He ran one hand nervously across his face.

"So then," he turned to Mitúch, "was our man Kalkbrenner staying with you?"

"Yes, he was," Mitúch replied into the wall, "but I didn't know his name."

"Did he give you some explosives?"

"No."

"Did you know Gizela Gábor?"

"No," Mitúch replied. "Never seen her."

"Right, Herr Ingenieur, you evacuated here, to Molčany – you have a very broad back, how come nothing ever hit it? – and who have you been in contact with –?"

"Some relatives."

"Ah but –" said Schrimm. "What ones in particular?"

"My brother –"

"Unteroffizier Wojkowitz!"

"Sir, Herr Oberleutnant!"

"Bring Mitúch in!" Schrimm ordered Wojkowitz, and with his eyes fixed on Mitúch's broad back he asked: "What's your brother's name?"

"Adam."

"Bring Adam Mitúch in!"

"Yes, sir!

The blood was pounding away in Jozef Mitúch's ears and inside his head in those final moments of the war, the final moments of darkness, fear and the utter despair that had overwhelmed him as he thought fitfully of his mother, Adam's wife Beta, their four children and his brother Adam himself. What had been the point of it all? Why had the partisans destroyed the bridge and blocked the road? He'd sent them the explosives to destroy the railway line beyond Rakytovce, if they were at all able. That would have made sense. That would have been a good thing for the whole area. But this? Because of Gizela and the partisans he couldn't hold his head up at home – Beta kept holding it against him, Adam as well sometimes – and now, because of the partisans, the whole village would turn against him. Beta and Gizela? Women of roughly the same age. In the final minutes of gloom and fear, it was they to whom Mitúch's thoughts turned.

At the Mitúchs' house the door flew open.

Into the kitchen marched four soldiers and Unteroffizier Wojkowitz. Without saying a word, they surveyed the kitchen before entering the front room, where they opened all the wardrobes, scattering clothes and underwear everywhere, looked under the beds and, leaving the door open, entered the back room, where old, deaf Grandma Mitúch was up and dressed, sitting on a chair next to the bed and, with a lighted candle on the chest and her prayer book in her hands, she was reciting a prayer, "... all-merciful God, who reigneth supreme over those in heaven, grant those who are wailing and drowning in this vale of tears to look up to Thee, grant these wretched people inspiration and the strength to turn aside from war in thought and deed, and if that be not Thy divine

will, stir them to knowledge through this great devastation...",
there, too, Unteroffizier Wojkowitz had everything opened
and thrown about and he fastened his gaze on the tall old
lady.

She raised one sallow hand with its network of bluish
veins.

"You wait," she said, "the Russians are coming! Just you
wait!"

"Was?"

Old Mrs Mitúch began again to recite in a whisper the
words of her prayer for peace.

The soldiers left the back room.

Unteroffizier Wojkowitz ordered: "Search the yard and out-
buildings!" and bared his white and yellow teeth as he grinned
at Beta. They were long and thin, wet and slimy with saliva as
his feeble lips opened and closed over them.

Beta watched him with her grey eyes and began to feel
muzzy, sensing nothing but the children clinging to her hips.
Her arms hung loose, with the slops that she'd been getting ready for the pigs dripping from her fingers; the slops
had been meant to stop the pigs squealing so the Germans
wouldn't hear them, and all you could hear now was the slops
drip-dripping into filthy buckets.

"Wo ist Ihr Mann, Midach?" he asked. He placed his right
hand on the big back holster that housed his pistol. "Du
weisst, wo er ist! Wo ist Kalkbrenner?"

Beta had no idea what he wanted, she couldn't say anything, but after a moment she blurted: "Your soldier ran
off – my men aren't at home – any partisans are up there in the
mountains – that way – not here in the village..." She paused
for breath. She pointed a wet, shaky hand behind her, roughly
in the direction of the Úplazy beech woods.

"Partisanen?"

"Ja, gut, ja!"

"Partisanen? Hier? In Molšany?"

"Ja, gut!"

Unteroffizier Wojkowitz undid the big black button on his big black holster.

"Nothing at all, Herr Unteroffizier," bellowed one of the soldiers standing at the open door of the Mitúchs' kitchen. "Nothing at all."

Wojkowitz turned to Beta and spat on her youngest child, Amalka. He left the kitchen.

Beta Mitúch stood over her buckets, deaf in the ears, blind in the eyes, hearing nothing, seeing nothing, in a stupor, only her skin showing endless tiny, cold ripples. After a while, she heard the children, "Mummy, mummy," as if from a distance.

"Mummy, mummy..." She eventually registered, as if from far off, their presence. "Mummy, Mummeee...!" she heard the children crying. "Mummeee...!"

She patted their cheeks with her wet hands. "Come!"

She grabbed the two large woollen shawls off Kalkbrenner's bed, one dark grey, one pale green, hurried the children out into the yard and ran towards the barn.

"Not the barn, Mummy!" her six-year-old, Betka, cried. "Not the barn! No, Mummy! Let's go to Petrová chase! There are trenches to hide in there!"

Beta Mitúch and the children dashed across the garden, ran over the new fence, now lying flat on the ground, and into the sunken lane, and then out of the sunken lane along a soggy footpath running between blackthorns and briers as far as Petrová chase. There she leapt down into a deep trench. The two boys jumped down after her, then the two little girls, Betka and Amalka, flung themselves down into her open arms. She covered the children in the shawls, wrapping them tight.

Back at the school, Schrimm glanced at his watch, stood up and barked at the lieutenant: "Leutnant! Have all houses and the road to Račany occupied from the south. Civilians! Grab whatever civilians!" And he glanced once more at his watch.

"Yessir, Herr Oberleutnant, sir!"

Time was flying.

Mitúch was staring into the corner. The blood was buzzing in his ears, drowning out the shouting, the orders given, the general hubbub inside the school and the heart-rending clamour of the starving cattle. He was trembling in anticipation of the moment when Schrimm and Gizela would perish.

"It's all gloom and fear," he'd told Gizela Gábor often enough. In the first week in January, Bürster's troop had left Molčany, and, because no new soldiers showed up, Gizela, inside the Stahl villa, had begun to fear the partisans who'd killed her husband. That was why she'd sent her maid to get Jozef Mitúch, believing that he would protect her from the partisans were anything to happen, and that the long, long and desperate hours of the night inside the villa would pass the quicker in his company. Mitúch had begun to visit her there, and after she'd begun to play the hostess, treating him to plenty of food and drink, he'd begun to feel better with her than at home. He noted how much safer from the Germans he felt with her, and they could have shown up at any moment, and after she began to play host to him with her own body, his interest in her became quite different. "It's all gloom and fear," he'd told her one evening. "What we've got today, fascism, Gizzie, it's a boundless unfreedom. You yourself know well enough what it is. The heart filled with apprehension, the head with humiliation, the bowed shoulders, the mendacious words or words obtuse and vacuous to the point of blasphemy, a world smashed to pieces, boxed in with borders, the disregard for human dignity and human worth, people in prisons, prison-camps, degraded, humiliated, many by now tortured to death, and more than many killed outright. Informers all round. All that is fascism and unfreedom. Today people lie as they speak, they lie in the papers, courts are no longer courts, they take away people's property at will, the papers are censored, telephones are bugged, people are herded into labour like cattle, people torture people, brutalize them..." Gizela Gábor tried to counter her fear of losing Mitúch and started to smile, baring her pretty, regular, dense, quite gapless teeth, and keeping her eyes fixed on his lean features as his dark eyes darted restlessly this way and that. She rubbed one leg against the other. "Jožo, my Joey!" – "What is it, Gizzie?" – "I find it ridiculous." – "Ridiculous?" Jozef Mitúch, engineer, was appalled. "You find all this ridiculous?" – "Of course!" – "You don't believe it?" – "No, I don't – no, the strongest belief today is belief in nothing." – "But you did believe Dietbert, the man you're always going on about!" Mitúch's words bore a tinge of reproach and mockery. "What? It's silly of you to bait me like that, Jožo. You're right, and that's why you're ridiculous, because you're right. The truth destroys people. Everything you just said is true. And it all applies to me as well, Jožo; you're a fool! I know one thing only and that is that I have only one life – and that's why I am the way I am. That's why I did all the things I did." Gizela Gábor registered the astonishment in Jozef Mitúch's expression. "It was me who talked my husband into taking over this villa of the Stahls, the brickworks and the estate, it was me who put him up to telling Major Dietbert about old Stahl, his wife, young Stahl, his wife and two children, all of them, who'd been hiding here up in the loft – they were then shot by soldiers out in the woods – it was me who put my husband up to showing the soldiers the way to the brickworks. There the Germans killed, captured and scattered the partisans. The Stahls were vile Jews! And the partisans? They were just scum! They'd killed my husband and stolen our horses from the farm. Fascism! You nitwit! Fascism is not only what you just said. Fascism is also an experiment in how to take control of humans. A modern attempt. But that's not enough where human beings are concerned. Controlling humans is not within human powers. Which is why these days everyone lives by their instincts. To avoid danger. I've also tried to avoid it, still do and will continue to do so. Jožo, Jožo! You don't understand living. You talk to me as if I were some little kid. It's a good thing you didn't tell me everything's unfreedom, bondage, slavery – the way we learned these words at school. The only way to live today is to let oneself be denounced – or to denounce others. For a time that rids us of the uncertainty that's so terrifying. You don't understand life, Jožo." Jozef Mitúch sat on the green sofa and looked in horror at his former classmate, Gizela. She used to sit next to him in a tight brown skirt and yellow jumper with a red stripe across her chest. At grammar school he'd rarely found the courage to speak to her – at the time the so fragile daughter of a judge. After their final school exams they'd gone their separate ways. As a student, when doing his military service and during the war, he'd forgotten all about her. "Is that why," he asked her, "you had Dietbert here?" – "Exactly." Her pretty wet teeth gleamed between her red lips. "That's why I had him, and others besides, Vogel, Bürster, plenty of them. It's why I've got you here too. And you just count your blessings, Jožo. You should be thankful you're here and that the Germans haven't sent for you. You've only got me to thank for your being here." After which they just looked at each other in silence. Mitúch, with all that had previously constituted his life shaken to its foundations, was wondering whether Gizela had managed to kill off her own conscience, and Gizela – she of the long white neck, white oval face, heart-shaped lips, blue eyes – was, out of fear for Mitúch's wellbeing, claiming victory over her own and his common sense. She tossed her head back. "Are you really capable of all that, Gizzie?" he asked. "That's none of your business, Jožo! Just don't hold it against me! It's who I've become. Nothing will change that." She rubbed one leg against the other. "Are you in love with me and is that what's making you angry? That's not good. Don't go thinking you have any claim on me! People today mustn't make demands of themselves, let alone of others. We don't know what's round the corner." She slipped off one of her shoes, leant against Mitúch and with her foot put out the light, a small lamp with a thick paper shade, on which ancient brown sailing ships, barques, brigs and cogs, seesawed amid blue waves. After a moment she used her foot to switch it on again. She was lying on the sofa. Mitúch stared dumbly into her eyes, which, as ever, meant less to repel than to beguile. "I don't trust you, Gizzie." Gizela Gábor said nothing, she merely smiled, and in that smile Jozef Mitúch discerned the abyss that had opened up beneath him, having seen that Gizela's oval face, her curvaceous body and her hair combed back behind her ears were all more beguiling than repelling, and Gizela was most beguiling thanks to the sheer awfulness with which she had presented herself to him. She steered one bare leg, velvety white and shapely, along the green sofa, letting her toes seek out the switch on the little lamp, which she switched off, and the ancient brown sailing ships on its shade stopped seesawing amid the blue waves, and at that moment Mitúch and Gizela were bathed in such savage rapture that all their misgivings, fears, conscience and common sense were driven away – Mitúch was bathed in the savage rapture of taking charge of Gizela Gábor's awfulness, and Gizela in the rapture of being temporarily safe from partisans. That night Mitúch failed to make it home from Gizela's, staying on for another two days and two nights, and thereafter he came to see her every evening until Oberleutnant Walter Schrimm turned up in Molčany with his troopers.

"So, Herr Ingenieur!"

Mitúch stared into the dark corner, believing now in one thing only, namely that the confusion that he and the partisans had stirred up in Molčany would be the death of Oberleutnant Schrimm and of Gizela.

Schrimm was staring at Mitúch's broad back. At the first opportunity he'd kill him, he suddenly thought, and he'd have all other civilians killed once he had no further need of them as protection for his retreating troops against partisans and Russians. He should have done that long ago! He should have passed them over to units of the SD! But... At that point Schrimm got a glimpse of the ghastly future that awaited him. Until the war ended, until he got back to Stargard, even he would become a murderer personally, his life would be in the same jeopardy as the rest of Hitler's murderers – they had believed his madness, believed in his grand idea – and whoever had so believed was like a member of the SS, and was like him, Schrimm, scared for their own life. That bitch Gizela! He looked away from Mitúch's broad back and flew into a rage because his men had rounded up the first batch of civilians and hounded them into the school, but only five men and three boys, among them Šimko's errand boy, Skittle.

Skittle, a small, dark-complexioned youth wearing filthy breeches fastened above his boots, and a check shirt with holes in it at the back, entered the school and at once smirked viciously at the sight of Mitúch standing in one corner with two soldiers next to him. Serve you right! So glad they've got you here too! He cursed him and he cursed himself and the moment when he'd first spoken to him.

That had been in the middle of January, when he'd gone to the Mitúchs' to sharpen his shredder blades on their electric grinder, and when, just as a joke, he'd said: "The Stahl estate's about to get a new landowner. Mr Mitúch, here, the engineer. Right?" Jozef Mitúch had said nothing. Beta, however, had responded: "Hm, and the whole village keeps winding us up over it." That had so irked Jozef Mitúch that a few days later he'd sent Adam's son Janko to Skittle with some cigarettes as a sweetener, to get him to stop him peddling gossip about him. And a couple of days after that Skittle had crowed to Mitúch: "If only you knew, sir, who smoked those hundred cigarettes..." – "Who?" – "Partisans," he said. – "Where?" – "Up on Úplazy!" After that they'd come to terms and, despite Beta's periodically kicking up a fuss about it, Adam Mitúch had given in and Skittle began paying regular visits to the Mitúchs to pick up the bread, bacon, lard and cigarettes that Jozef got from Gizela Gábor, and take it all to the parish odd-job man, Porubský.

In the school, Skittle was standing by the wall, thinking about Mitúch and about how he himself might give the Germans the slip.

"Bring the civilians in!"

"Yessir, Herr Oberleutnant, sir!"

"I need ninety civilians!" he bellowed as the anger surged inside him and with it an impulsive craving to have his revenge for Gizela, the horses, the bridge that had been destroyed, the concrete blocks that had been toppled, for Follen, Willich and Kalkbrenner, for Rottenführer Kolping and his squad. "Civilians – lots of 'em – ninety –" Schrimm hollered at his subordinates and the troopers, "– lots, not just a handful like these!"

"Yes, sir!"

"Stop the search for wagons and teams of horses! Find Kalkbrenner! And civilians – not just a handful like this, these won't use up so much as – as – a single revolver!"

"Yessir, Herr Oberleutnant, sir!"

The school fell silent, the candle flames flickered, and from outside came the heart-rending lowing of cattle. Oberleutnant Schrimm turned to see Mitúch and his broad back. Hang him! He cast a glance at Skittle. Hang the lot of 'em!

The livestock bellowed in chorus, one voice, two, many all at once.

At that point Schrimm suddenly felt a bit silly for requiring people like the ones they'd brought into the school as some kind of protection. He considered waiting till five for Gizela and then he'd make his escape with whatever soldiers happened to be there at the time! He'd escape with Gizela and her valuables – or stay put. He ought to kill her, plunder her stuff –!

Time was flying.

The minute hand on Schrimm's watch was ticking round fast. Seven minutes to five – six minutes to – five to! Kolping hasn't returned, he's copped it, Kolping, the Rottenführer, the road from the partisan villages is open to the partisans, to the Russians, the road to Račany and Čermanská Lehota is closed to him and his men, no sign of Gizela, maybe Gemert's killed her somewhere and stolen... At that point Schrimm's legs started to quake.

"Gefreiter!"

The little lance-corporal stiffened.

"Get me," Schrimm bellowed, "get hold of all lieutenants and NCOs down to the rank of sergeant!"

The lance-corporal turned and left the school running.

Five to five.

Five o'clock came, Gizela hadn't returned, out in the school yard the lowing of the starving cattle was heart-rending, the large windows in the school room were vibrating with the distant shellfire, Mitúch was on edge in the corner, Schrimm was on edge at the table, Skittle was cursing next to the wall, cursing Mitúch, Schrimm's chest had started perspiring, he took his pistol from its holster, examined it, slipped it back in the holster, and wiped his sweaty hands on the table top.

Molčany was on edge, it was having a terrible time.

Five o'clock came.

Schrimm, seated at the table, stared ahead of him and saw nothing. It hurt him badly that he was losing everything, that he'd even lost Gizela, and he was overcome with self-pity for having suspected her and for having mentally cursed her. She won't be coming back now – Kolping hasn't come back – Gemert hasn't come back... He's stolen her stuff, perhaps killed her... Schrimm was succumbing to the force that had destroyed the sentries Follen and Willich, Kalkbrenner, Gemert and Gizela, Rottenführer Kolping and his men, the force that held everything in its embrace. Nothing makes sense anymore, it's the same thing over and over again, every hundred, fifty, twenty kilometres... The force that had driven the regimental HQ out of Rakytovce was now pressing down on Schrimm like some cold, thick oil.

He stood up.

Some soldiers herded three civilians into the school.

Two lieutenants came in, stood to attention, NCOs began arriving and standing to attention, and Schrimm looked at them. We shall put up a fight," he wanted to say, "we have to, a German soldier..." He looked at the pale-faced men, standing rigidly to attention.

"Wait here!"

(228)

Time was flying, with Schrimm still waiting for Gizela.

The clouds in the sky broke up and Molčany was in for a nice day. The clear sky, a coolness in the air, a delicate pale green on the trees and fields. High in the sky, almost at its mid-point, one cloud left, all feathery as if shaped into tassels by some giant comb. Its tassels were ignited from below by the red fire of the approaching sun. The air was fresh and fragrant.

Adam Mitúch had driven his horses slowly to Barren Grove, the long beech wood that extended almost as far as Molčany parish boundary.

From one side of Barren Grove you could see the fields of Molčany, from the other the fields and meadows of the neighbouring parishes, Račany and Čermanská Lehota.

He drove his horses into a dip, fed them some dried clover, treating himself to a bacon sandwich, and as he ate he walked back up to see what was happening on the side where lay Račany and Čermanská Lehota.

Railway sleepers were no longer being shattered.

He looked down onto the road from Račany to Čermanská Lehota and the road to Rakytovce. Both deserted and forlorn, with no sign of life. Now and again he caught the sound of machine gun fire, and of submachine guns and rifles. After a short while, five tanks passed along the road to Rakytovce. "Aye aye, the Krauts aren't going to escape from Molčany now," he told himself out loud, "they're going to have to surrender." At that very moment a whizzing bullet took out an oak twig right above his head. He rejoined his horses.

He raised his arms, with the bacon, bread and knife still in his hands, above his head, because his handsome black horses were being admired by six men wearing top boots covered in mud and dust, thick, grey, padded army dress, short capes randomly decorated in green, brown and grey, and fur caps. He stopped, slowly lowered his raised arms and smiled at them.

"*Davay, davay,*" they called out to him. "*Davay!*"

Adam Mitúch gulped down his mouthful of bread and bacon and approached the soldiers.

"*Zdravstvuy, khazyay!*"

He had no idea what to say, switched the knife, bread and bacon to his left hand, and offered his large, work-worn right hand to the nearest of the soldiers.

"Welcome, comrades!"

He shook hands with the rest of them.

He walked back over to his wagon, took the bread and bacon out of the bag and handed it to the soldiers, along with the knife.

They began slicing and eating.

They were talking fast among themselves and although Mitúch had heard long ago, from men who had served during the Great War, that it's easy for another Slav to converse with Russians, he wasn't understanding a word they said.

After a time, one of the soldiers pointed to the horses.

"*Kakiye loshadi?*" he asked. "*Pad vyerkh, pad vyerkh?*"

Mitúch took a bite of his bread. He was thinking. He had no idea they were asking if they were saddle horses.

"*Pad vyerkh?*"

"Up there, *pod vrch*, up the hill?" he asked, "to Rakytovce? That's where Rakytovce is."

"*Da, da,*" said another soldier. "Rakytovce?"

He took out a map, turned it round and looked. "*Davay, khazyay, v Rakytovce!*"

Mitúch understood.

The soldiers waited while he offloaded the harrow, clambered up onto the wagon and Mitúch shoved his bit of bacon sandwich in his pocket and started to drive.

"*Davay, davaj! Gani, gani!*" they began shouting at him. "*Gani, gani!*"

Back in Molčany, Mitúch's house was deserted. Starving cattle began lowing in the stable, while a pig began to squeal in the sty, and in the small back room, on a chair next to the bed, sat old, deaf Mrs Mitúch. With her wrinkled features, distorted by weeping, and her tear-filled eyes she was looking at the lines, printed in large bold letters, of a book, "– and if such be not Thy divine will, grant them knowledge through this great devastation ..." She suddenly looked up from her lines at the German troopers who'd come charging into the room. She gazed at them with sunken eyes, out of which gaped the ruthless chasm of years and old age, an implacable immobility, and animosity towards Adam and Jozef, her daughter-in-law Beta and her children for having left her in the house alone.

"Haben sie was zu essen?" the sergeant roared at her. "Speck?"

She hadn't heard. "You wait!" She turned her unforgiving and implacable eyes towards him. "You just wait, the Russians are coming!"

"Was, du altes Luder?"

"The Russians are coming!"

The cold air started to pulsate to the drone of aeroplanes.

The sergeant booted the old lady's book from her hands and went outside with the men. With eyes filled with fury he glanced at the soldiers as they abandoned him in favour of the shelter of the Mitúchs' shed.

The air wavered to the sudden, sharp drone that had descended on the Mitúchs' homestead like a deluge of death and now drove the sergeant to seek shelter behind his men inside the shed.

The droning of the planes descended once more into the Mitúchs' yard and garden, and onto Petrová, the chase on the far side of the sunken lane beyond the garden. Adam's wife Beta and her children cowered down into the mud and water of the trench. She drew the dark-grey and pale-green shawls across the children.

The air shuddered with the clatter of machine guns, two explosions rang out and echoed, the ground shook, and following a deep silence during which Beta's mind was a total blank, the droning of planes came back, machine guns chattered in the air and bullets showered the Mitúchs' smashed-up shed and barn, slicing right through the cowshed and the already dead cow inside it.

The droning of planes ceased, then came back, two explosions hit the village, followed by a crackling sound, then all fell silent and before long Beta's ears were assailed by the heart-rending lowing of the starving and now frightened cattle.

Molčany remained deserted and forlorn. People were hiding in houses, outdoor larders and cellars. Outside the school, which no longer housed Schrimm's command post, or Mitúch, the engineer, or the eleven local civilians that the soldiers had manage to drum up instead of the ninety required, there were three heaps consisting of the shattered remains of four ramshackle carts and four pairs of dead horses. The mayor's handsome bays had also been killed. Cattle lowed, but otherwise there was no sign of movement, only slowly, very slowly, minutes passed, supplementing the complement of past years, months, weeks, days and hours.

It was almost half past five.

With its old, hoarse voice, the clock on the church tower struck a single note to a background of lowing cattle. That was its last stroke, its terminal voice, because a moment later, two minutes later, a shell exploded with a boom, in another moment another, and the top of the church spire, including the clock, flew into smithereens, bits landing on the reawakening spring grass around the church, on the rectory roof and in the rectory orchard among the serried rows of plum trees, long neglected and covered in a dense growth of lichen. One part of the clock's mechanism was left dangling from a plum tree, with it the dial, which continued to show five thirty-two.

At the Mitúch house the doors were wide open and the windows had no glass in them, because it had all fallen out that instant when death had descended on the German sergeant and his men.

Old Mrs Mitúch was sitting on a chair next to the bed, her hands folded in her lap, old sallow-skinned hands that time had interlaced with endless blue veins. She had turned her eyes, sunken, unforgiving, implacable, motionless and hate-filled vacant chasms of old age, towards the open door, because a huge shadow had flitted by it.

In the doorway stood a man so tall that he had to hunch down, though he still looked as if he were propping up the lintel. He was wearing a peaked forage cap and a motley cape with random blotches of green and brown that hung half-way down his top boots, and he was holding a long weapon, a light machine gun with a drum magazine.

"Are you the Russian?"

"*Da, babushka.*"

Although she'd heard nothing, a faint smile made its way out of the abyss of old, deaf Mrs Mitúch's eyes. "You wait, the Kraut's coming!"

"*Aaaa! Nichevo neboysya, babushka!*" He held his gun more upright so as to be able to enter the room. He entered, and when old Mrs Mitúch saw he was laughing and saying something she smiled back, even despite the tears that were flooding her eyes.

He bent down, picked her book up, placed it in her hands and with a smile on his lusty face went outside.

The Mitúchs' yard and others round about began slowly filling with the Soviet soldiers who'd come into Molčany from the villages in the foothills, Lipník and Greater and Lesser Hámre.

Any German soldiers left behind in Molčany were no longer trying to escape, but merely switching hiding places from one house to another, and if all else failed, they put up a fight.

Gunfire crackled in waves coming from rifles, machine guns and submachine guns, exploding grenades boomed, there were brief moments of total silence followed by isolated, solitary gunshots and detonations, then more waves of crackling.

The commander of the Molčany garrison, Oberleutnant Walter Schrimm was in flight from Molčany along with his officers, NCOs and troopers. He had already reached Monk's Lea and the sunken lane that cut across the parish lands and led towards Rakytovce through pine and beech woods. Four

German soldiers headed the rush along the sunken lane, overgrown at its edges with fresh grass and the odd bullace, hawthorn and brier, followed by Jozef Mitúch and behind him Oberleutnant Walter Schrimm. Behind Schrimm came two troopers, behind them the men and boys of Molčany, including Skittle, and last came some fifty troopers plus two lieutenants and the NCOs. Nobody had deployed them in that order, it was just the way it had turned out as they had fled from the school.

Schrimm feared nothing and regretted nothing, his sole concern being for himself and for a successful onward flight towards peacetime, towards which he would happily shoot his way if possible. There could be no thought now of retreating from Molčany, only escaping. He didn't care about the lean and mangy Styrian horses, or about the carts with the big thin wheels, or the equipment loaded onto them, he didn't care about the twenty head of lowing cattle left behind in the school yard. He didn't care about his own men, who, here and there and not being under orders, had put up a fight or surrendered. He'd seen the like before. He pressed on behind Mitúch, quite calm after the confusion in Molčany, and he knew what he was going to do. In due course, he would line up Mitúch and the civilians in a different order, and once he had no further need of them as protection for himself and his men against the Russians, he'd have them all shot. Although he couldn't shoot all of life away, he did mean to do this because killing can sometimes be like pouring oneself a nice glass of good wine. He should have dealt with the population of Molčany in that way long before, but he hadn't. His HQ had fled – possibly with Gizela... Maybe she was waiting for him... Maybe nothing had happened to her... He hurried on, sometimes breaking into a run, and sweat streamed down his back.

From the sunken lane they were in they could hear, coming from Molčany, waves of gunfire and isolated shots and explosions.

"*Davay, davay!*" shouted the six Soviet soldiers on the wagon behind Adam Mitúch. "*Khazyay, gani, gani, bystro gani!*"

Mitúch was driving his horses hard along the sunken lane towards Rakytovce, quite undaunted by all the gunfire and explosions coming from Molčany, he just charged on, his eyes fixed on the gasping, steaming, perspiring horses ahead of him.

"*Davay, davaj, gani, gani!*"

The German Unteroffizier Wojkowitz, the one who'd spat on Beta Mitúch's smallest child, Amálka, had made his escape from Molčany by zigzagging through the houses, and, without his cap, rifle in hand and his face covered in mud, he'd taken the sunken lane to Petrová chase, lain down in a wet field, waited a moment to exhale his fatigue, then looked behind him and spotted a trench. He crawled across to it, the trench where Beta and her four children were crouched down in the mud and water.

A droning made by aeroplanes was approaching.

"Eek!" Beta squeaked quietly as Unteroffizier Wojkowitz swung his legs into the trench. She held tight to the wet and crumbling side of the trench. "Oh, my God, the children!"

"Ruhe!" Wojkowitz squeezed back into one corner. "Ruhe!"

Wild-eyed, he stared at Beta, who – with the children behind her – was standing only one pace from him as he grinned at her with his white and yellow false teeth, long and narrow, wet and slimy with saliva, breathing through his grimy mouth from which saliva dribbled each time he breathed out. Beta Mitúch held tight to the sides of the trench, pressing her fingertips into the wet clay, which came crumbling down.

Flying low over Molčany and Petrová chase, two planes passed overhead.

Gunfire was crackling in the village.

The planes came back over Petrová.

"Sie kommen!" Wojkowitz lay down inside the trench, squeezing himself beneath the feet of Beta and the children so as to be hidden from the planes, which he knew were on the lookout for even one single German soldier. From down on the ground came "Gut, gut!"

The planes began circling over the chase and the trench, the piercing whine of the engines spiralling down into the trench wave after wave, they then flew upwards, tilted and dropped back down.

Beta, with the children clinging tight to her, saw them through her tears as terrifying birds, dark and rabid, and all that dwelt within her, heart, lungs and blood, rose up in an entreaty that sprang from her helplessness in the face of that circling of death. She saw long, sharp flames start to spout from one plane. The trench was covered in chattering waves of the planes' machine guns firing. She sank her hands into the clay and in her unspoken prayer to the planes she cursed Jozef Mitúch, the engineer. Kill *him*! Not us! She clung tight to the clay.

Unteroffizier Wojkowitz, who was lying beneath Beta and her children, lay with his face in the mud, thinking of nothing, desiring nothing, with but one thing oppressing his hag-ridden brain.

When hotfooting it away from a small town they'd razed and burned a year earlier, he and his men had taken a road that was all carved up. Here and there the town was still burning. Outside the town, following the road, wooden poles and on them power lines. The poles slashed down to the height of a man, because the Germans had destroyed them before they retreated. The poles were dangling from wires or lying, wires and all, on the ground. The remnants of the poles still standing – and Wojkowitz put them at about a hundred and fifty – were decked with children. Each pole had three children wired to it through their wrists. Children – dead – drooping down into the mud next to the poles, others hanging by their hands at an angle towards the ground. "These kids will be the death of us," a friend had told him at the time, "we shouldn't have done this!" – "Why not?" Wojkowitz had asked him. "Why does it bother you?" – "It's cowardly." – "Not really – cowardice is something else, this shows courage!" The road was deserted, the children tied up and hanging down towards it –

Wojkowitz lay there in the trench underneath the Mitúch children and Beta, pressing his head down into the mud, his hag-ridden brain now tormented by one thing only, that he would probably never again see... In the mud of the trench, he fished out a photo of a little girl in a featherlight white dress, the girl in the photo was three years old, and smiling –

The planes cut up the ground around the trench with a line of bullets, also cutting into the trench, after which they no longer flew back over Petrová chase.

At Monk's Lea Jozef Mitúch was getting closer, along the sunken lane, to the pine wood that had sprung up over the gully-eroded earth. It's about two hours on foot from here to Úplazy, he reckoned. How about turning off to Úplazy with them, to Porubský? The partisans were sure to have gone back there after destroying the bridge and blocking the road. He was aghast at his mad idea: seven partisans, hopelessly outnumbered by so many Germans! He was walking ahead of Schrimm, deaf to the words that Schrimm kept repeating: "Faster, faster!" Deaf now to anything at all.

They were approaching a crossroads.

Two aeroplanes flew past over their heads.

Schrimm and his men jumped sideways and leaned hard against the edges of the sunken lane rising above the trench.

The planes came back over the sunken lane.

Mitúch broke into a run.

"Come on, lads, let's run!" Skittle yelled at the top of his voice. He scrambled out of the sunken lane. "Let's make a run for it!" Thorn bushes grabbed at his legs and a bullet from Schrimm's revolver shot a hole through his back. With his legs caught in the bushes he collapsed, his head pointing towards the sunken lane.

"Down on the ground!" Schrimm bellowed after the fleeing Mitúch and fired a shot. "Get down!"

"Nieder!" roared the soldiers after the fleeing civilians from Molčany. "Nieder! Volle Deckung!"

Searing flames began shooting forth from the planes, bullets pounded the sunken lane, four shells exploded amid Schrimm's fleeing troopers, and once all had gone silent, two injured men were howling there.

Four Molčany men, three boys out of the eleven Molčany civilians and Mitúch made a dash for it, running across the fields towards the pine forest.

The planes came back over the sunken lane and carved it up with machine-gun fire.

Jozef Mitúch and two of the Molčany men, Kubica and Benko, made it into the pine forest.

The gunfire in Molčany fell silent, the last few random rifle shots and a few random grenades gave way to silence.

At Petrová chase, three Soviet soldiers came to a halt above the trench.

"*Vychadi!*" one of them said to Beta Mitúch, beckoning. "*Vychodite!*"

Beta Mitúch was shaking with fear for her crying children and for herself, unable to move, afraid of seeing them kill the German, and that the children would also see it, she stared numbly up out of the trench with her grey eyes at the three tall soldiers standing there above her and bidding her to come up out of the ground.

"*Vychadi!*"

"I don't have the strength – and I can't – there's a German here!"

"*Vychadi!*"

"There's a German here," she pleaded, "don't kill him!"

"*Davay, vychadi!*"

The soldier bent down and hauled Amálka out of the trench by her arms. He looked into her ice-cold features, especially her red cheeks. He bent down and spotted the German soldier in the trench.

"Ááá, German –!"

The other soldiers gathered by the trench.

"No – please – don't kill him –!"

The soldier plucked all four of Beta Mitúch's children out of the trench.

"*Vychadi!*" he shouted at Beta with an angry shake of his head. "*Davay, vychadi!*"

Then he looked briefly at the German Unteroffizier, who was lying there in the water and mud, face down, with his mud-coated head on his hands. In his fair hair, wet and coated in mud, there was a red hole. The mud round his head had a suffusion of pink foam, even the photograph was pink.

"*Myortvy, ubit. Davay!*"

Beta Mitúch retrieved her woollen shawls from the trench, rose up out of the ground and, with a profound sense of relief in which her mental cursing of Jozef Mitúch began to fade away, she set off on sluggish legs with her two eldest children, horrified every second that she and the children had been so close to death; ahead of her went one of the soldiers and behind her two, carrying her little girls. They dropped down into the sunken lane and then crossed the broken fence into the garden. They entered the yard. Beta Mitúch burst into uncontrollable tears at the sight of her shattered barn and shed, the fragments of dead Germans and her peaceful homestead.

Old Mrs Mitúch was standing outside the kitchen door. "God be praised, children, Beta!"

The older children ran up to her, and the soldiers having set the little ones down, they also ran up to her.

"Don't cry, Betka!" said the old lady. Then she looked towards the laughing soldiers and asked: "And the German's not coming back?"

The children's cries drowned out the laughing soldiers. "No, Gran! The German's lying in the trench."

The soldiers in the Mitúchs' yard laughed more and more.

"But where are those poor chaps?" she asked. "Adam and Jožko and that...?" Old Mrs Mitúch cast a fearful glance at the soldiers.

In the stable the cattle started lowing again, and in the sty the sow and her family began to squeal.

Beta ran across to the stable.

It was close on six o'clock.

Adam Mitúch, engineer Jozef's brother, was driving his team slowly towards Rakytovce, where he'd taken the six Soviet soldiers. He was approaching the crossroads at Monk's Lea. He was taking it slowly and quietly, with his eyes on the horses, whose coats were not shining in the golden sunlight blazing across from the horizon because they were caked in lather. He wasn't speaking despite the fact that next to him on the plank, with her back to the horses, sat Gizela Gábor. He was thinking about her, how she'd stepped out in front of him near Rakytovce, frightened, shaking, and how she'd begged him to take her to Račany. As a girl she must have been pretty. Even now she's pretty, the bitch! He thought with envy of his brother, the engineer, who'd known her ever since grammar school.

They were getting closer the crossroads.

The horses started to snort, then pulled up.

Mitúch looked ahead, stood up and pointed with his whip. "What's that over there?"

The road beyond the crossroads was green with German uniforms and Caesar, the Mitúchs' black stray dog, was licking at some red blood.

Mitúch shuddered.

"We have to turn round, Mrs Gábor," he said to Gizela after a short pause. "Look!"

Gizela Gábor stood up, turned round and looked ahead. "But when," she began, her voice quavering, "when will we get to Račany, Mr Mitúch? Please, just keep going. What do I care about them! The Germans are swine! I'm terribly afraid of being on my own, I'm quite worn out, and I'm so scared. There are Germans scattered all over the place, and Russians... Do keep going –!"

Mitúch looked at Gizela, at her pale frightened face. "What?"

"Just keep going, I'll give you a watch –!"

"Now, now, Mrs Gábor," he said, "look – even my horses aren't going to get through that lot. So you can get off my wagon!"

"Mr Mitúch –!"

"Did you hear me?"

Mitúch's horses started snorting again. Caesar was licking blood.

"Get off my wagon, and now!"

Gizela Gábor got down from the wagon.

Mitúch turned off with his team onto a side track away from the dead Germans, away from dead Skittle and the two men from Molčany. He lashed at the horses and headed off with his wagon, making a great detour, to Barren Grove, where he'd left his harrow.

Gizela Gábor stood at the crossroads gazing helplessly after Mitúch.

"Worse than that swine!"

All sweaty in her large, yellow fox fur, weighed down with her watches, rings and bracelets, once the property of the Stahls, from whom she'd coaxed them on the pretext of hiding them somewhere, she now skirted the track where the dead men lay. She had her hands in her pockets, no longer carrying her small but solid suitcase, because Karl Gemert, the bookseller, had yanked it from her grip before they reached Rakytovce and booted her out of his car. She walked on, fatigued and frightened. "You can't stay here," Schrimm's words rang inside her head, "here you'd either perish or certainly not live like a human being! Gizela-Gazella." She hadn't perished – though she might perish yet... She looked back at the dead men in the deep sunken lane and was slightly shaken by the almost drunken eyes with which the Mitúchs' Caesar was staring at her.

The Molčany men, Kubica and Benko, who'd managed to escape from Schrimm's men at Monk's Lea, now lay hidden in the pine forest among some dense thorn bushes growing under the roots of one tree, from beneath which the soil had slipped into a deep gulley, and were gradually exhaling their fear. Sweat was still dripping from them and they were shaking.

"I wonder if anyone was left behind in the lane," Jozef Mitúch pondered aloud. "I do wonder, can they all have escaped? Unlikely."

Kubica and Benko said nothing. All three just breathed silently in and out until Mitúch suggested they go with him to Úplazy.

"Why?" asked Benko, the hall porter on the Stahl estate. "What'll we do there? Let's just wait awhile and then head slowly home. Who knows what's gone on there! We have to restore some order to the village. Like we wanted to do in August."

"But do come with me. We can tell Porubský –"

"Porubský's there?" asked Kubica, the Stahls' coachman. "I thought he'd been done for ages ago."

"Why d'you put it like that? After all, Porubský –"

"Never mind!" said Kubica, who was afraid of Porubský and remembered how he'd sent Porubský packing when he'd come to get him to join the partisans. "I don't like his sort!"

"Why not?"

"Because! I'm sure he was the one as killed Gábor – who he shouldn't have, he should have done for his missus, 'cos she's a –"

"So you're not coming?" Mitúch asked the pair. "I'm off."

"There's no point anyway, Porubský won't be there now."

Mitúch left them, running.

They gazed after him, at his brown tracksuit and the bloodied arm that he still had bound up with a blue handkerchief.

Far from wanting to go up to Úplazy, Kubica and Benko just wanted to get back home and keep telling people how ghastly it had all been, that not much had happened, only Mitúch got that arm injury.

They got to their feet and headed out of the forest into open country.

By this time, minutes in Molčany were no longer precious. The living who'd been in hiding all over the place surfaced from cellars, outdoor larders and houses, from trenches, returning home from field and forest, the late Skittle and the two men were lying in a deep sunken lane at Monk's Lea, this side of the pine forest. The Germans were gone. Those captured were being held in the school, dead ones were scattered about the village, in what was left of the Mitúchs' shed and at Monk's Lea. Also lying there was the commander of the last German garrison at Molčany, Oberleutnant Walter Schrimm. His right hand clutched the pistol with which he'd shot the fleeing Skittle and then fired at Jozef Mitúch, the engineer, and his back had two bullet holes in it. His large new forage cap lay a step away from his head.

In Molčany, minutes were no longer precious, but precious they were, very precious, up at Úplazy, outside the partisans' bunker, where the twittering birds had been joined by a song thrush. And precious they were for the German soldier Kurt Kalkbrenner, who'd been captured by the partisans Hriška and Stanko, dressed in old clothes in an anti-tank trench not far from the Stahl brickworks.

Kalkbrenner was lying on the ground, his hands bound with his narrow trouser belt, watching the four partisans with his bright green eyes, hardened with a reproach he had nobody to utter to. He took even old Porubský to be a partisan.

After seven o'clock young Porubský, Zubák, Mezej and Mikuláš also turned up on Úplazy, the latter two bearing the rifles of the two German sentries, Follen and Willich, whom they'd killed by the bridge leading to Čermanská Lehota. They were all covered in soil and mud, Porubský being soaked almost up to the waist.

"What's this...?" he asked huskily. "Who's this?"

He pointed his rifle at Kalkbrenner, whose hands were bound as he lay on the ground. Next to him, lying where it had been dumped, was his black satchel and the German uniform taken from it.

"Who's this?" He threw the rifle taken from the German sentry at his legs. "Who've you got here?"

"Ask him," said Hriška, laughing. "He'll tell you."

"Where'd he get that peasant outfit?" Porubský asked. "He shoulda changed into the kind o' clobber we wear round 'ere!"

The men standing over Kalkbrenner all burst out laughing.

Kalkbrenner lay on the ground, his arms ached beneath the narrow trouser belt and he looked up at the eight men standing in a semi-circle above him.

The little chap, the parish odd-job man Porubský, looked uncomprehending from Kalkbrenner to his own son Mišo, whose grimy cheeks had turned red with the effort of coming up to Úplazy, cheeks with the prominent cheekbones he'd inherited from his father. This one isn't going to do them any more harm! he thought to himself. Why do they need to torment him? Uneasily, old Porubský was smoking his stubby, curly pipe.

The other seven men, impatience readable in their eyes, looked down at the prostrate Kalkbrenner.

What Kalkbrenner read in their eyes was a terrible desire. You want to kill me so you can get back to Molčany as soon as possible and make merry. In the torpor that brought only sporadic moments of clarity into his thought processes, he scoured his past life for things for which he was blameworthy and which might be the cause of his present predicament. He found nothing either up to thirty-eight, when he had enlisted, or in the years that followed, during which, as a soldier, he had been across France and the Soviet Union as far as Karachev. German troops, he thought, as he saw the young men above him making their own plans without reference to any superior officer, wherever German troops came, they tortured and destroyed. People cannot carry on being bastards for long, however much they might enjoy it, but what can one man do to oppose it? Even what he had done in Molčany was pointless and perhaps detrimental. Maybe Jozef Mitúch, the engineer, was also dead by now. Kalkbrenner lay there, his mouth dry, and he wanted to shout out. He didn't know what, because he'd already told everything to Hriška and Stanko, who'd driven him up to Úplavy.

"He's a German partisan," said Hriška, scratching his incurved nose. "I bet the Germans also leave partisans behind them."

The others nodded.

"Don't be silly!" Porubský berated them. "If he was, he'd have worn our sort of clothes."

"That's the very point, Dad," young Mišo Porubský retorted. "If he were wearing our sort of clothes, it would look as if he was trying to hide and have done with the war. But in these peasant clothes...? Goodness knows where he sprang from! And then he *is* German!"

Porubský the partisan pointed his submachine gun at him.

"Ich," Kalkbrenner said to the partisan Porubský, "hab' dem Ingenieur Midach den Sprengstoff gegeben – Dynamit, Ekrasit – und deshalb die Brücke –"

Pavela, Hřiska and Stanko burst out laughing again, far from the first time since that morning.

"He keeps saying," said Hriška, "that he's an engineer and he's got dynamite and ekrasite. We've already searched him, shaken his uniform out, and he hasn't."

The eight men stood over Kalkbrenner.

"Mišo!"

The partisan Porubský looked at his father.

"And suppose he's come a long way like this to follow his army home?"

"Ach –!"

"But he doesn't have any weapon!"

"Dumped it somewhere – I don't trust him."

The sun was over the horizon now, against a clear sky, lighting up the backs of the eight men on Úplazy and offering some pleasant warmth after a cold night. The damp black earth smelled nice, as did the forest, waking up to a new day with all its tiny pale-green buds. To the west and north the earth juddered with gunfire, near and far, because it had already passed beyond Molčany. The twittering of small birds was invaded by the high-pitched melody of a song thrush.

"Get yourself over there, Dad!" said partisan Porubský to his father, pointing to a spot behind some rocks covered in moss, ivy and grey lichen – they were above the partisans' bunker. "So you don't have to watch."

"Watch what?" old Porubský asked, taking his stubby, curly pipe from between his lips. "What am I not supposed to watch?"

Zubák pointed his submachine gun at Kalkbrenner.

"You mean you're going to kill him?"

"So what –?"

"That's not within your rights, lads!" he told them brusquely. "Who do you think you are? Dealing with the Germans is now down to the Russian army alone, not you. Only the Russians have actually fought the Germans. What have you done? Not much. Apart from getting in their way a bit. Don't you dare kill him! I'll report you at once. And it wouldn't be very nice of you anyway. What's he done to you? You don't know who he is. And me, look at me, I couldn't even shoot a stag when it was lying down. I've always thought it degrading to shoot at any quiet living thing."

His son Mišo looked rather abashed, as did the other six men, who stood a while longer over Kalkbrenner, staring down at him. Then anger and exasperation at old Porubský began to get the upper hand.

At that moment Kalkbrenner wanted to shout, to get Jozef Mitúch to come to his aid, but that struck him as utterly ludicrous. Why shout for him if he was no more? Not even this lot were really to blame... Kalkbrenner suddenly recalled the long deep ditch that he'd seen in a wood in Russia, the people in the ditch all shot, the soldiers shovelling soil on top of them – and here and there one, only wounded, had stirred, tried to rise and get away from the dead and the soil. They were like him... And Kurt Kalkbrenner, lying on the ground and staring at the semi-circle of men, started mentally cursing himself for having come through the war blameless and also cursing the men standing over him. Be as you are – like us – don't trust one another or anyone else, keep an eye on one another, steer clear of one another out of fear, disparage one another, demean one another, haul one another away from towns and villages, exterminate one another, and there's just one thing I wish for you, that you'd feel good about it for a long time and that you'd kill off your own selves – terrible things await you... Kalkbrenner lay on the ground in silence, shivering with the cold that was passing from the ground into his back.

"Let's go down to the village. Lord knows what's gone on there!" Old Porubský looked from one partisan to the next. "We can take him with us. Down past Dead Fallow, it's shorter that way."

After a pause young Porubský agreed and once Kalkbrenner had donned his uniform they left with him for Molčany.

Jozef Mitúch was hurrying to Úplazy. He wanted to meet up with the partisans and tell them what was what, tell them that a German, one Kurt Kalkbrenner, had been billeted with them. He was in hiding somewhere, but he'd show up and was going to need help. In Molčany, the word of partisans would count. Their word would be that Kalkbrenner was not to be harmed by anyone – and something also needed to be done about Gizela Gábor, because she will certainly have done a runner. It would be tricky, but... Mitúch hurried on up towards Úplazy, he wanted to welcome the partisans back and rejoice with them that there were no Germans left in Molčany, except for the dead and those held captive. He had a bullet hole above his right wrist, bound tight with a blue handkerchief to stem the bleeding, though he'd actually lost very little blood.

He wished he was up there, on Úplazy, bringing the partisans the good news: You can head home now! Then he meant to rush home himself, to see his mother, his brother, his brother's kids and his wife Beta, then wait for Kurt Kalkbrenner to appear. Kurt Kalkbrenner, a very odd German soldier who wanted to see the war out in Molčany. He was bound to drift back from somewhere. There was no knowing where he'd been hiding. They hadn't had time to fix anything. But it wouldn't have been in the liquid manure under the decking in the cowshed, as he'd intended.

As he thought back, Mitúch caught a flash of Kalkbrenner's good-humoured smile.

The forests above Molčany were deserted. All was quiet. The old beeches in the sparse forests stood in silence as they reached up to the spring sky, as did the young ones in the dense, uncoppiced stands. Silence reigned, only birds twittered and a song thrush was singing away, as if trying out a flute somewhere.

Úplazy was an elongated hill. From Molčany you could see two slight cols and three humps.

Adam Mitúch knew Úplazy well. As a boy, he, Porubský and Zubák had pastured cows there. He knew that the partisans' bunker was by some rocks in the right-hand col. That's what Skittle had told him. He hurried on, now and again breaking into a run wherever the path was level or rising just slightly. His arm was smarting. A slight trickle of blood ran down into the palm of his hand, where it began to cake.

It was almost eight o'clock when he reached the rocks, covered in green moss, ivy and grey lichen. He looked for the bunker, couldn't find it, stood beneath the rocks and called out.

"Mišoooo!" He tried again: "Porubskýýý!" He waited.

Úplazy responded with a faint echo.

"Mišoooo!"

He waited. Just a faint echo.

Could they have already gone down to the village? he wondered. Had they known it was now safe to?

He ran across from the rocks to a clearing with a dense stand of young beeches. He paused. The pain in his arm with the gunshot wound burned like a sharp, searing flame. He stood and stared, the pain in his arm stabbing and slashing the more as his pulse beat faster. He looked across the burgeoning beech stand at the remnants of his clothes scattered about on the reviving grass. The once white trousers caked with soil and mud, the mud-stained linen shirt, the no less filthy shabby old twill coat. A step or two beyond the clothes lay cast aside his hat with holes in it and a black satchel.

He stared and stared, not hearing the fluting of the thrush, then he lowered his head, made a move and descended slowly towards Molčany.

Suddenly he turned, left the track in the small beech stand and took the footpath down to Dead Fallow because he wanted to save time and still help Kalkbrenner if he could.

The people who'd fled in every direction were now returning to the village.

Around nine o'clock, Adam Mitúch, the engineer's brother and Beta's husband, was returning from the fields. He was impatient to get back, but he wasn't driving his handsome black horses hard. They were worn out, their shiny coats caked in lather, with scattered patches of new sweat, they weren't shining in the golden sunlight as they plodded along, their bodies swaying from side to side with each step they took. He was also letting them have their own way because he was conscience-stricken: what would he find at home? Would it not have been better if he'd stayed in? Why had he suddenly let go of his common sense and gone off into the open at night? He thought angrily of his brother, of Kalkbrenner, Gizela Gábor and his dog Caesar. He had to kill him... He checked to see if everything was still on his wagon. The harrow with which he'd also meant to work over any unploughed parts, and the bag which, however, no longer contained any bread and bacon; there was still some dried clover, chopped straw and oats for the horses, and he had a metal water bucket, blankets and the axe with which he'd knocked down their new garden fence. Gravely and with apprehension he looked ahead of the horses.

In the garden he was seized with impatience, but he entered the yard only very slowly.

Gunfire sounded to the north and west of Molčany's forests. It had swept across Molčany, its fields and forests like a sudden thunderstorm.

In the young beech wood through which Jozef Mitúch was hurrying down to Dead Fallow all was quiet. The slender, smooth beech trunks, grey and black, were driving sap into the the emerging new twigs, the pale-green buds, damp and glistening, lit up by the golden sunlight, on either side of the footpath birds were twittering, joined by the fluting of a song thrush.

Mitúch registered none of this, such was his haste. His brown tracksuit stained with soil and mud, no beret, the burning, stinging pain in his arm, and his features filled with uncertainty and anger. He kept mentally repeating to himself what he would say to the Porubskýs senior and junior and to the rest of them if Kalkbrenner were no longer alive. "You've killed an innocent man," he would tell them, "not just innocent, but someone who'd helped you. You took matters into your own hands without waiting for orders. That's why all this has happened. But for that German, hunger would have driven you back down into the village, because I wouldn't have been able to send you things. I don't know who could have. The Germans would have got you. And if it weren't for him, you wouldn't have succeeded in waylaying those Germans. Why have you done this to Kalkbrenner? You'll be put on trial for this!" That's what he'd tell them and he'd see to it that it came about. He paused for thought. But Gizela Gábor could say the same: if it hadn't been for her, the partisans up on Úplazy wouldn't have had anything to smoke. Had there really been any point to this whole thing? Could they help it? Had there been any point carrying on with what was over after he'd shed his uniform in Stakov and changed into those old white things? It was because of those that they'd caught Kalkbrenner and dragged him off somewhere. In what, where was the point of it all? Mitúch hurried on through the young beech wood towards Dead Fallow.

A thrush chimed up.

Deep inside his lungs, Mitúch could sense the fragrant spring air. He halted, gazed about the forest, and took a deep breath. He was seized with an odd, unexpected calm that surprised him. What was called for, he suddenly thought, for a person to be able to breathe like this? He carried on down the path.

He stopped short, as if something had stopped his legs working. He'd never smelled it before, but he knew what smell it was that was suddenly drifting through the forest, he walked on, not knowing he was walking.

Before long, the young dense wood began to thin and give way to the first clearing at Dead Fallow, a large felled area coming back to life with pale-green grass – and Jozef Mitúch slowed right down, taking very small strides, because right there, on the pale-green grass, right there where the Romanians had had their huts and where the youthful Porubský, now the parish odd-job man, had fallen for a pretty Romanian girl, white as white butter and raven-haired, lay two groups of dead men, shot in October and left unburied.

Mitúch's heart was pounding.

On legs filled with pain, with his whole body aching, he dashed across the clearing, fleeing from the field of the dead, pursued by two on whom his eyes had settled, two killed men in military capes, still holding hands, gunfire rumbled in the distance, he ran on and on, hounded by horror, as fast as he could go, then covered in perspiration and completely groggy, he slowed to a walking pace with his head hung low.

At half past nine he was re-entering Molčany.

Even from a distance he could see, outside the village, men filling in the trenches left behind in the fields since the autumn by Borek and Dietbert's troops. The sun shone in his face, slightly burning his sleep-deprived eyes and warming up his benumbed body that had been drenched in sweat more than once that night. People were standing in gateways, outside their homes, wandering up and down in droves, calm and relief written all over their faces, and children were running about and shouting. He looked up and began saying hello to acquaintances and strangers, both those he'd seen on Wednesday and those he hadn't seen for over two years. People smiled at him and he sensed from the sparkle in their eyes that they were welcoming him. He began greeting Soviet soldiers, exchanging pleasantries with them and with other people, and he strode through Molčany more jauntily now because he now felt no pressure in his back and no question inside his head about whether someone might be about to ambush him, who any such might be, who might be meaning to denounce him, questions that had long been lurking there. He passed burned-out houses, where men were already getting down to work, walking round their burned-out houses, creating piles of burned planks, roof beams and other timbers, he called across to them: "May God be your helpmate!", "Be He so!" they called back, he walked to the Stahls' villa, above which he saw a red flag and a red-and-white flag with a blue triangle. Now and again the spring air flapped the flags gently with a slight breeze. Everything might have been made up for by this moment if there weren't those – up there at dead Fallow – lying in wait for passersby... In the front garden of the Stahl villa he was greeted by the yellow flowers of a sprawling forsythia. He glanced round at the pair of lads who were taking huge packs of hay to the cattle lowing fit to rend the heart in the school yard.

At the gate that gave access to the villa he stepped aside for the tiny widow Plátenička, Skittle's mother.

"How goes, Gammer?" he called to her. "How are you?"

Plátenička didn't look back, she was hurrying to the village.

He entered the Stahl villa.

There was no Gizela in the Stahls' rooms, just lots of Molčany men, the Stahls' hall porter Benko, chairman of the former, underground, National Committee, was conferring with the men. There were countless Soviet soldiers in every room, and there were also some partisans present. There was quite a hubbub and faces looked calm and relieved.

Jozef Mitúch began exchanging greetings, somewhat awkwardly, with the partisans. There was a chill to their handshakes. Amid the hubbub and the questions flying this way and that, smiles broke out on faces after he mentioned old Porubský, that is, until he mentioned Skittle.

"Skittle's dead," said Porubský in the husky tones rising from his sore throat. "Poor guy!"

"Where?" Mitúch leaned against wall. "Where is he?"

"On the track at Monk's Lea – with some Germans. Plátenička, his mother, has been here, crying her eyes out."

Mitúch faced Porubský and blanched. "I went up to Úplazy to find you and tell you..." He faced Porubský, the gaiety dancing on whose cheeks and prominent cheekbones had passed at the mention of Skittle. "I went –"

"Where? Where d'you go? Like that?" Porubský pointed at his blood-soaked arm. "With your arm like that? What happened? We caught..." Porubský led the pale-faced engineer, Jozef Mitúch, out and into the Stahls' sitting room, sat him down on the green sofa next to the tiny electric lamp, on which brown barques, brigs and cogs seesawed amid the blue of waves. "We caught a German soldier. He was dressed in rustic clothes. How had he strayed that far?" Porubský dropped to a whisper. "He kept saying he was an engineer and that he had some dynamite and ekrasite... Wait though, could he have been talking about you?"

Mitúch shook his head, waiting.

"They're up on Dead Fallow," said Porubský. "God Almighty, it's ghastly up there! The dead Stahls are there, some partisans... The Germans didn't bury them... Do you have any idea where Gábor's wife is?"

Mitúch shook his head.

"Have you seen her?"

"No."

"The word is that she ran away with the Germans, but where could she have run to?"

"No idea."

"What's wrong with you? Why are you so pale? It's ghastly up at Dead Fallow! My father didn't want us to let that German have it, not even a dog would want him, but when they saw that dead baby at Dead Fallow – it still had its dummy in its mouth...! The German's lying there next to it. My father didn't want to have him killed, but up at Dead Fallow he had no more to say – maybe he'd just remembered the Romanian girl, he's mentioned her often enough... That's where the German is, after all he was partly to blame, they were all to blame –"

Mitúch gaped wide-eyed at Porubský. To blame?

"What's up? You're very pale."

Jozef Mitúch silently raised his left arm. "It's this arm," he said, "I need to see a doctor."

"So you don't know about Gizela Gábor?"

"No."

Mitúch left the Stahl villa and slowly walked off home. He reached the gate and was immediately surrounded by the children, his brother greeted him with a smile, the latter's wife Beta and his old, deaf mother with anticipation. For a long time none of them could utter a word, whether good or ill, because his arm was coated in blood and his face was pale.

"We're all here now," Beta broke the silence. "Where's the German? The poor man was so sorry to leave. He seemed on the verge of tears –"

"Adam!" Jozef Mitúch, the engineer, addressed his brother. "I'm aching all over. Could you drive me to the doctor's in Račany? We could find a way across the fields – through Barren Grove."

He pointed at the bullet wound in his arm.

Adam looked at him with a hint of a smile.

"It won't be that easy," he said. "We have to go to the Stahl villa, get a permit, and only then. Teams of horses are needed for other things now – there's a lot of clearing up to do in the village. Lots of corpses, dead Germans, Russians – and others."

"Russians as well?"

"Some Russians also fell. Nine, I've heard. We've got a huge job on our hands. The bridge is down, the road to Račany is buried, there are all the burned-out houses, an anti-tank trench to fill in – then there's the Stahl estate and brickworks to be sorted out –" – "But none of that's yours to bother about!" said Beta with a look of pity for Jozef in her grey eyes. "Just hitch up and go! He's not going to get there on foot. The sooner the better!"

At half past eleven, the Mitúch brothers set out with the fine black horses, now cleaned up a bit, along the field track to Račany to see Dr Hlaváč. Adam drove the horses harder wherever possible because he could see that his brother was very pale and could barely even speak.

* * *

In Prague, Gizela Gábor didn't speak to Jozef Mitúch when he got off the plane, nor on the way to the coach, nor on the coach, and she couldn't bring herself to speak to him even outside the airline office. In the evening that same day she phoned round all the hotels in Prague, which took her over an hour, but failed to find him anywhere.

She wanted to meet up with him because she couldn't shake off the impression she'd had from their silent meeting on the plane from Košice – or from their last encounter in Račany back in forty-five.

That time she'd run into both Mitúchs, Adam and Jozef the engineer, in Račany, at the surgery of Dr Hlaváč, whom she knew well. Adam was steering his brother, by then very weak, along the corridor. "Gizzie?" Jozef had asked at the time, "You here – in Račany? What – are you doing here? Why didn't you run for it – with the Germans? That – that might have been – the wiser thing to do. You – you don't belong here. You won't be able to live here as – as a normal person." Gizela Gábor had said nothing in reply, treating both men to a somewhat timid, but disdainful glance and walking away from them. Dr Hlaváč, aided by some Soviet soldiers, had Jozef Mitúch transferred to

(255)

hospital, and when he got back Gizela Gábor asked: "What do you think will happen to him, Cyro? Will they be able to help him?" – "Not very likely," Dr Hlaváč replied. "Blood loss, septicaemia, all the chaos – I doubt it, Gizzie, I very much doubt they'll be able to do much for him." Dr Hlaváč shrugged and was mildly surprised to note the gleeful expression on Gizela's face. "You know that joke?" – "What joke? No." – "In Rakytovce a Russian soldier burst in on some old biddy and shouted at her: '*Davaj chasy!*' She took her clock off the wall and handed it to him. The Russian turned it over and over in his hands and a cockroach fell out. It began running about on the floor and the old dear stamped on it. Now wait for it, Gizzie! The soldier shouted at the old lady: '*Job tvoju mať! Ty ubila mashinista!*'" Gizela Gábor and Dr Hlaváč had a good laugh.

In Prague, Gizela Gábor sought Jozef Mitúch, the engineer, in vain. She couldn't trace him anywhere. Two months later she did catch up with him, but only by letter.

Jozef Mitúch received a letter from Adam, from Molčany. Adam gave him all kinds of news from Molčany, about how the village was tearing itself apart, how Kubica and Benko were making a strange go of running it, a job much better suited to partisans, especially Porubský and Zubák, but there was not one partisan to be seen or heard of, they could, it was rumoured, have all been locked up somewhere, and he wrote about his family, adding at the end: "Mum is still well and her sight's still good, though she's deaf as a post and is still praying only for peace, for the war to end at last, and I'm also sending you a letter that came to Molčany for you, we don't know who from, must be from some woman you know."

The engineer, surprised, read the other letter with considerable curiosity, not having expected that anyone would still be writing to him at the Molčany address.

The letter was brief. Mitúch read it quickly, pausing to stare at the lines that said: "Your prominent standing doubtless means you travel frequently to Prague. Be so kind as to pay me a visit next time you are here." He read it over and over again.

He'd found the two letters in his box when he came in from work. He'd been alone at home, sitting in an armchair by the radio and listening to the deep tones of some Negro spirituals.

He read the letter from Gizela yet again, re-reading her address several times over.

He folded it, put it in his pocket, switched the spirituals off and headed towards the Danube, where his wife and two children were out for a walk. On the way there he thought long and hard about himself and Gizela Gábor. On the tram he watched four girls, all pretty and prettily dressed. Each had a tennis racket in a blue canvas case under her arm. They were chatting about school. He sat there, lost in thought and looking at them.

By the National Theatre he alighted and walked towards the Danube. On the embankment there were lots of mothers and lots of children. The mothers were strolling or sitting around on benches and the children were running about.

Mitúch smiled and bent down.

"Daddy!" cried his two boys, the twins Peter and Ivan, as they ran towards him. "Daddy!"

Peter got there first and flew into his father's arms. Ivan hadn't been fast enough, he stopped and burst into tears.

Mitúch rose to his feet with Peter and hurried over to Ivan. He took both by the hand and all three hurried to where Peter was pointing.

"Mummy's over there!"

"What brings you here??" Jozef's wife asked, smiling to veil her surprise. "Has anything happened?"

"No, nothing."

"So how come you're here?"

"I wanted to see you."

"Are you going tomorrow?"

"Yes." The following day he was in Prague at yet another geological research seminar. The meetings ran over into the next day, and, the session over, he went, that same afternoon, to visit Gizela Gábor.

"Look about you," she said after he'd been sitting in her bedsit for about ten minutes, in a red armchair, and after he'd heard how Dr Hlaváč had swindled her, conning her out of her savings and her more precious knickknacks, and fled to the West. In some agitation, Mitúch breathed the warm air, which was steeped in cigarette smoke, alcoholic vapours and perfumes, for all that the flat was clean and the window open to the Maytime street. "I'd love to get my life back together – everyone's got a right to that much, to living as a proper human being, no? – that's why I'd been to Košice that time – but Molčany's a problem. I could have a better life, and get a better job than what I do now with Department Stores, but I don't know what kind of appraisal I'd get from those who rule the roost in Molčany these days. You know what I'm really like, don't you?"

Mitúch said nothing, his elbows resting on the arms of his chair, and he watched Gizela. His dark restless eyes flitted now and again over the seven yellow tulips and one purple one in a vase on the back ledge of the sofa. More than what she was saying now he was hearing what had stuck in his memory from January 1945: "Jožo, Jožo! You don't understand life, you're a fool." He looked at Gizela, ample-bodied, wearing a flimsy silk dress. Her long neck and oval face had, as ever, lovely white skin, and her blue eyes – as it struck Mitúch – had a self-assured smile.

"All right, then," he said coldly, "you're telling me that that thing with the Stahls and the partisans just slipped out and that it wasn't true. You're claiming to have said it just to keep hold of me at that terrible time. You claim to have been terrified of the partisans."

He glanced at his watch. He had four minutes left.

"With the Stahls it was as I've been telling you, and with the partisans."

Jozef Mitúch, the engineer, pondered. "What's it to you, Jožo? This is why everyone lives by instinct today. Avoiding all risk. I've always tried to avoid it, and I still do and always will." He began to grope uneasily in his pockets for a cigarette. "Don't be making any demands of me! There's no knowing what'll happen next. Jožo, Jožo! The only way to live today is to let oneself be denounced – or to denounce others."

"Help yourself! There are some cigarettes on the table here."

"Thank you."

"That's the way things are," said Gizela Gábor. "If you happen to go to Molčany or write to someone there, that could help me a lot. I could get a proper job... After all," she said, leaning back against the cushion on the sofa with its delicate floral design, "it's all a sham anyway, the things that are going on."

"What's a sham?"

"Everything."

"What?"

"Everything that's going on here –"

"Are you trying to provoke me?" Mitúch's voice was more brusque, with a hint of mockery. "Why is it a sham?"

Gizela's oval white face flushed slightly. "Why? All of this, all the life we're living is gloom and fear. In anyone around me I see my own private enemy, I have a sense that someone's out to destroy me, I have to exercise humility among people, speak to them in humility, swallow their inanities and falsehoods, accept their disregard with humility. It's not easy, living like that. I expect you've reached the same conclusion. It's not easy living with a frightened heart, a mortified brain and a bent back, having to keep listening to the doltish, vacuous things people say – once in Molčany you said something about it being humanly blasphemous – not easy living when you're thinking about those people in prisons and labour camps. Gloom and fear – the only way to live here now is off the gloom and fear. I work at Department Stores – I may work there, but even I'm only living off gloom and fear – and I've had enough – in the name of God, you're a engineer with a respectable qualification, prove to people that I..."

Gizela Gábor turned pale, smoking in a nervous silence, then suddenly her oval face reddened.

"... but no, not that, just prove to me at least that even I might still be able to live a normal human life, not like this – all based on people denouncing one another –!"

Jozef Mitúch sat there in Gizela's red armchair lost for words. "Jožo, Jožo! It was me who talked my husband into taking over the Stahls' villa, brickworks and lands, me who talked him into betraying others – the ones those soldiers later shot in the woods – me who talked him into showing the Germans the way to the Stahl brickworks." Mitúch's restless, dark eyes began to dart this way and that. He glanced at his watch. The Stahls, the partisans, Kalkbrenner at Dead Fallow, Skittle, the men in the sunken lane at Monk's Lea – and now Gizela Gábor here. He glanced at his watch.

He stood up.

"You're trying to provoke me, you're twisting my words," he said, "but it's not me saying them, it's you, Mrs Gábor. You told me it was pangs of conscience that drove you to write to me. You haven't studied your Hitler properly."

"What?"

"You haven't studied him properly. Do it now!"

"I beg your pardon!"

"Study him closely and you'll find there that it's the chimera of conscience and morality that stops you doing what you're doing. What pangs? Pangs over the Stahls and the Molčany partisans? Pangs because of all you've been through since the Germans wanted rid of you? Because of all that you're going through now? No, no, Mrs Gábor! You are afraid of people getting at you, but only the living do that – I'm being got at by the dead, those left in the forests around Molčany, at Dead Fallow. No – no – people like you can't live like human beings. You can live as a being, but not a human being! Do whatever

(260)

you want, but expect no help from me. Provoke me as you will, I still won't help you! I myself am finding it hard to live as a human being. Not one of us is entirely guiltless where others are concerned, but I don't want to live off guilt either now or in the future –"

Gizela sat there on her red sofa, legs crossed, her hands resting behind her on the back of the sofa, her head tipped slightly backwards and directing a hint of smile at the flushed Mitúch. "Aren't you taking rather a liberty, sir –?"

"In your case, surely," Mitúch replied sharply, "but you've nothing to gain by trying to provoke me, nothing to gain by threatening me, because if you do inform on me and destroy me, that won't have turned you into a human being!"

"You have taken quite some liberties, sir –!"

"Of course, quite a lot," said Mitúch. "I shall not give you that assurance that you count as a human being. You disqualified yourself on that score long ago, you don't count as one – and you only have yourself to blame...!"

"Mr Mitúch –!"

Jozef Mitúch turned and left. He rushed to the airline office but missed the coach. He took a taxi to the airport.

Inside the plane he developed a headache, and his restless dark eyes stared forward between the heads of the other passengers.

The plane began to descend, listing to one side. An irksome feeling passed through Mitúch. He looked fearfully out at the huge grey wing, covered in rows of rivets and, next to the wing, at the slanting green world that lay far, far below.

Mišo Belica had been forcibly removed from Veľké Dvorce, and two years later they installed a lawyer, Dr Štefan Malena, who'd been forcibly removed from Bratislava, in his vacant house.

Some believed that that was when it had all started, others thought not and said it wasn't until the autumn of fifty-three, when Ignác Dugas had started boasting: "That cross? Not a problem! I'll get a tractor, wind a chain round the cross and out it'll come! It's intolerable!"

Dugas's words had upset the village of Veľké Dvorce and Ignác Dugas became a target of the inhabitants' fury.

Thanks to a letter from her father, Eva Dubovský, whose parents lived in Veľké Dvorce and who'd mentioned the cross more than once to her husband, also knew about what Dugas was planning to do with it.

It was a nice day in October.

The vast MZ works housing estate, in part built and in part still awaiting completion, about fifty kilometres from Veľké Dvorce, was lit up by the warm, setting sun.

Playing out in the rutted, unmade street outside block XIV were two boys, one aged six, the other five, and a little two-year-old girl. Their parents, the works GP, Dr Martin Dubovský, and his wife Eva, were at home, sitting in their living room and reading.

"I can't stop thinking about that cross, Martin," Eva suddenly said to her husband. "It keeps bugging me."

Dubovský didn't respond. He was immersed in a handbook on the statistical classification of ailments, injuries and causes of death.

"This affects everybody," said Eva, "nobody's spared."

"What?"

"The kind of society we've got."

"You're right, Eva," her husband said. "It's a pretty merciless struggle, but basically right. The scientific organisation of society naturally means there's a price to pay, there may be a degree of violence, but the price is still lower than in a society left to drift forward elementally – and it's fairer. The struggle is basically right-minded, and just –"

"I'm not so sure."

"It's the right thing, Eva."

"I'm not sure it was right to remove Belica and resettle some Bratislava lawyer in his house. So far it strikes me as just cruel and ludicrous. It undermines trust in socialism. And socialism shouldn't be jeopardised through such absurdities."

They both, the factory GP, Martin Dubovský, and his wife Eva, came from Veľké Dvorce, though Eva only because her parents had lived there since the war, since 1940, and despite their lack of interest in the village at that stage, while Martin hadn't even been there since 1945, because he was afraid of the locals; Eva sensed that the latest events in Veľké Dvorce concerned them both.

"It's not right, Martin," she said after a pause, "I don't like the Belica case either, or that lawyer's part in it, or the way Dugas is carrying on. We can't look at it just from the angle of reason and the scientific organisation of society."

"How then?"

"I mean," said Eva, "you're on the wrong track. You rely on reason, science – you're like that handbook of yours on causes of death. Everything's like that. We've learned to call many things by new names and accept and acknowledge them under those names. What does 'class struggle' or 'the socialisation of the village' actually mean? You name causes of death by numbers and symbols – and we've learned to conceal many, very many other realities under new names and symbols. The Belica business, and the lawyer, it bothers me, and the cross as well. One's labelled 'class struggle', the other 'fighting obscurantism', but there could be quite different things involved, Martin –"

"Well, I'm not bothered about the cross thing."

"No?"

"No, Eva."

"Nor about Dugas, or Belica, not even about that lawyer?"

"No?"

"Don't you think, Martin, that this attitude is just you trying to assuage your conscience with regard to Jankovič?"

"No."

"Jankovič bears us a grudge. He doesn't come to see us – more's the pity... You should have stood by him and not backed down!"

Dubovský failed to respond.

"Well I *am* bothered by the cross, because in my view, despite everything, that cross is a symbol of the struggle for love and respect for man – and man, that isn't just –"

"What of it!"

Dubovský dismissed her words with a wave of his hand, gave a moment's thought to Jankovič and stared at certain lines in his handbook: "E 883 Random poisoning by caustic aromatic substances, acids and corrosives. E 884 Random poisoning by mercury and its compounds." With commando-soled shoes on his feet and wearing a new, grey shepherd check suit, he leaned back in his armchair, half-knitted his overhanging brows and twitched his lips.

"Eva," he said, "a cross is a symbol of a superstition, so too the one in Veľké Dvorce, and Dugas may well be doing the right thing in wanting to remove it."

"Symbol of a superstition?"

"And isn't it?"

"No, Martin. To me it's a symbol of love and respect for man, and infinite love and respect at that... Just think back to your late brother and your mother!" Eva fell silent and stared down at her book. She thought it better not to annoy her husband over Mr Jankovič, a highly qualified engineer, and the Veľké Dvorce cross, because she feared that might precipitate a condition in which she had no wish to see him and which she had not seen him in since the summer, savage moods that had taken hold of him from time to time over the previous two years. She snuggled down in her armchair, raised her feet in their red slippers and tucked them under her light-brown skirt. She fixed her dark-blue eyes on her book and read a passage that reiterated all those words about the difficulties involved in the spread and growth of the new society that was to come.

After a while, she glanced out of the window.

Outside, the red of four unfinished, brick tower blocks sprang into life. They had turned magenta in the dying sun as it sank into the red clouds.

"That cross *is* a symbol of a superstition," said Dubovský after a pause. "If my mother hadn't been superstitious –"

"She wasn't superstitious, she believed –"

"Same difference," said Dubovský. "Today's way of life seeks to overcome superstition and personally I'm convinced that that will help us a lot. Look at it this way, Eva, and see that our way of life, which has been like a jungle for centuries, is being permeated with a science that is wiping that jungle out. Don't try arguing back at me, you're simply wrong, Eva."

"You know I'd happily be proved wrong over such matters, but what if I'm actually right?"

Dubovský shook his head. "Is Soňa coming?"

"She should be," Eva replied. "She promised she would. She's an odd girl. I'm very fond of her. Even with all the work she puts in here, she still has time for some biology. Was she studying medicine perhaps?"

"I don't know."

Eva went back to her book, still troubled by Belica, who'd been forcibly removed from Veľké Dvorce, by the lawyer who'd been forcibly removed from Bratislava into Belica's old house in Veľké Dvorce, by their friend Jankovič, the engineer, and by Ignác Dugas, who'd begun his menaces over the Veľké Dvorce cross. "And what about your brother, and your mother and father?"

Dubovský was looking at his book.

"Martin!"

"Yes?"

"What have you got to say about your brother, Fero, and your mother and father? Or those dreadful victims, the ones shot, the ones burned to death?"

"Victims?" Dubovský looked at his wife with his calm, deep-set eyes, veiled by a shadow. "Those victims tormented me for as long as I remained disgusted by life in our times. But not anymore. The cross, that cross – it's ridiculous, Eva –"

Dubovský tried to dispel the relentless tremor of bitter remorse that he was having for speaking to his wife in such crude terms and for speaking like that only because she'd mentioned Soňa. Did Eva know something, or not? Soňa's parents lived in Veľké Dvorce. If she hadn't come to work at the factory, he might never again have seen anything good in life. He felt a twinge of unease. Soňa – and here was Eva fussing about a cross, and Dugas.

"Listen, Eva," he said, "be so good as to write home to your father, or to tell him while he's here, not to keep writing to you about such things! What's the point in writing about some cross or the goings-on in their local politics?"

She declined to reply and both Dubovskýs stared at their books, not reading, their minds being tied up with Veľké Dvorce, of which they knew plenty from Eva's parents, her father in particular. That cross...! Why write about that, why give yourself a headache over it? Maybe it's not about the cross at all, thought Eva, maybe it really is about something else... The cross being a nuisance to Dugas... The cross that was such a nuisance to Ignác Dugas stood in Veľké Dvorce, a village spread across hillsides and former upland meadows, above the topmost cottage, at Bukovec Rise, on Belica's Meadow. About five hundred paces from the cross lay the cemetery. Whenever a body was being borne to the cemetery, the procession always paused at the cross. The pallbearers would set the bier down on the ground, either for a rest or for others to take their place, and at that point the priest would chant: "Non intres in judicium...", a Latin hymn entreating the Almighty not to place his servant before His judgement seat, because no one can measure up to Him until and unless all his sins be forgiven, then the priest would end with the words "Kyrie eleison!", the organist would respond with "Christe eleison, Kyrie eleison!" and intone the beginning of the Lord's Prayer: "Pater noster..." The people would always kneel down, whether the path was dry or muddy, because they had known since times long past that they had to pray for the deceased, so they prayed, and the Our Father line having been recited by the rugged voices of overworked men, the thinner voices of women eaten away by poverty, woe and disease and by the thin voices of rosy-cheeked children, the priest would sing: "Et ne nos inducas in tentationem..." The organist would respond with: "Sed libera nos a malo!" Then the pallbearers would raise the bier with the coffin and the deceased onto their shoulders and everyone proceeded to the cemetery. That's how it had been in Veľké Dvorce since time immemorial, and since time immemorial the people had said their Our Father and listened to the words of the priest and organist. And while they did not understand them, they sensed in and behind them the voice of the other world to which they had borne countless people from Veľké Dvorce. "Everyone will get an allotment out of it," Ignác Dugas had often heard his father say, whenever they talked about the cemetery, "and everyone will come and grow things on it." Since time immemorial the cross had stood by the track across the meadow latterly known as Belica's. When, back in the days of Austria-Hungary, Mišo Belica had married into the household of a rich old maid and acquired, besides her and some other plots of land, the meadow on Bukovec Rise with its wayside cross, he had a new cross planted on the meadow, carved from the pure core of a handsome oak tree that he had bought for the purpose from an oakwood in the nearby parish of Slanica. In the town he had invested in a brand new figure of Christ, coated in gold paint, and had the crucifix consecrated. And in Veľké Dvorce life went on as before. People were born and people died, priests at the foot of Belica's cross chanted unintelligible words about ordeals by God, and people, for all their trepidation due to the words' unknown meaning, would say their Our Father at the cross when the men carrying the coffin paused to rest or to let others take their place. Mišo Belica owned a lot of land because, before getting married and entering the rich old maid's household, he had made it a condition that she sign all her property over to him. That way he acquired fields, meadows, pastures and woodlands. Eventually, the younger folk of Veľké Dvorce, who no longer worked on its fields and meadows, but, after 1945, had taken up jobs in sundry factories and building sites nearby, in the MZ works, or all manner of office jobs in the nearby district town, and now only came back to Veľké Dvorce to spend Sunday there, began considering forming a cooperative. Among them Ignác Dugas. The regional national committee gave them its backing and when the village national committee all agreed that the only obstacle to any cooperative would be Belica, they expropriated his farm and homestead in 1951 and physically removed him, his son, his son's wife and their nine children from the village. All the livestock and farm equipment were divided up among cooperatives in neighbouring villages, especially Slanica, after which Veľké Dvorce waited to see what would happen next. Two days later, a grey car, covered in mud, arrived in the village and moments later the village odd job man, gravedigger and watchman, the still young Jožo Faraga, scowling at anyone he bumped into, went round the village with his drum: "Oyez, oyez, oyez..." He fell silent for a brief moment before announcing austerely: "This evening, at 8 p.m. a meeting will be held in the village hall. This is to set up the preparatory committee of the cooperative, the united agricultural cooperative. Everyone should turn up at eight o'clock because applications to join the collective will already be being signed." Veľké Dvorce failed to show up at its village hall. Neither then, nor later, did anyone put in an appearance, even though Jožo Faraga went round more than once to drum the citizenry up for such a meeting. "You've not a hope of sending me round to drum up interest in the cooperative yet again!" Jožo Faraga told Benc, the chairman of the local national committee a fortnight later, treating him to a scowl filled with resentment, "because people keep taking the piss, all they do is make fun of me and say my drum's driving the cooperative right out of the village. Not a hope...!" Jožo Faraga pulled his old, greasy, green hat down over his glowering forehead and added: "And listen here, Chairman, it's high time Veľké Dvorce had a public address system like they have in Slanica. There's no drumming goes on there! Everything's neatly broadcast!" – "But for that you need electricity, wise guy!" – "What?" – "For that you need electricity, I mean for a public address system." – "You don't say!" – "Obviously! It doesn't run on lamp oil! And what would you be doing if we already had such a system?" Chairman Benc asked raising a quizzical eyebrow. "You can be sure you'd be..." – "Don't you go taking me for an idiot or a clown, Chairman. What would I be doing? I'd be busy twiddling my thumbs!" Jožo Faraga replied, and he left. Benc followed him with his quizzical gaze and open-mouthed. After that Jožo Faraga did no more drumming. Belica's fields needed to be ploughed and sown, his meadows also needed looking after, and so they were divided up among the population. Those who had plenty of fields and meadows received plenty, those who had few received few, but anyone who had a team of horses, oxen or cows got something. The people had been given the fields and meadows and along with the fields the duty to turn in a prescribed quota, and although they'd fought hard against Belica's land, they decided, ultimately, to yield to the inevitable, to avoid being forcibly removed, and start cultivating them. That was preferable to having to form a cooperative. "Whatever next," they said, "fancy setting up a cooperative in a village like this! Cooperatives are all well and good for folk in the lowlands, but here?" – "Sure, down there! Up here you sow poverty and harvest penury!" – "Heigh-ho, such a poor village and just look at the crackpot ideas they come up with!" – "And by force! If it were all voluntary, so be it!" – "And there's all that stuff they rant on about, in the papers and on the radio, how cooperatives can only be set up on the basis of voluntary action." – "And they ought to have said what needs doing, how to go about it! You can't set up cooperatives just like that." Belica's Meadow, including the wayside cross, fell to Mišo Dugas, Ignác's father, he would mow it, leaving quite an area round the cross untouched – suppose there's a landmine at the foot of it it! – that SS man is also buried somewhere hereabouts! – and his wife used to turn the swathes. It was like that for two years. And now? Why has Eva started going on about it? Does she sense something? Does she know? Dubovský glanced at Eva as she stared into her book. This can't really be about the cross, there's something else going on... "Where are the kids, Eva?"

"Out in the street."

A week passed. In the middle of October 1953 the sky turned grey and damp days set in. The Veľké Dvorce valley turned grey, the green pine forests and reddish brown beech woods turned grey, wet roofs acquired a glint, as did the pots hanging on wooden fence posts.

Walking along the road that wound like a snake across the hillsides and former upland pastures on which Veľké Dvorce had been built were two gentlemen. One tall, robust, slim, dressed in an old trench coat and with an old grey hat on his head, the former lawyer Dr Malena, who'd been forcibly removed from Bratislava in February 1953 and installed in Belica's old house in Veľké Dvorce, and the other in a black plastic mac with a black hat on his head, the teacher Moravčík, who'd been transferred to Veľké Dvorce from the regional capital during the war, in 1940. They took the steep path up towards Belica's cross.

At the foot of the cross they stopped and turned.

"Doctor Malena," said the teacher, Moravčík, cocking one large, black, bulging eyebrow, "to be strictly objective, one has to concede that the common people are on the up and up. I've heard that building plots are going to be handed out here."

Malena leaned on his bamboo cane and surveyed the meadows on Bukovec Rise that Mr Moravčík had pointed to.

"They say that was the really terrible thing about concentration camps," he said soon after, as they were heading back down the steep path from the cross, and he came to a halt, "a planned jungle: conditions so regimented as to drive people to mutual destruction. The camps were also on the up and up, as you put it, with new buildings going up in and around them all the time, but the people lived like in a jungle, having to engage – to use our modern terminology – in class warfare. Oh dear, that wretched Soňa of mine! She's been everything under the sun, and now she's a kultprop and leading one awful life, don't you know... Depraved, that's what she is. She had a son, Jurka, we've no idea who the father is, and she's dumped him on us, for us to look after him while she lives just for her own self, answering only to the call of her body... She does nothing to support us, contributes nothing for her son, never gives us a penny –"

Moravčík, lost in thought, gazed down into the vast lowlands, split into four small valleys, dotted here and there with white cottages, and at the hills that were vanishing in the grey mist. Skalka, the highest of them, was completely veiled in mist, along with its fir forest. Three small white clouds had broken away from the grey mist, they were drifting down and spreading out over the pine trees. The road that wound like a snake had turned a shade of grey.

Malena and Moravčík moved on.

"Why do you speak of your daughter in such awful terms, Doctor? It's bad enough having to hear such things said about one's own offspring, but actually to voice them, well, it's –"

"They keep going on and on," Malena, the former lawyer, replied, "about how this regime is all for the good of man. Every regime has said the same. Even in prison you're ordered to write home and say you're doing okay. This much I can say to *you* at least, that nobody cares anymore about us oldies. I've come to terms with that despite having been forcibly removed here from Bratislava all because I had a lovely villa there, not large, not small, just lovely – but this regime doesn't look after young people either. I can tell *you* that this regime may be building factories and houses, but it's demolishing souls – demolishing the souls of the young, and if it can't win the young over by anything other than being frivolous about sexual matters, there'll be no point in its filling the prisons, the camps – it'll lose the day –"

"I'm not sure I quite believe that. If one looks at it objectively –"

"Ah, that daughter of mine, Soňa –!"

"I praise God," said the teacher, Moravčík, that my daughter gives me no cause for complaint."

"It's ludicrous really, but I'm moaning about her to you with gratitude. In you I've found someone who doesn't shy away from me as if I'd got the mange. All my friends and relations, on my own and my wife's side, have begun to shun me as if I were a leper. But you, dear friend, not you... My Soňa, she – she's a downright bitch, debauched she is – how else could she have become a kultprop –?"

They carried on downhill. Malena's once expensive trench coat had now turned a dull shade of grey, while Moravčík's cheap, black plastic mac glistened.

"And where's your daughter now?"

"Some company called MZ, Emzed," Dr Malena replied, "they need all sorts of people. They took her on and that's where she works as their kultprop. I don't know what that is, or what the company makes. Weapons, as like as not – those doves of peace –!"

"At Emzed?" the teacher queried in some surprise, and he thought of his own daughter, Eva, and her husband, the GP, Dr Dubovský. "At MZ Engineering by –?"

"That's right –"

"I didn't know your daughter was there, and that she is your daughter."

They both lapsed into silence and walked quietly on down. Malena, filled with loathing for his daughter Soňa, a loathing that drowned whatever else he had inside him, and Moravčík, fearful for his Eva, the wife of Dubovský, the factory GP.

"There was Soňa," said Malena after a while, "then came the Party secretary, then that Vlach fellow and many others, then Dugas, the worst is yet to come, my friend – and all that's left is Soňa, such as she is!"

A wet week passed by and they began allocating the building plots, Belica's Meadow on Bukovec Rise having been added in to the planned distribution as a single oversized parcel because it wasn't big enough to divide into two, and it was made over to Ignác Dugas, including the wayside cross.

Ignác Dugas, the youngest of the many sons of Mišo Dugas, now scattered worldwide, the Mišo Dugas who had subsisted on his not quite two-hectare smallholding, was secretary to the local national committee in the nearby village of Slanica.

He was well pleased with the building site allotted to him, and having sensed that the locals assembled in the Veľké Dvorce village hall wanted to ask him a question, but were too timid, he said: "That cross? Not a problem! I'll get a tractor, wind a chain round the cross and out it'll come! It's unthinkable! I won't have it outside any window of mine!" He looked round at the men.

"You're overdoing it, Ignác," his father, Mišo Dugas, ventured to tell him. "Better not to go overdoing things. Don't get too big for your boots!"

The good people of Veľké Dvorce waited to see what Ignác Dugas would do.

Ignác Dugas wasn't liked. Not even by his father, an old man now, but still a fine upstanding figure. He'd once raised his fist at him and said: "I'll have your guts for garters, Ignác!" – "Come on, Dad, there's no need for that!" – "I'll give you no need, right in the chops!" his father had bawled back at him. "You say one more word about the cooperative! That's

no way to go about things, trying to force people into something! People have worked hard to win a bit more land, so you
can't go taking it from them by force. Each of our folk works
hard to win a bit of extra land, they work very hard... And
you? All you've ever done is loaf about, about as much use as
the pong in your pants! What do you know about winning a
bit more land?" The man's got money, people would whisper
about Ignác Dugas, he does, he gets more than his quota of
wheat, potatoes, meat, for Korea, and then sells it all on the
quiet! Some were surprised and shook their heads in disbelief,
while others spread the word that he'd even done well out of
the currency reform. "What of it! I'm going to build a house!"
One Sunday, when he was bragging to the men in the Veľké
Dvorce pub, the men just listened in silence. "How can Jano
Jakubec, the agriculture chap on the regional committee be
building a posh house for himself? And how can Števo Kun-
kel, the regional Party chairman, be building a posh house for
himself? And he already has one new house in Dvorce, *and*
he'll inherit his father's cottage! It's unthinkable!" Ignác Dugas
was no oil painting. He had five front teeth missing. He'd had
them knocked out by the Gestapo during the Uprising. Girls
would joke that when he opened his mouth it was a gaping
hole. And he was frail. During the war he'd been a farm hand,
knocking about from village to village, and during the Uprising he'd been first a partisan, then a bandit, and then, after
the war, when he'd joined the Veľké Dvorce militia and slung
a rifle across his shoulders, the men would shout after him:
"That thing's bending you down like a blade of grass. And
mind it doesn't give you a blister on your shoulder!" In 1947 he
joined up, and when he'd done his stint in the army and come
back with two white teeth and three of dental gold, which
did a fair job of filling the gap in his mouth, he took a job at
the MZ works. There he found himself a girl, Paulína Ambro
from Slanice – "Rosy-red Paula" they called her because of her
ruddy cheeks and blonde hair tinged with yellow – married
her and moved in with her parents, the Ambros, in Slanica.

With the passage of time, the people of Veľké Dvorce began saying: "That Ignác Dugas isn't all he seems. They say he's up for a secretary's post." – "Secretary?" – "You heard me, secretary. At the village national committee in Slanica." – "You're joking!" – "Yep. Honest! Just ask around!" – "Good grief! How can a scab like him be a secretary? What's the world coming to...?" Ignác Dugas did become secretary, in charge of the agenda of the local national committee in Slanica and the surrounding communities, and he liked his tipple: within Slanica and the surrounding communities there were two cooperative distilleries that produced pretty good plum brandy. And as a married man he would also go to village dances, and even if there wasn't one he would often be out till dawn anyway. He was forever wiping his clammy forehead with his sleeve and shouting: "Dear wife, my dear in-laws, we're going to be living in paradise!" Some of the citizens of Slanica were happy with him, because with Ignác Dugas in charge all sorts of things could be achieved, whether at threshing time or in how quotas were broken down. Only when it came to those extra quotas for Korea was there no getting round him: they had to be. He kept saying it was unthinkable, and that it was their patriotic duty. The people of Slanica turned in their extra quotas, and even after they'd set up their cooperative they continued to do so as its members.

The main reason Ignác Dugas was so pleased at being allotted Belica's Meadow was that it was the largest building plot in Veľké Dvorce, and he began stocking building materials on it.

"Are you pleased, Paula?" he asked his wife when one late afternoon he drove her up to Belica's Meadow on his motorbike to show her the piles of bricks, stones, sand and timber. "Quite something, eh?"

"I'll be happy enough with the house, but hardly with you."

"Why not, why not, Paula?"

"You drink – and I've heard tell you want to uproot this cross. Is that true?"

"Yes!"

"Your dad won't let you, nor will mine or my mum. Such things just aren't done! And Moravčík won't allow it either, nor his son-in-law, that doctor chap."

Ignác Dugas just laughed, baring his white and dental-gold teeth in a grin.

"Well, I'll be...!" he said. "Such small fry! Mr father, your father, your mum! Moravčík and that partisan woman of his – what a bitch she was! – and Moravčík's son-in-law? A doctor? He needs his neck wringing as it is!" Ignác Dugas pointed towards Skalka from which a grey mist was drifting down onto the fir forest. "That way, beyond Skalka, that's where Moravčík's son-in-law, that doctor, had my brother bumped off. Why did he do that? Anyway, come on, Paula, let's get off home. And you stay out of my affairs!"

"That SS man's buried here somewhere," she said. "Are you going to have him dug up?"

"Leave off, will you! What's it to you anyway?"

He mounted his motorbike, Paula the rear seat behind him, and they set off down the snaking road with the engine off.

On his bike Dugas was thinking about people. He concluded that people were a mixed bunch: Belica was forcibly removed ages ago and Chairman Benc is pleased he'll never have to pay his money back. Thirty thousand! And back then that was a massive sum. Benc, he's a bright guy! His own father was angry when Belica was hauled off from Dvorce. Said he was a decent chap. He'd borrowed two hundred crowns from him and Belica had never asked for it back. His father has always been distressed at not being able to return it. The longer Belica's been gone, the more it bothers him. Benc is quite happy that Belica's gone. But what about Malena? Where to have him removed to? Will he be wanting it back, or not? He's a strange fellow. He took fright and it wasn't long before he turned up with the money. He's scared. He certainly won't be asking for any back. Twenty thousand, now this, and that, a drip here, a drip there – and there it'll be, a house on Belica's

Meadow! Paula's just stupid. She doesn't know anything. She's scared of the cross, and the SS man – silly ass!

The people of Veľké Dvorce knew plenty about Dugas, spread rumours, whispered together and gossiped about him, but they also feared him, and the village teacher, Jozef Moravčík, also knew plenty about him, and once more he mentioned what was going on in Veľké Dvorce in a letter to his daughter, Eva, who was married to the doctor, Martin Dubovský.

It was a grey November day.

A fine drizzle was coming down everywhere, onto the village of Veľké Dvorce, spread across hillsides and former upland meadows, it was drizzling on Belica's cross, which had acquired a slight lean since the Uprising, having been dashed by fragments of landmines, and the drizzle was also coming down on the MZ works and its housing estate.

Eva Dubovský, a teacher at the MZ works, was at home, reading a letter from her father, written in a rangy, shaded script.

"Dear Eva," she read on with some curiosity. "We are well, thankfully, and trust you are, too, and that everything is as good as you wrote.

"Nothing new here, everything as it was.

"Except that I've come to know a lot better that lawyer who was forcibly removed from Bratislava and resettled in Belica's house. He's a Dr Štefan Malena. I occasionally go for a stroll with him. He's a strange man because it strikes me that he's totally preoccupied by one thing: he's forever complaining about his daughter Soňa, who works at Emzed, where you are. I was surprised when he told me, and I wondered whether he had particular trust in me, or he's just not normal. In my hearing he complains about his daughter, going on and on and in quite harsh terms. I don't know what bad things come to his knowledge. They must be awful, because he does complain about her a lot. He says she's already caused him a lot of grief already, and still it goes on. She's dying to find a suitor who'll boost her chances of a career. But then what girl wouldn't?

"Dr Malena, the lawyer, may well have grounds for complaining about his daughter, because she has a son who's here with her parents, and they say they don't even know who the boy's father is. She'd love to find a suitor with a good career. That's pretty obvious.

"Except where would you find one such today? It would have to be some unscrupulous individual given that these days it's still possible to make a fortune at least through fraud and thievery. Certainly not through honest labour. Such a suitor would have to be something like our local committee secretary Dugas, who's about to build himself a house on Belica's meadow, here in Veľké Dvorce. He keeps talking about using a tractor to uproot the wayside cross that must have been on his patch forever. Such harebrained ideas are ludicrous, but they also sadden us greatly, because to us the cross is a serious memorial and reminder of other people who didn't meet their end the way that SS man did who'd been laying landmines at the foot of the cross.

"I didn't know that the Malena girl you mentioned as a close acquaintance was the daughter of our Dr Malena, the lawyer, and I was very surprised at all the things he told me about her. It made me both happy and sad that I'm so much luckier than he, for one quite natural thing: the nice, unsullied life you have with Martin and the lovely children the pair of you have. If what her father tells me about her is true, you'd be well advised to avoid her as far as possible. It's a pity to waste time with people like that.

"Dr Malena plainly trusts me a lot, treats me as a friend and tells me unbelievable things about his daughter, as if to unburden himself. So, my dear Eva, do take my advice –"

Eva went on reading her father's letter, absorbed by Soňa Malena and by Ignác Dugas and his plans for the Belica cross, and having reached the end, she began, her mind filled with thoughts about all that and about what had gone on at Veľké

Dvorce during the Uprising, to get ready to take the children for a walk, though it wasn't very nice outside. Her mind kept leaping from Soňa Malena and her father, the lawyer forcibly resettled in Veľké Dvorce, to Ignác Dugas, Belica's cross, the Uprising and her husband Martin. In the past few months she had enjoyed her husband's company, though she couldn't agree with his ideas and attitudes regarding the events in Veľké Dvorce, because in the past few months he had changed. He was no longer being harried, as he put it, by irksome states of mind and had begun to believe in his work again and enjoy it. That made Eva happy. But why did that coincide, she wondered, with when Soňa started working at Emzed? Why has he changed so? Why does he see, in her, the sense of those victims, past and present? According to him, Soňa is just what a young person of today ought to be – and Soňa's father is a lawyer who, for no apparent reason, was forcibly removed from Bratislava – and apparently he isn't quite right in the head if he complains so much about his daughter. Soňa has a child, she's morally compromised, but she's no ordinary girl –

"Where's Daddy?" the older boy, Igor, asked. "Mummy?"

"Yes, dear?"

"Where's Daddy?"

"He's at a lecture in the Community Centre."

In the lecture hall on the ground floor of the unfinished six-floor building which, according to the plans for the MZ works housing estate, was to become the hub of the community's social and cultural life, a department store and later an entertainment centre, the cultprop Soňa Malena had been lecturing on the new socialist man's attitude to work, going into questions of care for the individual, and now she'd drifted slowly, she had no idea how, into questions of morality.

The factory GP, Martin Dubovský, stretched, leaned back on his chair and looked at Soňa. He watched her, listened closely to what she was saying and, when Soňa Malena registered that he'd been sitting there all that time without making notes, she stopped and waited.

"That comrade there," she said after a pause, pointing at Dubovský and raising her pale, smooth face slightly, "might consider making the odd note! Right?"

"Sorry?"

Some half-hearted laughter went round the lecture hall, diffusing satisfaction that something unpleasant had gone the way of someone else, and while it lasted, Soňa Malena, who was standing behind her table, felt a suffusion of warmth across her blushing face.

"I'll start making some then, comrade," said Dubovský angrily, "so I don't forget anything?"

"I should think so, comrade! Be so kind!"

This was all for the sake of appearance, this entire brief, seemingly unpleasant exchange between Dubovský and Soňa Malena, because Soňa and Dubovský had colluded in agreeing that, in the presence of the public, whoever might be listening, be that workers, engineers or officials, they would resort to this buffoonery so that people would see that they were distinctly cool, at other times simply indifferent to each other.

Soňa Malena went back to her lecture, while her audience duly took notes.

The lecture hall was vast. It could seat up to three hundred people. The walls were adorned with slogans in large white letters on a red background, posters, pictures and banners.

Although the exchange between Dubovský and Soňa Malena had been concocted, Dubovský felt chagrined.

Soňa went on with her lecture.

The Dubovskýs had arrived at the MZ works early in 1950 and since then Dubovský had succeeded in building up a health service that made itself felt not only within the works in the form of preventive and protective public health measures, but also within many of the people, who had begun to understand care for their own health as an obligation vis-à-vis others and a prerequisite for doing their jobs well. He wasn't satisfied with the results. "People are very demanding, Eva," he told his wife. "More is required of me than of a manual worker.

I'm harassed by a sense of not having done enough – and that people are exploiting the work that I do. They also exploit me, many people see me as a means to helping them avoid work. People of a fitting class background demand more care from me than I can give them, and people who feel victimised on account of their class apparently blame me in private for not receiving even minimal care. There was no way I could have helped Jankovič... That pains me..." – "You should have... you should have stood by him, Martin, You shouldn't have given in. If we were to back off in the face of every absurdity..." – "I'm just so sick of it all..." He'd been dismayed by the case of his friend Jankovič, a highly qualified engineer, and Eva watched with disquiet as Martin slowly lapsed into a state that neither he nor she had foreseen. He began to hate everything which made up his life. He hated his job, its milieu and people, he kept drifting into moods of some savagery, in nothing could he discern the sense of his past sacrifices, he occasionally sank so low as to hate his wife and children, but just as he was at his worst, when, early in August 1953, Soňa Malena appeared at the MZ works and was accommodated in the Community Centre, he became a changed man. Soňa arrived and immediately came to see Dubovský at the works surgery – with a dark tan, her face darker than her sandy hair, red lips, flaming pale-blue eyes, a gleaming white dress, enlivened with tiny red and black circlets – and asked for a check-up. "Comrade Doctor," she had said the Dubovský, "in July I went to help with the harvest and while I was having a swim I caught a chill and then flu. I'm worried it might have left its mark on my lungs or pleura." Dubovský picked up his stethoscope and, having checked her over – the dark-bronze skin on her back and shoulders had a variable glint to it – he noticed she was getting dressed rather slowly and with charming ineptitude. "May I?" he asked and at first had no idea how it could have happened, but he helped do up the buttons on the back of her dress. She stayed at the surgery longer than any ordinary patient and as Dubovský chatted to her he could tell that she was a feisty lass, self-confident, almost aggressive. She made him feel like an unattached young man, unencumbered by anything, one who was enjoying life and delighting readily in some new existence. "Forgive me," he said, "I'm happy to say you're fit and well." She smiled. "You've nothing to fear, your lungs are quite unaffected. I could do with more patients like you. Where will you be working?" – "I'll be their cultprop." – "Really? Excellent! You'll have your work cut out. You'll have to start from the very bottom." – "I'm really looking forward to it, Comrade Doctor," she assured him with a flash of her white teeth, densely packed like a tiny keyboard, "though I've never done anything like it before, let alone in such a large factory." – "I'll help you with any advice I can." – "I shall be most grateful." With his stethoscope in his left hand he saw her to the door and felt an unaccustomed sense of pleasure, holding the stethoscope, and even after he'd set it aside. For several days after that he would pick up the stethoscope with that same sense of pleasure, and after he'd got to know her a lot better during their stint volunteering with the harvest at the local state farm, he was hugely pleased to have found in Soňa a genuinely precious free spirit. He'd introduced her to Eva and was glad Eva made friends with her. "All those sacrifices, past and present, made sense and they still do," he said, "if it means the rise of more people like her." Dubovský was a changed man, the savage moods went away and his wife, Eva, as well as the children, were glad of his company. She was also glad of the company of their new acquaintance, Soňa Malena, who popped round for a quick visit now and again, giving Eva the chance to chat with someone she found agreeable.

"Marx, Engels, Lenin, Stalin," Soňa went on with her lecture, "proved, beyond the shadow of a doubt, the untenability, the absurdity of pre-bourgeois and bourgeois doctrines regarding morality –"

In the Community Centre lecture hall Martin Dubovský was sitting with his mind fully engaged as he listened to Soňa's spirited, warm voice.

"What a pity, Soňa," he jotted in his large pad, "that you don't believe all this yourself, and that you had us put on that charade today instead of having a discussion – if you did believe in it, but no, you can't believe in it –"

Then he began drawing a large house, next to it a spruce tree, in the background a spruce wood and beyond that a hill. On top of the hill he drew a trig point.

He glanced at his watch. Bored stiff, he watched the second hand, which was going very slowly from one minute marker to the next, then clumsily, with his left hand, he wrote: "Marx, Engels, Lenin, Stalin – like with the Bible, anyone can read into them whatever suits them best, anyone can use them, many abuse them –"

"So take this down, comrades," said Soňa Malena, "because it is very important!" She paused. "This is a fundamental precept: Pre-bourgeois and bourgeois doctrines regarding morality are untenable, absurd, because they assert the existence of an eternal and immutable moral code, eternal truths in the domain of morality. A morality for mankind that stands above class differences and above any memory of them will only be possible when society has evolved to a stage where class differences will not only have been obliterated, but forgotten as far as the daily round is concerned."

Soňa Malena went on dictating and her audience continued making notes, bent over their exercise books, notepads or jotters, but Dubovský took down nothing. He stared at his watch and added some toadstools and flowers to his drawing of a house, some spruces and a hill.

She shouldn't have done it, he mused, she shouldn't have suggested they play out that charade in this group. His mind was on the kind of people who attended his surgery. They paraded past, pale-faced, hyperaemic, disfigured, their limbs and chests deformed by disease and the hard lives of earlier generations, their teeth missing or decayed. Soňa had reawakened his belief that the point of his work was to ensure that there would be progressively fewer such people, that too was where her whole morality thing was directed – and she was happy to put on a charade, she didn't believe her own words, it was all bluff... What a pity, Soňa...! His thoughts turned to Eva, who'd told him more than once that his view of people was quite superficial, rather like his handbook on causes of death. Eliminate poverty, eliminate disease – that way many causes of death will be largely eliminated... He'd believed that as long as he believed Soňa. But Soňa evidently didn't believe in her work, her own words... What had happened to her? Why had she suggested they indulge in that charade?

In the lecture hall all was quiet, the audience were quietly writing down their notes, and in the moments of silence between the sentences Soňa was dictating in her spirited, warm voice you could hear the scratching of pencils and pens.

Outside it was gloomy, there was a fine drizzle and the grey November day was drifting down towards dusk. The huge housing estate of the MZ engineering works, brick-red, half-built, awaiting completion, was silent, because the unmade muddy streets, rutted by the wheels of trucks and dumpers, brown with the broken-up earth of what had been fields, and grey with the shingle dredged up from rivers, were quite deserted, not a single adult, nor a single child in sight. The ground was wet, bits of panels and sawn timber were soggy in the drizzling rain, and the concrete baseplates and rusty iron pipes for the future railings round the blocks gleamed in the wet.

Dubovský's wife Eva was getting the children dressed, ready to go out for a walk.

The Dubovskýs lived in Block XIV.

On the estate there were still lots of blocks at various stages of construction, awaiting completion. They were red with their kiln-fired bricks. Everyone called the estate 'Palermo', though no one knew who the name was down to. Someone might have meant it in jest, or someone might have begun living the good life there. From the estate it wasn't far to the works, just a ten-minute walk, and all the residents of the estate, apart from some of the women and the children, worked at MZ, the Emzed works. The estate was new. People had only been living there a year, and they were manual workers, engineers, office workers, a hugely disparate community all brought together by their working at MZ. They lived in one- to three-roomed flats and in the dormitory block for singles, twelve bunks to a room. There was a Community Centre with a canteen, club rooms and lecture halls, a library and rooms which were planned as temporary accommodation for visitors, short-term employees, lecturers, and actors and the members of visiting choirs and dance companies.

That November afternoon the estate was immersed in a gentle, thin mist and the fine drizzle.

From Block XIV Dubovský's wife emerged with their three children.

The children, two boys and a girl, were dressed for warmth, with white plastic macs over their coats and white rubber snow boots on their feet. Their mother, a slim woman with a pale face bearing a slightly sceptical smile and fulsome red lips, was wearing a green coat, also with a white plastic mac pulled over it. Round her head she had a pale-green scarf decorated with the major sights of Paris and texts in black; her legs, thin from the ankles up, had their feet protected by brown shoes with thick crepe soles.

She walked with long strides, slightly hesitantly, as if she were about to stop after each step as she led the children along the rutted, unmade street.

"It's raining, Mummy. Let's go home."

Eva held the older boy's hand tight.

"No, Igor! Not yet –!"

"Why not, Mummy?"

"It's been ages since we went for a walk and you haven't been outside at all today. We need to stretch our legs."

They reached a crossroads.

"Hello!" Mr Jankovič, the engineer, greeted her. He was middle-aged, pale, with a stoop and terribly thin, and he was wearing a shabby, green ulster. "Where are you off to, Mrs D., in such horrible weather?"

"We're just out for a short walk," said Mrs Dubovský. "The children haven't been outside all day –"

Mr Jankovič gave a slight shrug because he thought it quite odd going for a walk in such horrible weather and her voice had had a noticeably thin, diffident ring to his ear.

"How are you, Mr Jankovič?"

Eva was troubled by the question the moment she uttered it.

"Not good, Mrs D."

Eva turned her pale, slightly bedrizzled face to the engineer, whose own face was as pale as a cotton sheet and wrinkled with endless tiny furrows. His large, seemingly colourless eyes shone palely and reproachfully out from his face.

"Not good," he repeated. "And getting worse and worse. The times I've been to see your husband – the works doctor, a GP, a specialist, then this doctor and that, one board of inquiry after another... I've found it quite offensive. It's been dragging on for years now... I'm of the wrong class, Mrs D. – and I missed out on treatment while there was still time... And now? I don't think there's anywhere that could help me now. And your children, are they all well?"

The boys hopped up and smiled at Mr Jankovič.

Eva was troubled by his question.

"They're fine, fine for now –"

Olga started walking in circles round her mother and tugging at her white plastic mac.

"I can say this to you..." Engineer Jankovič's wrinkled features wrinkled even more. I'm sure you'll understand me, even though it's your husband who's the doctor. It's immoral, what doctors are doing. They've backed down, bowed their heads... They should have made themselves heard and got themselves more scope for their own sense of moral obligation, if they still have one. A doctor is duty bound to treat an enemy on the battlefield, at the front, and not let disease slowly kill a person in peacetime... During the Uprising I met a German officer, a medic, and he, Mrs. D., a German, released our wounded partisans and placed them in the hands of our doctors in our hospital. That was in Martin. What goes on today, it's not right. The sort of thing that went on in the death camps... I experienced that myself, I know what I'm talking about – though, truth to tell, that was modern warfare, and now, with modern peace... I can be as useful to the works as anybody else and I'd be of even more use of it weren't for my heart, these nerves... But even that shouldn't be an issue. As he preserves people's health, no doctor should be asking himself whether the life of this person or that is the more useful. Forgive me, Mrs D., it makes me feel so much better to be able to share the odd word with someone." Jankovič began to tremble slightly. "I found it all quite offensive and, to be quite frank, with you, it took away my will to work and my will to live – I seek no act of charity from anyone hereabouts. I hold nothing against your husband. I know he'd be suspected of reactionism if he'd taken my part that time, me, an engineer, a friend of his... That's where we are today. Vets are better placed than doctors: their victims can be put to some use. But what use are the victims of doctors –?"

Jankovič was shaking.

Eva stared at the ground.

"Good bye, Mrs Dubovský," he said. "And please forgive me –!"

"See you sometime, Mr Jankovič."

Jankovič entered Block VIII.

Eva's gaze followed him, she watched him go through the door, watched as the door closed slowly and silently behind him, then she turned her gaze to the long, rutted street ahead, and looked round to check if anyone was coming and might have been listening to them. The long street, wet and deserted, behind the red high-rises reared the Community Centre with its white façade.

Four shiny figures in white plastic macs, Mrs Dubovský and her three children, walked slowly along the street, the brown and grey street, glinting in the fine drizzle, unmade and rutted. Her and her three children's faces were getting wet from the fine drizzle and the grey damp air, which was still punctured here and there by the yellow foliage of alders and willows, and their faces were also kept wet thanks to the evenly and deeply greying overcast sky.

"Mummy," Ondrej asked, "why was Uncle Engineer shaking like that?"

"He's poorly."

"Daddy's a doctor, why doesn't he make him better?"

"My dear little lad," his mother replied, "not every illness can be cured."

She must tell Martin... Eva Dubovský walked silently on with the children. She must tell him –

Eva Moravčík had married Martin Dubovský, a medical student, shortly after they returned from the mountains in forty-five. At the time, Martin Dubovský couldn't imagine life without Eva, a fine figure of a girl with chestnut hair, dark-blue eyes, steeled by the Uprising and five months spent in the mountains, a girl who he sensed, body and soul, was bracing him for his future life, and because, following his return from the mountains, he'd found no one and nothing except the wretched bare walls of his parents' cottage in Veľké Dvorce, smoke-stained and rain-soaked, he'd been thrilled when she said: "We might contrive to live in such a way, Martin, as to replace everything that we two have lost." After the war, Martin truly believed that everything was going to be possible, that there were no limits to personal happiness, and he gloried in having Eva as did she in return. "Eva," he said one time, now as a married man, "we may have promised each other a lot, you may have promised me too much, but things are good as they are..." – "No," she told him, "I didn't promise that much... I'd love to... If indeed any one person can ever replace another. I don't believe one person could replace another. It can't be done. Anyone who happens along after someone who's been lost, be they more or be they less, they can never be *the* one who is no longer. But the effort put into creating a new life can easily push old losses into oblivion. You must agree that it would be no bad thing if one person did try to compensate another for people who've been lost, and it's no bad thing if they do so desire." – "If it hadn't been for you, Eva, I don't know what I'd have done at the sight of the remnants of my father's cottage." Martin Dubovský, his wife and their three children lived well, even though working at the MZ factory and living on its housing estate were evidently not easy, because, until Soňa Malena showed up at MZ, Dubovský had been sinking deeper and deeper into his savage moods as he sought in vain the point of past and present sacrifices, but could not find it anywhere.

The four figures all shiny in their white plastic macs carried on slowly down the street.

"Dear children," said Eva Dubovský jokily, the way she'd heard it on the radio, though her mind was on Mr Jankovič, the engineer, and on what she'd learnt about Soňa Malena from her father's letter, "don't worry about the awful weather! You won't get soaked to the skin because we've all got good macs on and good shoes, and it certainly doesn't matter if your hands and faces get a bit wet. We can just wipe them dry when we get indoors. You have to get out a bit every day and get used to every kind of weather, then you'll be so fit that you won't ever catch cold or get ill. You need to keep well."

"Mummy," Igor wanted to know, "where's Daddy now?"

"He's at a lecture."

"What's he lecturing about?"

"He's not lecturing himself, just listening and learning," Eva explained to Igor, "because Daddy's a doctor, he has to know a lot of things so he can treat people, and so that he can, he has to a lot to learn. Sometimes he does give lectures himself, but not today."

"Can I be a doctor as well?"

"Of course you can," Mrs Dubovský said to Ondrej, "when you grow up you'll learn things, you'll be a student – "

"Me too?"

"You too, Igor, you'll – "

"When I become a doctor," Ondrej said boastfully, "I'll cure Uncle Engineer?"

"It's waining!"

"Yes, Olga sweetie, it is raining a little," Mrs Dubovský said to her little girl, "but never mind."

"Rain, rain, go away, Olga wants to go and play – "

"It's waining, it's pouwing...," Olga made her own contribution, "and Gwandad's snorwing!"

Igor and Ondrej laughed at Olga's little ditty.

"Mummy?"

"Yes, Ondrej?"

"Is it going to rain again tomorrow? When will it stop?"

"Maybe it won't rain tomorrow, it's gone on for so long now, it's been this horrible for such a long time."

Eva and the children walked slowly on among the brick-red high-rises, chatting now and again, otherwise saying nothing, they walked over the brown earth left over on the unmade roadway from what had been fields, and over the grey sand dug out from under the soil – and Eva resolved once more, as her thoughts turned to her husband, Mr Jankovič the engineer, Soňa Malena and Ignác Dugas, that she'd tell Martin –

"It's waining," said Olga, "it's waining, Mummy!"

"I know, darling. We won't stay out long. We'll soon be back indoors, we'll make the dinner, then Daddy will come home, we'll eat, you'll go off to beddy-byes and Daddy and I will still have some work to do."

She must tell Martin, Eva's mind was on Soňa, Dugas... But no, perhaps better not tell him, and not mention Mr Jankovič either... Right now Martin's like he was after the war. "The dead remain dead, Eva." She suddenly recalled the words Martin had used when, in April 1945, they'd been staring at the bare walls of the Dubovskýs' cottage in Veľké Dvorce, "we're left with ruins, but self-assurance, the determination not to jeopardise freedom, love, respect for others – those are the main things that survive, Eva, as they must! If people live with this in mind, the sacrifices won't have been in vain...!" A great deal had changed since then. She won't say anything while... Jankovič might be the source, the product of the savage moods into which he had gradually sunk after Olga was born... No, she won't say anything... He may be right in what he believes, after all, she herself, under Soňa's influence, has begun to believe that all the things that are going on might be right, for all that they sometimes seem quite wrong. Society organised scientifically, the class struggle, socialisation of the village, the fight against obscurantism – maybe it is all right, even though it has produced Dugas in Veľké Dvorce, Soňa's father, the lawyer in Belica's house, Belica, the cross, new victims, new injustices, Jankovič – for Martin all these things are right, he's begun to have faith in it all again, because he has faith in Soňa – and you cannot live with faith – but where's the love and respect for others, dead or living? Maybe it's about love and respect for people who are yet to come... No, for now she'll say nothing to Martin, let him not find out about Soňa from her, maybe he'll get to hear everything some other way, when father or mother comes to see them, they'll tell him –

"Mummy," Igor began, "why doesn't Uncle Engineer come to see us anymore?"

"He's poorly, he's not feeling well."

"And will he come after he gets better?"

"Of course," she replied, "then he'll start coming to see us again, he'll tell you more stories – "

The new and old injustices, the sacrifices of times past and present, Eva was thinking, it's all there somewhere inside Martin, it used to torment him, he detested life... He may be right to look for the sense of it all in people like Soňa, all those things that often seem cruel, pointless and ludicrous... And if Soňa is as Martin sees her, if all this can make her a person of worth, then Martin is right. But, for him, is this not too trifling a boon in exchange for his brother Fero, his mother, father and others slain and burned to death?

Eva Dubovská and the children came to a more level street. They ran off from her, started chasing each other, the boys then surrounding little Olga, who was still striding along with lumbering steps.

Eva smiled at her children, her features marred by her want of conviction. For they, too, her children, were a boon in return for the sacrifices, maybe their promising future will be an even greater boon. The sacrifices were terrible, but there must have been some point to them –

In August 1944, some partisans, Slovaks and Russians, had reached Veľké Dvorce, Martin, along with a number of other men from the village, had joined them, as had his elder brother, Fero. By October, Martin, still a student at the time, had become the company commander and his brother Fero had become envious. "Listen, Martin," he said, "what do you suppose I'm going to do? Take orders from you? I'll work my hide off digging out bunkers and trenches, the Germans will show up and that'll be the end of us. We've eaten everything there was in Veľké Dvorce, so if we stay, we'll starve to death!" – "Quit talking like that! It's bad for discipline," Martin called him to order. "Take some men and get digging!" – "Discipline!!! I'll be doing the digging while you're lounging about with Eva Moravčík, eh? You call that discipline, lounging about with your girlfriend! I'll take some men, but...!" his brother Fero replied, then talked four of his pals, Ján Furdík, Michal Berec, Jozef Dugas and his brother Ignác, into joining him and then they left the company. They took submachine guns with them and Martin Dubovský put out a search party to find them. The valley in which Veľké Dvorce lay was wide and very long and dipped gently down towards the plain where there were several piedmont villages. This was where Fero Dubovský prowled with his four friends and, armed, threatened to kill anyone who refused to give them ample food and drink. Late in October the villages were occupied by German troops, and when they learned that partisans were sleeping in the house next to the chapel, they blew up the two houses on either side of the chapel and burned them down. Fero Dubovský and his comrades had withdrawn to Veľké Dvorce, where they were all, except Ignác Dugas, who'd succeeded in escaping, captured by a partisan patrol, which led them, disarmed and bound, to their commander, Martin Dubovský. After the four bandits were subjected to a brief trial, Martin Dubovský's features were quite pale and his eye filled with tears as he read out the sentence passed on his brother Fero and his three comrades: "The accused, Ján Furdík, Michal Berec, Jozef Dugas and František Dubovský, who became deserters and bandits and so sullied the clean slate of the partisan struggle, caused the death of thirteen people and brought about considerable material damage – are sentenced to death by firing squad... The sentence to be carried out with immediate effect!" Martin Dubovský and twelve other partisans led the bandits off to the gamekeeper's lodge in the fir forest on the far side of Skalka, illuminated by the autumnal October sunlight. The yellow light of the setting sun played about the trees' needles as the four condemned men dug a grave. "I'll be lying here," said Fero Dubovský, "but where you'll be, Martin, you yourself have no idea! You've no idea – you shouldn't have done this to me!" Martin Dubovský was grief-stricken, but daren't let it be seen, because his company discipline depended on it, and when he gave the order to fire, there was such a noise inside his ears that he didn't hear what his brother Fero shouted at him. "Martin," he shouted, "you'll never know a moment's peace after this, not until you kick the bucket yourself. Don't you shoot me, don't you give the order, get someone else to give the order!" The four bandits toppled into the grave and that same day Martin Dubovský drank himself stupid at the teacher Moravčík's, where he'd been invited home by the teacher to meet his wife and daughter, Eva. "Eva," the inebriated Martin moaned, "I've had my brother shot – d'you know what lies ahead for me? All the things I'll have to do to make myself forget? How much evil I – I – shall have to wipe from the face of the earth, all by myself?" That time when he lost his brother, who was two years older, Dubovský did wonders for discipline in his company, and when a troop of Germans tried to capture Veľké Dvorce, they had to do battle with Dubovský's men for a full four weeks before eventually driving them back into the mountains. Then more German soldiers entered Veľké Dvorce under the command of a Major Gerhard, who decided that in his battle with the partisans he would observe restraint, and they also had an SS man with them, whom his younger companions had nicknamed Pif-Paf-Russe, because he had made quite a mark on the eastern front with the number of Soviet soldiers he had "dismantled single-handedly".

That was morality in combat, Dubovský thought in the lecture hall of the Community Centre as he drifted down into one of his savage moods. That was morality, albeit immoral, and the morality of class is also combative, they say –

"Evil is evil," he told Soňa after the lecture, keeping up with the charade, if now against his will, "and good is good, irrespective of time, place or class, and there has always been evil, and always will be, comrade. And proverbially speaking, the worst evil is that which masquerades as good."

Soňa gave a scornful smile. Her pale, smooth features, aglint with her pale-blue eyes, rippled with apprehension.

"You're wrong there, comrade," she said. "Definitely wrong, because such things as good and evil have to be seen in terms of class. Whatever is prejudicial to my class, the working class, which is the very medium of progress, is evil, and that has to be constantly brought into the light and destroyed!"

"Will you permit me a question, comrade? What happens next if some evil should crop up even among us, if we perpetrate some evil among ourselves?"

"That also has to be seen from the point of view of class! Look, comrade, think logically! Has the working class been called upon by history to be the medium of progress?"

"Yes, we can agree on that."

"What is evil and what is good from the class point of view? Is evil that which harms the working class or that which benefits it?"

"That which harms it."

"Does that have to be fought against?"

"In the class sense, yes, when the working class is assuming power and for as long as it is stabilising that power. But what then, comrade?"

"Right, Comrade Dubovský," said Soňa Malena with a slight smile, a slight smile only, but Dubovský registered it as particularly scornful. "Should any evil raise its head within the working class itself, it has to be treated as no more than some residue of past social formations, whether withered away or still withering – and, naturally, it has to be destroyed, brought to light and destroyed. Any enemy, a saboteur or subversive – and such is in any event a class enemy – may come from without or within. We have to bring them to light and destroy them. What then, after class oppositions have all vanished? Evil will vanish. Until then we have to keep destroying it."

"How, comrade?"

"Come, come, comrade," said Soňa Malena with her scornful smile. "Surely that's why we have our organs of national and state security, the courts and so on and so on... You need be in no doubt as regards this philosophical aspect of our doctrine. It's plain and simple, isn't it?"

"Permit me another question, will you, comrade? Can this really be called a philosophical doctrine?"

"Of course it can, comrade! The essence of our philosophical doctrine is to seek out the enemy and destroy him."

"Permit me a comment, will you, comrade? It strikes me that you've actually got it wrong!" said Dubovský. His brother Fero sprang back to his mind. "No, comrade! What you told us about morality, or morale, it's all so superficial, things that might hold up during a war or revolution. Like I said, when the working class is assuming power and is still stabilising that power. Later, as socialism is being constructed in peace, class oppositions are inevitably blunted, or vanish, as I might put it, and the issue of any acute class hostility ceases to exist. Evil then manifests itself in a different form, not in class antago-nism. Classes will have been ceasing to exist – and with that the class struggle. Evil as a constant, as an objective reality, will take on a different form... At which point I would permit myself another question, comrade: what happens if the work-ing class becomes its own enemy...? We know from experience that even within the working class people lie, they steal, kill, murder and so on and so on... I think instead of class morality another kind of morality has to step in – societal morality, state morality, human or –!"

In the quiet of the lecture hall all eyes were now turned on Dubovský.

"Comrade!" said Soňa Malena to the now sullen Dubovský as she brushed him aside. "Your questions have taken us beyond the purview of this discussion... And I believe I have already answered them. I ought merely to add that quite the reverse: with the building of socialism the class struggle gains in intensity and class morality becomes ever more warrant-ed... Don't go thinking, comrade, that the class struggle and the attendant issues of class morality need to be jettisoned. Far from it. A society that is building socialism needs to organize the class struggle, seek out the enemy, bring him into the light and destroy him... Your views, comrade, reek of Bukharinism or the petty bourgeoisie, they're reactionary, idealistic, counterrevolutionary... Does anyone have anything else to add?"

She looked at Dubovský.

"All right, then, comrade!"

"It's all very well," he said, "having this kind of debate. Slapping a label on your opponent and shutting him up, and a highly dangerous label at that, and not just one, but many. An entire arsenal! I have no desire, comrade, to return the compliment, and with interest!" Dubovský was starting to be gripped by anger. "Most of all I'd like to know whether anyone, amoral by nature and in private, can be moral, say, in the workplace, or not, in his public life, in his attitude to other people and so forth. To my way of thinking, he can't. I think we should discuss this more instead of –"

"I think, comrade, that that is a matter of maturity and consciousness. A mature and conscious individual will subordinate all his personal and private issues to his work and the common good, and live in line with the interests of the working class."

Dubovský asked no further questions, just glowering at his desk, while Soňa Malena cast her contented and triumphant gaze over her animated, surprised and smiling audience of ordinary workmen, fitters, engineers and office-workers. She began giving out instructions regarding the next meeting. From their unspoken acquiescence in what Soňa had been saying Dubovský also sensed their unspoken derision.

He was harming the cause, and himself... He was making fun of those who'd been duped...! Taking a cankered view of himself, he closed his notepad full of sketches and scribbles, picked up his green retractable ballpoint and kept clicking it up and down. Larking about with charades, it's not on – not like this...! She doesn't believe her own words, he doesn't believe the things he's been saying, they've been playing the fool, taking the mickey out of people who want to have something to believe in so they might –

"Excuse me, comrade," rose out of the silence, "would you mind?"

Soňa, Dubovský and the audience looked at Mokrý, chairman of the one of the workshop branches of the Party, a thin, dried-up, swarthy-looking chap, whose scalp glimmered white through his sparse black hair.

"Yes, comrade?"

"You've got it all wrong," said Mokrý. "All wrong. I disagree. Marxism teaches us that, once there's socialism, poverty and war will be things of the past. I believe that – and anyone who doesn't like it, who wants poverty and war, let them clear off, we need to be rid of all such!" He paused, smiling at Dubovský with his dark eyes. "I'm sure Comrade Dubovský doesn't believe a word of what he's been saying. If he did, he wouldn't bother treating us. He'd just say being sick is being sick, an evil is an evil – can't be helped. But he does help us, driving our sickness away. Those who want poverty and warfare – that's also sick. They have to be driven away! Comrade Malena doesn't believe what she said. Otherwise all of us here would have had it. One would just shout at another that he's a class enemy... Things can go wrong, true, even a dentist can extract a healthy tooth – but that doesn't mean, comrades, that healthy teeth have to be extracted. I think it's like this, that – that it's hard to find a genuine class enemy – and so sometimes we just grab anyone, call him a class enemy and away with him! And away he goes! He's copped it...! That really isn't right, it's not what Marxism teaches us... Explain this to us, comrade, how it's –!"

Dubovský smiled at Soňa and Soňa, whose pale, smooth face had turned a shade of pink, began explaining, repeating what she'd said in her lecture. Now and again she stuttered slightly. Her audience watched her, some grinning, others bewildered – and Dubovský, his retractable pen in one hand and his note pad in the other, became self-absorbed, Soňa Malena's words passed him by, as did those of workshop chairman Mokrý and such other members of the audience who'd plucked up the courage to join the debate. His mind was on his executed brother, the other bandits executed and the thirteen people shot in Slanica. So awful that, after all this, people should be bickering about who their enemy is, floundering about in pointless uncertainty – and he himself saw in Soňa alone, in that hypocritical, inexperienced, maybe stupid girl, the sense of those victims, those old injustices, the new... Mentally, Dubovský began to laugh at himself. The sense of the victims wasn't in Soňa, nor in all that hot air, not in any persecution, but maybe somewhere in that place where Eva suspects it –

Soňa Malena's wan, smooth face was flushed and her pale-blue eyes looked reproachfully at Dubovský.

The lecture hall was growing darker.

Someone put the lights on, large white globes hanging from shiny tubes.

Almost an hour of sterile debate passed, brought to an end by Mokrý when he rapped his knuckles on his desk: "We have always worked honestly – and – and I know plenty of people who would have been working with us, but couldn't. They're in jail. That's not class warfare – that, Comrade Malena, is sabotage. After all, socialism – it's like a gift that we mustn't go destroying like this… Comrade Dubovský said there'll always be evil. He's right about that, because there'll always be bad people. I was once told by Comrade Eva Dubovský –" Mokrý smiled at Dubovský – "that socialism is a gift of history that comes at a great cost, that's how she put it, and we, we have to prize it and, I would say, cultivate it. Socialism can only be cultivated and built up by decent, principled people, not by scoundrels and all kinds of – in a word by people! We know what this is about, don't we?"

"No," Soňa Malena interrupted him nervously, "no, comrades. From now on we must treat these matters purely from the class angle – until such time as class antagonism and any recollection of it have disappeared… What Comrade Mokrý has been saying merely proves how easy it is to slip into idealism and commit errors that the class enemy can craftily exploit… This is taking us beyond the framework of an open comradely discussion –"

Soňa Malena went on, granting a modicum of truth to each discussant, especially to workshop chairman Mokrý, and brought the meeting to a close.

The people in the audience rose from behind their dark-brown, lustreless desks, carried on the debate in groups of three or four and began making their way out. Dubovský re-opened his notepad, clicked his retractable ballpoint to expose the tip, pretended to be jotting something down and waited for everyone to leave the lecture hall.

"Sorry, Soňa!" he whispered as he walked by her. "Don't be mad at me!"

"By all means," she said, so loud that it could be heard by the people out in the corridor. "What is it, comrade?"

She smiled at Dubovský, now neither condescendingly nor scornfully, then shook her head as if about to apologise to him.

Dubovský was no longer just one member of her audience, but Martin, a man with agreeable, sharp, always somehow slightly restless features, deep-set eyes overshadowed by the prominent forehead hanging over them, eyes that were care-free, always with a hint of a smile and now and again with a flash of caution in them, a fine figure of a man, just short of tall, wearing a grey, fine shepherd check suit.

Soňa glanced behind her through the open door into the corridor.

"Come upstairs," she whispered. "Will you?"

"Now?"

"Any time you like."

Dubovský nodded and walked out of the lecture hall.

Then Soňa Malena pensively bundled together her note pads, books, two exercise books, her record book and her little red bag, staring down at the table.

Her fingers were white, thin and long, her hands smooth and with red fingernails, the sleeves of her long red jumper rolled back to just beyond her wrists, the jumper itself drawn tight across her hips and billowing over her breasts. It covered her neck almost to her chin. Round her invisible neck she had a little gold chain with a tiny gold hammer and sickle dangling from it. Her face was pale, smooth, the left side of her mouth curled slightly upwards.

Dubovský hurried down the long corridor then stopped outside the clubroom. He opened the door and a rush of voices filled the corridor. He stepped inside.

The rush of voices in the corridor died, the only sounds left being the pinging of a table-tennis ball and the brisk, tiny footsteps of Soňa Malena.

On her feet Soňa had a pair of beige shoes on medium-high heels, her shapely legs were slightly hampered at the knees by her tight skirt with a slit at the front over her left knee and behind over the right, which sat close round her mildly broadened hips, while her long red jumper had a slight fold above her hips, and on her head billowed waves of her sandy blonde hair.

As yet, the Community Centre had no lift, just an empty shaft. Fixed crosswise across its doors were odd bits of deal floorboard, and because the doors had only black plastic handles and no lock they all carried red warning signs saying CAUTION! LIFT! SHAFT! lest anyone try the wrong door and come to a sticky end. This was intended as a temporary security measure to cover the few days before locks were fitted.

Soňa walked with her brisk, tiny steps up the stairs and arrived at the sixth floor.

"Oh!" she let out a faint yelp. "Have you been waiting for me?"

"Yes – I need –"

"Come on in!"

"Have you got any...?"

The former lawyer, Malena, Soňa's father, leaning on his bamboo cane, wearing his trench coat, all wet at the shoulders, and a wet, wide grey hat, held out his wide hand but without looking at Soňa, his eyes being fixed on the door to the lift.

"Will a hundred crowns do?"

Soňa took a hundred-crown note from her little red bag and handed it to her father.

"Who are you seeing these days?" Malena stuffed the banknote in his coat pocket. "Don't stick to anyone regular, you might fall in love... Love's been the undoing of more than one woman like you –!"

"Father! For God's sake, get out!"

"I've got nothing left, Soňa. My last things went on that Dugas fellow, as a loan, he said. You've destroyed me, Soňa – that Party secretary, the Vlach chap... Nobody wants to buy my furniture or pictures. Now you'll just have to carry on as you began with that secretary –!"

Soňa looked away from her father.

"You bitch!"

Soňa unlocked the door to her bedsit, which was next to the lift.

Malena left.

Soňa's door closed with a bang that echoed right round the long corridors.

From the first to the fifth floor of the Community Centre the parquet flooring had yet to be put down in the rooms and hallways of the bedsits. There was no furniture anywhere, because they'd forgotten to plan for it!

Soňa Malena, the cultprop, who hadn't wanted to live in the dormitory, had been given a bedsit next to the lift shaft and they'd furnished it for her with items from the offices of the MZ works. She'd had her parents send her a bed.

Outwardly, 'Palermo' was a quiet estate.

Maybe it will liven up a bit, people thought, once it's complete and once, according to the plan, thirty thousand people come to live here.

The rutted and unmade streets, the concrete baseplates and the rusty iron pipes for the fences round each block, the bits of planking and raw timber left lying about the streets, the brown earth and the grey sand – all of this was now sunk in darkness, with just the odd glint of something in the light from the provisional street lights, each one set very far apart from the next. It had stopped drizzling, but the air was heavy with the dank fog that was sinking earthwards. It was a grey, very raw November evening, drowning everything in that damp, heavy fog.

Eva Dubovský and the children were heading back from their walk, her husband Martin was sitting in the clubroom, watching a pair of passionately preoccupied, battling chess-players with berets pulled down over their foreheads, and Soňa Malena, up on the sixth floor, still dazed after the discussion in the Marxism-Leninism circle and her father's visit, was airing and tidying her room. She wiped the dust from the frame round a photo from when she'd been volunteering at harvest time.

And how nice Soňa looked in that photo. Wearing shorts and a flimsy chequered blouse, she was sitting on a sheaf, her bare legs with her arms round them and her feet stuck in among the spikes of corn, her breasts were squashed together by her shoulders and the wind was playing with her hair, blowing it upwards, her eyes were half-closed against the wind and she was laughing boisterously with her wide lips and teeth, the latter straight and densely packed like a white keyboard.

"Dear children," said Eva Dubovský in the tone of a radio programme for kids, as they approached block XIV, "here we are, home again –"

Olga ran to the door of No. XIV and reached up for the big, black handle.

Eva and the children went inside No. XIV.

Half an hour passed, several minutes passed.

"Come in!"

Soňa, waiting in bedsit for Dubovský, looked in eager anticipation towards the door.

"Good evening!"

She failed to respond, went pale and sat down on the bed. She stared in terror at the production planner, Vlach, who had closed the door and was now standing in the middle of the room.

He was wearing a green, army-style raincoat, slightly damp at the shoulders, with his hands stuck, clearly restless, deep inside the pockets.

"Soňa," he began, "Quit fooling about with Dubovský! There's no point. Go for others."

"Why?"

"He hasn't got any money and you've been dallying with him since August. Give him up. You don't even know how to goad him – at that thing today it was ludicrous, positively dire. Making a fool of yourself like that in front of everyone."

"Sit down, Peter."

"No, I'm leaving. You'll have to get me money from other sources – like your father."

"My father? He hasn't got any left. He lent his last to some chap called Dugas, who wants to build a house in Veľké Dvorce."

"I don't believe it!"

Vlach stood over Soňa, his hands restless in his pockets, staring mockingly into Soňa's pale face. He took out a cigarette, lit it and spat some tobacco out through his thin lips.

"I'm going to need that money," he said, "urgently! Are you expecting Dubovský? There's no point. Leave him! We'll come back to this again. I don't believe you, Soňa, or that father of yours."

His thin lips formed into a smile, his hands twitched inside his coat pockets and he left.

Soňa remained seated on the bed with a sudden headache and shaking all over.

There wasn't a living soul in the wide corridors of the Community Centre, and they were wide, long and deserted as Dubovský left the chess-players in the club room and trudged silently in his commando-soled shoes up to the sixth floor in the foul mood that had gradually and unsubtly come over him at Soňa's lecture and in the discussion that followed. He wasn't so much mortified by how Soňa had publicly called him all those dangerous names, Bukharinist, petty-bourgeois, reactionary, idealist and counterrevolutionary, as by his loss of faith in her and by the charade that had been so damaging to him, to Soňa, maybe to Mokrý and the other discussants as well. He'd begun having pangs of conscience about Jankovič, which Soňa's appearance quelled somewhat after she arrived at the MZ works in early August.

He was annoyed at having let himself be lured into that charade at the Marxism-Leninism circle because he loved Soňa deeply and would have resisted in vain, but now he'd begun to suspect her and see in her something other than what he'd seen at the outset. People hadn't died for his conscience to be blunted by some Soňa. While he was watching the young chess-players he'd sunk into a savage mood. He knew that mood well because it used to creep up on him now and again even before he met Soňa. He made his way slowly and silently up the stairs. Charades shouldn't be put on, least of all one like theirs, he thought. The savage mood into which he was sinking ever deeper stemmed from an ancient injustice that had persecuted entire families in Veľké Dvorce, his own forebears and closest kin. It was an ancient injustice that kept changing shape during and after the Uprising, and if it hadn't been for Eva Moravčík, he would scarcely have been able to come to terms with the new life that bore the injustice along in ever new forms. The constant peril that had, during the Uprising, loomed over him, Eva and the people around them, had stirred in him a sense of living for the moment, and not for some unseen goal. What had it all been for, he mused, as he plodded up the stairs, and what's the point of having other goals, so lofty and remote? The way we're living, trifling, short-term, everyday goals suffice. Eva had stirred in him a yen not to live for the moment: he had graduated, married her, then came the first child, a second, the third, he'd learned to be patient, to do without things, but having registered the growing pressures of day-to-day life and that the world was sinking back into wars, he was once more plunged into thought: What's the point? What's the point of squandering life, his young life, of which he'd already lost so much in the Uprising? Where were his comrades in the Uprising now? No trace of so many of them. Everything was lost in the Uprising, youth and that untrammelled sense of freedom even in the face of imminent death. Where had it all gone? It got lost there. And afterwards? He had come through, he was a doctor now, moderately well off – but where were the others? What became of them? No trace of them, of so many of them! They'd languished as he had, and vanished. They'd filled their lungs with something or other, then once the war was over, it had begun to stifle them. Then came lots of pointless work, and with it servility – and plenty of men of the National Guard were as good as he was, maybe better and more worthy. What's the point of squandering one's only life on lofty goals, far ahead, what's the point of trying to make up for a chain of past injustices by seeking to secure a better life for oneself and one's children, though, again, by a chain of injustices both now and in the future? No one knows what's to come. Everything changes from one day to the next, what was sacred yesterday is to be cursed today. The world is divided, it's darkening towards war, with provocations on every side... There's no truth anywhere, they're all lying, proclaiming one thing one day and the next day something else – where's the way out of this chaos? How on earth can one look for distant goals in it? No one believes anything or anybody and everyone's putting on some kind of charade. The old ills have gone on their way, new ones have appeared, and they're all the worse for being unexpected. We have to live for the moment. He'd been naive to believe Soňa... He'd believed her because everything about her said that out there, somewhere inside people like her, the new people, young, unencumbered, readily receptive to the new way of life and capable of relishing its positive aspects, was the sense of... He found that laughable. His brother Fero, his mother, his father and so very many others – and Soňa, sense in Soňa? We have to live for the moment, in Soňa he'd found a momentary goal, Soňa had stirred in him – as Eva had once, though this time more potently – the will to seek after sense, to seek remoter goals, and it was this Soňa who'd put him up to that charade at the Marxism-Leninism circle, playing it out with him in front of those decent folk, he playing along with her... In front of decent, deluded folk... In his savage mood he reached the sixth floor, passed the lift door and knocked on Soňa's.

Soňa came to the door.

"Well hello, Martin!" she whispered. "Wait, I'll lock it."

"Nice place you've got, Soňa."

"You think so?"

"Like in some den of iniquity."

"What makes you say that?"

Dubovský sat down in a metal armchair, Soňa on the metal bedframe.

"That was the first and last time, Soňa," he said eventually, "there'll be no more stupid charades like today's. That was a sick thing to do in front of those decent and maybe deluded people."

"What's got into you, Martin? Not even you go along with everything that goes on here."

Dubovský said nothing.

"What's got into you?"

He gave a shrug.

"Martin!"

"I believed you, Soňa," he said after a pause, "and I believed other things besides, and all because I believed you. Now? After that charade today – ?"

"Let's not be kill-joys, Martin," said Soňa, "It'd be a shame if – "

After that there was a long silence in Soňa's bedsit.

Dubovský was looking at Soňa as if seeing her for the first time, with a feeling of having done ill by her with that charade – he'd been downright beastly to her! – and he began to relate everything he knew about her to his own life.

In October forty-four he'd had to withdraw to the mountains with his company, twenty-seven of whom had fallen. The troop of Germans who'd driven the partisans out of Veľké Dvorce consisted mostly of Waffen-SS. They occupied almost all the houses and cottages and were getting ready to launch an attack on the partisans' camps and bunkers. They kept a close watch on the few people who hadn't fled Veľké Dvorce, mostly old men, women and children, though in a village sprawled out across hillsides and upland pastures that was quite a task. Veľké Dvorce had sprung up along a snaking track that wound over the hillsides, and at Bukovec Rise, beyond the last and topmost cottage, on Belica's meadow, stood Belica's cross, already old back then, made of oak, blackened with age and having the odd long, wide cleft in it. The cross had nailed to it an old, sheet-metal human figure, now almost grey all over, and on its round metal top a few scattered sharp, spiky stars were still welded in place. Every day, early in the evening, Mária Dubovský would come to pray at the foot of Belica's cross, she, mother of Fero Dubovský, whose own brother Martin had had him shot for becoming a bandit and causing death and destruction at two houses in Slanica. Every day, early in the evening, Mária Dubovský, dressed all in black, would kneel down at the foot of the cross, wind a black rosary round her work-worn hands and say a prayer for the dead, one that she knew, adding a supplication for her executed son Fero before finally saying a rosary filled with pain. Once it was an early evening in October, the sun was submerging into the dark fir forest on Skalka, its yellow gleam shivered by the trees as it shone down on Mária Dubovský kneeling before the cross. "– turn, oh, Lord, Thy merciful gaze upon a soul that abideth in purgatory…" The SS man Pif-Paf-Russe happened to be passing the cross and paused beside her. "– and," she prayed aloud, "deliver that soul if it be suffering for its sins…" – "Nee, was machst du hier?" Pif-Paf-Russe asked, directing his question at her back. "Betest du für die Partisanen? Ja? Du alte Pfütze! Warter nur mal…!" "– be merciful unto his soul," Mária Dubovský prayed, "– grant unto him eternal peace there where Thou Thyself reignest in the heavenly heights beside Thy dear Son and the Holy Spirit…" Pif-Paf-Russe, that elongated face criss-crossed with vertical creases around the mouth, disfigured across its purple brow that had been first shattered then operated on, the eyes out of line, the right one pressed down by the purple brow towards its cheek bone, eyes filled with distrust, as if the higher one were constantly checking the lower one, Pif-Paf-Russe glanced at the cross, at Mária Dubovský, lit a bent cigarette and looked down at the ground, at the still green, dense grass. He walked off, away from the cross. He had been well-schooled politically and knew that a powerful race, called upon to play a part in history, would drive out weaker races, exterminate them, because the mighty torrent of its vitality would shatter the ludicrous obstacles of the so-called humanity of individuals and smash a way through to the humanity of nature. Nature destroys the weak to provide space for the strong. That was why the Führer had built those camps, that was what all those new armaments were for. Pif-Paf-Russe strode down the path, pondering how he should fulfil his moral obligation. It would hardly be worthy of a German soldier to have shot the old woman in the back, even if she had been praying for the partisans. That's no way to dispose of anyone, there's no fun in it. Touching a woman like that with a bullet makes you feel squeamish, because the bullet leaves the pistol that you're holding in your hand, so it feels like you're thrusting your hand into some muck... He strode on down the path, smoking thoughtfully, and suddenly he recalled the dense green grass at the foot of Belica's cross, and landmines. Such fun it had been in Russia, he thought. Wow, the sheer rapture of it! In his mind's eye he could see the Russian captives who'd been ordered to walk in a prescribed manner across a field that had been mined to clear the way for a body of German troops on the attack. They had rendered the minefield harmless, flying high up into the air. But those had been elements politically beyond the pale, commissars, rabble-rousers – but what about that old woman? Is she not a dangerous rabble-rouser, is she not worse than a Russian commissar? She must have been praying for some partisan!

The only ones who pray these days are people hostile to the grand Idea that drives us Germans. The sun finally sank down among the dark fir trees on Skalka, the yellow glow went out, and by the time Pif-Paf-Russe arrived back at the local command post he knew what he was going to do. "Great idea!" the restrained Major Gerhard said to him, "Give it a go! Maybe it will summon the partisans from heaven, if not from the mountains! Be careful though." – "Yessir, Herr Major!" Night fell and Pif-Paf-Russe gathered up two landmines, took them to Belica's cross, dug up a small area of grass at the foot of the cross, buried the mines and carefully replaced the turf over them. Next morning, he went back up to the cross, casually, to check that the grass still looked as it should. Well done, lad! He was satisfied and waited to see what would happen. In war, anything goes, especially in a war like the present one, one what forges a way for the strong, and a strong man doesn't look round to see what's happening to the weak – his sole concern is that things have to go forward so that the weak are gone for good. The weak have to be broken, in body, heart and spirit – or conversely you break their spirit, heart and body. Inoculate them with fear, inject fear into them, because he who is afraid only lures death to him. Such was what was going on inside the head of SS man Pif-Paf-Russe, and all day, till late in the afternoon, he and his comrades watched with their telescopes from the distant hill slope beneath Skalka and waited to see what would happen. Around him he had people who were just like him. Most were just young lads, two still just fifteen, and they were sitting on a fir tree that had been felled by a shell, watching the cross and chatting – Pif-Paf-Russe, a forty-five-year-old one-time double murderer and a "green" from Birkenau, being the oldest and most experienced of them, led the conversation and was teaching them things. "You're young," he said, "you still don't know anything, my young jackasses, still wet behind the ears. Aiding the Führer, the party, the government of the Reich – that has to be the most glorious goal of any male German, and if anyone

happens to kick the bucket, my young jackasses, that's imma-
terial. And what *is* that woman? Nothing! You might see that
for yourselves any moment now. Are you thinking the woman's a human being? She isn't. She's a smelly old bag of wind
because she lives without a grand idea." – "This is gonna be
great!" – "Not half!" – "You can bet on it, jackass," said Pif-Paf-
Russe, putting his telescope to his eye and focussing on the
cross, "like the first time you get drunk or have it off with a
woman. Second time it comes easier – and after that...! After
that it becomes an insult if anyone suggests you keep off the
booze or the women...!" – "She's gonna fly right up to her
Christ!" – "You've got it, jackass," said Pif-Paf-Russe, "She'll
give him a hug!" Above Veľké Dvorce, on Skalka, the sun had
begun to submerge into the dark fir forest, its yellow gleam
lighting up Belica's cross. Mária Dubovský, dressed in black,
mother of two sons, Martin the partisan and Fero the executed bandit, and clutching a black rosary in both hands, made
her way up to the cross and knelt down. From the distant
hillside below Skalka, Pif-Paf-Russe and his pals focussed their
telescopes on her. "This is it!" – "Not quite!" – "What's wrong?"
Pif-Paf-Russe asked as he twiddled the eyepiece of his telescope to refocus from the cross to the woman in black. The
chromatic colours surrounding the woman in black and the
cross caused him to smile. "Has she spotted something?" –
"Perhaps she has, the old hag!" Mária Dubovský, her black
rosary wound round her crippled, work-worn hands, was
praying. "– be merciful unto his soul," she pleaded out loud,
"– grant unto him eternal peace there where Thou Thyself
reignest in the heavenly heights...!" – "Come on, gran," said
Pif-Paf-Russe, "get on with it! You're not kneeling close enough
to the cross." Mária Dubovský then began to pray her painful
rosary. Her knees started to ache. Pif-Paf-Russe's pals' hearts
started beating out loud as they waited and waited, staring at
the cross and the woman in black. "Come on, gran." – "Pif-Paf-
Russe," one of his fifteen-year-old pals wondered, "have you
also got a glow round the woman and the cross?" – "That's not

a glow, you jackass, it's the colours of the spectrum. Come on, gran, get in closer!" Old Mária Dubovský looked at the long, deep clefts in the black oak wood, raised her twisted hands to help her lean against the cross, "– fruit of Thy life, Jesus," she prayed, "who was crowned with thorns...," she raised her arms once more and as she shuffled closer to the cross on her knees, that was when her son, Martin Dubovský, lost his mother. Pif-Paf-Russe and his pals shouted for joy when, through their telescopes, they saw three large bits of black clothing fly into the air, outlined by the colours of the spectrum. "I did think," said Pif-Paf-Russe, "I did think she was going to give Christ a hug – but this will have to do! Well, what did you think of that, my jackasses?" His pals were breathing fast. Belica's cross had recoiled in horror, started to lean slightly, its wood splintered by shell fragments, with three new holes in its metal crown, but it hadn't tumbled over, and when those people who'd remained in Veľké Dvorce heard about it that same evening, Eva Moravčík, a young lass of twenty-two, who'd stayed at home instead of going to Bratislava, where she'd been studying philosophy, went off into the mountains to join the partisans. She left Veľké Dvorce, because she could stick it out no longer in the atmosphere of green German fear, and she left to find Martin Dubovský. She needed to tell him everything about what had befallen his mother, she needed to be beside him, to console him, because when he'd come to their place after the execution of his brother Fero and got totally drunk, she was seized by pity and admiration for him. Thus had Martin Dubovský lost both his brother and his mother during the Uprising.

"Soňa –!"

The Community Centre on the MZ works housing estate was still awaiting completion. It had no lift yet, just a deep empty shaft, wires were poking out of the walls of its corridors wherever an electric lock or light was to come, with just the odd naked light bulb attached to some of them, only the exterior wall had been plastered, with some ceramic decorations stuck on it, in places some of the roof was still missing, but inside it was warm. The radiators were hot, if unpainted as yet – and it was also cosy and warm in Soňa Malena's bedsit on the sixth floor.

In it, she had a low, metal-framed bedstead, a wardrobe, two metal armchairs and a coffee table, a metal desk and a small bookcase.

"Soňa –!"

She was stretched out on her bed, on the pale-green bedspread, with her body still lightly tanned since the summer, and with her smiling white face she looked up into Dubovský's as he bent down close over her.

"Soňa –!"

Dubovský lay down on his back and pointed to the photograph of her volunteering at harvest time.

"Don't you like me in the photo?"

"Oh yes, there and here," he said. "There you look like 'Come lads, come and get it!' – and here –"

"And here like what?"

"Here?" Martin asked with censure in his eyes, which were hidden in shadow, as he hugged the tanned Soňa to him. "Here you look like 'Sup thy fill, my country lad, as custom dictates'... – but that's a nice photo. Do you mean it as promotional or just promoting yourself to yourself?"

"There's some call even for that if one's to have faith in oneself."

"I don't like that, Soňa."

"Why not?"

"It's what people with an inferiority complex do."

"Oh, you, Martin...! The greater the inferiority complex, the larger the photo, and this one isn't very big... Sup thy fill, my country lad, as custom dictates –!"

Martin Dubovský lay there a moment on his back, staring at the harvest-time photo, then he turned his face to Soňa's.

"Soňa," he began after a longish pause, "why did we put on that charade today? What had got into you?"

"By that stage we had to," she said, parting her lips slightly to reveal between them her glistening teeth, straight and densely packed like a tiny keyboard, and breathing fast, causing her breasts to undulate and the tiny chain with its gold hammer and sickle to dangle onto Dubovský's chest. "We had to, Martin, we had to – and let's put it on some more, it helped me, things livened up a bit in the club, though it got Mokrý a bit excited, but then others play charades as well, everyone does, you too, Martin, we both do so people don't get the idea we're going out together, everywhere calls for it – let's keep it going as long as possible! "We have to, Martin, we have to –!"

Soňa fell silent for a brief moment.

"Let's play, let's keep playing, we too, let's play, Martin, Martin –"

In Block XIV Eva Dubovský, Martin's wife, was settling her children in their chrome-plated cots, troubled by her father's letter and by Soňa and Martin. Why was he so changed since Soňa's arrival…? Her father had been forcibly installed in Belica's old house – maybe she's just one very unhappy lass, but able to get on top of it… Who knows? What does Martin see in her…? How is it possible to see in her the sense of anything, all the things, that have hit Martin? Martin has changed quite strikingly – he believes in his work, his life, though Jankovič –

"Mummy?"

"Yes, Igor?"

"Are you coming to bed as well?"

"Not yet."

"And why not?"

"I still have to iron your clothes for tomorrow –"

"And why doesn't Uncle Engineer come to see us anymore?"

"He's poorly – now go to sleep, Igor."

"Yes, mummy."

"Mummy," Olga called out, "good night!"

"Good night, Olga."

"Mummy?"

"Yes, Ondrej?"

"Will Auntie Soňa be coming to see us?"

"I don't know," Eva replied to her children, "maybe she will, maybe she won't – now, off to sleep, children, good night!"

"Good night!"

In the bedroom, Eva went from cot to cot, tucking the children in nicely while her mind was on Soňa and the knotty problem of whether or not to tell Martin what she'd learned from her father's letter. She can't tell him... Let him see something illusory in her... She came out of the bedroom and crossed the living room to the kitchen to a mound of children's shirts and dresses.

Dubovský knew quite a lot about Soňa, because Soňa loved him and sometimes told him things about herself, like the little son she had at her parents' place in Veľké Dvorce, but he didn't know everything.

They were silent, Martin and Soňa, on the sixth floor of the Community Centre, in a bedsit flooded with a yellowish green half-light. The heads of both of them were filled with a rush of memories, half-formed ideas, ponderous and importunate thoughts, and questions.

The twenty-three-year-old girl, pretty, daughter of a former lawyer, an only child, she'd completed secondary school after the war and enrolled to study medicine... Towards the end of her second year, the party secretary at the university, a nonentity, had her brought to him and told her: "Comrade Malena, the choice is yours: either, or...!" – "What's this about, Comrade Secretary?" – "You know very well what it's about, surely?" – "No, I don't," she said, though she had more than half an idea from his pale-green gleaming eyes. He had the eyes of a serpent. She watched him, a young fellow, with a narrow forehead and wide puffy cheeks, a wide mouth wearing a constant smile, with thick lips, soggy at the corners. "I've told you before. I could help you conceal your class background, we could contrive something with your file if... It can be done – anything can be done if..." – "And – then what?" – "You'll be able to complete your course, you'll complete it, or..." – "Is that your word of honour?" – "Of course, comrade...!" Out of fear for her future and that of her parents she indulged the party secretary for two revolting months, and after two months – in 1951 – she was expelled from the university. She was completely crushed, complained to her parents and her father said: "You did wrong, Soňa!" Then he beat her and shouted at her: "You've wrecked your own life and ours. Don't come complaining to us, don't come asking our advice! It's too late now. Since you could disown us before such nobodies, I'm disowning you...! You should have held your ground...! You should never have given in...!" From that moment on her father had maintained a stony silence, gradually become alienated from her mother and from her, and a few days later she abandoned her parents. She found a job as a secretary, another one two months later as a lab assistant at a pharmacy, forever switching jobs until finally, in Bratislava, she wound up in the Peace Factory and with the help of friends she made on holidays and voluntary stints at harvest time she got into workers' education. She was pretty, she continued to garner useful acquaintances, exploiting them, beating herself and others up because of that party secretary, for a time she worked in physical education at the regional national committee, fell foul of the official in charge of physical education and left, she gave birth to a baby boy, fathered by...? She placed him in a nursery, then with her parents, and finally she'd arrived here, at the MZ works because they needed a cultprop. Abused, laid low, she can't believe in anyone, not even in her work, because so far as she can tell, no one believes in what they do, except Martin. A person has to have something in order to go on living, whether that's making goods that are a laughing stock quality-wise, or trumpeting things one doesn't believe in oneself, it's all one. Work is work, a necessary evil that everyone has to perform – and life is life, and that has to be lived. She organises her work at MZ and on the estate herself, and she does it well, she mixes with lots of different people and everything's going well. Many sing the praises of her bulletin boards, finding them smart, lively, topical, while others claim that their element of folk art comes agreeably to the fore and that the Marxism-Leninism circle really does enhance the workforce's understanding of theory. Her lectures are described as being of a high standard – and meanwhile it's a charade... Visiting theatre companies and choirs are invariably major events of a high order artistically. What a shame, Soňa...! Martin is someone who would reclaim her for living, he would even help her little boy Jurko and perhaps her parents as well. Martin comes to see her, having basically abandoned his wife and children by this stage... What a shame it was, Soňa, to have believed you, to have believed a single word you uttered... You've had a hard life, but you have failed to stand your ground, you've always lived, and still live, on impulse, you preach – without believing your own sermons, you con honest, deluded people with falsehoods, the warped products of your own life story, honest people have seen and still see something in you – it's a perilous charade you're putting on –

The heads of both, Soňa's and Martin's, were filled with a rush of memories, half-baked ideas, ponderous and importunate questions that demanded answers, all these things jumbled up and colliding together. Soňa wanted Martin's response to many issues, Martin wanted Soňa's, and both were waiting for answers to all manner of things from themselves as well. Are they perhaps lying to each other... Could Soňa be lying... Could Martin. He does lie to his wife and children – and who does Soňa lie to?

"Listen, Martin," Soňa interrupted Dubovský's musing, "how about I pay you a visit to keep up appearances?"

"What's the time?"

"Half past eight."

"Okay then."

Soňa Malena got dressed, combed her hair, put on some mauve lipstick and as on any other occasion when Martin Dubovský had been with her, went off to pay his wife Eva a brief visit.

Dubovský drew Soňa's pale-green bedspread over him, reached across to the bookcase and picked out a brochure, opened it from the back and, locked away inside Soňa's bedsit, looked at the lines "– chemists have enthusiastically played their part in the socialist restructuring of our country, in the planned, single-minded, creative task of industrialising and chemicalising the country...", he stared at the lines, not reading them, not thinking about what he was seeing. Pity about you, you kids and Eva, pity about you, Soňa, it was a pity about you, Mum, it was a pity to have had you killed, Fero, all for this, this nothingness, a pity about you, engineer Jankovič... Suddenly Martin Dubovský's head was filled with a rush of people and things that swept everything along, from everywhere he'd ever been, people who came to his surgery, who needed him to do something to help them – but not this, not Soňa, not Soňa's dissembling – Dugas, Belica, Malena, the cross – poor Eva, she may be right – the scientific organisation of society, class struggle, old victims, new victims, the fight against obscurantism, class morality, of this kind or that, ridiculous nonsense – and he, a doctor, who's supposed to care about people, is here – and Soňa, for God's sake, ever since August he's been sending her, almost every time, on these visits so that Eva can have someone to discuss things with or just have a chat for an hour or so, so it could never cross her mind that he's at Soňa's – the kids, Eva – it's vile, nauseating – and it was for all this that his father had died, his own father –

Martin Dubovský suddenly laughed out loud, as if he'd gone mad, then the laughter suddenly turned to silence, there in Soňa's bedsit, having been dashed by the thought of Eva: Eva doesn't do this, because she is mindful of Fero, who was executed, of Martin's mother, who'd been killed, of what had been played out at the cross –

At that point, Dubovský fell into a stupor. He lay on his back, the brochure on the chemicalisation of the country in his hand, and his eyes, staring into a void, turned towards the little lamp hanging on the wall.

In Soňa's bedsit silence reigned. Dubovský registered the ticking of his watch.

In Block XIV Eva and Soňa were sitting in the grey, florally decked armchairs in the sitting room, chatting.

"The way it goes with construction, Eva," Soňa objected, "is like the accelerated cultivation of food crops. In accelerated fruits there are gaps, there's something missing – accelerated fruits are often flavourless –"

With Soňa being all keyed-up thanks to the session at the Marxism-Leninism circle, the two visits, by her father and Vlach, and the moody Martin, and Eva thanks to the letter from her father, their conversation was distinctly forced, and now the two women, twenty-three-year-old Soňa and thirty-two-year-old Eva, lapsed into yet another of that evening's silences.

"Have you heard the latest joke about Kohn and Grün?" Soňa asked Eva.

"No –"

"Kohn and Grün," Soňa began, "bumped into each other on Wenceslas Square and Kohn said: 'Listen, Grün, I've had the most awful dream.' – 'What about?' – 'They expelled me from the Party and took away my Party ID card.' Next day they met again and Kohn said to Grün: 'Don't worry about it, Grün. I dreamt that Eisenhower came to Prague and when they offered him the keys to the city he got on his high horse – he was sitting on his white horse anyway – and refused them saying: 'One moment, gentlemen! I don't mind accepting the keys – but first you must return Grün's ID card!'.'"

"Kohn's, wasn't it?" Eva queried.

"Grün's, no?"

"So which one got expelled?"

"Grün, I think."

"No, Soňa, it was Kohn they expelled – you're not with it!"

The joke about Kohn and Grün remained unlaughed-at, both women sitting in silence.

Eva rose from her chair and went into Martin's room.

"Where's Martin?" Soňa asked her when she came back with the slightly battered November issue of a magazine filled with photographs and drawings of fashion designs. "Isn't he here?"

"No. He's off playing table tennis, or chess, or he might be at the works. He's hardly ever in of an evening –"

Soňa relaxed and sank deeper into her chair.

Eva sat down again and opened the magazine.

"What do you think of this one?"

They began scrutinising the girls and women in sporty jumpers, sweaters, cardigans, practical skirts and blouses and chatted about fashion.

"Nice, if one had the money!"

"Ah," said Eva, "looking at fashions, it's like travelling in the mind."

"Travelling? I don't know what you mean –"

"Yes, travelling in the mind – and not being able to afford it."

"Ah –"

"How come you're so out of it, Soňa?"

"Worn out."

"Oh, look! I forgot to close her cot!"

Out of the bedroom had come Eva's Olga, wearing blue pyjamas dotted with tiny trucks, bobbins, ducks, planes, cars, cats and houses.

Olga ran towards Soňa, her wide pyjama bottoms flapping about her legs.

It took them a while to coax Olga back into bed.

An hour had passed and Eva had said not a word about what her father had written, and after that hour Soňa went back to the Community Centre.

"Any news from our place?"

"Everything as normal – Eva's not quite with it –"

Soňa began to undress, Dubovský watching as she did so, and once she was undressed, the time flowed quickly and quietly by in the bedsit and midnight drew close.

"Martin," said Soňa, "we have to keep up that charade, but unobtrusively. Today you went a bit over the top and stirred up quite an unpleasant debate, as if it you were seriously interested."

"But I am interested," he said, "because –" Martin sensed a foul mood rising inside him, "I don't know what'll come of it if people really take your views on board –"

"They're not my views."

"Whose then?"

"No idea. They're put about from up top. They're what's been decreed. They have to be believed in. People here can't go having their own ideas, they need to be made not to think, just to believe things that have already been thought out... Why were you so interested at that session today?"

"But come on: I, as a doctor, would have to kill off the sick who were undesirable in class terms, the sick well-to-do peasant, factory owner, lawyer –" he remembered the engineer, Jankovič, "– and so forth –"

"And don't you?" Soňa snuggled up to Dubovský. "It's what's done, Martin, even you do it, perhaps without realising it, you put in for treatment for people with a desirable class background and leave the undesirables to fester – and the same goes for lawyers, judges – and so on and so forth, even my father stopped working because his conscience rose in revolt; in the end he did want to work, but then they wouldn't admit him to the chamber of barristers – though what's that to us, Martin? Enough debating! We're not at the club now. It's only there that... It might all be different one day, once we're together – and then I too might complete my studies... Doctors do all right even today if they're clever enough, they always have – and if we both worked well, shut up our surgeries for the summer and travelled – Martin! Let's keep up the charade, everybody else does, to the best of their ability –!"

Dubovský, mulling over the Jankovič thing, wasn't listening.

"Let's just not play it the way we did today!" said Soňa. "It would be a bit too obvious. I'm sorry for all the things I called you. Nobody takes it at all seriously anymore. Keeping up a charade is a lifelong business –!"

"No!"

"Why not, Martin?"

"I always thought you believed what you said, that you believe in your work. One needs to believe...! As you also should have – I believed until you –"

"In what, Martin?"

Dubovský failed to reply.

"What I said at the club today, it's impossible to believe, because to believe it and act accordingly, well, that's a crime," she said. "Nor is what you said to be believed. Do you realise what it would mean, the cataclysm that would hit people if they believed it and started being nice to one another? This entire social order would collapse. One thing does have to be believed in and that's the need for charades," she said in her sprightly, warm voice. "Come, Martin, let's compile a new creed! I believe in the Goddess of all goddesses (the first with a capital G), in the Charade of all charades, the Creatrix of heaven and earth, and in Her son... Who can be Charade's son?"

Dubovský failed to reply.

"She has many sons already," said Soňa, and she went on: "On May Day they carry them all in parades... I believe in the Goddess of all goddesses, the Charade of all charades, the Creatrix of heaven and earth, and in Her son –"

Dubovský, his face above hers, remained silent as he listened to Soňa, with his amazement and anger growing apace.

"– and in Her son, Yusuf Vissarionovich –"

Thus did Soňa Malena, a girl who'd been laid low, the cultprop girl at the MZ works and housing estate, compose, in bed in her room on the sixth floor of the Community Centre, a ludicrous and macabre creed. The room was bathed in the yellow-green aura of the little lamp hanging on the wall and turned inside its dark, moulded-plastic shade towards the yellow-green paintwork. Her bedsit was like a hot beech wood in May, when its young leaves are being scorched by the bright sun. Soňa's bright eyes flashed, as did the tiny keyboard of her white teeth, her fair hair dangled over Martin's forehead, illuminated at the edges by the yellow-green glow. Soňa Malena had composed a creed, but Martin Dubovský, who hitherto had let himself be captivated by every moment spent with her, was composing nothing, merely listening to her as she took such pains to make a mockery of everything that she made a pretence of teaching others. Soňa's words and their content began to nauseate him, her work at Emzed and on the estate, because he saw nothing in it all but self-serving hypocrisy.

"Soňa, are you out of your mind?"

"Why do you ask, Martin?"

"Who do you want to endear yourself to by this? Yourself?"

"Don't you find it endearing?"

"No, I don't," said Dubovský, "because you're poking fun at endeavours aimed at helping others."

"You call this an endeavour aimed at helping others?" she queried. "This? What matters is not who some endeavour aims to help, but who it harms. This endeavour put paid to my life, and my parents' –"

Soňa fell silent, her pale-blue eyes, fixed firmly on Martin's face, were seething with rage.

"What's happened to you, Soňa?"

"My father came today. Sorry, Martin...! I wouldn't want to add to your dejection, you're in a bad enough mood as it is. When you arrived something was already gnawing at you."

Soňa, still sporting her summer tan, cuddled up to Martin.

"Look, Martin," she asked in a whisper, "can I tell you something about my father...? I trust I can tell you... Who could I tell if not you. I've told you quite a bit today, but not everything –"

"Go on then."

"My father came today – oh, and someone else we know came today, someone we know – you also know him." Soňa briefly shifted her gaze to the pale-green bedspread as if wondering whether she should go on. She frowned. "My father was

(323)

here, he's started coming to see me, he needs money. Everything's gone, jewels, watches, fur coats – and now? Nobody wants to buy his pictures and furniture, and my parents are forever arguing. And now my father will keep coming here. The last of his money was winkled out of him, allegedly as a loan, by some fellow called Dugas in Veľké Dvorce – my father gave it to him so he'd be allowed to live there."

"Dugas, that functionary?"

"Yes. Dugas. Claims he wants to build a house. And I've also dug a big hole in my father's pocket because I met someone –" Soňa lapsed into silence, waiting a moment, "– anyway, he came here today, he works here at Emzed – and I can't go on, Martin. I can't any longer. Please don't be cross with me over that charade, today... I can't go on because I love you –"

Her breathing revealed the state she was in.

Martin stared woodenly into her face, which had grown jumpy and was animated by her darting eyes.

"No, I can't take it anymore, Martin. I love you, I can't deceive you any longer." Soňa fell silent. "I can't go on deceiving your children, Eva, or you." Soňa fell silent again, then, after a brief pause, she went on in a low voice: "Last winter, I had a visit from the local production planner, Vlach – I knew him from way back, in Bratislava, my little boy Jurko is his. Oh, God! When will Jurko be as lucky as your children? – this Vlach, this production planner, he's a provocateur, a blackmailer. He used to guide people illegally across the border. I loved him – and last winter he came to see me, said he would help us all. I talked my parents round, we went with him, and he cheated us. The money that cost my father! They caught us, and him, brought us back and let us go – and that was more money up the spout, and we lost our villa in Bratislava and my father was forcibly removed to Veľké Dvorce – and there he was done out of his remaining cash by some Dugas fellow, and today Vlach came to see me, he wants money... Oh, God, Martin!"

Martin stared woodenly at Soňa. Her lips were quivering.

"It was Vlach who found me this job," said Soňa, "here at Emzed, he talked me into showing an interest in you, to get round you politically, financially... But no, Martin – forgive me! They'll put my parents away, and me... It cost us my parents' house to cover everything up. But now, Martin? That's why I've been dithering about all this time, why I made up that thing with the charade, because I thought... But no, Martin, I love you and I can't go on like this –"

Tears began to stream down Soňa's white cheeks.

In Block XIV, Eva Dubovský's three lovely children were asleep, each in their own chrome-plated cot. Igor was lying on his right side with one leg on top of his little duvet, Ondrej on his tummy with his right foot poking through the red net, and Olga on her back with her arms spread out as if raised to catch a falling ball.

The Dubovskýs' flat was small, three small rooms, a tiny kitchen, and an even tinier hallway the door of which you had to open with great care to avoid smashing the low-hung light. In their case this had already happened more than once and Dubovský had often totted up how many such hallways were being built and how many such lights were going to get smashed; this came to him especially at the moment the slivers of lamp glass hit the floor.

The air in the flat was dry and warm.

At half past eleven Eva Dubovský came out of the bathroom, in the bedroom she slipped her dressing gown from her smooth, white shoulders, popped her feet into her red slippers and crossed into Martin's room. Her steps were measured and slightly hesitant as if she meant to stop after each one. From the desk she took three newspapers and the letter she had received from her father in Veľké Dvorce, put out the lights and went into the bedroom. She placed the papers and the letter on the bedside table and glanced at the children, Ondrej had now extricated his foot from the red net, and after she had drawn her rucked-up nightdress over her head it drifted down over her smooth white body all the way to her tiny feet.

Once in bed, she lay out flat, stretched her relaxed, freshly bathed body, plumped up her pillow and took her father's letter out of its blue official envelope, on which the address had been typed.

"It was by that cross that Martin's mother died," she read, "and you then went off to join the partisans, she'd been put through a lot and we were put through a lot with you. There's no way Dugas's rampaging can be deemed proper, because people are sickened and incensed by it and it means defiling a sacred landmark. If the cross were to rot away of itself and no one was even contemplating a replacement, all well and good –"

Having read her father's letter, she glanced through the papers. Glanced through them, pausing now and again to read an item and then tossing them piecemeal on the floor.

Half an hour later, she fell asleep as she was thinking about telling Martin nothing relating to Soňa. He sees in her a person worthy of those people killed and burned, of his executed brother Fero, of his mother who was killed, and of his father. Martin inclines to ready enthusiasm for certain people and things... Since Soňa's been at Emzed, he's been different at home and at work, a changed man... Poor Jankovič... The night light on the bedside table glimmered, filling the bedroom with a pale-brown half-light.

Two hours passed.

The estate was immersed in mist and darkness as Dubovský made his way back to Block XIV. He was walking over uneven, sticky soil, the pebbles in the gravel wobbled and grated beneath his feet and he kept tripping over broken and split wood panels and odd bits of sawn timber.

Dubovský, like many others before him, had taken an instant liking to Soňa's youthful, lively and apparently unfeigned belief in what she was doing. It revitalised in him positive imprints from the Uprising, and Soňa's presence restored his belief that the old values had not been destroyed in vain, nor the people destroyed with them, and that Soňa was the embodiment of what had been achieved by the new endeavour to do good by people. That afternoon, he'd suspected that he could have been wrong and when, in the evening, she had railed against her father and her own life, he had sunk into a foul mood which bred foul thoughts that sucked him deeper and deeper into a perilous maelstrom. Soňa's charade and Soňa's way of life now made him revile his work at the MZ works and on the estate, and now he saw in Soňa nothing but the embodiment of the hypocritical way in which she managed her day-to-day existence.

His sullen state on the way home to Block XIV also sprang from having heard her blasphemous creed and from having been knocked back down to a place where he had no desire to be, the place where he'd been before he met her, a place of trivial goals all too close and attainable. Through his mind flashed a dull glimmer of the future: working at the MZ factory without Soňa would become dreadfully dull and all that would remain to him would be his work, Eva, the children, Eva with her mind forever on Veľké Dvorce – Belica, Belica's cross, Malena, Dugas – all that would remain to him would be caring for the sick who would need more help than he could offer and for the well who merely exploit him – and Jankovič, a proud man who is now rejecting his help – and Soňa will remain a beautiful, alluring body with no soul, an animal, naked, vapid, abject, tossed aside now into the blazing heat, now into the freezing cold, Soňa will remain for him as for others an abject, lustreless creature... it's inconceivable that people should have perished for the sake of this... It was pitiful to have had you killed, Fero, it's a pity about you, Mother, and you, Father – all for the sake of this skulduggery... Outside Block XIV Martin Dubovský shook a bit of wire from his trouser leg and unlocked the main door, determined to avoid Soňa Malena from then on and never again to enter her flat.

No, he can't, he mustn't ever again... Dubovský walked slowly down the long corridor. How ghastly is this! Vlach, the Emzed production planner... Soňa must have put on that charade because of Vlach. And what will become of her now?

He unlocked the door of the flat. He felt as if he were flying down inside a dark pit.

On the MZ housing estate the night passed, so too the next day, and many days more, then the full length of autumn, now bright, now misty, then with a hint of snowy whiteness, or the glint of meltwater, sometimes the winds sent flurries of fine dusty sand around the estate, or scraps of paper, and now and again a yellow leaf, and autumn having passed, winter came and blew snow all over Veľké Dvorce.

"It's not that bad here even during a winter like this one," Mr Moravčík, the teacher, wrote to his daughter Eva, "because we get on so well with the Malenas. We sometimes go to see them and sometimes they come to us, and so time passes.

"Malena can get quite bitter sometimes and moans that if the kind of things that have befallen him and his daughter have to be done, then the new people at the top should have rented Hitler's old camps and used them to turn people who get in their way into artificial fertiliser. How the Malenas keep body and soul together I have no idea, because they do nothing and I am worried that he sometimes goes to see his daughter Soňa and she helps him out now and again. He goes on about how she has ruined her future prospects and I am just surprised a father can talk the way he does about his own child. If it were anyone else I would hold it against them, but Malena is an intelligent man and it is with sorrow and bitterness that he dismisses his daughter as a trollop and a slut. He calls her even worse things that I cannot put down on paper. Perhaps any father would be the same if his daughter lived like she does. And it is barely to be wondered at that a man in Malena's condition and state of mind even starts going out of his mind.

"The other day it was awful to see Malena and Belica, who sometimes comes back to Veľké Dvorce, to see them as a pair of unfortunates and to listen to them complaining to one another. Belica comes back to check the state of his house and land. He is even said to have been to the Local National Committee to ask whether their people are cultivating it properly. I also wonder how Chairman Benc is feeling; he only had Belica forcibly removed from Veľké Dvorce because he had borrowed money from him and had no intention of paying it back.

"I believe that they are tearing the cross out of people and putting nothing back in its place. Doing exactly what Ignác Dugas is about now that he is set on building a house and keeps boasting about how he will yank the Belica cross out of the earth. He is a strange man, impulsive, but not, let us hope, actually dangerous. I find it odd that so many people, even old and honourable Communists, are afraid of the swaggering good-for-nothing, who has no respect for anything or anyone apart from himself, not even for his wife and her parents, or his own parents either.

"Over Christmas we could come and see you and at least help out a bit with the children –"

Christmas arrived and the Moravčíks did come to visit the Dubovskýs, and Belica's cross, Veľké Dvorce, the Uprising, Ignác Dugas and Belica himself, who'd been forcibly removed, all came up in conversation. And the Moravčíks also mentioned the Malenas and their daughter Soňa, her little boy Jurko – and after New Year's Day they went back home.

"I do admire Soňa anyway," Eva told Martin on the first Sunday afternoon in January. "I don't believe the things they say about her – and if she were as terribly wrong in the head as her father makes out I'd admire her even more, because she really does prove herself to be as you've always described her."

Dubovský was sitting in his room, pretending to read a manual on how the health service in a large enterprise should be run, and he didn't respond to what Eva had just said, being battered by his conscience for having been so brutal to Soňa. He'd abandoned her, having failed to convince her of his own truth... Soňa needs to be bucked up, harnessed to the times, to be torn away from her father, helped to cope with life, or at least with some advice – as things stand it lacks humanity –

"Working as she does," Eva went on, "it's quite something, her efforts are to be seen all around, and on top of that having a child to care for, parents to support – isn't it though...! Isn't it, Martin?"

Dubovský closed his manual and looked obtusely at Eva, whose white face and dark-blue eyes were turned idly towards the sky. What was to be done? Wait until everything sorts itself out? This is unbearable. Leave? Where to? Somewhere to live, the move –

Eva gave a toss of her chestnut hair

"The lives of young people," she said, "are the very sense of all that has happened and is happening – everything keeps changing so, meaning I can't begin to imagine what our children will be like by the time they reach Soňa's age –"

"And where are they?"

"They went next door – they're almost more used to being there than at home –"

"Fetch them back."

She went.

Dubovský rose and wandered about the room as if trying to drive out the still living presence of Soňa Malena, more alive and more painful since he'd stopped seeing her and was now keeping her at arm's length. Does Eva know...? Was she speaking in irony? If not...? Dubovský was seized with pity for Eva.

The children, Igor, Ondrej and Olga came back.

"Come!"

Dubovský sat down on the tiles.

"Daddy," Olga squealed as the first to run up to him, "let me show you my teddy-bear –!"

"No!" said Dubovský. "We're going to play at Little Red Ridinghood! You can be her, Igor the wolf and Ondrej the huntsman."

"And you, Daddy?"

"Er," he said in answer to Ondrej, "I shall be the director."

"And Mummy?"

Dubovský's children were standing around him, their laughing faces filled with expectation, and their wide blue eyes with gleaming smiles.

"Mummy," he said, "she'll have to be the mother *and* the grandmother because they're aren't enough of us."

"Yippee!"

The children scattered.

"Martin," a smiling Eva began, "listen, couldn't you go over to Veľké Dvorce at some time and have a chat with Dugas? Get him to leave the cross where it is or at least let the villagers resite it as they see fit."

"Why? There's no point!"

"I think there is," said Eva. "Where I'm concerned, and for Veľké Dvorce. Your late brother, your late mother...! I'm not concerned about the cross just for its own sake, as a cross, but it will do no harm to anyone – not even you – if there's at least something as a reminder of the good and the bad sides of the Uprising."

"Why are you telling me this, Eva?" Dubovský snapped. "I don't propose to meddle in Dugas's affairs. He can do what he wants! I haven't been to Dvorce since forty-five – and you'd have me go there now, when it's in turmoil? What would the locals do to me after everything that happened during the Uprising? Dugas –"

"But he's a gangster!"

"As if there weren't worse ones!" said Martin. "To hell with him! The cross, my brother, my mother – there's no point going over all that again. Old sacrifices, new sacrifices – all of them pointless, all that effort wasted –"

"You talk like that here, but you're different at the factory!"

"Just like anyone else!"

The children came running in, Olga with a little basket, in it a small piece of dry bread, and an empty bottle, two apples and a packet of dates left over from Christmas, Igor with his fur coat on inside out and a wolf mask on his face, and Ondrej with a toy rifle and wearing his father's green hat, and they came and stood in front of their father, who was sitting on the tiled floor.

The director, works GP Martin Dubovský, began: "Once upon a time, there was a pretty little girl..." – and when her mother-Eva had dressed Little-Red-Riding-Hood-Olga to go and see her grandmother, she lay down on the sofa and picked up a book ready to play the sick, old grandmother praying in bed.

There on the sofa she lapsed into thought, irritated by the children's shrieking and by Martin's story-telling, and it struck her how happy Martin had been to play with the children of late – he'd begun spending his evenings at home, he never said much, he studied a lot and he did his job at the factory as never before, people spoke highly of him, and Chairman Mokrý had recently said what a really nice chap he was! – and then there was an almighty clamour as the wolf-Igor gobbled up the grandmother-Eva along with her book about life in a circus, gamekeeper-Ondrej slit him open with a wooden knife and pulled grandmother-Eva out from inside his inside-out fur coat, Olga started crying because she didn't want to be gobbled up by the wolf-Igor, and Dubovský was laughing.

The play came to an end and Eva suddenly remembered Jankovič, the engineer.

"How's Jankovič, Martin, do you know?" she asked. "How long's he been at the sanatorium? A month or thereabouts?"

"I guess so," said Dubovský, "about a month. I've spoken to his wife – but he's still the same. His treatment's going to take time. If –"

Dubovský broke off.

If he'd gone into the sanatorium earlier, he thought, then maybe... That's where it all began, with Jankovič. He, Martin, had been the one who persuaded him to seek treatment, he'd arranged the sanatorium for him, but Jankovič had needed help long before that – you have to help people who've been duped by Soňa, Dugas, or Vlach, and Soňa herself needs help –

The doorbell jangled.

"See who that is, Igor." Eva eased herself up from the sofa. "Just Igor, not all of you!"

All three children ran out into the hallway and welcomed in Soňa.

"Hi, kids!" Her buoyant, warm voice reached them from the hall. "Hello there!"

The children ran back into the room.

Eva rose from the sofa, went out to greet Soňa and brought her into Martin's room.

Martin took a step towards her, offered her his hand and relieved her of the four hefty volumes that she'd borrowed from him.

"Did you study them properly?" he asked, gesturing to her to take a seat. "Do join us!"

"Thank you."

Soňa sat down in the red armchair.

"Pity you didn't turn up earlier. You could have taken the part of the grandmother –"

"That's right, Auntie Soňa," said Igor, "come on, let's play Little Red Riding-Hood again, there are enough of us now –"

"I'll be Little Red Riding Hood –!"

"I'll be the wolf –"

"Me the gamekeeper –"

The children clustered round Soňa.

Martin Dubovský looked askance at Soňa, at her pale, smooth features, enlivened by a smile playing round her wide lips and in her pale-blue eyes, and at her dark eyebrows and eyelashes – he could feel his heart pounding as his eyes took in her grey-green dress, drawn tight across her breasts, hips and legs.

"Soňa –"

She turned her face towards him, shining with the reward of that smile playing round her wide lips, but shadowed by the reproof in her eyes.

"Do you want to borrow some more books?"

"I'd love to."

"Take your pick." He pointed to the bookcase. "Take whatever you need, whatever you find, there's stuff on biology – and suchlike... Eva, if you don't mind," he said, his eyes fixed on Soňa's breasts, "get the kids dressed for me, I'm going to take them outside. Sorry, Soňa! We couldn't have had a proper chat with the kids around anyway –"

"Come on, Daddy –"

"– outside, behind the Community –"

"– we can have a snowball fight!"

Eva, with a look of surprise on her face, gently rose and began getting the children into their winter coats, Soňa looked on, bewildered, noting her slim, supple lines, wearing that grey dress, moving from one child to the next, Dubovský also putting his coat on, and then he left with the children for the snow-covered, churned up ground of the MZ housing estate.

He'd had to get out, he couldn't stay there with Eva and Soňa, with his pity for Eva and his loathing for Soňa, coupled with his desire to have her.

Soňa and Eva remained alone.

Martin Dubovský and the children left Block XIV, for a brief moment he gazed at the high-rise that was the Community Centre, at the window of Soňa's bedsit, then walked on in silence following his children, who were running all over the snowy, wintery landscape of the estate.

On the waste ground behind the Community Centre, with its high, randomly scattered drifts of crumbly frozen snow and its random bare patches, the children were hurling white snowballs at each other, and as the sun began to sink towards the horizon, the snowballs took on a shade of purplish pink.

Deep in thought, Dubovský stared at the horizon, at the straggly pink and purple clouds. He had behaved badly, cruelly, he thought. Jankovič had been hospitalised too late, and he had believed that Soňa was the gift of a lifetime, that she was worth even letting Jankovič suffer, and Soňa was a poor girl in a chaotic state of mind, kept above water by the blackmailing

Vlach – but where to turn? There was simply no way to put matters right with the Malenas, Soňa, Vlach, Dugas... For God's sake, what mattered here was himself, Eva, the children. He had made his own contribution to Soňa's mental chaos, and what was Soňa up to now apart from what anybody could observe? Who was she living with, who was she sponging off in order to keep Vlach quiet and help her parents?

Dubovský's boys' hands were wet and red, and Olga ran up to him with her gloves sopping wet.

"Come on, kids, home! It's cold."

"Not yet, daddy!"

"Come on, let's go!" He picked Olga up and dusted the snow from her coat and legs. "Come on, Igor, Ondrej!"

The winter, now mild, now cold, as if it had one cheek made of sunlight, the other of ice, went on.

Ignác Dugas, the chairman of the local national committee at Slanica, had secretly turned to account the five hundred litres of plum brandy that he'd had distilled from the secret hoard of illicit ferment that he'd confiscated. The snow had left barely a mark on the building materials that he'd had brought up to Belica's meadow, and when the hard frosts were followed by the warm and sunny days of spring, they rapidly melted the snow on the piles of stones, bricks, sand and timber that various men with carts had brought up to Belica's meadow for him. And, without delay, Dugas took on men from Veľké Dvorce, workmen he called them, booked some masons and the workmen began digging and the masons began concreting the foundations of his new house, a villa with five rooms and a garret.

Ignác Dugas wasn't the least bit concerned that there might still be a landmine at the foot of Belica's cross or that an SS man lay buried there. Around the cross there were now bags of cement piled up, now bits of wood tossed aside, at other times mortar mixing tubs were propped against it, or again wheelbarrows, or a pile of planks, smeared white with lime or grey from concrete dust.

The house grew and grew. By March the walls were up and in April it also acquired its roof timbers. At the bottom it was grey from the concrete foundations, but depending on which side caught the sun, they were streaked with the bitumen that the sun had softened and allowed to trickle out of the layer of insulation. Above the foundations it was red from the bricks and above the brick walls it was also starting to show red from the roof tiles. By Easter the roof was finished.

The work had proceeded very quickly. It had had to, because that parcel of land could only remain in the hands of whoever could build a house on it within a year. Ignác Dugas knew what he was about: he wanted to be the first to get a house built on the site allotted to him. And he was. While the other parcels were still only receiving supplies of building materials, Dugas's, next to Belica's cross, was gaily adorned with his red villa.

Easter in 1945 was very cold. All round Veľké Dvorce a fresh wind blew, driving white, or sometimes greyish, clouds across the sky and strewing odd scatterings of tiny clumps of snow down from them. It also blew right through Dugas's new house, through the openings yet to be filled with doors and windows, and through the unsealed-off loft space.

Ignác Dugas was strolling about his future living quarters, and the kitchen, wearing a new grey suit and a green trench coat, which had a warm sheepskin lining, and explaining to his wife, "Rosy-red Paula", who had some new black shoes on her feet and was wearing a brown skirt and a short, warm, dark-blue coat, where everything was going to be. He wore a constant smile that exposed his false teeth, two white and three of dental gold.

Around the cross, encased in left-over red roof tiles, the cold wind blew, fluttering the faded red paper ribbons tied round the dry wreath that had hung there since All Souls' Day.

Dugas turned away from the cross, bent back and looked down at his wife. He looked sideways at one half of her red face, at her yellowy blonde eyebrows and hair and at her white headscarf decorated with blue and red flowers.

"Paula, you make me laugh," he suddenly said to her. "You said I wouldn't become secretary, but I am, you said I wouldn't get a plot to build on, but I did, you said I wouldn't build a house, but I have done, and you joked at the idea of me becoming a candidate for election at regional level, yet a candidate I am! Anything goes if you know the right people or you've got friends in the right places. Paula – and you make fun of me not yanking out this 'ere cross and people not voting for me – it's intolerable, Paula, just admit it!"

"I don't make fun of you," said Dugas's wife, "but you're not going to get the cross out. Remember that!" Paula's red face paled somewhat. "You won't get it out whatever else you might do!"

She stared at her husband with a look of reproach and curiosity.

"Not right now, maybe." Ignác Dugas looked pensively at the cross. "Once the house is completely finished and I set about making a garden outside the windows, then the cross will go. It won't be able to stay. I can tell you that much. I'm a member of the Party and that means that a great deal is expected of me – and then there's my candidacy for the region. If I were elected, I'd have to do something to make my mark – but wait! – wouldn't that be better *before* the elections?"

"And when do you propose to make yourself known to the electorate?"

"I don't know yet, but sooner rather than later." He watched his wife for a moment. "I'll have that cross out – and neither your father, nor mine, can do anything about it, nor your mother, nor mine. Remember that! That teacher, Moravčík, won't get anywhere, nor that partisan woman of his, nor her husband, the doctor, even though his mother was killed there. I know where he works, I know how he lives, and I know what he does. They're reactionaries the lot of them, they listen to Radio Free Europe and Voice of America, and they'd like noth-

ing more than for President Eisenhower to come visiting...
but I'll show them! If ever that doctor, or any of them, starts
blabbering –!"

"And what will you do with the SS man?" Dugas's wife
asked. "The one said to be buried hereabouts?"

"He's nothing to worry about. He'll have rotted away by
now!"

Dugas's wife turned, went the few paces into the hallway
and looked up the concrete steps leading to the future attic.
The wind gusted through the opening above the stairway
and blew some dust and fine sand off the steps into her face
and eyes.

"Let's go, Ignác," she said, wiping her eyes which were
closed and half-hidden by her yellowy-blonde eyelashes, "it's
cold here. I don't know...! People keep grouching about you,
they're envious – do be careful...! As for me – I – I refuse to
live here with you the way things are, see. I don't want to be
frightened the whole time that someone might set fire to the
very roof over my head, see. And that someone might do you
in somewhere, see! I refuse! Build your house and – and – live
here on your own...! Then there's the cross thing and the SS
man –!"

"It's going to be nice living here, Paula," Ignác Dugas tried
to reassure his wife as he started the engine, "a smart little
villa on a hillside! Believe me. We'll have a well dug, because
there'll be water, there's a spring can be drawn on from under
that slope over there –"

"And there's that SS man buried here – ugh! – you know!"

The bike's engine spluttered and died, Dugas dismounted,
his wife dismounted and they headed back down to Slanica on
foot. Dugas, having been lashed by the wind of Veľké Dvorce,
fancied some smoked ham and hard-boiled eggs. Paula's a
right silly goose! If only she knew... She thinks the house is
coming out of her money. We need to wait a while then get
Vlach to help squeeze more money out of Malena. Malena's
still got some... What does Vlach need money for? Not for

building a house, obviously. He's, he's just a lady-killer, crafty sod – he's got women everywhere, by the crateful.

"I have been hearing," Moravčík wrote to Eva after Easter, "and I forgot to tell you about this when we were with you at Easter, that most of the materials going into the new houses being built in Veľké Dvorce have been filched. There is talk of one case where some young chap after building a new house took all the cement he needed from a large building site in the town nearby, bringing it home little by little in his briefcase! And they steal timber from the forests, for all that every tree has been recorded nine times over, and mostly at night, so it is only recent owners of hunting licences who go on about them and get into arguments with them because there is such a racket and so much movement in the forests at night that the game is abandoning the reserves. It is enough to make you laugh sometimes. Belica was here a while back and said he had told Dugas that he will be for it when the tide turns. He told him he would have to remove the house from his meadow. He was not going to put up with it there. No one had asked him, Belica, if it was possible to build on his meadow. If there were no other way, he would have to take the house away piecemeal in his hat.

"Not long from now and I shall have been a teacher for forty years, and I have never been able to afford a house. And I am prepared to think I do deserve one, having always served well as a teacher.

"The world is so unjust, to everybody. Malena and his wife are not getting along together at all, forever quarrelling and fighting, and he even rants at Jurko, Soňa Malena's little son, and as Mrs Malena told me recently, he has even tried to kill him. And he blames her for bringing their daughter up badly, letting her loose on the world, spoiled and ill-equipped. Sometimes, Malena has fits of total stupefaction when he talks to nobody, cuts himself off and if he does speak, then it is only to reply in terms that suggest he had not been listening. The other day, I asked him how it had come about that in Bratislava, out of the blue, they had bundled him and his furniture onto a lorry and installed him here, and he replied that Soňa lives by prostitution and told me to write to warn you to keep a close watch on Martin. Really, my dear Eva, do keep an eye on him and do not let him get trapped by Soňa, because things would go bad for you and your lovely children if that nice husband of yours fell in love with a prostitute. It is terrible when they cast a man like Malena into penury and passivity, a condition in which all he can think of is how to carry out some evil deed.

"There are other things going on in Veľké Dvorce as well. Agricultural researchers have been here, probing the ground and the district in general and explaining to people that there is going to be cooperative farm here, with a focus on growing fruit and fodder crops and on pasture-management. People, some at least, think that is a good thing, and I would not be against some such arrangement myself, seeing that Veľké Dvorce and all its lands are ideally suited to it. I have also been hearing that Veľké Dvorce is soon to be linked into the electricity grid. Faraga will no longer have to go around banging his drum once he has been replaced by a public-address system."

At Veľké Dvorce, Dugas's house had been rising up on Belica's meadow, and the MZ estate had seen more new high-rise blocks erected. But the estate was still awaiting completion. The inhabitants complained about the unfinished streets and pavements, that there was no street lighting at and after dusk, no parks and no green spaces. They moaned about the lack of a cinema, the still scruffy Community Centre, that there were no playgrounds, shops and stores, and no day-care centres or infants' schools. Inside the Community Centre the lift still hadn't been installed, leaving just a deep, empty shaft and, on every floor, a board nailed across the lift doors bearing the warning sign CAUTION! LIFT! SHAFT! On the sixth and fifth floors, someone had scrawled on the lift doors a skull and crossbones in thick black felt-tip.

Soňa Malena spent the working day as the kultprop at the MZ works, sometimes she would go to visit the Dubovskýs, though less often than she used to, because since that Sunday when Martin had left her and Eva and taken the kids for a walk, she'd detected in Eva a degree of reserve and even peevishness, she'd been trying to take her work more seriously and, shaken by the break-up with Dubovský, she'd tried to sort her life out, though without knowing how, her life with her little boy, Jurko, who was in Veľké Dvorce, with her father, who kept coming to her for money – she wasn't coping – with her willpower in tatters, at a loss since her previous life with Dubovský, having little faith in her job and recoiling at her own latest views – and she was saving up so as to be able to help her father and was now toying with the idea of leaving 'Palermo' and the MZ works, escaping from Vlach, who kept demanding money from her, claiming he didn't trust her and now threatening her; there were moments when she lost the will to carry on living; at other times she enjoyed the new and unfamiliar sense of actually being quite fond of Eva and the children, and a sense that Martin's treatment of her was right. Otherwise there was nothing for it, this was all... No, no! Just because of Vlach she wasn't going to do Martin any harm. The works GP, Dr Martin Dubovský, was avoiding her and getting on with life, as if cut in two, worse than before he knew her: he loathed Eva, but was attentive and kind to her; he loathed his children, but forced himself to play with them; he loathed the hypocritical Soňa for casting him, too, into hypocrisy, and he liked the Soňa who was lost and unhappy; he pitied the pensive and sincere Eva and her children and he sometimes insulted them by using cutting terms of abuse; alone with Eva he would complain bitterly, sometimes venomously, about the hypocrisy, falsehood and wrongdoing in public life, and at the works, in the presence of patients, at meetings and conferences, at training sessions and in debates he played the part of one wholly convinced of and committed to whatever theory was being mooted at the given moment; at times he was horrified at his loss of vision and that somewhere the cruel truth was lurking in wait for him; in everything, in every step he took, there was Soňa, in whom he had once placed faith as in the sense of all those sacrifices, past and present and constantly being repeated, because through her life and work she had laid bare the hypocrisy into which he himself was sinking; he sought a way out in his work, in studying, then once again in work; he was tormented by pangs of conscience for having hurt Soňa, and he was seized constantly by a growing urge to help her, because deep inside him was resurfacing, unobserved, the belief that Soňa was a person of real merit; Martin's wife Eva taught at the school attached to Emzed, she was left suffocating by what she knew about Soňa, she mentally fought back against her father's letters because she didn't want to see Soňa as her father, the deranged Malena, saw her, she didn't want to say anything to Martin lest he see in her just a silly, jealous woman; yet she constantly accepted Soňa, even pitying her now and again – and there were moments when she began to be afraid of her.

April was in decline, and one Friday morning Eva came in from the shops, carrying milk, some pastries and butter, and she said to her husband: "Martin!" Her tone was unusually brusque and reproachful.

"Yes, Eva dear?"

"I met Mrs Jankovič while I was out –"

"And –?"

"She's off to see her husband, maybe her late husband – attempted suicide – poison – he did it at the sanatorium –"

"What?"

"He took some poison."

Dubovský stopped buttoning up his shirt.

"All Palermo's full of it... Perhaps if he'd been allowed a course at a spa previously... No, no, that's a ridiculous thing to say...! If this, if that...! As a doctor you should have done all the necessary two years, one year ago...! Jankovič needed peace and quiet – and I know you've arranged spa treatments for people who were fit and well – and just because they aren't qualified engineers – not friends of yours – because they have the right class background...! Jankovič didn't fit in with your ideas of a society organised scientifically –!"

Dubovský's lips puckered, his deep-set eyes sharpened and the skin over his cheek bones twitched up to his eyes.

"Eva!" he said angrily, paused, then yelled in a strangled voice: "I've had just about enough of this! Always Jankovič, Jankovič! The people most entitled to treatment are those who haven't been able to seek treatment for entire generations. From the class perspective I acted correctly, even if I didn't agree with it in my mind, and all those commissions that looked into the Jankovič case also acted correctly. Who's to blame for that? Later, Jankovič refused treatment himself, having taken umbrage. I'm surprised at you, Eva, the way you cling on to some weird kind of humaneness. What was in the past is bad, do get your head round that, will you? – and it has to be banished once and for all! We need to cultivate the young strengths in the new, up-and-coming class and sweep the old garbage away. We need to foster new relationships among people...! That's the order of the new day and –!"

"Are you saying Mr Jankovič was garbage to you?"

"And –?"

"Now you listen to me, Martin!" Eva's pale features reddened with rage, her dark-blue eyes gleamed, and her voice conveyed fear for her husband and a degree of loathing for Soňa. "No, no! Don't you talk to me like that! You can save that kind of talk for people who live by deception. And Jankovič was *not* garbage. He was a good friend to both of us, don't forget that means you too! – and that's the only reason you were afraid to help him. Carry on like this and you won't be a doctor. Carry on like this and you won't be a human being –!"

"I beg your pardon –?"

The boys came running in, stopped in the doorway and stared with their wide blue eyes at their father and mother. Olga came trotting along behind them and she came to an abrupt halt beside her mother.

Dubovský turned up his shirt collar and took his tie in both hands.

"I beg your pardon –?"

"You know very well what I'm getting at, Martin," said Eva, "you know exactly what I mean. You won't be a doctor if you just cling to this version of morality or that. There is only one morality, the human one, no other. We've heard plenty about all kinds of moralities, national, racial, class – but that, my man, is nothing to do with morality, it's national, racial or class egoism, nothing else. Since when has egoism been elevated to the status of morality? You have given in to egoism, whether it's your own, or someone else's or some class egoism – or perhaps just the egoism of what happens to be convenient: think nothing, do nothing – let others get on with the thinking and doing, let others take responsibility for me...! On the one hand you don't agree with anything that's going on in our own time, and on the other you're governed by some crazy class egoism. Let class get on with the thinking and doing on my behalf...! You're too compliant, Martin. I now realise why things are the way they are. People like you say nothing and truckle to egoism – and then Jankovič poisons himself. Why should the elderly poison themselves? What harm do they do to others? Belica goes to Veľké Dvorce and everyone makes fun of him. The only reason he was forcibly removed from Veľké Dvorce was that Party chairman Benc once borrowed money from him and subsequently didn't pay any of it back. You know that just as well as I do. You knew Belica well and you know what kind of man he was... He never deserved what he got – not even from your class-based point of view...! Is this the class struggle, is this that scientific organisation of society? This is a new-age jungle...! In Veľké Dvorce that madman Dugas is threatening to uproot a cross and antagonising people, the one-time lawyer Malena is losing his mind, and his Soňa, a moral wreck of a girl, is engaged in organising political training and development – and who knows what else, and you –"

Dubovský blanched.

"Please, Eva...!" Dubovský yelled in a strangled voice, hurled his tie down on the table, then picked it up again. "What are you going on about? I hope you're not suggesting that I work hand in glove with some egoism and that – and that I'm to blame for Jankovič and that I'm responsible for all of this!"

"Who else?"

"If anyone's to blame, it's other people."

"Other people again! That's all so easy, to go blaming others. But you're in their service!"

"And you aren't?"

"I am too," said Eva, "but my service isn't as dangerous as yours! It doesn't affect people's lives. But I always try not to be in service to class egoism –!"

"You stupid thing!" Dubovský retorted scornfully, and he began knotting his tie. "You're so stupid, Eva! We all serve in the same way. One lies, another steals and a third commits murder. Sometimes that's all done by one and the same person. That's the way it goes, there's no other way – in today's battle there's no way of taking into account the personal problems and vagaries of some Jankovič...! Jankovič took umbrage and refused treatment – and you know the trouble I had persuading him to go into the sanatorium –!"

"But by then it was too late –!"

For just a moment, Eva looked insensibly at her husband, her dark-blue eyes shining out from her pale face, the upper half of which seemed ablaze with chestnut ringlets.

"Where's that love and respect for others gone, where's the self-assurance, the determination to do nothing more that might place freedom in jeopardy, things that had you have your own brother executed, for which you actually brought death to your own mother and father? You're wrong, Martin, and forgive me, but if I hold you responsible for Jankovič, you can hold me responsible for similar things, because I don't want to live with the awareness of aiding and abetting falsehood, theft and murder. I don't want that – and I don't even want to live under the same roof as someone to whom these things are a matter of indifference. Certainly not, Martin –!"

"But, but – all right, have it your way!"

"Yes, Martin!"

"Do whatever you want –!"

The children stood there woodenly as they listened to their parents.

Dubovský sat down in his grey floral-patterned armchair and finished doing up his tie.

"I have acted in the way society demanded of me –!"

"A society deluded!" said Eva. "Completely misguided. Even you must acknowledge that no society, and a completely new one at that, can be constructed on the basis of mutual destruction. You may think of me as lacking in social aware-ness, old-fashioned or whatever, but I would merely remind you that the Jankovič case pains me. He was a good friend, a close friend, and far from being a bad person, on the contrary, he was helpful to us, and I believe you neglected him for your personal convenience, so that you wouldn't have to argue with anyone, so that you wouldn't have to take the part of a friend, because, admittedly, it's easy to make excuses one way or an-other – but you, Martin, you were even able to make sacrifices for others, there's your brother, your mother, your father – and what's with you now? Once again you get these foul moods, here, at home – and you see people in terms of some bizarre class-based egoism in order to reduce me to silence and still your own conscience!"

Dubovský's brow twitched as it hung over his deep-set eyes.

"Come, children!"

Eva took Olga, Igor and Ondrej, who'd been staring, be-wildered, at their father with their wide, blue eyes, into the kitchen and gave them their breakfast.

Dubovský remained seated in his grey armchair with its floral pattern, exasperated by Eva's criticism. His head was buzzing. He had been shocked by the sincerity and private pain of her strictures. He had been pained by her mention of his brother, father and mother. He began to be ashamed of himself over Soňa. Did Eva suspect something? She was right about the impossibility of slipping easily into the course of events, into some vacuous submission just because Soňa wasn't the person he saw in her when she first showed up. Respect for others...! Self-assurance...! Freedom – doing nothing to jeopardise it...! That hadn't been the point... Eva was right, even right about the things she'd left unsaid – never before had she exploded like that... That hadn't been the objective, certainly not the objective that the morally wrecked Soňa should, with his assistance, deceive people who were waiting, seeking, people who wanted something to believe in.

Eva took the startled children to the lady next door, with whom she would leave them whenever she was at work, teaching at the Emzed primary school.

"Come and have breakfast," she said when she came back. "Come."

Martin rose to his feet and followed her into the kitchen.

"I'm sorry, Martin," she said after they'd eaten, "but I do think you should have said something when it came to Mr Jankovič. He meant no harm to anyone, and even if he did, you, as a doctor –"

"Listen," Dubovský yelled in a strangled voice. "Do you seriously think I'm not sorry about Jankovič?"

"Well, well!" she retorted sarcastically. "Sorry, eh?" She laughed. "But you say he was just garbage to you... Why bother about him, Martin? He's poisoned himself, he might die, conveniently disposing of himself! His case, and Belica's, and others, they all come under the same heading, the category labelled 'class struggle' – and that's that! You don't believe in anything... You've been deluded by something. You ought to be believing in what you believed in the past... You used to be different, Martin. Your willpower has been sapped. Where is your commitment of old: the things you said you needed do in order to get over your brother? How much evil you needed to sweep away – just you, by yourself! What's left of all that now? Nothing. Nothing at all! You've been surrendering – and spreading evil! You were in the Uprising, so was I – and do you suppose that was on our own account? We did it for others, Martin. What's happening today, that's no class struggle, it's –"

Dubovský looked in silence at the slim figure of his wife, her chestnut hair, her pale features and her shining dark-blue eyes, watched her slim figure slip into her green coat, then donned his own brown Ulster and picked up his hat.

"Come, Martin," she said, taking him by the arm. "Respect people and do them no harm. Ever...! A human being is no guinea pig for testing political passions on – or your own passing fancies –"

Dubovský remained silent. He knew that Eva was speaking from suspicion. Eva knew about Soňa – maybe she knew a great deal, otherwise she couldn't be so... He remained silent to give Eva no cause to mention her.

"You ought to be at least like you were at the end of last year, since the summer. You worked, you believed it was worthwhile, but like this...? I didn't like your attitude to people even back then, but try being at least as you were then –"

Dubovský was shaking and, to conceal his embarrassment, he, slowly, with his back to Eva, opened the flat door and transferred the key to the outside to lock up after them.

They came out of Block XIV.

The MZ housing estate was feeling the late arrival of spring, which was tinged in the distance with a veil of grey-green. Closer by, the grassy areas were a lively green, spangled with the yellow of dandelions and the white of daisies. In the bright sunlight, 'Palermo', still awaiting completion, gleamed red, while the buildings of the MZ works were gleaming white.

In his surgery, Dubovský was thinking, hesitating, wavering, but in the end he phoned Soňa to come and see him. Surprised, she nonetheless came, and Dubovský asked her to find out, discreetly, whether or not Vlach knew Dugas. The following day Soňa told him she'd got nothing out of Vlach. Vlach had just laughed and denied everything. Soňa was curious why Dubovský wanted to know, but he declined to tell her, merely indicating that it would help him if they did know each other and were friends even.

"One more time," said Soňa, "I'll have another go."

"Thanks, that'll be very kind of you."

Soňa made to leave.

"Does your father know Vlach?"

"He does," she said, "but I don't know what would happen if they ran into each other. He hates him –"

"My apologies, Soňa, for bothering you with this."

Soňa flashed her pale-blue eyes at Dubovský and left.

The late spring was getting warmer.

They had managed to save the engineer, Jankovič, some people did think back on him, some felt sorry for him, giving vent to low mutterings directed at Dubovský and the various commissions that had not deemed him worth releasing from work long before and sending for long-term treatment at a spa. Gradually, people forgot about him, being overwhelmed by petty cares of their own, and the silent estate lived silently on.

Veľké Dvorce was not living silently. They envied Dugas, they were angry with him and they loathed him. Dugas could get away with anything! He had the cement, lime, bricks, timber! He was particularly loathed by people who'd had to take enormous pains to secure house-building materials.

Ignác Dugas came to give his house, still awaiting completion, a once-over.

He would come on a Sunday or a weekday because, he reflected, when you're building a house, you have to keep an eye on the masons and other workmen to see that they're making a proper job of it and not fiching things.

He'd come on his motorbike. It was the end of April. And a lovely day. The masons were plastering the insides of the brick walls and whistling a song about the gendarmes of Detva.

"So how's it gonna be with these 'ere elections, comrade?" one of the masons asked Dugas, standing for election to the district national committee. The mason hammered at the bits of brick round the frame of the tripartite kitchen window, picked one brick fragment up from the ground and turned to Dugas. "I don't have much faith in 'em, like, 'cos they say as we can't, like, vote for who we want, only the ones they give us."

"That's not true," said Dugas. "My dear comrade, these are going to be elections like never before. It's unthinkable! These will be the freest elections this country has ever seen, elections based on the most democratic principles and foundations." Ignác Dugas wriggled his grubby hands out from the sleeves of his trench coat and pointed at his coat, once blue, but now all patchy grey and white with lime and white powder. "Think about it, in the past people only voted for political parties and knew nothing of the people they were electing. Nobody knew them. Did you, comrade, or your father before you, ever know who you were voting for?"

"Well that much is true," said the mason. "But they was good elections anyway, like, for the very reason you didn't know who you was votin' for. Now we 'ave to vote for people and I for one, Comrade Dugas, I shan't be votin' for you." The mason stuffed the fragment of brick between the wall and the window frame and hammered it into place. "In the past we knew the parties, like, but we didn't know the people, I mean the candidates, like, but now we do know the people – like you – and we don't know the party, because –"

"But what are you saying, comrade?" It had come as a bit of shock to Ignác Dugas, who could only smile, baring his white and dental-gold teeth at the mason. "You still lack any political awareness... Don't you know all the things our Party has achieved? Have you been asleep? Just think of all the construction work, the factories, think how the living standards of working people have improved, how much better everything is, because wherever you look about you, it's all changed, different from how it used to be –"

"Okay, things might be different, like, even better, that's true, people 'ave never 'ad such nice shoes, like, or clothes, an' they've not 'ad 'omes like now, nor eaten so well, like, but the thing is, like, that people like you 'aven't 'ad much to do with it all, all you do is ruin what's there before you –"

"Why? What makes you say that?"

"Well, like –"

"You just don't have the proper understanding, my dear comrade." Dugas put on a wry, dismissive face, laying bare his teeth. "Either you're stupid, as well as lacking political awareness – or you're trying to be funny. Where could you make as much as you do here? What you're getting here –" Dugas gestured towards the house, "it's pretty good, isn't it? Today not even doctors are paid as much."

"Non intres in judicium cum servo tuo, Domine," the Slanický parish priest Zima intoned drawlingly in front of Belica's cross and Dugas's house, reminding Dugas that any death knell rung out from the little old chapel at Veľké Dvorce, encased in scaffolding right up to the tiny cross on its tower, could be heard from there all the way to the road to Slanica.

The mason, followed by Dugas, passed from the kitchen to the living room. Through the empty window frames, painted brown, they could see, standing on the path at the foot of Belica's cross, Father Zima, wearing his long black chasuble and white surplice, and a black biretta, and behind him the sacristan, an altar boy carrying a black cross, the organist, a bier with a black coffin on it, and next to them the pall-bearers resting and a whole crowd of people in black, mostly women.

"Kyrie eleison."

"Christe eleison, Kyrie eleison."

"Pater noster –"

The people knelt down on the drying mud of the track, which had been churned up by cars and carts and was flecked with the white of lime mortar and the red of brick dust. "Our Father, who art in heaven...," prayed the work-worn men in their rough voices, the poverty-stricken, care-worn and sickly women in their thinner voices and the red-faced children in their high-pitched voices.

The mason removed his white cap. Ignác Dugas vacillated, but the mason having shot him a second enquiring glance, he removed his grey hat.

A black car drove slowly past the praying throng, followed by a huge brown-and-green bus.

"– Thy kingdom come, Thy will be done, in earth as it is in heaven –"

"Who's died?"

"Some living being," said Dugas with a nasty smirk. "Some old biddy or other."

"And so many have come to her funeral?"

"It's always like this in Veľké Dvorce..." Ignác Dugas paled slightly and sank deep in thought. He fixed his eyes on the faded red paper ribbons tied round the dry wreath that had hung there since All Souls' Day. "It's always been like this in Veľké Dvorce – round here whole crowds turn up at funerals –"

"Et ne nos inducas in tentationem –"

"Sed libera nos a malo."

The people rose from the muddy track, the men lifted the bier onto their shoulders and the black procession moved off towards the cemetery.

Not speaking, Dugas left the mason's side and looked after the funeral procession, which had left the air with a churchy whiff of thyme, and once he saw they had all reached the cemetery, he mounted his motorbike and hared off down the track to Slanica.

The track to Slanica went downhill, passing through trees, meadows and fields, winding left and right, here and there as twisty as a piece of discarded string.

Ignác Dugas was contemplating one tricky business. His mind was on Moravčík and the Malenas. That perishing lot! They scheme, they conspire about all sorts of things, some-times the priest joins them – and who's to say it wasn't they who'd talked him into shedding any misgivings and continuing to chant away at the foot of Belica's cross? And the other lot, at EMZED! Dubovský thinks that just because they killed his mother by the cross – that... I bet he can get round his father-in-law and his father-in-law then gets round the priest... It's politically unthinkable! Okay then! Ignác Dugas began weaving a plan of attack against Martin Dubovský, his wife Eva, and her father, but with Dubovský himself as the main target, because he knew that Malena and the priest sometimes visited him.

He arrived back home, in Slanica.

Outside the house where the Ambros, his in-laws, "Rosyred Paula's" parents, lived, stood a black motorbike and next to it, wearing a green trench coat and a floppy green cap, Vlach, the EMZED production planner.

"Labour be praised, Comrade Dugas."

Dugas slowly dismounted from his own bike and chased off the Ambros' mustard-coloured dog.

"Hi, Peter! Come on in."

"I won't," said Vlach in reply. He reached into his pockets, took out a cigarette and set it between his thin lips. "Comrade Dugas, I've told you this several times already: I need money."

"I can't let you have any right now."

"Comrade Dugas," Vlach went on, smirking and blowing a puff of smoke out through the tiny gap between his compressed lips. "Remember the elections!"

Dugas blanched.

"Why?"

Vlach, his free hand in his coat pocket, smoked and smiled and fixed his grey eyes on Dugas's pale face.

"I don't believe you. We do understand each other, don't we?"

"We do."

"Fancy a vodka?"

"No, I'd prefer a really good plum brandy," said Dugas, grabbing Vlach by the arm and steering him out of the yard.

"I've got a mate round the corner, he's got some great stuff. We can chat there."

They left.

Two hours later, Dugas came back home, somewhat the worse for wear and in a foul mood.

"There's no point you going on about it," he said to his in-laws, his furious mother-in-law standing there all red in the face, "I'm just not going to put up with Belica's cross there. It'd me who'll be living there, not you. I'll be living there, me, and every funeral's going to stop outside *my* house. Enough, do stop going on at me! Who could possibly put up with having the priest stop outside the house at every funeral and chant whatever it is over every corpse – making people pray their hearts out outside your very window!"

"You're a bad egg, Ignác," said Ambro, his father-in-law. "But don't you dare lay a hand on that cross, or things will get nasty! I'll be keeping an eye on you!"

That same evening, Ambro flicked the crumbs off his brown corduroy trousers, drawn tight above his clodhoppers, rose from the table and headed for bed. In the doorway he turned to ask Paulína, Dugas's wife: "Where's Ignác?" He stood and waited for her reply, blinking with his light-brown eyes and flaxen eyelashes.

"At the Community Centre more than likely."

Ambro lapsed into thought.

"Your husband's a bastard," he said. "A right bastard. What do you need a bloke like that for? You go to work at EMZED – all that way every day! – you give him money and he's building himself a house and planning on some other monkey business. It's pointless you worrying. And you're up to something, the pair of you. You could have had children by now. And you could have been living round here even. What's the point of building a house in Veľké Dvorce? Where's Ignác?"

"I already told you."

"You're another –!"

Ambro went into the living room and switched the light on. He came back after a moment and said: "Listen, Paula, if Ignác does something stupid in Veľké Dvorce, things will go very bad for him! Just tell him that! He'll be sorry!" Ambro went back indoors.

Paulína was sewing buttons on her new blue blouse. She kept her eye on the living room door through which her father had passed. Her light-brown eyes darted about the door.

"I think I'll keep them here in the kitchen," said Mrs Ambro, who had suddenly appeared in the kitchen with a huge saucepot in which some tiny ducklings were chirruping away. "It's too cold for them in the closet."

Paulína was bent over her blouse, pulling her thread through a button hole.

"Ignác isn't home yet?" Mrs Ambro asked, having lodged her pot with the ducklings safely on top of the warm tiled stove. "Where is he?"

"No idea," said Paulína. "He'll be along eventually. He always gets in late at the moment. He could be at the Community Centre or the campaign headquarters."

"Come off it!"

"So where then?"

"Someone said he'd gone off on a tractor somewhere. With Kubiš!"

"On a tractor –!"

Paulína tossed her blouse to one side and ran out of the kitchen.

Ambro emerged from the living room just in time to see Paulína running off in her blue tracksuit.

She kept running, tying her headscarf as she ran, running to ask after her husband Ignác and Kubiš.

Kubiš and Ignác Dugas were in Veľké Dvroce.

It was silent and dark, here and there, there were lights on behind the windows, some higher up, some lower down, revealing just how deep the valley was, with its cottages and houses scattered up and down the hillsides. A stream babbled along the valley bottom, extra full with snowmelt coming down from the hills around. The air smelled damp and wafted warm about the face.

The tractor driver Kubiš was sitting on his tractor outside Dugas's new house, its engine idling and shaking Kubiš all over the place, so he was holding tight to the seat and steering wheel so as not to fall off. His head was buzzing and he had pins and needles in his hands and feet – and Ignác Dugas was fixing a heavy, solid chain around the cross.

"Come on, Ignác, what's all the – the –?"

"Hang on and keep your voice down! Christ! I can't loop the hook on!"

"Try the string you use to keep your pants up!"

"Arsehole!"

"Nearly there – or not quite –?"

"It's like this chain's got a mind of its own, dammit!"

"Hurry up! Somebody might – they might catch us at it, and then what –?"

Kubiš was holding on to his seat and steering wheel, his head was buzzing, he'd got pins and needles in his hands and feet because of the plum brandy, and Dugas, sweating like mad, cursed and swore and kept wiping his sweaty brow with his sleeve.

"Come on! This is intolerable – for Christ's sake!"

The tractor gave a loud cough, its hefty tyres slithered and spun, then got their powerful grip back on the track and Belica's cross fell onto the track. It tumbled out in one piece, right from the base, including the round section of the trunk of Belica's oak, left untrimmed to give the cross a more solid foundation.

"Haul away!" said Dugas as he hopped casually back onto the tractor. "To Slanica!"

"Slanica?"

"Well –!"

"Why there?"

"What's it to you, just keep hauling!"

Kubiš the tractor driver set off for Slanica, dragging the cross over the ground, driving the tractor hard down the zigzag track, and the cross's protective metal roof clanked against any projecting stones on the track where it had begun to dry out. The tractor's lights bobbed from the track to the ditches and trees.

Midnight was long past and now it was three in the morning.

"Where've you been all this time?" Paulína asked her husband, having caught a whiff of booze from the living room. "How come you're so late? I was looking for you! Where've you been? Where did you go on Kubiš's tractor? You weren't at the Community Centre or the campaign headquarters."

Dugas took off his coat.

"Where've you been?"

Dugas sat down on the bed and removed his shoes.

"My dear wife, it's like we'll be living in paradise –!"

"Where have you been?"

He took off his trousers.

"Where have you been?"

"Out canvassing!"

"Where?"

"Dvorce. My dear wife, dear in-laws, it's like we'll be living in paradise, you'll see –!"

"My father's angry. With both you and me. Just forget about the cross. They're angry about the cross, and because we don't have any kids –"

"All right, I'll forget about the cross," said Dugas and got into bed. "Did they come looking for me from the district party office? This is intolerable!"

"No, they didn't."

"My dear wife, dear in-laws, it's like we'll...! Come, darling Paula, lift up your nightie!"

"Phooey!"

"Come on –!"

"You drink, you go out boozing – and you stink like a barrel!"

Dugas lay down, and before he drifted off he had a vague sense of satisfaction at having achieved great things. He'd palled up with Vlach, talked him round. Talked him round... Vlach's an arsehole! He'd threatened to do the dirty on him – now, at election time, if he didn't give him some money. But then he had to win, he had to have a higher position so Malena would be afraid of him. What Malena has Malena must give him... He'd uprooted the cross, people were going to be afraid of him, everything was going to go nice and smoothly... It's so good when people are afraid... Vlach now, he's worldly wise... He knows everybody, he's in cahoots with the secret police – he really could do the dirty on him... Before long Dugas was fast asleep, snoring contentedly.

The night passed.

In the morning, Dugas's wife was in tears, her mother was sitting in the kitchen wringing her hands, and her father, Ambro, was lashing out at the cattle in the cooperative farm's cowshed. He kicked the cows' legs with his own robust, long legs because they wouldn't get out of his way as he tried to muck out the dung-soaked litter from under them.

"The stupid swine!" the men of Veľké Dvorce would unburden themselves above the great pit where the cross had stood opposite Dugas's house. "What can you expect from a swine like him? A bit of pork at best!"

"Oh, dear God!" the women of Veľké Dvorce wailed. "Dear God!"

"He's a flaming idiot!"

"He is that!"

"But what's he done with the cross?"

"Hauled it off somewhere, buried it, junked it –!"

"Or chopped it up and burned it!"

"Oh, dear God, dear God!"

"That knucklehead's going to rue the day!"

"Where did you put the cross?" Ignác Dugas's father, Mišo Dugas, asked him; he'd arrived at the Ambros's in Slanica that morning. "Where've you hidden it?"

"That would be telling!"

"Now wait here!" Dugas's father's tall, erect figure went red in the face. "You have no idea what's allowed and what isn't. I'm also a communist, have been since before you ever were, and I know that such things just aren't permitted. You need to be taught a lesson, you nerk –!"

"Where *is* the cross?" Paulína asked. "Where'd you put it?"

"Just shut up and leave me alone!" Ignác Dugas bawled at her and kept yelling at the others till he had saliva running down his chin: "Leave off, will you! It's not you who's gonna be living there – it's me – not you –!"

He was all atremble with helpless venom.

"My dear Eva," Mr Moravčík, the teacher, wrote to his daughter. "Just a brief note this time, it's as much as I can manage. That Ignác Dugas has used a tractor to uproot Belica's cross at the foot of which Martin's poor mother met her end, and the people of Veľké Dvorce and round about are outraged, and they're making threats against Dugas. We are both utterly dismayed that such a thing could have happened. With heartfelt grief we think of Martin's late mother, and of you. Yours as ever."

Eva handed the letter to her husband and, having read it, Dubovský stood pensively for a moment, there in the living room, his hands shaking as he held the letter, before saying: "The weather's nice, tomorrow's Sunday, let's go over to Veľké Dvorce!" He looked at Eva, who was quite surprised.

"And what will we –?"

"We'll go and visit your parents – and your father needs to be told not to write letters like that one. And to think he had Paula Dugas deliver it! Was it really she who brought you the letter?"

"Yes."

"We'll go!"

(359)

"All right, I don't mind." Eva thought about it briefly. "I haven't been there for ages. Aren't you afraid of going there? You've never wanted to."

"No, we'll go!"

Veľké Dvorce had fallen silent, not even Father Zima, the Slanica parish priest, had said anything in church that Sunday, although there were more people there that day than at any time in the past and although very many of them expected the priest to have at least a word to say about what had happened to Belica's cross in Veľké Dvorce, but he never mentioned the cross once. No one was saying anything in public, people had simply stopped, they were afraid.

Ambro, Dugas's father-in-law, was withdrawn, determining how not to let matters stand and make things hot for his son-in-law, Dugas's mother-in-law kept silent, as did his wife, Paulína.

Both villages, Veľké Dvorce and Slanica, were seething, and Ignác Dugas, secretary of the local national committee, fearful and enraged as he sat alone in his office, was typing a letter. They all need their gobs shutting! he kept thinking. And to stay out of it and quit messing about...! It might get through to them that even worse things could come their way!

He finished his short letter and spent a long time re-reading it, and again. Was it enough? For now, certainly. Ignác Dugas sat in the office of the Slanica national committee, wearing his trench coat, his hat on his head, pondering as he stared at his letter. He had a headache, because ever since the evening when he'd ripped out Belica's cross he'd been drinking non-stop, for the third day in a row. He wondered if he hadn't overdone it. The very next day, May Day, people he knew at the district committee had patted him on the back, but then lapsed at once into a stony silence, smiling maliciously. Moravčík's to blame for this, or if not, he will be...! He began reading his letter again, while worrying about the elections and the money Vlach was demanding from him. Only Malena could have let on to Vlach, or that whore of his!

"Reactionaries," he said aloud, "reactionaries, the lot of 'em! "

That Sunday afternoon, the day after May Day, saw the Dubovskýs, Martin and Eva, their two boys Igor and Ondrej, and Moravčík, the teacher and Eva's father, strolling around Veľké Dvorce. People stopped them to say hello and some were very welcoming. They didn't stop and chat with anyone, merely exchanging the conventional questions and answers: "How are you?" and "Very well, thank you." They weren't saying much to each other either, as if sensing that they didn't have anything particular to say. From the pile of earth that had once been their cottage, now overgrown with burdock and nettles, they walked in silence up to Dugas's house, still awaiting completion, cast a glance at it and at the framed sign: CONSTRUCTION AUTHORISED, and then stood staring in silence into the pit opposite, where once Belica's cross had stood. After a little while they moved on from Belica's meadow to the cemetery and the great tomb crowned by a black marble memorial bearing in letters of gold the names of all those who had been executed, fallen in battle, been beaten to death or burned. Besides the names of the four bandits – Ján Furdík, Michal Berec, Jozef Dugas and František Dubovský, who'd been buried in a common grave because of Martin's mother, killed next to Belica's cross – there were the names of Mária and Štefan Dubovský, Martin's parents – and many others.

The Dubovskýs – Martin and Eva and the boys, Igor and Ondrej – stood in front of the black marble panel, decorated with letters of gold.

Igor and Ondrej were dumbstruck.

In 1944, Ignác Dugas, too, as a seventeen-year-old lad, had been one of the bandit gang led by Fero Dubovský, Martin Dubovský's brother, as its commander. After the bandits had caused death and destruction at the two houses in Slanica and Martin Dubovský had despatched a group of partisans to seek them out, Ignác Dugas had managed to escape. He got rid of his automatic and army belt, roamed about the villages and, after his brother was executed, went off to the town to report to the German command post and avenge himself on the Veľké Dvorce partisans for his brother's execution. On his way to the town he was caught by some German soldiers and taken off to the command post. There he was attended to by the Gestapo, who knocked out five of his teeth, ordered him to take his shoes off, then hung him up by the arms and placed two red-hot electric rings under his feet. He was interrogated and, although, bleeding at the mouth and with his bare feet dangling over the electric rings, he no longer wished to avenge his brother, he did betray Martin Dubovský and the other partisans, but that brought no harm to anyone, because the commander of the German troops in Veľké Dvorce, a Major Gerhard, who thought of himself as a very easy-going person who anyway believed in the principles of collective responsibility, had all males between the ages of sixteen and sixty picked up, entrusting them to the care of a Truppen-führer who was to lock them up and torture them, make a show of interrogating them and then set them aside for future use. Moravčík, the teacher, managed to hide for a time before escaping from Veľké Dvorce to join his brother in the town. One very rainy day in early November, with Veľké Dvorce covered in water and mist, Eva Moravčík dressed now like any of the locals, went down into the village and, having learnt that all the men were locked up in the school for the fifth day in a row, she hurried back to report to Martin on what had happened. As she passed beneath Belica's cross she saw a soldier nailing a sign to the cross bearing the words ACHTUNG! MINEN! BETEN VERBOTEN! Was he mad? Who was the sign for? Who'd be likely to pray here? The soldier turned. Eva froze at the sight of the elongated face, with vertical slashes round its mouth and with its deformed and purple forehead that had been smashed and operated on, and she was horrified by his right eye, depressed by the disfigured purple brow towards his cheek bone. She turned her fulsome lips into a smile at the depressed, sideways-looking eye lest the soldier detect they were quivering. The soldier, SS man Pif-Paf-Russe, was holding the large hammer with which he had nailed the notice CAUTION! LANDMINES! PRAYING FORBIDDEN! to the cross. Pif-Paf-Russe was expecting someone else to come to pray for the partisan and that he would despatch them just as he had that woman, but to keep the German soldiers safe, the easy-going Major Gerhard had ordered the warning sign to be put up. Eva stared at the horrifying, deformed face. "What's that?" she asked, pointing to the sign and went on to ask in her broken German: "You pray?" – "Me?" Pif-Paf-Russe jiggled the large wet hammer he was holding and smiled a chilling smile. "Not me. Have you come to pray for the partisan? Don't you pray, you're young, and pretty…" – "Sorry?" – "Have you come here –" Pif-Paf-Russe pointed to the spot beneath the cross where he had just planted two landmines and covered them over with turf, "– have you come here – to pray? Have you got a dead partisan somewhere? Don't you pray, it would be a shame to kill someone so young…" – "No, I have no partisan – but let me have that hammer!" – "What for?" Eva glanced about her and had another shock when she looked back into the soldier's eyes. They were pale grey and the distrust in them was fading away, as if the higher eye had stopped keeping check on the lower one, which looked out sideways. "I need to kill a pig –" Eva pointed to the nearest cottage on Bukovec Rise, "– he musn't squeal. I'll call you when it's done." – "No," said Pif-Paf-Russe, "I'll come with you, to help." – "No, you stay here – to keep watch – we mustn't be seen together…!" Pif-Paf-Russe jiggled the hammer he was still holding, compressed his face into a chilling smile and handed the hammer to Eva. "Thank you very much!" Eva seized its clammy wet handle, turned away from the soldier, swung round, aimed a blow at the purple forehead and felled the soldier at the foot of the cross. She tossed the hammer away, and with all the strength at her disposal, as if she were being supported by some unfelt, mighty wind, she then fled from the cross to the far side of Belica's meadow, and on towards some hazel and dogwood bushes, then through them, and a beech wood, horrified at having killed someone, into the beech wood and out again, then through two clearings into a pinewood. Back to Martin, oh, God, to find Martin – get back there, walking or running, and tell him she'd killed someone... They'll seek revenge... Eva ran, hot sweat trickling into her mouth, like rainwater, running, she didn't hear the explosions from the direction of the cross, where Pif-Paf-Russe had been rolling about on the ground and brushed his hip against the landmines. "Martin," she said to Dubovský in the gamekeeper's lodge the other side of Skalka, "I've killed a man – they'll come, we're done for!" – "You've nothing to fear, Eva. Let's just wait for them. They'd show up anyway. Come and get changed. You're all wet, drenched – quick!" Eva followed Martin, shivering with cold, trembling with fear, all a-quiver over everything, she held onto him with both hands, "Dear Martin...," she said, her teeth chattering as she let herself be stripped and dried off, "dear Martin...," she kept on saying long after, upstairs in the lodge's cold guest room, lying feverish on the wet clothes she'd removed as the sense of guilt for having killed a man faded from her. With her eyes motionless and knowing, gleaming and resigned, she looked into Martin's eyes, deep-set and overshadowed, flashing white at odd moments, "Dear Martin...," she whispered, "whether you'll want me to or not, I shall make up to you everything you have lost and are yet to lose...," and after a pause she asked: "Have I killed, Martin?" – "No, Eva, you've killed no one." Martin Dubovský dressed Eva in her uniform and put her boots on. On Belica's cross the sign saying ACHTUNG! MINEN! BETEN VERBOTEN! was still there, Pif-Paf-Russe's remains were buried by his younger comrades, arseholes, at the foot of the cross, and their commander, the easy-going Major Gerhard, on orders from above, launched, along with the men gathered up from Veľké Dvorce as a shield against the partisans, an attack on the partisan camps and bunkers in the mountains. Dubovský's company fought well against the Germans, but failed to hold Gerhard's men back at the gamekeeper's lodge beyond Skalka and scattered, leaving behind them dead men on both sides. Those captured included both Martin Dubovský and his father, and Eva Moravčík. Major Gerhard stood on the gamekeeper's pile of trimmed logs, had his men set fire to the lodge and ordered them to shoot anyone who made a run for it. "If there are any," he said, "and that's not very likely. They'll be warmer inside than out here in the cold and rain. It's much nicer by a warm fire." The soldiers drove their captives into the kitchen, used incendiary devices to set fire to the loft space, stairs and the rooms on the ground floor and waited with guns at the ready for any who might try to run. Major Gerhard and three officers stood on the woodpile and watched as the roof, upper storey and walls blazed. In the ground-floor kitchen, the room furthest from the burning walls, were crammed the sixty captives. "Look there, Father," said Martin, "that axe! Lie down next to the stove, here, and hold it between your feet, blade up!" – "Martin – I... Who can save us now?" – "Just lie down!" Dubovský, shaking with fear and cold in his sopping wet clothes, lay down, raised the axe between his feet, blade up, and his son Martin cut through the rope binding his hands. He took up the axe, cut through his father's rope, then Eva's, then everyone else's. Under the weight of the roof and upper storey the burning wall gave way, the captives huddled together in the kitchen, their eyes glinting with the red flames of the burning walls. Martin took Eva and his father by the arms and watched for a gap in the wall through which they might escape. Suddenly it was if a gust of wind blew a body of suffocating, acrid smoke in on them. The burning wall collapsed, bringing down with it part of the burning ceiling. The men all lurched back, crushing Martin, his father and Eva up against the huge oven and knocking them to the ground. Martin hauled Eva out from under them, opened the door of the bread oven, rejoicing at its sheer size and volume, pushed her inside it, went in after her, and, from under the swarming, trampling and struggling men, from under all the groaning, shouting and general hubbub he began dragging his father in after them. The choking men spotted them, two of the younger ones yanked his father from his grip and crammed into the stove themselves, if only to the extent of their heads and half their chests. Another piece of ceiling came down and the choking men began clamouring in utter terror "oh, mother – dear wife – oh, God – save me, save us – us, my kids...!" the men yelled and clamoured in voices rough and feeble, a clamour that issued from their whole being, Eva watched the two terrible faces crammed into the oven's jaws, the clenching and unclenching of Martin's father's hand, above the oven the dry blazing timbers crackled, the lodge was cracking and collapsing, Eva closed her eyes so as not to have to see the two terrible faces, mangled with pain, she opened her eyes – the faces, heads, the hand, all covered in embers, the men stopped yelling and clamouring, lapsing into silence in the red-hot coals, the fire and the smoke. "I told you no one would be leaving the lodge," Major Gerhard told his officers as he sat on the woodpile, "because it's warmer there than out here. What an awful day it is. More rain!" – "Yes, Herr Major," said his lieutenant, "but mightn't they have hidden in the cellar?" – "No, the entrance to the cellar's over there, from the outside." "Oughtn't we to blow it up?" – "No, just take it easy, it might still bring some partisans in because it's not nice in the forest and can only get worse!" Major Gerhard and his officers, wearing shiny rubber capes, stood a while longer on the gamekeeper's log pile, watching the mound of burning and smoking beams, beds, tables and cupboards before clambering back down. "Oberfeldwebel!" – "Yessir, Herr Major!" – "Give the site of the fire a once-over and shoot anyone still alive. They'll have had enough by now!" – "Yessir, Herr Major!" Inside the oven, Eva and Martin stared at the lifeless black heads in the oven's jaws, covered in dying embers, and at the convulsively twisted hand, they choked on the stifling smell of burned flesh that was drifting through the baking chamber from the exhaust.

Close by the oven the crackle of automatics, two bursts, a third, a fourth. Then came a long silence until the embers in the oven's jaws started to hiss with the water produced by the rising cascade of rain, until the blackened and hot oven began to cool. It was then that Martin Dubovský, now alone in the world, no brother, no mother, no father, held the sobbing Eva tight and, looking up through the oven's exhaust, saw that the sky was now black, he used his feet to push the burnt faces and burnt hand, blackened with soot, out of the jaws of the oven and finally he and Eva left the mound of burned remains. Eva was crying, and Martin carried her, most of the time lifeless, off into the forest. "My dear Eva," he said each time they paused to get their breath back. "Eva – survival, that's the only thing, to get through all this and devote our whole lives to seeking redress..." A week later, Ignác Dugas was released from the German command post to drag himself home to Veľké Dvorce on his burned feet, to stay at his father's cottage. In the fullness of time, Martin Dubovský's minor burns cleared up in the bunker up in the hills round Veľké Dvorce, when the war was over, he completed his studies, as did Eva. "You rose from death," said Mr Moravčík the teacher, as he gave them his blessing at their marriage, "you will not be able to live one without the other, give your lives to each other and to others besides. Cleave to each other and accord each other all respect." Then while bursting into tears of joy, he also trembled with apprehension. Time passed and the Dubovskýs moved to the MZ works' vast housing estate, still awaiting completion. They lived well, contentedly, until Martin began to give in to foul moods following Soňa Malena's arrival at Emzed; in her, Martin saw the sense of all that had come to pass in Veľké Dvorce and in its hills and forests, and for a time contentment was restored between himself and Eva.

Completely mad, he thought angrily of himself, as he and Eva, Igor, Ondrej and Moravčík stood beside the pile that had been the gamekeeper's lodge beyond Skalka, and when they visited the spot where he had had his brother executed.

They left and, back in Veľké Dvorce, ran into old Mr Furdík, whose son Dubovský had had executed.

"Hello," said old Furdík, "and welcome, Doctor!"

"Hello!"

Dubovský was shaking, and as old Furdík tried to relight his pipe, his hand dithered and twitched all round it and he couldn't aim his match at the tobacco.

"So, old friend, how's things?"

"Not good," he said slowly, "not good at all, Doctor. Everything would be fine if there were no Dugas. Are such things permitted?"

"No, they aren't."

The Dubovskýs tarried awhile with Furdík before returning to Eva's mother's; she had been looking after Olga in the meantime, and before dusk they set off to Slanica on foot, pausing by the chapel and the two mounds that were the houses that had been burned down, before heading for the station.

Just as they were leaving the chapel, Ignác Dugas shot past on his red motorbike, on his way to inspect his house at Veľké Dvorce, still awaiting completion.

He was overcome with venom when he saw who Moravčík was accompanying.

Ignác Dugas knew all there was to know about Soňa Malena, Martin Dubovský and his wife, Eva, and he had plenty of things to worry about: Belica's cross, now uprooted, his wife, his own peace of mind and the elections. He was afraid of Moravčík, his daughter Eva, and his son-in-law Martin, which was why he wanted to intimidate them, and because he had things to do the following day at the district committee office in town, he sent a letter from there to Moravčík in Veľké Dvorce. He was afraid of his pals at the district committee, who said little and were given to smirking, and he was afraid of people, including Vlach, the production planner at Emzed. He was afraid of many of the people of Slanica and Veľké Dvorce who worked at Emzed, and there were times when he was afraid of his wife Paula. People get about, spreading who knows what, gossiping – and what if Paula or anybody else tells Dubovský everything and if Dubovský starts getting at him? He's been here, causing trouble! Paula's so argumentative, forever nagging... Stupid cow! Ignác Dugas's hand was shaking as he posted, in the town, his letter to Moravčík, the teacher who lived in Veľké Dvorce.

"Bastards," he muttered to himself as the letter slipped down inside the postbox, "bastards everywhere you look! Reactionaries! You haven't heard the last of me! Enough's enough!" He paused briefly by the postbox, still thinking about his letter.

"Mr Moravčík!" the letter said, and what it said further down, that terrified Moravčík, Eva's father. "There's something I need to tell you –"

Having re-read the letter, Moravčík went round to the Belica house, home now to the Malenas.

What had been Belica's yard was deserted, everything seeming coated with a layer of dust, a dark-brown square in the middle where his stolen dung heap had been, silence in the yard, no dog, no chickens, geese or ducks, no cows mooing, no pigs squealing, holes in the barn roof and the shed next to the barn on the point of collapse, and the contents of a wheelbarrow tipped out next to the animal houses. Next to the dark-brown square a red doll's pram and the red and blue carriages of the toy train Jurko used to play with, thrown about all over the place. On the veranda three large wardrobes covered with sheets.

"Good morning, Doctor Malena –"

"My wife's taken Jurko shopping," said Malena in the kitchen, cluttered up with a large white dresser and some white kitchen furniture. "I was about to do the dinner. She'll be back shortly."

Malena pointed his grubby hands at the pile of potatoes on the table, wiped his hands on his old brown trousers, opened the door to the sitting room, which was chockablock with cupboards, an escritoire, two beds, an oval dining table, dining chairs and some deep leather armchairs.

"Do come in, sir, enter our people's-democratic lounge –!"

"Doctor –!"

"We've got to sell all this stuff," said Malena and waved his arm around the room, "but we don't have a buyer. Who'd be likely to buy furniture and pictures these days? But we're going to have to –"

Mr Moravčík, the teacher, sat down on a large leather settee and opposite him Malena on the piano stool.

"I'm here, Dr Malena," Moravčík began, his voice shaking, "over a quite awful business –!"

"You know, I've never peeled potatoes in my life, not even on military service."

Moravčík produced his letter.

"I'll read it... Let me read it to you... It's a letter I've received about your daughter... Mr Moravčík!" he read. "I have to write to you because we have discovered that you really ought to look to your son-in-law, who during the great Slovak National Uprising... But, no," said Moravčík, "I can't read it, Doctor. Please – if you wouldn't mind – you – you read it –!"

He passed the letter to Malena.

Malena took Dugas's letter, ran his eyes down the first few lines and read on: "– who during the great Slovak National Uprising had a certain Jozef Dugas an innocent man killed and is now having an affair with a certain Soňa Malena, she's employed as the kultprop at the MZ works and she has it off with any bloke willing to pay well her well enough. We have established that he has had a child, a boy, with her and he is living with her parents at Veľké Dvorce by Slanica and her parents are one-time lawyers and reactionaries then there's you and Zima the Slanica parish priest and there'll be others stirring up trouble in Veľké Dvorce. You rant on against the United Agricultural Cooperative you rant on but you'd better look out the lot of you or you could be got by something nasty or even worse than nasty!!" Malena burst out laughing.

"What do you say to that, Doctor?" Mr Moravčík, the teacher asked, horrified. His dry face had blanched, his blue eyes fixed on Malena's pallid complexion. "So that's why you complain about your daughter, going on about her like that to me, her fancying my son-in-law, the medic, Dr Dubovský –?"

Moravčík's dry, pale lips were quivering.

Silence descended on Belica's sitting room. The room, crammed with costly urban furniture, crowded in on Moravčík with its warped walls, missing their plaster here and there and full of cracks, and its low, rotting ceiling, its two small windows admitting only a greyish light, and the whole reeking of putrefaction and fragrance.

"So you," Moravčik shrieked, "this – so your daughter is as you've said – and my son-in-law, daughter and the children have –?"

"Belica was here yesterday and he, too, went so far as to demand, my dear friend, some rent money from me for this house – and he's right, he ought to be being paid something – and that Soňa of mine, she was my daughter, but not anymore, she's a daughter of the times we live in," Malena said calmly, watching Moravčík's horrified, dehydrated features, his great, mobile, projecting black eyebrows and the white hair above his ears, and he handed him back the letter. "She's a daughter of the times. She fooled me so as to let herself be fooled by others, and now she fools everybody. If she were not like that, how could she have become a kultprop? You can't begin to imagine what it's like to have such a bad apple for a child..." The lustre had gone from Malena's pale-blue eyes and his pallid complexion had grown even more pallid. "It's all her fault, hers – she was a medical student and so that she might continue with her studies, some Party secretary at the faculty snared her, forced her to repudiate us, her own parents, to conceal and falsify her background, her class background, and to yield to him – which she did, repeatedly – and in the end they expelled her anyway – and since then? – after that she came to us to unburden herself of the whole thing, and as much as up to that point, up to that point, my good friend! – you yourself know what it is to have a child – we had loved her, terribly, she was after all our only child – after that I came to hate her – she should never have yielded, not to that nobody, she shouldn't have yielded, she should have held out, stood her ground, but she didn't – and now she's taking it out on herself and the world around her – all she is now is a prostitute, that's all they made of her – prostitutes don't just roam the streets, but higher spheres as well...! And then Vlach, a certain Vlach! It's a terrible thing, my friend, I've never harmed a fly, but that Vlach I would kill if I knew where he was – and finally there's Dugas, and my Soňa serves people like that... How's she to be dealt with? How, tell me, my teacher-friend! What does she deserve? Wherever there's carrion, there you'll find vultures, and my Soňa is leading plenty of vultures, and against me –"

Malena fell silent, blinked his lustreless eyes and watched Moravčík, whose lips were quivering in horror.

"I, I'll – I'll go there – and I'll –!"

Malena seemed not to hear.

"I'll go there –!"

"I can assure you of one thing," said Malena, gazing into a void, "that that thing about our Jurko isn't true – and about your son, the medical man – because my daughter already had him when she left to join the factory where she now works. The rest I don't know – but I'm going to find out, my dear friend, and I can assure you that I'll sort that daughter of mine out myself – myself! Don't worry about a thing! As for believing all this stuff, I don't. The letter's unsigned. We don't know who wrote it. It's certainly, certainly, some lousy swine who wants to remain anonymous, and it would seem, would seem to be some kind of provocation, possibly dangerous, possibly just plain silly. Just don't you worry, my friend!"

"And will your daughter tell you the truth?"

Moravčík folded the letter, sitting there in the huge leather armchair as if torn to shreds, quietly breathing in the Belica putrefaction and the Malena fragrance and with his blue eyes fixed on Malena, his pallid complexion and the small quivering muscles beneath his gently perspiring skin. The room that was once Belica's seemed to come alive inside Moravčík's eyes. The deep leather armchairs crowded in on him, as did the high-backed dining chairs with their leather facings, the oval table fidgeted, the beds, bedside tables, bookcases and shiny desk all kept moving, and everything shone with a toxic sheen, the piano, the gold frames of the pictures piled up on top of a wardrobe, the old walls pressed in on him and the old wooden ceiling pressed down.

"My daughter...!" said Malena quietly, with a hint of self-pity, then added: "Now she does tell me the truth! It's getting late – don't you worry, my teacher friend –!"

"Soňa!" Malena said the following day to his daughter at the Emzed housing estate, in the Community Centre, in her bedsit on the sixth floor. "Do you have any cash?"

"No, Father, I don't, I can't give you any –!"

"You're having an affair...!" Malena stood there, at his daughter's, and he hadn't even sat down, with his wide grey hat on his head and his bamboo cane in his hand. "You're having an affair with the doctor at this place, a certain Dubovský. Let me have some money unless you want me to –!"

"For God's sake, Father –!"

"I wouldn't want it," he said, "to become permanent, you could fall in love, you won't make a penny out of it –!"

Soňa's lovely white hands were shaking, there were tears in her eyes as she made up her mind that she had to do everything possible to prevent Eva hearing anything and as she took five hundred crowns from her little red nylon bag. She handed them to her father. Her smooth pale face paled even more.

"For God's sake, Father, go!"

Malena took the money and left without a word, and when he looked in on the agitated teacher, Moravčík, in Veľké Dvorce, he reassured him in the pleasantest terms.

"You've nothing to fear, my friend," he told him. "It's not true. It's just a stupid provocation, a ludicrous falsehood, a... I've also been to see your daughter and remembered you to her. She's a very lovely woman and I think she leads a very lovely life with her husband, they have very lovely children, three... I should be surprised, my good friend, at your son-in-law. Fear nothing!"

Moravčík was somewhat relieved, he re-read the anonymous letter with mistrust and in secret and having thought everything over, and in a dismal state of mind, he wrote to Eva from home and told her everything as it occurred to him.

"Veľké Dvorce, 4th May 1954," he wrote in his rangy, shaded, slightly shaky script. "My dear Eva, I am writing to you on a very grave matter, although Mr Malena, the lawyer, who has been to see you, told me that I should not write to you about it at all. I feel so terribly sad, with such anguish and pain in my heart, that I have to write. I have always known and always feared that people today have been demoralised by the war –"

Moravčík finished his letter, hesitated for quite some time, and finally posted it.

Ignác Dugas was drinking. He was afraid because of all the things that he'd done, he was especially afraid of his comrades at the district committee, silent, wearing malicious smiles and looking away from him. He was drinking and thinking, with a splitting headache and his legs and hands shaking.

His wife, "Rosy-red Paula", had gone off to the MZ housing estate and found herself accommodation in the dormitory block for singles because she'd had a row with Ignác and told him she wasn't going to live in a house opposite which he'd uprooted a cross and close to which an SS man was buried, and Ignác had left Slanica and the Ambros for the town, where he was lodging with a pal from the district national committee.

From its earliest days, May was alive with canvassing at the agitprop centres, which were open from early morning till late at night. The agitprop centre for the MZ housing estate was in the lecture hall of Community Centre. For most of the day it was deserted.

"You playing charades, Soňa?" Dubovský asked, having run into Soňa, alone in the lecture hall. It was the sixth day after Ignác Dugas had uprooted the cross in Veľké Dvorce. "This is no time for playing games."

"It isn't, Martin, I know," she whispered. "I have my regrets – today I see things differently –"

"How? How differently can you be seeing things? You're deluding yourself, and me, you're letting your child down, your parents, people who need to have something to believe in. Maybe you have to, maybe not, but that's what you're doing!"

"You've no right to speak to me like that!"

"I think I have, especially after everything that's gone on between us –"

"Martin!" she whispered. "Martin, you're being unfair."

Dubovský felt a tremor as he caught the glimmer in Soňa's watery, pale-blue eyes.

"And you couldn't even find out for me – maybe you didn't actually want to – whether Vlach and Dugas know each other or not."

"And why do you need to know?"

"Don't you worry about that!" Dubovský replied curtly. "It's none of your business!"

He turned to leave.

"Have you been looking for me?"

"No," came Dubovský's curt denial, "not me –"

"Martin!" Soňa grabbed Dubovský by the forearm. "I don't know what to do. My father keeps coming to beg me for money. He may actually have gone mad... He spends more on fares than what I give him... Please, Martin, won't you help me? Why do you avoid me just when I need you most? I haven't got you, I haven't got anybody, just a deranged father. I'm hoping that there's at least a whit of human feeling in you... Could you come and see me this evening? We can have a talk and you can give me your advice –"

"What time?"

"Whatever suits you," she said. "I won't come here this evening, I'll wait in for you."

It was a warm evening on the MZ estate, a gentle breeze blew among the red high-rises, those completed and those awaiting completion, the evening was also warm in Slanica, where people, enraged over Belica's cross, were streaming into the agitprop centre, the tavern, all awash with banners. This was where, among others, Ignác Dugas, was to present himself to the electorate. They were curious about this person, who was not only standing for election to the district national committee, but was the man who had had the gall to rip out a cross in his own village, and they had come streaming into the agitprop centre.

Three cars were parked outside the agitprop centre, one grey and two black, and Dugas's red motorbike, while inside were the canvassers, candidates and the electoral commission.

Many had had their say, and now it was Ignác Dugas's turn.

He rose to his feet, dressed in a new grey suit, leaned back slightly behind the long, red-decked table, and because each candidate himself had to acquaint the voters with who and what he was, he began to read from his prepared speech – though he did so without verve, constrained, and he felt like a naughty child being force-fed porridge made of ashes, he read quietly, quickly, the sooner to be able to sit down again, and knowing that there was now no point reading what had taken him more than a fortnight to put together – in quiet tones he read about his grandfather, a poverty-stricken peasant who had put every ounce of energy, as had his wife and children, into their meagre existence on their tiny farm, and then he read about his father, who had been an itinerant seasonal labourer and gained first-hand experience of the rapacity of the landed gentry and their henchmen, and then about himself, who had accompanied his father to his seasonal employments and worked as a farm hand for wealthy, grasping farmers, who often hadn't even fed him, then he read about how, before the glorious Slovak National Uprising in 1944, he had been in contact with Soviet partisans in the hills and forests of Veľké Dvorce. "And then I took part in our glorious Slovak National Uprising," he read, his white and dental-gold teeth gleaming, "I fell into the hands of the Gestapo, who brutalised and tortured me, and after we were liberated by the glorious Red Army, I joined the militia in my home village, Veľké Dvorce, and with other comrades we twice defended the village against remnants of the defeated fascist German Wehrmacht. After that, I enlisted in the Czechoslovak Army, where I conducted myself in exemplary fashion, my father even being sent a letter of commendation from our command HQ, then I got a job at the MZ engineering works, left there for a course in politics, after which I became secretary at the local national committee here in Slanica."

The packed agitrop centre was silent. The good folk of Slanica, crammed together on the long fir-wood benches and standing alongside the walls, had sat, or stood, and listened in silence. Some looked at him, but most were staring into the ground, leaning forward, blinking and pondering. They shrank in horror that such a pack of lies could be listened to, let alone uttered, but they just pondered, blinked and stared into the ground. That people like this man could –!

"– in the course of my current activities, I have always sought to ensure that our united agricultural cooperative, which we set up and have led from strength to strength, grew into a superior kind, in order that its lavish products might feed working townspeople and be among the best in the district – and even before the cooperative came into being I insisted that the breakdown of quotas be fair – always and in all things, and I have tried to ensure that our community of Slanica, but other communities also, made their contribution in aid of Korea's struggle, the Korea that is now under reconstruction –" Why bother reading it? From the district committee, from the Party itself, a report had been sent about his uprooting the cross, but nothing had arrived yet, and maybe won't. The bastards! "– Korea is under reconstruction... That, comrades, is no laughing matter!"

Canvassers, candidates and the electoral commission, they all looked at Dugas.

As he spoke, a flicker of fear flashed across Ignác Dugas's face because from the men and women bent forward, seated, standing, silently listening, meekly blinking and staring down at the ground, he'd been expecting the question: "And what became of those extra quotas?" Ignác Dugas needn't have worried, nobody had heckled him, nobody was asking any questions, because the people just carried on sitting or standing in silence, meekly blinking and staring down at the ground. He gained some comfort from a strange new idea that had come to him, that there was no truth in what people had been and were still saying about him. Maybe nothing that he'd done was true – maybe that report from the district committee, from the Party, had not even been sent, maybe – he *had* to win this election, it was even of concern to Vlach that he should win. If he gets a superior position, Malena will give him more money, he's still got plenty –

"– and now I do whatever I can to assist," Ignác Dugas read on, louder and more assertively, "our Party and government's intent to construct socialism in this country faster and better, and I personally have always and in all things, despite the reactionaries, fought obscurantism, and I saw to the successful removal from a certain kulak's meadow –" he raised his voice confidently "– to the forcible removal of a certain kulak of Veľké Dvorce from his meadow and so stopped him hampering the foundation of the united agricultural cooperative – I saw to it that on that former kulak's meadow there is no longer the cross that was such a sorry and shameful reminder of the atrocities of the Nazis, because people, still backward and lacking in political awareness, would stop by the cross, pray and secretly pity Belica, the kulak, and I did this solely because our Party and government –"

"Put a sock in it, Ignác!"

The people froze and looked round towards one corner at an elderly, but still erect, tall man who had pushed in front of the others, put his spectacles on and held aloft an open red book.

"Wait, comrade," the chairman of the electoral commission called from behind the long table, "then you may speak once Comrade Dugas has finished."

"I'm waiting for no such numbskull!" said the tall man in spectacles. "Ignác Dugas is my son, and I can speak to him at any time and in any place... And I reckon that includes here! He's a crook and an impostor! A cheat! This book here, from this little book he taught me the way things are and the way they're going to be, I believed him and I'll read you something from it. I'm an old communist, and whatever our Party has put out in newspapers and books in the past, it has been as good as it word. I believe it's still like that."

The noise, the clatter and laughter, that broke out in the agitprop centre abated and Mišo Dugas adjusted his spectacles and began reading slowly, glancing now and again at Ignác, who was staring at him wide-eyed and thunderstruck. His lips were parted slightly, his arms and legs were trembling, and his papers were shaking in his hands. The light bulbs shone feebly and his white and dental-gold teeth glinted in the poor light.

"– priests were not put on trial," Mišo Dugas read, slowly, "whereas spies, traitors to the people and warmongers were. Questions of religion were not brought to the courts. Not a word was said about religion beyond statements that the accused had abused it for their own ends." The father cast a long glance towards the son. "In 1949, the President of the Republic, Klement Gottwald, said: 'No one wants to take away or suppress our believers' religion, no one wants to lock up churches and priests or even prevent people taking part in such rituals as are prescribed by this or that religion.'" Mišo Dugas folded away his spectacles and looked at his candidate-son. "So now what, Ignác? This is how you fool people? Have you no shame? And aren't you the least bit concerned about mouthing such words as Party and government? Do you know what this is? Don't you know that what the government or the head of government says is sacred? You don't know and you're working against the government! Are people supposed to vote for a candidate like you? Uprooting a cross, that's like demolishing a church. And our Party and government are spending vast sums on churches and repairs to them. Even in Veľké Dvorce they're repairing the old chapel, which no one has bothered even to whitewash for over a century! What is said and written should be put into action. If the Party and government you talk about are anything like you, then we could have spared our legs the effort of coming here. I don't believe the Party's like that, because I know it, but I know you're different. Nobody's going to believe you ever again, because you say one thing and do another!"

Mišo Dugas looked around at the people present and rolled up his red pamphlet.

His son Ignác, red in the face, shut his mouth and sat down, then got up. At the long table, there was great confusion among the members of the commission, the canvassers and candidates, canvasser leaned towards candidate and candidate towards canvasser, some of them with a smile on their faces. The people clattered with their benches, grumbling, some even laughing.

"A fine specimen of a candidate that one!" shouted Ignác's father-in-law, the yellowish-haired, red-faced Ambro and he got up to go. "God Almighty! Is that what we're meant to vote for? What did happen to those extra quotas?"

Ignác's father, Mišo Dugas, took fright. He sensed that that was one word that shoudn't have been raised.

"And where's the meat, Ignác?"

"And that wheat?"

"And those spuds?"

"They certainly didn't make it to Korea, Ignác has his own splendid Korea, there – there in Dvorce, where he's building a villa like some foxy lawyer!"

"The crook! Sold the lot!"

"At the time of the currency reform, he cheated! Put his money in his brothers' savings bank accounts, boasted about how much he had in the bank, how he hadn't lost out and had done well out of the whole thing. Now he's building a villa – and wouldn't we all like to!"

"He's always been a cheat, even during the Uprising, he was just a bandit – good grief! – the things that happened here in Slanica because of him!"

"Just what did happen at the Gestapo, Ignác? That time they roasted your feet? Your brother!"

Mišo Dugas, a tall, upright man, stood there with his rolled-up red pamphlet and stared at all the people cursing and shouting, horrified, he hadn't meant to do this to his son. The agitprop centre was buzzing and roaring with coarse voices, and Ignác's father trembled at having gone about it badly, worse than he'd meant to, the uproar pitched this way and that in short and long bursts, the shouting seemed to toss waves of sound from wall to wall and from the middle of the throng to the long, red-covered table, to the electoral commission, the canvassers, the candidates and to the terror-stricken Ignác Dugas.

"Is that what we're meant vote for?"

"They're all the same!"

"Scum!"

"Comrades," the electoral commission chairman bellowed over the shouting and general hubbub, "calm down now! Stay where you are!"

Mišo Dugas, Ignác's father, squeezed through the cursing and shouting crowd, squeezed his way towards the door, went outside, followed by the rest, one at a time, in twos, in fives.

"He milked us for those extra quotas –!"

"He drinks –"

"He boozes –"

"He's a right drunkard –!"

"He gets into fights with his father, and his father-in-law –!"

"Because of him the Germans burned down two cottages, and thirteen people they shot, in Dvorce, beyond Skalka, sixty people burned to death because of him –!"

"The Gestapo shoulda burned 'is feet an' legs right up to 'is arse, tools an' all –!"

"Comrades," the chairman shouted in vain, "comrades, don't leave, settle down, all will be explained –"

In vain did the chairman of the electoral commission keep shouting, in vain did he try to save Ignác Dugas.

The agitprop centre dispersed and fell silent, the only ones left were the canvassers, the candidates and the electoral commission – and that same day at something before midnight, Ignác Dugas drove to Veľké Dvorce on his motorbike, drew up outside his father's cottage, thumped his father in the face with his fist, knocked him to the ground, knelt on his chest and started bellowing.

"– and why did you do that to me?" his bellowing took on the clearer form of words, while saliva dribbled from his mouth, "in the name of your stinking Christ all-bloody-mighty, why did you do it to me, why did you have to disgrace me like that? I'm gonna break every bone in your body –!"

"I didn't mean that to happen," the battered Mišo Dugas struggled to say, "certainly not... You should have left the cross alone, you should have left Belica alone, he was a good man, he lent me money and I still haven't paid him back... You shouldn't have treated people so badly. I didn't mean this to happen, Ignác."

"I'll give you didn't mean it! Christ all-bloody-mighty –!"

"People don't want people like you, Ignác –!"

By the time the kicked and battered Mišo Dugas got up off the floor, his son Ignác was charging down the winding road to the town on his motorbike.

On his bike he mulled over ways he might avenge himself on all those he had his suspicions about: Dr Martin Dubovský, his wife Eva, her father Moravčík – the Malenas, Father Zima, his father-in-law Ambro, Paulína, his own father – it's intolerable, there's no end to them...! If only one could have the entire nation put away...! That's not possible...! There wouldn't be anyone to do the work...! But they need to be put away, perhaps...! But then *they* will put them away, it was a great slur on them all – they won't leave it at that, they can't –! It's Dubovský's fault. What was he doing here on Sunday? Fomenting unrest!

After midnight, at Belica's meadow on Bukovec Rise in Veľké Dvorce, the roof on Dugas's house, still awaiting completion, got burned away, the dry fir wood having flared up and shone briefly out into the dark, warm night, so briefly that the fire brigade didn't make it in time.

On the MZ Palermo estate, that night in May was very pleasant, a gentle breeze blew among the red high-rises, those completed and those awaiting completion, the Dubovský children, Igor, Ondrej and Olga, were asleep as usual, each in their own chrome-plated cot, Igor lying on his right side with one leg on top of his little duvet, Ondrej on his tummy with his right foot poking through the red net, and Olga on her back with her arms spread out as if raised to catch a large falling ball.

Just before one, Eva came out of the bathroom, in the bedroom she slipped her dressing gown from her smooth, white shoulders, popped her feet into her red slippers and crossed into Martin's room. Her steps were measured and slightly hesitant, as if she meant to stop after each one. From the desk she took three newspapers and a letter, the fifth since the time Ignác Dugas said he was going to uproot Belica's cross, put out the lights and went into the bedroom. She placed the papers and the letter on the bedside table and glanced at her lovely children – Ondrej had now extricated his foot from the red net – and after she had drawn her rucked-up nightdress with its pattern of tiny flowers over her head it drifted down her smooth white body all the way to her tiny feet.

Once in bed, she lay out flat, stretched out her relaxed, freshly bathed body, plumped up her pillow and took her father's letter out of its blue official envelope, on which the address had been typed.

"Veľké Dvorce, 4th May 1954," she read, "My dear Eva, I am writing to you on a very grave matter, although Mr Malena, the lawyer, who has been to see you, told me that I should not write to you about it at all. I feel so terribly sad, with such anguish and pain in my heart, that I have to write. I have always known and always feared that people today have been demoralised by the war –"

"Soňa –!"

Inside Soňa's bedsit on the sixth floor of the Community Centre, her room was bathed in the yellow-green half-light cast by the little lamp hanging on the wall and turned inside its dark, moulded-plastic shade towards the yellow-green paintwork. Her bedsit was like a beech wood in May, through whose young leaves the bright sun is shining.

Soňa was sitting on her bed, on the pale-green bedspread, like in the photo from when she was volunteering at harvest time, no shorts and no flimsy chequered blouse, her body now white and just waiting for sun and wind.

At the table, sitting in a metal armchair, was Martin Dubovský, wearing his shepherd check suit.

"My father comes here," she said, "he keeps coming to see me and ask for money because he's afraid that if he had money coming to him by post he could be seen as a person with unearned income – and I do not have any money, I need... I fear for my father because he seems deranged to me. I need money... At least for now, until my father or mother finds a job... Vlach has stopped pestering me. I think he's come to some sort of arrangement with Dugas and that Dugas is milking my father for his benefit, making out that we'd once meant to flee the country and that we'd let ourselves be fooled by him –"

Dubovský sat woodenly in Soňa's armchair, staring at her as if she weren't there, in a state of shock, he was sinking into a foul mood because Soňa, a lovely, alluring body without a soul, an animal, a naked, obscure, menial creature, an outcast now left to roast, now to freeze, a lightless creature – pity about you, Fero, and you, Mum, and you, Dad –

"Look, Soňa," he said, "don't ask this of me, I'm not for it in a case like this, or in any other case –"

"Why not, Martin?"

"No!"

"Why have you put your coat on? Don't go yet –!"

Martin offered no reply. He sat in the armchair, staring at the white Soňa, whose white, smooth face and pale-blue eyes had a hint of pleasure tripping about them, that he had come, that he was still with her, joy was dancing in her eyes, ever so slight, barely a twinkle, as if it were trying to get under the feet of the fear that was crushing Soňa in every thought that came to her, in every word she spoke. Martin, despairing of himself – he'd come to see her thinking that his former attitude to her was gone for good, and now he sensed it flickering back to life – his mind plunged in darkness, he could see nothing before him but his devoted wife, his children – and Soňa, an unhappy, menial creature, lost, wretched and disturbed.

It was as if Soňa, on her pale-green bedspread, was staring through half-closed eyes into the wind, trembling with fear that, for the sake of her father, mother and Jurko, she was having to risk everything, Martin and any future with him.

She made up her mind before she was ready.

"You'd be making good money," she said, "you'd have more money for yourself, it pays well, you'd help me for as long I was here, though I plan to leave, I won't be in Palermo – and I could put cases your way, if you wanted me to. I'd put my father's mind at rest... My father knows about the two of us and keeps threatening to tell if I don't give him money – he sometimes gets quite mad and I worry that – and that would make me feel bad – you have a lovely wife and lovely children –"

"What are you getting at?"

"My father knows."

"How? Who told him?" Dubovský shifted in his seat. His eyes glazed over and his lips developed an odd twist. "Who told him – you?

Soňa burst out laughing. Her keyboard of white teeth sparkled.

"But Martin, how can you be so...? Do you suppose I go blabbing about myself over such things, that I'd blab about what I love most...? Don't be so naive!" Soňa drew her legs up, lay on her side and propped her head on her hand. "There's something wrong with you, Martin, since this has all been going on for a long time now. Things like this get out of their own accord. We've been going together for a long time now, you repeatedly promised to marry me, a promise you haven't kept, you've kept putting it off, you're still putting it off, you avoided me when I needed you most, but now you either accept my proposal, or –"

"Or what?"

Soňa was offended by Martin's question, uttered deliberately in a tone of incomprehension. She raised herself up on the bed, the right side of her mouth twisted upwards.

"Because of you," she began, "I've gone without all manner of things, because I loved you so much, and I love you the more, the less I see of you, I've given up, if I can put it this way, prostituting myself, because – Martin, you're being naive if you think I don't consider myself that which I am, or have been. I became a prostitute so as to be able to study, and I remained one up until I met you, Martin! It was because of you that I stopped, because of you that I began to believe that there is some sense to it all – and you? You yourself made me prostitute myself to you, too – and for that you're going to help me! What else have I been to you today? And now you're going to help me in return! I wanted to live with you, have children with you – you didn't. In return you're going to help me, because I have to help my boy, my parents, my father –

help them! If not, I'll go and see Vlach, other than that I don't know what I'll do –"

Dubovský fixed Soňa with his eyes ablaze and, giddy with rage at himself, thought that Soňa was entitled to adopt that tone, that she was right.

"You could even carry out the terminations here, at my place – temporarily."

"Hang on there, Soňa!"

"I've been hanging on a long time already." She gave him a look of disdain. "A long time, Martin."

At that moment, Dubovský grew thoroughly disconcerted. If he did what Soňa was demanding of him, he was going to feel, in the company of Eva and his children, like some pitiful wretch, a criminal, he'd be forever a pitiful wretch and criminal to himself, a pitiful wretch and criminal to Fero, his mother, his father... If he didn't do it – he'd be, to Soňa, a coward, Soňa would be penniless, her father would tell Moravčík, and Eva, everything – what would Eva do, what would she do when she found out...? What would Soňa do? Was this some act of provocation?

Soňa tossed the pale-green bedspread across her white body, covering herself up to her breasts. Dubovský looked at her. She was yellow-green in the yellow-green half-light, like a cloud after a storm and after sunset, an expectant, menial creature, a hazy form, her face looked as if a wind was blowing right in her eyes, a distant wind coming from a frightening future, for which Martin suddenly felt responsible.

"When, Soňa?" he asked quietly, "When?"

"Sorry – what?"

"The termination."

She gave a faint smile with the keyboard of her teeth, faint and bitter.

"I'll fix it for you for tomorrow at – wait! – at four in the afternoon."

"Here?"

"Here."

"I'm not a specialist."

"Never mind that. Everyone learns from their first cases."

"Who's this about?"

"That's no concern of yours."

A moment passed in silence.

"What's Eva going to say?" Soňa asked eventually.

"Why?"

"I didn't pay her my regulation visit today – and you're here –"

Dubovský shifted, his face now bright red. He stared towards Soňa's little bookcase. On top of the books she'd borrowed from him she'd left a bit of bread and an open tin of 'Chatka' crab paste.

"Is this some kind of provocation, Soňa?" he asked. "Are you doing it to get at Vlach, like the time we put on that charade at the club?"

Soňa shook her head and tears ran down her cheeks.

Then for quite some time Martin Dubovský remained seated in Soňa's armchair as she lay silent, shrouded up to her firm breasts by the pale-green bedspread. Their minds were blank as if blocked by an iron gate that had creaked, jammed and banged shut, as if it were the gate to some endless, filthy street to return along which meant nothing but misery and pain.

In Block XIV Eva was wide awake.

She read through all six letters that her father had sent since Ignác Dugas had first said: "That cross? Not a problem! I'll get a tractor, wind a chain round the cross and out it'll come! It's unthinkable!", and some parts of the letters she read over and over again. She had a sense of the world crumbling beneath her feet. She had never been either God-fearing or of any kind of religious disposition. Neither her father, nor her mother had been that way inclined. Their prime concern had always been that their Eva should never do anything bad to herself or others, but Ignác Dugas had started making threats about that cross and she had become oppressed by all that had befallen her in her lifetime. Martin's brother Fero, executed, Martin drunk and complaining to her father, Martin's mother killed and splattered around Belica's cross, the flight to join the partisans, Martin again, the soldier nailing the ACHTUNG! MINEN! BETEN VERBOTEN! sign to the cross, the wet hammer and its clammy handle, her flight to join Martin in the hills, the promise given that moment when Martin had freed her of the feeling that she'd killed a man, "Martin, whether you want me to or not, I shall make up to you everything that you have lost and are yet to lose...", Martin's father, burned to death inside the gamekeeper's lodge on the far side of Skalka, his hands in the jaws of the oven, and the nights spent with Martin in the hills. Eva was being oppressed and tormented by all of that. She had a vague sense that people had not planted the cross for no particular reason. It had been a means by which to stir in others love for their fellow men, respect. Having no such love and respect meant being reduced to the level of the soldier who'd nailed the sign to Belica's cross. All those victims and other sacrifices, life as lived in her own day – what had it all been for? If only love and respect for others could be revived... The cross in Veľké Dvorce had not been a symbol of some superstition, as Martin said. His mother had perished at its foot out of love and respect for her executed son Fero... Had she believed she could help him through her prayers, had that been mere superstition, then it was a good superstition... Maybe one day it will have been made redundant, but those who still needed it were not to be chastised –

"It isn't possible to expect much love from people," she read in her father's letter, "because that would be like expecting mud to have roses grow from it, but, as it is, one has to strain every sinew to have love for others be born within one. If there were no love for other beings, there would be no heroes, there would be no times like the present, when – so far as I am able to judge – there are many of the prerequisites for love for others, for a better life, though it does strike me that people have squandered that precious opportunity and begun cultivating nothing but a sinister enmity. You know yourself what came of the enmity fostered by the Germans, when they sanctified it as a moral obligation.

"Today people are afraid, they do everything they are told to do. We are also afraid, and the Malenas likewise – everyone is afraid of something. I feel the same as when you went off to join the partisans and when the Germans were keeping tabs on everyone. It strikes me that Malena, a lawyer when all's said and done, is taking leave of his senses. Not that that surprises me, given that he has to live here. I cannot imagine what a man like that has to live on, when he also has a wife and the little boy left in his care by that bad apple of a daughter of his. What kind of a mother is it who refuses to raise her own child, what kind of times are these, when women give birth and leave their children with grandparents or some matron or even to fend for themselves? It is pretty much the same with you. You leave the children at your neighbour's – and what kind of job is it when you are bound to be on edge in case anything should happen to them? As soon as term's over, we'll come and give you at least a little assistance. We shall be happy to come, because for a time at least we will be rid of Dugas and his roistering about the local villages. He even suspects me of agitating against him, but I have done nothing of the sort, nor do I have any such intention, because I believe that thwarting a nonentity like him is a job for others. If no such exist, then I cannot think what the world is coming to."

In her younger years, Eva would often smile at her father's teacherly way of putting things, and more than once she'd said: "Stop lecturing me! I'm not one of your pupils!", which her father acknowledged and blushed somewhat at her reminding him of the fact. "I sometimes forget, Eva, that you're no longer a little girl," he used to say, "though there's nothing wrong in what I've been saying." However, of late, she hasn't found her father's words either comical or teacherly.

"The only way for the world to be a nice place," she read, "will be if everyone cultivates a love for other humans and at the same time has enough sense to tell who is or is not human, because it is clear to me that the individual who laid landmines at the foot of Belica's cross cannot be thought human –"

And then she began re-reading the letter her father had written on May 4th, 1954.

"Veľké Dvorce, 4th May, 1954," she read, and her heart began to pound away with sheer emotion. "My dear Eva, I am writing to you on a very grave matter, although Mr Malena, the lawyer, who has been to see you, told me that I should not write to you about it at all. I feel so terribly sad, with such anguish and pain in my heart, that I have to write. I have always known and always feared that people today have been demoralised by the war. How could they not be when one thinks back to the terrible suffering? After the terrible suffering inflicted on the world by war, anyone who has survived it will be in a sense cut off from anything that had been good about the world and stand in fear of the dreadful task that lies ahead: that of living in a manner that matches up to that terrible suffering. It is a dreadful task and people today are barely up to it. Which is why everything in us is turned inside out, and all because of the huge demands placed on us and of the trifling things that we do.

"And that is why I think, my dear Eva – but do not be alarmed! – that Martin, that kind husband of yours, has fallen into temptation and let himself be beguiled by Soňa Malena. All I know has –"

Eva spent a long time over her father's letter, finally reaching the end, after which she set it aside and stood up.

She wandered about the bedroom, from one cot to the next, seeing how Igor, Ondrej and Oga were nicely asleep. "Martin, my dear, whether you'll want me to or not, I shall make up to you everything that you have lost and are yet to lose..." She burst into tears above the peacefully sleeping children, staring blankly into a void, and, gripped by a sadness and an awful premonition, she choked back her tears. Who, what had she made up to him for? With what? With her own self, the children? They have to be taken from him, and she must kill, kill herself...! "My dear Eva," she was rent by the words Martin had uttered that time as they fled from the burned-down lodge the other side of Skalka, the damp, cold fir forest, dark and silent, "survival, that's the only thing, to get through all this and devote our whole lives seeking redress...", then her mind was pierced by Martin's promise back then "I've had my brother shot – d'you know what lies ahead for me? All the things I'll have to do to make myself forget? How much evil I – I – shall have to wipe from the face of the earth, by my own devices alone?" – and what is Martin now? What is he? A human being who is ceasing to be one... At that instant Eva's mind was jabbed by words in her father's letter: "– because things would go bad for you and your lovely children if that nice husband of yours fell in love with a prostitute," the words jabbed her like a sharp stone piercing a bare foot. How was she to quell all this going on inside her...? There was no way –!

She went back into the living room and sat down in her grey floral armchair. She rose, scrabbled around for a cigarette and some matches, lit up and exhaled the hot smoke. She sat down again.

If it's true..., she couldn't free herself of one single thought, of the jumble of thoughts, memories, emotions. Because Martin had been crushed, she had done a lot, all she could, to help him, and she had wanted to make it up to him, with her own self and the children, for all that he lost because of the Uprising and the war... Maybe she hadn't done enough, maybe such effort – no, that's rubbish, nonsense... She was benumbed. If it's true... No, she doesn't want to foist herself on him with her making up for things, with all that effort – that's ludicrous – and her, Soňa... She comes to visit, discusses things... Not, it's not possible, a person can't be like that... Maybe she's giving her father's words of warning too much credence – and her father maybe gives too much credence to the demented Malena... Martin – he's being racked by the sacrifices made because he is so nauseated by today's way of life –

She turned towards the other grey floral armchair in which Soňa Malena sat so often, discussing things, debating matters, telling jokes, asking Martin where she might read up on this area of biology and where that. Eva stared at the chair in which, four hours before, that very evening, Paula, the wife of Ignác Dugas, had sat, complaining about Martin.

Paula had been at the Dubovskýs' that evening, dandling Olga on her knees and complaining: "I went to see the doc, your husband, today – and they chucked me out. They said I was as fit as a fiddle. But I hadn't gone there looking for treatment, but tell him he needed to do something, because my husband Ignác is cooking something up against him – he might even get him locked up." – "What?" Eva had asked, "What on earth for?" – "He's a right bastard! People are against him and there's an election meeting tonight where he'll introduce himself to the voters, but he's bound to get his fingers burned – and he'll want his revenge, him and the others who'll have been there to back him." – "I don't believe it, my husband hasn't done anything." – "That makes no difference, Mrs Dubovský. It's all because of that cross of Belica's... I didn't want my Ignác to..." Paula sat in her chair for over half an hour, and after she left the chairman of the works council, Mokrý, came, hesitated and then sat down on the edge of the same armchair. "What's going on with the doctor, your husband?" he asked after a long pause. "Today they threw some woman called Dugas out of the surgery. She came to me to complain..." – "Apparently," she told Mokrý, "they want to take my husband into custody." – "That's what the Dugas woman also told me, but don't worry, Mrs Dubovský, we won't give him up lightly." Mokrý kept his darkish face, dry as paper, turned towards Eva, his white forehead showing through his sparse black hair. "The doctor is a wonderful man – we won't give him up. He's done a great deal for our factory. Anyway, I'd better be going." – "I can't believe this, Comrade Mokrý," said Eva, "but if anything of the kind does happen..." – "Don't you worry, Mrs Dubovský!"

Eva stared at the chair, seeing them both, "Rosy-red Paula", the red face, the yellowy blonde hair, yellowy blonde eyebrows, and Mokrý, the hard, dry, swarthy hands, the black fingertips, sharp black eyes.

"Why has Soňa stopped coming to see us so often?" Eva Dubovská asked the absent Mokrý and the absent Paulína Dugas, her voice sounding deep and cracked, "Do you happen know?"

Mokrý and Paula stared mutely back at her.

Eva shuddered, she rose, burst into tears and dropped her burning cigarette into the ashtray. Even a dog is pained when his service isn't appreciated, let alone a human... She crossed to the bedroom, gathered up her father's letters, put them in the bedside table drawer, tossed the newspaper onto the floor and lay down.

She lay there and waited.

Morning approached.

"Where've you been, Martin?"

"Why?" Martin was taken aback by Eva's deep, cracked voice. "Why, Eva?"

"It's very nearly dawn –"

"We had a lecture at the agitprop centre," he said, "then I stayed behind for a game of chess –"

The Dubovský bedroom was dim, a dimmish blue light coming in round the striped roller blind, and it breathed with the breathing of the three children and Eva, who was lying under a lightweight white duvet.

"Forgive me, Martin," said Eva, meaning to hint that she knew about him, "but Palermo is just an estate with all the drawbacks that go with estates. It's brought in all kinds of people. Everybody knows everything about everybody, adults and children alike know about the adults and I wouldn't want our children to hear from other children... Have a bath to freshen up, there was plenty of hot water, and come to bed."

"There's nothing for them to hear."

"Not so far. I haven't told you anything yet. I haven't had any sleep and I've been thinking –"

Dubovský undressed in silence, had a bath and cleansed himself of Soňa Malena.

"Well then, Eva," he began as he returned from the bathroom, "you've been thinking – so tell me what about."

Eva remained silent for a moment.

"I've been wondering," she began eventually, "whether any one person can be a repacement for another."

"I don't understand."

"I mean whether the departure of one or more people amounts to a loss that's irreplaceable. In our own times, people get treated in all sorts of ways, people have been subverted, they treat themselves badly – and I think that's wrong – the thing is, should anything happen, could anyone replace us, for you?"

"What are you actually talking about, Eva?" Dubovský asked. "You say person, but what do you mean by person?"

"You don't know? You've lost a brother and your mother and father. Weren't they persons? They were, no? I have tried to be a replacement for them. How have you replaced them? How have you substituted another for them...? I also take myself to be a person, and your children –"

To that Martin offered no reply.

"Eva," he began again, after a long pause, "don't you get a sense that you've been wallowing in some odd superstitions of late?" He suspected that Eva knew all there was to know about himself and Soňa and went on ask: "Haven't you caught yourself believing things that don't exist?"

"What superstitions am I wallowing in –?"

"My brother, mother, father, Belica's cross – today those are all superstitions, victims of superstition, the partisans, me, you – they were all victims of superstition, some dreadful superstition. Where are our comrades, the ones killed and the living? We've let ourselves be hounded by superstition into some things that haven't been properly considered, into fighting for respect for others – yet that lies yonder, in Veľké Dvorce!"

"Respect for others isn't fought for with rifles alone –"

"– and what exactly are you trying to say, Eva? Do you want all this, this entire ghastly existence, to drive me back into the kind of insanity the Uprising was? Into some kind of illegal underground existence? Everything you've been saying is superstition – the cross, religion, I got that all sorted out ages ago, I've left the church, you don't even know about that. Why be there? To trouble one's head with superstition, be warped by it? I don't want to be warped by superstition ever again – I want to live! Respect for others –"

"What illegal underground existence are you talking about?"

"Today it's illegal to think well of others, to cultivate respect for others, today that's illegal, underground activity – and it's not allowed – the only things that *are* allowed are those that have been decreed –!"

Dubovský let out a great guffaw.

The children began to stir in their cots.

"Martin!" Eva whispered sharply, terror-stricken that the abyss beneath Martin was even deeper than her own. She recoiled at the laughter erupting from his rage and despair. "I'm happy to be guided by any superstition that sustains in me respect for you, the children and other humans worthy of the name, I'd rather let myself be warped by superstition than kept straight as a die by science – which is science only for the deluded and deceived – which teaches me distrust and blind hatred. The kind of superstition that is stirring within me at this moment tells me I was right, and committing no wrong, in following you into the mountains and in wanting, once we were back, to fill your life with a kind of replacement for the people you had lost, except that –"

"Don't be ridiculous, Eva."

"All right," she said, "to you it might be ridiculous, but not to me. If such things are going to be ridiculous as far as you're concerned, you'll slide into doing things for which there'll be no one to judge and punish you... Your conscience alone will be your judge and executioner, and that is the most terrible executioner that ever was. It will be executing you every day of your life... I've given you quite a lot, Martin, myself, children... You know, even I could have lived, could live even now, as a single woman, live for the benefits, the recognition, money, a career – but I haven't done, and all for your sake, whereas you...? Even a dog is pained when his service isn't appreciated, let alone a human... If, Martin, someone is to replace me and the children for you, I shall –"

"How is it possible to replace someone for someone?" he asked. "A person can't replace himself, if part of him goes missing – so how could he replace someone else?"

Then Martin stopped listening to Eva's deep, broken voice, instead sinking into the unrelenting, foul mood of his that was eating away at anything that might yet amount to the very point of living.

The bedroom filled with more of the blue-grey of morning, Martin stared at the two blue-grey strips at the edges of the striped roller blind, he wasn't listening to Eva.

"One person hates another these days," said Eva, "the way that SS man hated your mother – and if people today could, they might well act the way he did. Maybe they do. I've no desire for a life like that and I don't want to give my children one, especially when the person nearest doesn't want... What are factories for, and these modern housing estates, if the people who live on them just hate and devour one another...? I don't want to have my children live in a world like that...! I don't want to expose myself and my children to the wreck you've become... There's not a bit left of the you that once was... I've spoken to Mokrý, and to Dugas's wife... People are out to get you –"

Martin wasn't listening. At odd moments, his brain was penetrated by Eva's bitter words, which sprang from her father's letters and her painful decision to stop living. He sensed what Eva was threatening to do, and he didn't care, his mind being absorbed by swirling images of Soňa and the sense of her that he'd had ever since that summer, the way his blood pulsated at the sight of her, as it had ever since she first took him to her bedsit with the photo of her volunteering at the harvest, and that night he sensed her again, his mind now overrun with images of the terrible things to which he had to accede for Soňa to be able to support her parents and her little boy, and for the whole thing to be kept under wraps for as long as possible. And to what end, to what end...? Soňa is Soňa no more – yet he has to help her! He has to, for the time being he has to save her from Vlach, from Dugas... That's all that matters now... Martin Dubovský, blighted by Soňa and blighted by pity for Eva and the children couldn't sleep. Nor could Eva.

The lightening blue of early morning passed and a new day dawned.

Some fitters arrived at the Community Centre, ripped away the planks nailed crosswise across the lift doors, fitted the doors with patent locks and handed the keys in to the caretaker, Bučko.

Dugas's wife, "Rosy-red Paula", told both the Dubovskýs, Martin *and* Eva, what had happened at Veľké Dvorce and assured them that nothing would happen to them now, because her Ignác had got badly burned at the pre-election meeting. His house had also been badly burned. Dubovský felt a twinge of fear, told himself that he didn't care about anything anymore, and went to see the production planner, Vlach, dragging him out of the office into the quiet corridor.

"I don't know who you are, Comrade Vlach," he said in a shrill whisper, "and I don't know who your contacts are, but I do know that you've been smuggling people across the border and that you are extorting money out Soňa Malena and her parents. I'm warning you, leave off –!"

Dubovský's eyes grew darker and Vlach kept opening and shutting his mouth, his narrow lips crinkling like paper.

"Don't you take liberties with me, comrade –!"

"I shall be taking far worse, you'll see! You'll be doing plenty of time for this," Dubovský whispered shrilly. "And another thing – Dugas came a cropper yesterday."

Dubovský left. Vlach lit a cigarette and stared after him in alarm.

During the morning, the sky clouded over, the air stilled, quite windless, and down out of the sky came the rain, noiseless and falling straight down.

That afternoon, Soňa Malena had a visitor.

The muscles on the ashen face of her father, Štefan Malena, which appeared round in profile, were quivering faintly and glinting with raindrops. His tall, powerful frame seemed completely to take over the metal armchair, which sagged beneath him. His grey, wide-brimmed hat was wet, and his trench coat was soaked through at the shoulders.

"Can you?" he asked a third time. "Can you spare me a little, or not?"

"No, I can't – Dad, for God's sake, go!"

"I gave all I had to your mum – she's taken Jurko to Komárno, taking the money with her. I want to join her there... Do you love Dr Dubovský?" Malena ran his hand over his small chin, furrowed down the middle. His forehead was perspiring slightly. "A prostitute mustn't love anyone, love is financially unproductive... Prostitutes used to be recruited from the dregs of society, to serve the upper classes, but today...? It's all back to front – they're recruited from the upper classes to serve the dregs – it's terrible –!"

"I don't have any money," she screamed, "and even if I had some... I also need some, I also want to eat, to dress properly...! Dad, for God's sake, go!"

"You mustn't love Dubovský!" Malena's eyes flitted about the room as if seeing nothing. "Your first duty is to your parents, and Jurko! You managed to have a baby, but you dumped it on us so you could live the way you like... And you do live the way you like, because otherwise you couldn't have landed that job. But no, Soňa! Enough is enough! You have to live like this...! You don't want to live like a mother, so you have to live as a prostitute! You won't give me any money then?"

Malena stood up. With his tall, strong frame he seemed to fill Soňa's tiny bedsit.

"You've got none!"

"No! I'll get hold of something during the day. Come back tomorrow, or wait somewhere! Though not here. Dr Dubovský's coming and –"

"Dubovský...! Dubovský's coming –!"

Soňa Malena started, with sheer venom in her eyes, but at brief intervals also imploringly, she gazed at her father's perspiring, ashen face.

"You mustn't love Dubovský. You look nice, you're a pretty lass – and you should have money. Men pay very well for a pretty woman, they'll give her all they have, but Dubovský wont give you anything, because you love him –!"

The pale Soňa was shaking.

"Dad, for God's sake, go!"

"How much would blokes pay you for a night? Dubovský won't be coming anymore, I'll see to that...! You have ruined us, you... You'll carry on doing it with that Party secretary, with Vlach and others – but I won't have you messing up Dubovský's life, or that of his wife and kids!"

Malena clamped his hat back on his head, picked up his bamboo cane and left Soňa's bedsit. He marched down the stairs of the Community Centre, then along the churned-up street, and having reached Block XIV, he stopped, looked about him briefly, began walking up and down in the rain that veiled the red housing complex in a grey mist and finally rang the bell next to the door on which a rectangular card bore the legend "Martin Dubovský, M.D., General Practitioner to MZ", and when Eva came to the door, he took a step back, paused and smiled.

"Mrs Dubovský –"

"Yes," said Eva, somewhat taken aback, "I'm –"

"Permit me –" Malena offered her a damp, broad hand, "– I'm Dr Malena, father of Soňa Malena – your resident kultprop – now isn't that a ghastly word, makes you want to choke!"

"Pleased to see you," said Eva, fearfully. "We've met before. Do come in!"

Eva conducted Malena to the living room.

"Children, stay in the kitchen and play!"

"I bring you regards from your father in Veľké Dvorce," said Malena as he sat down in the living room, "and I was keen to see you because your father often mentions you – his only child, right? – and I thought that... Your father is a treasure, the only person not afraid to talk to me, for which he is to be thanked, as are you, Mrs Dubovský –" Malena fell silent, watching Eva Dubovský in some surprise as she sat down gently, softly in her grey floral-patterned armchair, a good-looking woman with a white complexion, dark-blue eyes, chestnut hair, a slightly alarmed expression on her face, trim lips, a light, lissom body, spry, then his eyes began to flitter about her living room, pausing with utter loathing at a picture on the wall, a small oil painting of women, with packs on their backs, on the way to market, "– a lovely place you have here, plenty of lovely space – I thought... Mrs Dubovský, your husband, the doctor – and my daughter Soňa... Keep your eyes open! He loves her, she him, they may even be living together... He's about to pay her a visit right now –"

Eva froze.

"It's not good, him forever going to see her... She's a hussy... I know a thing or two about life... and it's not something I like to see. Your husband is committing a mistake, and so are you, Mrs Dubovský. You're a lovely woman – with lovely children – and where are they? – do keep things in check as far as you can! I'm very fond of your father because he's not afraid either to lend one an ear or bend another's ear –!"

Eva suddenly flushed bright red.

"That's my advice to you, Mrs Dubovský –!"

"May I ask you a favour?"

"My daughter Soňa, she's a –"

"Would you wait here while I pop out?"

Eva rose, went to the kitchen, brought the children to be with Malena in the living room and then dashed out of Block XIV into the rain in search of her husband. Not finding him at the MZ works, she ran back home, soaked to the skin and her feet splattered with mud. She found the flat open, no Malena – and the children sitting on the carpet, playing with a large rubber ball like the leather ball footballers kicked around.

"Mummy," said Ondrej, looking wide-eyed at his mother, "the nice man's gone and he told us to play –"

"Where did he go?"

"He didn't say."

"Come with me!"

"Where to?"

"Now, Mummy, but it's raining –!"

"Where to, Mummy?"

"For a walk – to find Daddy, and that nice man, come along –!"

He has to know! That one thing now suddenly left Eva's mind clinched. He has to know! Eva's mind came crashing down as when a landslip crashes down and buries any waters. There was but one thing that now occupied her mind, all else was too painful and would not let her breathe, and she matched action to thought. He has to know!

"Where are we going?"

"For a walk, Ondrej!"

"It's raining. It's raining really hard, look!"

"We're going anyway, Ondrej, Igor!" Eva shouted at the boys, who were running around the flat. "Olga!"

"Raincoats, Mummy!"

"No need now –!"

When a landslip crashes down and buries any waters, the waters remain inside it, they find the only, the easiest way

(402)

out, and when Eva came out of Block XIV and dashed with the children to the Community Centre with a view to shouting at Martin from behind the door to Soňa's bedsit – after which she would toss the children out of the window and jump out after them! – her mind was taken up with the easiest, neatest way out because it was the most terrible. She would have avenged herself with what he held dearest and in what he had always seen as a replacement for his brother, mother and father, even though he used to laugh at the idea. Avenged herself with herself, for all that would leave him cold, but he could not live without the children. He couldn't live, not by any means, not even he – he'd be living as their killer... Killing his children! He has to know! She couldn't live without Martin –!

Eva and the three children, with Olga in her arms and holding Ondrej by the hand, ran inside the Community Centre, CAUTION! LIFT! SHAFT!, she halted by the door, pressed the moulded-plastic handle down, the door was unlocked, she was jubilant, looked down into the shaft, closed the door, rushed up to the first floor, the door there was also unlocked. And on the second, and on the third... As water streams from a landslip, and the more fiercely for having fought its way out by the only route possible, so, too, Eva, the faster she breathed, the more strenuously she ran and dragged her children along with her, Olga now crying as she dangled from her right arm only, leaving her left hand free to drag the boys up the stairs, the more her mind screamed: get at him by killing them and killing myself...! So that he'll be a murderer, the most terrible of murderers...! The door on the fourth floor was unlocked.

She ran on up to the fifth.

On the sixth floor, her husband, Dr Martin Dubovský, carrying a package, the instruments with which to perform a termination, and wearing a wet plastic mac, with a wet hat on his head, knocked on Soňa's door.

She came out.

"She's here," said Soňa, "but so's my father – it appears he's expecting you –!"

Eva's shouting and Olga's crying, followed by shouting from Igor and Ondrej, flew up the staircase to the sixth floor and Dubovský's eyes clouded over, the shadow across them clouded right over, and they flashed once. He leapt towards the lift shaft door, opened it, stood cautiously on the smooth iron ledge, grabbed hold of the iron door frame with his right hand, in which he was holding his package, pulled the door to after him and in order to shut it properly, he slid one half of one of his commando soles out over the shaft then one half of the other, then, still clinging onto the iron door frame with his right hand, in which he was holding his package, he quietly closed the door behind him.

Soňa Malena, frozen to the spot in terror, stared at the CAUTION! LIFT! SHAFT! and at the skull and crossbones that someone had scrawled on the lift door in thick black felt-tip and heard neither Eva's children, nor Eva.

"Oh –!"

Soňa Malena's eyes glistened, they watched Eva, a slim woman in brown shoes with thick, light-brown crepe soles, the shoes covered in mud, her stockings splattered with mud, her wet brown-and-green skirt, her wet grey jumper, her wet chestnut hair, her spattered face, the strip of hair sticking to her forehead.

"You're here –?"

Soňa sensed from Eva's voice that she was at a loss for words.

Eva sprang towards the lift door, stepped back from it, and at that point her lower lip began to tremble.

Behind the lift shaft door, Dubovský was standing on the narrow, smooth iron ledge that extended from under the door out over the shaft, holding onto the moulded-plastic handle, and as he leaned out over the black pit, intersected in seven places by the dim light entering the shaft through the matt glass of the small round windows set in seven doors, he gripped his package in his right hand. Beneath him, almost twenty metres of darkness and gloom, a deep rectangular prism of darkness and gloom like the nights and days and the days and nights of the terrible, mysterious peregrination that is human life... He held himself on the smooth, narrow iron ledge by his commando boots, shoes with thick, knurled rubber soles, and with his left hand he kept hold of the door handle. Both his hands were sweaty, as was his forehead. He tried desperately to make himself believe that his shoes couldn't slip off the smooth iron ledge and that his clammy hand couldn't slip off the black, moulded-plastic door handle. "The handle's secure," he mentally reassured himself, "it'll hold, it'll hold, even though there's only a small piece of metal inside it...!" Then he felt a tightening in his lungs, he took two deep breaths, breathed out and breathed in again.

"Why did your path have to cross mine," he heard his wife Eva cry out in a broken, full voice, "Comrade Malena? Why here as well? Why did you cross paths with my children? Speak out – why won't you answer me?"

Soňa Malena didn't answer her.

Dubovský sensed that if with one hand he kept gripping the door handle and if he kept hold of his little package with the other, his stamina would be split in two and his body weaken.

"Why have you crossed my path yet again, now?"

Dubovský could hear his children rampaging about in the wide corridor, Igor with firm steps, Ondrej lighter-footed – and Olga trotting around on her tiny feet, until suddenly she stopped short.

"Pursh, Mummy!"

Dubovský knew that Olga was asking for her purse. She would often play with it if she could lay hands on it. He was badly shaken, as if his breast had been split with self-pity.

Soňa watched numbly as Eva picked the wet-haired Olga up and gave her her purse, including the money.

"Down, Mummy!"

Eva clasped the little girl to her bosom.

"Er, do – please, do come in," said Soňa, "we can talk inside, if... I don't know what this is about... The boys too, come on, Igor, Ondrej!"

"No!" Dubovský caught Eva's voice coming into the shaft. "Martin's in there – and I'd never set foot inside your place. Least of all with the children –!"

"What Martin?"

"My husband!"

"I beg your pardon! Mrs Dubovský!"

The two women, Soňa Malena and Eva Dubovský, Soňa in a lightweight brown dress, leaning slightly forward, Eva glaring with her dark-blue eyes, looked at each other in stupefaction, as if they'd turned to stone as a pair of motionless statues, pale in complexion, paling like the pallor of the moon as the cloud veiling it thins.

"Mummy," Dubovský heard Olga, "down, Mummy!"

Dubovský's strength was beginning to break down, as if half was passing into his left hand, with which he was clutching the door handle, and half into his right hand, in which he held the heavy package. He heard a coin clink on the concrete floor of the corridor the other side of the door, then the clink of two, three more, another clink, and suddenly all the coins spilled out of the purse and hit the ground in one go.

"Mummy, down!"

"I refuse to enter your room," Eva told Soňa, "least of all would I ever take my children in there – but just tell me, where's Martin!"

"I don't know."

"You do know, Comrade Malena," Eva snorted, "You're lying, because he's in there, I know he is, you're lying – or your father's gone mad –!"

"Mummy, down!"

With his feet and commando-soled shoes Dubovský was holding up on the smooth, narrow ledge overhanging the shaft, holding tight to the door handle with his trembling left hand, pressing tight against the door, levering the handle upwards to stop it moving, and a pain suddenly shot through his left forearm. He raised his right hand with the package as if to make a grab the far wall, prop himself against it and lever himself back against the door. The boys' footsteps clomping about in the corridor, Ondrej shrieking and Igor yelling. The children, Eva...! The package slipped from Dubovský's grip and seconds later his ears were assailed by the bang, crash, wallop that flew up from basement, up through the rectangular prism of darkness and gloom and up into his ears. Dubovský was soaked in his own perspiration, he grabbed the door handle between his right thumb and forefinger and gave his left hand and forearm a degree of relief, now that he could barely feel them. He pressed up against the door, resting his head on it. A stabbing pain returned to his left forearm.

"Show me where Martin is," said Eva to Soňa, "to make him feel ashamed of himself, and you with him –!"

Soňa Malena opened her door.

The pale-faced Eva took four steps forward, then swivelled to take in the whole bedsit, tiny, filled almost chock-a-block with a bed, bedside table, wardrobe, a small metal table, two metal armchairs and a desk.

In one of the metal armchairs sat old Malena, tall, sturdy, trembling all over, his broad hands shaking on the arms of his chair, in the other a woman of about thirty with stern, robust features, dressed in the kind of folk costume worn in the villages that surrounded the MZ works.

"Forgive me – Mrs Dubovský," said Malena in a tremulous voice, "please be so kind – and forgive me for – for leaving your flat in such a rude way – and leaving it open... I was in a hurry to come here – and I don't want to have to take the late train home."

Through the gloomy-dark shift Dubovský's ears were assailed by banging and rattling.

Someone's locking the doors...! Fitters...! Dubovský stopped breathing as he glanced down into the gloomy, slender depths, plunged into darkness. He was terror-stricken by the sense that somewhere the cruel truth was lurking in wait for him. He had betrayed himself, betrayed that moment when he and Eva had left the burned-out gamekeeper's lodge on the far side of Skalka, determined to live and to right all wrongs... He tried to allay his conscience, drown it out – along had come Soňa to help him drown out his conscience, persuade him by some device or other that he didn't have Jankovič on his conscience... He could have taken his part, fought on his behalf – he hadn't. Along came Soňa and he'd tossed aside Eva, his children... The fitters are coming... They'd forgotten to lock the doors as they left... He took his left hand off the door handle and wiped it on his chest. The fitters are coming... They're going to lock this door...! What was left of him? Nothing – sites of fires overgrown with burdock and nettles, a hole in the ground where a cross had been uprooted... He was about to get out, and face Eva and Soňa. He leaned out over the slender rectangular prism of darkness and gloom. He may have put paid to Dugas, his being in Veľké Dvorce sufficed there, but he hadn't put paid to Vlach, Soňa was now beyond his help, he was about to get out –

"Mummy, down!"

"No, my dear little Olga!" said Eva to her little girl as she turned to Soňa. "Forgive me, Comrade Malena!" She turned to Igor and Ondrej. "Ondrej, Igor, come along! We're leaving now!"

The boys trotted up to their mother.

"Gather up the coins."

Igor and Ondrej gathered up the coins and gave them to their mother. Eva tipped them into her purse.

"We'll put the pursh in a safe place, shall we darling! All right?"

"All light!"

"Labour be praised!"

"Labour be praised!"

"Bye-bye!"

Dubovský, scared witless and put to shame by Eva, humiliated, resentful of Soňa, listened from the top of his slender shaft as the footsteps retreated, as the boys' shouting the little girl's squealing faded away, and as a door banged and keys rattled from the second floor.

The production planner, Vlach, on his way from Slanica to Veľké Dvorce, stopped his black motorbike outside the Community Centre and dashed inside in his soaking wet rubber cape and hurried up the stairs.

Soňa was standing outside the open door to her bedsit and in front of the closed door bearing the red sign CAUTION! LIFT! SHAFT!

In a moment of intense relief that he would soon be leaving his post above the abyss, and of profound humility with regard to Eva and her children, Dubovský, infused with a determination to treat people the way he had after he and Eva had left the site of the burned-out gamekeeper's lodge on the far side of Skalka, gripped the door handle tight, his left forearm and the fingers of his right hand were unbearably painful, he leaned out over the deep, slender, rectangular parallelepiped of gloom and darkness, pressed the handle down and heaved at the door with his shoulder. The door opened out into the corridor. He grabbed at the wall for support and, his whole frame a complete wreck, he ignored Soňa Malena and stumbled on into her bedsit, coming to a halt before her father.

Soňa followed him inside.

"Martin, if you don't mind – I –"

"What about you?"

"I –"

"What?"

"Martin –!"

Soňa's father leapt from his armchair, yelled "What about you?" Soňa, you're not going to do this...! You scum, you've destroyed me, you've destroyed us all...!", hurled her down onto the bed and snatched the gold chain with the tiny gold hammer and sickle from her neck.

Dubovský sprang at him, dragged him off Soňa, who was flat out on the bed, and shoved him into an armchair.

The woman with the stern, robust features ran towards the door.

On the fourth floor, the caretaker, Bučko, with a large key ring in his hand, was just closing the lift door.

"What are you up to, Mr Bučko?"

"I'm like – " old Bučko turned round and watched as Vlach hared up the stairs to Soňa's without waiting to hear his reply, "good afternoon, Comrade Vlach! I have to lock all the lift doors to prevent any accidents. They fitted the locks, then didn't lock the doors, the slobs, just threw the keys at me... So, we have the keys, but where's the lift! I heard some children shouting their way up the stairs and I says good grief, I should make sure the fitters locked all the doors, so I tries the first floor, gave me quite a shock, it did. And than Mrs Dubovský came down the stairs with the kids, praise be...! Right – I'm off now, Comrade Vlach, up to the fifth... Good bye, Comrade Vlach!"

Vlach – somewhat disconcerted – arrived at Soňa's bedsit door, hesitated, knocked and opened it. He went inside.

"That's," Dubovský yelled, "sheer provoc- –!"

Soňa tore herself from Dubovský's grasp, screamed "leave me alone!" and ran out into the corridor.

The woman with the stern, robust features and Vlach ran out after her.

The slamming of a door thundered the length of the corridors of the Community Centre, followed by its echo, and a dull thud coming from the shaft just as Bučko was locking the door on the fifth floor.

The moment passed and the MZ housing estate had an edginess to it as people tried to figure out who had thrown Soňa Malena down the lift shaft, or if she hadn't jumped down it herself, the people in the factory were edgy, just standing beside their machines that were still running, and people standing out in the rain on the churned-up, unmade streets talked about Soňa Malena. Many were sorry for her, knowing her for a good-looking, hard-working lass. A crowd stood out in the rain, outside the Community Centre, for a long time.

Evening came and time moved on towards midnight.

"Who's been arrested?" Eva asked her husband as she hesitantly entered the bedroom. "Malena?"

"They've taken Malena, Vlach, some woman and, the care-taker, Bučko into custody – they'll be arresting plenty more."

"But not you?"

"Why me?"

"You, not responsible for the lift, for Soňa...? How can you ask such a silly question?"

Eva lay down.

"Poor Soňa," she said. "How would you classify her death?" Then she began icily: "What group would you place her in? I've had a look in your statistical handbook, but I couldn't find anything except 'E 902 – any other fall from a height'. It really was some other fall from a height, completely other, peculiar... You're a broken man, Martin... Study the causes of death of your brother and your mother – your father, and study the causes of Soňa's death...! I'm only saying this in case they happen to come to get you and we don't get a chance to say good-bye – I have this strange presentiment, Martin, it both-ers me – if we were unable to talk more about this. I'm even starting to believe Dugas's wife and Chairman Mokrý. Think about the causes...! You'll understand them without the need for science –"

Martin remained silent.

"What's to become of us, Martin?"

"They might lock me up – I don't know. Don't keep saying such awful things!"

Then they both fell silent, avoiding each other's gaze, not speaking, shaken each by their own horrors, and expecting some harsh days ahead. They lay on their beds, awake well into the night. Martin was shaken by the horror of the lift shaft, the horror of Soňa's death, and by the cruel truth that had been lurking in wait for him inside the shaft, the cruel truth that betrayal of oneself and of the victims of the past meant the abyss, death. Eva is a human being... Soňa and her father aren't, they had turned into creations of the enemies of mankind, maybe that's what they wanted, maybe not, but they hadn't passed muster, and nor had he... He had been outdone by humility, respect, he was quivering with admiration for Eva's, and his children's, remaining alive. Eva, Martin's wife, was in dread of herself, of her father's words of warning, of Malena, who was increasingly demented, and her dread only grew worse, the longer she listened as the bedroom breathed the secure breathing of her children.

"Eva," said Martin into the quietly breathing bedroom, "if we don't have enough time to talk all this through – Jankovič I could have helped, I know – but I didn't help him, I was afraid... Back in the day, Jankovič had operated underground, and he took part in the Uprising and then, while there was still time, I was too scared to help him – we are cowards, Eva – and they'll be arresting plenty more because of Dugas and Soňa."

* * *

And so in early August 1954, Ignác Dugas, no longer secretary to the Slanica local national committee, or a candidate for, or elected member on, the district national committee, merely the clerk in charge of allocating building materials for the construction of private houses, arrived on his bicycle in Veľké Dvorce to take a look at his own new house, which was still awaiting completion and had been partly burned down. He came by bicycle, being no longer the possessor of a motorbike. He stopped in front of his house, where he passed Jožo Faraga, the parish gravedigger, watchman and odd job man.

Jožo Faraga was carrying a pickaxe and a spade over his shoulder.

"Who are you going to mark a plot out for?"

"You don't know?"

"No."

"Really?"

"No."

"Your father's died," said Jožo Faraga, adjusting his pickaxe and spade on his shoulder and pulling his greasy green hat, dented above his right ear, down over his forehead. With his wrinkled face he cast the deathly pale Dugas a dirty look and then screwed his wrinkled face up further into a wicked grin. "This morning. Passed away sort of sudden like, no one expected it. He was very old, and since that election meeting he hadn't been himself. And he hadn't spoken to anyone since he got out of clink." And then Jožo Faraga went on to console Ignác Dugas. "Everybody has to sooner or later. People are like flies, so then – it can't be helped really!"

Dugas, fearful, pushed his bicycle up against the wall of his house, still awaiting completion, his hands weak with fear, he went inside, did a tour of the empty rooms, doorless and windowless, treading over the lime-mortar floors, bits of broken bricks, odd pieces of charred timber, planks, and cracked and broken roof tiles. He hadn't been back to his house since the fire, having been kept away by anger and self-pity. He sat down on an upturned mortar mixing tub, coated in the white of lime mortar and charred round the edges, stared at the soot-covered, bare walls and choked back his tears. He felt sorry for his house, for Paula and his dead father. Poor old Dad! He'd believe anything! He'd believed it impossible to close down and demolish churches, and he'd even believed a cross meant as much as a church. He'd believed such things and hadn't been afraid to say as much in public, that time at the agitprop centre. He hadn't meant to do his old man that much harm when he went to see him after the calamitous election meeting. The poor chap had believed the stuff he'd read... Then he'd been poorly, poorly, still poorly when they let him out of jail – and here was Jožo Faraga surveying a plot for him... The funeral, no – what about the funeral? How could he attend his old man's funeral? How could he possibly attend his old man's funeral? His mother would burst into tears at the sight of him, the people there might well drive him away... People – best left well alone – they keep silent for a long time, but once stirred... He was overcome by another wave of self-pity. He rose, took another look about him. Oh well! He left the house, mounted his bicycle and drove to the cemetery.

"Jožo?"

"What?" Faraga asked from the pile of red-grey soil he'd dug out. "What do you want?"

"When's the funeral?"

"Tomorrow, late afternoon," Faraga informed him. "But you stay clear! It'd be pretty nasty if folk beat the shit out of you at your own father's funeral!"

Faraga's wrinkled face beamed with a smile.

Ignác Dugas rode off to the town and came back the following day to his house that was awaiting completion, but had been damaged by fire. Once more he surveyed the damage, choked back his tears and soon set about gathering up the tiles and stacking them up in the corner of one room. He went on stacking, tossing any broken pieces to the far side of the room and waiting for the procession that would be taking his father to the cemetery. He wished to see at least his father's coffin on the bier, waited, and his waiting was rewarded.

He removed his hat and sat down on the upturned mortar mixing tub. He stared at the spot where Belica's cross had once stood.

The new parish priest, name of Stolárik, who'd come from Slanica in lieu of Zima, who was still in jail, did not stop opposite Dugas's house, though he knew that priests had paused there since time immemorial. He strode straight past. His long black chasuble and white surplice billowed about him. He was followed by the sacristan, an altar boy carrying a black cross, and the organist. The men carrying the long, black coffin containing the late Mišo Dugas came to a halt, set the bier down on the ground, knelt down and the others present also knelt down. They all knelt down in the mud opposite Dugas's house.

And waited.

Father Stolárik took a look round and rejoined the kneeling people with the sacristan, the altar boy and the organist.

"Arise," he said, "and let us move on."

"A Lord's Prayer for the deceased!" reached Dugas's ears and the room he was in. "It's what we always used to do!"

"Non intres in judicium...," Father Stolárik intoned, and having reached the end of the hymn about divine judgement, he continued: "Kyrie eleison."

"Christe eleison, Kyrie eleison!"

"Pater noster –"

"Our Father," the rugged voices of overworked men, the thinner voices of women eaten away by poverty, woe and disease, and the thin voices of rosy-cheeked children, began to pray, "– Thy kingdom come, Thy will be done, in earth as it is in heaven –"

Ignác Dugas sat there, elbows on knees, staring at the dried, white lime mortar and the red and black fragments of bricks and tiles, clutching his grey hat and listening.

"Et ne nos inducas in tentationem –"

"Sed libera nos a malo."

For several days, Ignác Dugas kept himself to himself, preoccupied with his father, his house, which was awaiting completion and had been damaged by fire, and with the people in prison – his father-in-law Ambro, Moravčík, Dubovský, Malena, Father Zima... Which of them was to blame for the fiasco at the election meeting and for the fire at his house? Ignác Dugas wondered. Maybe one, maybe all, maybe even others... Five days passed and on the fifth day after the funeral Ignác Dugas went to see Father Stolárik to ask him what it was that priests in Veľké Dvorce had always chanted before Belica's cross.

"But Dugas, there's no such thing as Belica's cross anymore," said Father Stolárik. "Do have a seat, Dugas."

"There isn't, but there also is," said Dugas, and he humbly sat down on a chair facing the priest, "though not there, somewhere else."

"What the priests sing?" Stolárik queried. "There is, you see, this ancient custom in Dvorce. It's been kept going for around four hundred years. At the local rectory there's a deed, about four hundred years old, and it contains a brief account of what happened on Bukovec Rise. You see, it's where what were called trials by ordeal were carried out as a test of divine judgement. It's where bandits were put on trial, and if a bandit wouldn't or couldn't confess, they would sear him with red-hot irons. They believed that if he were innocent, the iron would leave him unscathed. Admittedly, everyone who went on trial proved guilty, because the red-hot irons seared them all. But on one occasion they happened to be trying a particularly notorious bandit, called Kajdušek, and, it is said, the red-hot iron just wouldn't touch him. Kajdušek was released, and as he continued with his wicked ways, he was suddenly struck by lightning on Bukovec Rise and killed. The people duly erected a cross and, ever since, priests have sung about divine judgement at the spot – though I've no idea as to the truth of the matter. It could well be just a legend, a folk-tale. You find all sorts in old deeds. But a custom is a custom, Dugas. Some are of long standing, others only short-lived." Father Stolárik then reached for a black book, flicked through it, pointed at certain lines in it and said to the blenching Dugas: "Here it is."

Ignác Dugas took the book from him and read: "Set not, oh Lord, Thy servant before Thy judgement seat, for no one in Thy sight can stand the test unless Thou forgivest him all his transgressions." Dugas read on. After a moment he turned the page and began reading from the other side: "– a great day and filled with gall – when Thou comest to judge the world by fire."

"That'll do, Dugas," said Father Stolárik, "that's no longer sung by priests at Belica's cross."

"Not that bit?"

"No." Father Stolárik watched Dugas with a somewhat startled expression. "So tell me, Dugas, where did you put the cross."

"I can't."

"Really? You could tell me." Father Stolárik's young, swarthy features bore a smile. He took some cigarettes from his desk and offered Dugas one, and when Dugas declined, he lit one himself. "I'm not going to put the cross back where it was."

"Not you? Who then?"

"People."

"Really!"

"They'll find it and put it back, and if they don't find it, they'll put up a new one." Father Stolárik gave a light shrug. "There can be no question of not having a cross there, Dugas. Take my word for it – it's going to be bad for you, living in that house."

"I know –"

"And are you worth your salt?"

"Why d'you ask?"

"You must know plenty of people," Father Stolárik said. "Look them up sometime and tell them they've got certain blameless people locked away – your father-in-law Ambro, Moravčík the teacher, Dr Dubovský the GP, Father Zima, and even old Malena –"

Dugas got to his feet and shrugged.

"I did know plenty of people," he said, "but they've all started shunning me, as if – as if I'd got the mange –"

Ignác Dugas left Father Stolárik, spent two days and nights on the bottle, skipped work, and, having finally sobered up, went to the MZ housing estate to see his wife, "Rosy-red Paula".

She greeted him without a word, but came back to life when he told that her father, Ambro, had been released home.

"Paula," he said as they went outside the singles' dormitory block and sat down on a pile of blackened sawn timbers, "what's to become of us, how's it to be?"

"Living with you is horrible – poor Dad! And here some woman has also been let out, and the fitters, and old Bučko, the Community Centre caretaker, but –"

"But Paula!" Two white and three dental-gold teeth gleamed inside Dugas's mouth. "Let's get away from here! I'm not going to stay, either here or in the town, or in Veľké Dvorce. I shan't earn much, I've shaken off the money thing, I've stopped building that house, everybody's watching me, spying on me, and the friends I did have now steer clear of me as if I was flea-ridden – and they're refusing to release the ones they've locked up – and I'm not going to finish that house, not now, Paula, there's no living there now, they could burn us out again, they'd kill me –!"

"And what'll you do with it?"

"Sell it, as is!"

"You got a buyer?"

"One'll show up – things are looking bad, Paula."

"I know that," she said, "bad – and with you things have never been good. I once tried living with you, Ignác, after I married you – and I will give it one more try."

A sparrow was hopping about the churned-up street, there were some children playing on a patch of grass, it was windy and the wind was scattering dust from a half-spilled bag of cement, very fine sand it was, and from the churned-up soil. A little column of dust formed itself on the flat roof of the tall Community Centre building.

The children on the patch of grass were joined by two boys and a little girl skipping along with tiny steps.

"Ignác," said Paulína, "d'you see those three kids?"

"The boys and the little girl?"

"Yes, they're Dubovský's, the doctor they've put away. And that's Eva Moravčík, his wife." Eva was strolling towards the patch of grass.

"What d'you reckon, Paula?" asked Ignác Dugas, having watched the slim figure of Eva Dubovský in her flimsy, yellow floral dress. "What d'you reckon? Shall we move out to the border area?"

Paulína stared ahead of her with her rosy-red face and light-brown eyes, smiling and with her yellowy-blonde eye-lashes flickering.

"What's funny about that?"

"Can you just imagine it, Ignác? Us two? How shall we begin life there? As we are? With just our bare hands? We squandered all we had on that house. Imagine living like that, Ignác."

"But not us two alone, Paula. We won't be alone there. Think cooperative – there even bare hands suffice... In Slanice I couldn't dream of joining the cooperative, or in Veľké Dvorce – one's been set up there as well now, and old Belica, he was in on it at the outset and said how he'd survived so many things, so he could survive the cooperative as well."

Paulína looked at her husband.

"We haven't been together for such a long time now," he said, "and that's another reason why I'm here; I was feeling down – and I got to thinking about all sorts of things... It's intolerable, Paula, and I can't stay here, because over yonder in Veľké Dvorce there's a cross buried, and an SS man – and I'm only human, as a human being you go for one thing, then another, we humans are all the same – I can't stay here... You can come with me, if you want, but if not, just say so. I can't live here."

"And where is the cross?"

"In Slanica, at Oakwood Bottom, in your father's field, buried. Me and Kubiš, we buried it there that time – the field was due to be ploughed by Kubiš anyway – that's where it is – not a word to your father now! Things were so bad when uprooting the cross was in the air –" Ignác Dugas glanced towards Eva Dubovský and his eyes sought her three children among others on the patch of grass. "– don't say anything to your father so things don't get any worse when they set it up again."

Paula's light-brown eyes twinkled as she watched the sparrow hopping about. The wind blew a cloud of dust through the air above the street.

"Shall we leave, Paula? I'll never finish the house anyway –"

"I'll give it one more try, Ignác."

Ignác Dugas smiled, heaved a happy sigh because of the sudden sense that his wife's words had freed him of the burden of the house awaiting completion and half burned down. He gave Paula a hug.

In Veľké Dvorce, that large village spread across hillsides and former upland meadows, two houses stood vacant and abandoned. Belica's, because old Malena's wife had come and sold off the furniture before going back to Komárno to rejoin her sister and Soňa's little boy, Jurko, and Dugas's, awaiting completion and half burned down, because no buyer had been found for it.

And so time went on. Time's footsteps spread bloody dust everywhere, as if Time had been mercilessly trampling people down and as if the bloody dust was being flicked off legs, here leaden and weary, there brisk and sprightly, but legs that had been blood-spattered by war. In September, the teacher, Moravčík, left prison to rejoin his sorrowful daughter Eva and his wife – and time went on. The summer came and went, autumn came and went, winter, spring arrived and the red 'Palermo' gradually turned white. The brick-red high-rises acquired a coating of white mortar, concrete walkways were created between them, gradually covered with a layer of tarmac, the streets were levelled, rolled flat and paved with small granite cubes. The residents of the blocks of flats prepared their gardens, and volunteers created flat open spaces for parks and flowerbeds. In the Community House and the unfinished blocks, parquet-layers, electricians and plumbers were hard at work – 'Palermo' was growing apace. And time went on, on legs here leaden and weary, there brisk and sprightly – and Eva, whom they let stay on in Block XIV because she had three children, received letters from Martin in prison.

She would read them, as once she would letters from her father.

She remembered all that was in them, as she remembered all that had been in her father's, and lines that caused her pain or gave her pleasure she saw clearly even in her mind's eye: "– accustom the children to the self-sacrifice that protected us during the Uprising, teach them, to the best of your ability, respect for others, teach them self-confidence and pride in being human, because all else may well be superfluous!" – "– I wish to come back to you only in whatever way in which I may be worthy of the promise you made me, during the Uprising, of wanting to be a replacement for the people I had lost..." "Dear Eva, I am pleased to be able to write to you again. All is well with me..." She lived in expectation of Martin's return.

Came the autumn of 1955.

Eva received a letter from Martin.

"5 Oct. 1955," she read. "Dear Eva, I am pleased to be able to write to you again. All is well with me. What are you up to? How are you? What are the children doing? Igor's started school! What are they doing, Igor, Ondrej and Olga? They'll have grown some, surely. How are your Mum and Dad? I was pleased to receive your letter and have been thinking about what you wrote. Do write and tell me what you, the children and your Mum and Dad are all doing! I'm pleased Igor has started school. Thanks for passing on regards from friends –"

Every day for eleven days Eva re-read Martin's letter and on the twelfth day he came home.

He hugged Eva in silence, and the children, who didn't recognise him immediately, he hugged Eva's parents, who had moved from Veľké Dvorce to Block XIV on the MZ housing estate.

That evening he had a shave.

"Martin," she asked him in the bathroom as she took him a towel, "what's next for you, for us?"

"I'll know that tomorrow."

"And you yourself, Martin?"

"Me?" Dubovský took a deep breath in and out. "I've done my stint in jail, Eva, now I'm back." He smiled with his still patchily soaped, thin face. "I'll take a chance – get a decent honest job somewhere or other –"

Eva burst out laughing.

He had a bath and got into bed, opened the bedside table drawer to check if there was a book in it, because, in the bedroom, he always put books in the bedside table so that the children wouldn't take them, and because the Dubrovský household had increased by two, Eva's parents, and the Dubovský flat had a jumble of additional furniture, he found no book in the drawer, just some papers, letters, mostly his from prison, but including some sent to Eva from Veľké Dvorce by the teacher, Moravčík.

"Veľké Dvorce, 4th May 1954," he began reading. "My Dear Eva," he read on for a while, went back to the dateline, "Veľké Dvorce, 4th May 1954", was acutely embarrassed, felt a pain inside his chest and began again: "My Dear Eva, I'm writing to you on a very grave matter, although Mr Malena, the lawyer, who has been to see you, told me that I shouldn't write to you about it at all. I feel so terribly sad, with such anguish and pain in my heart, that I have to write. I have always known and always feared that people today have been demoralised by the war. How could they not be when one thinks back to the terrible suffering? After the terrible suffering inflicted on the world by war, anyone who has survived it will be cut off in a sense from anything that had been good about the world and stand in fear of the dreadful task that lies ahead: that of living in a manner that matches up to that terrible suffering. It is a dreadful task and people today are barely up to it. Which is why everything in us is turned inside out, and all because of the huge demands placed on us and of the trifling things that we do do.

"And that's why I think, my dear Eva – but do not be alarmed! – that Martin, that kind husband of yours, has fallen into temptation and let himself be beguiled by Soňa Malena. All I know has only come from an anonymous letter. I do not believe anything in the offending letter because it also claims that the little lad Jurko, whom the aforementioned Soňa Malena left in the care of her parents, who live in Veľké Dvorce, is Martin's son, and that, to the best of my knowledge, cannot be true. My sole reason for writing to tell you this is that, if any such thing as a relationship between Martin and a woman described by her own father, poor man, as a slut and a prostitute were remotely possible, you should not yield to any instant fit of manic emotions, but wait and act with reason for the good of your husband, yourself and your lovely children. It would be misguided of you to imagine that you would do anything rational in the first fit of rage and heartbreak..." Dubovský read his father-in-law's letter, trembling in bed, and having read it, he looked back at the date, "Veľké Dvorce, 4th May 1954". He quickly hid the letters and closed the drawer.

Eva came in.

"What's today's date?"

"October twelfth," she said, "Why?"

"Just asking," he said. "I was thinking it was about now that they killed my mother and you came to find me –"

"No, that was the eighteenth."

Eva's nightdress, with its hint of sky-blue, drifted down over her smooth body, and as she turned her head to one side, her eyes sunk deep into Martin's, which were covered in shadow and glinting with a gleam of wonderment, she smiled with her fulsome lips.

The doorbell rang, and when Eva's mother, who was always the last to bed, opened the door, she, with the words, "Oh, do come in, they're still awake," led the two visitors straight to the Dubovskýs' bedroom, the older one, extremely thin and with a stoop, a face like linen that had browned with age, furrowed with countless tiny wrinkles, and the other, lean, with darkish, sunken cheeks.

"We've come to welcome you back, Doctor," said Mr Jankovič, the engineer, "Comrade Mokrý here and I bumped into each other, and he told me –"

"Greetings, Doctor," said Mokrý, "welcome to Palermo –!"

"Thank you, thank you very much –!"

They both shook Martin Dubovský's hand and having stood awhile smiling at the two Dubovskýs and saying they'd better be going, Eva bade them wait and asked her mother and father to bring some chairs in.

"Do stay," she added, "he hasn't told us either what it was like inside!"

"No, not that," said Dubovský, "you tell us what's new."

"Nothing," said Mokrý with a shrug. "Nothing really worth mentioning. What people are like says what to expect of them. Today I had a visit from Paula, Dugas's wife, she cried her eyes out then asked if she could have a job at our place, and at the end she told me her husband had been jailed. I can't really say, but something about what she said had me thinking she might have spilt the beans on him herself." Mokrý glanced at the surprised Eva and smiled. "Here, Mrs Dubovský, it's true, that thing you told me once, that socialism is a gift of history whose initiation and preservation come at a great cost – and we wreck it every way we know how. What we need is a large body of decent, principled people... Really!"

The Dubovskýs' bedroom sprang to life as all six chatted together, enlivened further by questions from the three children, who had woken by turns from their brief sleep.

Dawn was barely breaking that verdant Sunday morning when old Mr Bajkovský from Koštice, "Old Dry-thorn Jano" as they called him, was already grazing his son's cow by the Koštice mineral spring. He was standing in a green willow carr, looking ahead of him, and the cow was calmly grazing the herbage. From behind the sparse foliage he stared at the pale-grey concrete block out of which, through a spout, the springwater gushed down to the ground, splashed among the stones, then ran along a little channel worn out of the ground to get lost in a brook nearby. The mineral spring, the spring, the waterhole, the names the poor thing gets given by the locals! All sorts of people come here and refer to it by all sorts of names, the water, our springwater or mead of the earth, and it has also been called, since time immemorial, our spring with a tang. "Come and taste our spring with a tang!", "Hey there, I've just taken a sip from your tangy spring!" – and so on. Other mineral springs taste quite different, with a sharper tang, or more mild, their bottoms have various different colours, grey, red, some jet straight out of the ground at will, others depending on what man lets them do or helps them to do, by means of hollowed-out tree trunks, curved wooden troughs like bits of a barrel, or, like ours, they come out of concrete blocks through metal spouts. The community at large care for them in various ways, depending on how many people, more or fewer, actually use them, and yonder – in Teplice, well, there they're nicely fenced round, even the ones where the water is drawn down and sent off to the towns. There each spring comes up and out through a nice header. Our one, though, it's not any old mineral spring, spouting acidy water – it's our very own tangy spring, as people have always described it, and it's kind of walled up inside a cube of concrete. Mr Ondrkál the bricklayer walled it in – but what does he know about anything! He's never been anywhere, seen anything. And how proud of himself he is! What a great job he did, sorting our tangy spring out like that! Oh, my dear tangy spring, you're so good to drink from! Some water this is! And what a kick! And you deserve a prettier surround, made of stone, nicely decorated and with a sign... He looked about for the cow. She was grazing away peacefully. It's good water, he thought, excellent, but not to be drunk by those as shouldn't! Anyone who's already dying of something certainly shouldn't drink it. It really ought to be coming out of a nicer wellhead, it deserves one. He looked across beyond the concrete block at the green bank lining the concrete roadway a bit higher up and at the sandy footpath leading down from the road to the spring. It's good water, but with a kick. He took a puff of his short curly pipe and let the grey smoke out through his drooping lips. Eh, our tangy spring! He's drunk a fair amount of it in his time. He's been alive for many years now and has been drinking it ever since he first set eyes on the world around him. And he's done some travelling in the wider world, not much, just a bit, on military service, or working away, in Prussia and Austria, he'd meant to take a trip to America, but suddenly war broke out at the wrong moment – so you can never know what makes the world go round, only here, by our tangy spring. And it's nice here, first thing in the morning like now, fresh, crisp... Ah well, what's to be done? Old man Bajkovský had passed his few scraps of land to his son and his son had passed them on to the cooperative farm, and now he comes here to graze his son's Lysaňa, and now and then you get to hear about things going on in the world, there's so many people of every kind come here for the water. And they've got all sorts of names for our spring... The world's different from how it used to be, ever since they built this road – and now! My, oh my! Good water it is, but not to be drunk by those as shouldn't! All kinds of people have tried it. Even some German soldiers turned up once for a drink. This water – and then, but this was way, way back, there was this little blind girl, they say, grazing a cow one time, and a beggar came by and the little girl gave him a piece of bread, all she had. The beggar then got thirsty after he'd eaten, and he hit the ground with his stick and said: "Water, flow!" and the spring gushed forth right there. "Have a wash in that water!" the beggar then said. The little girl had a wash and suddenly she could see. She looked about her, meaning to say thank you to the beggar, but he was no longer there by the spring. That's just a fable, I know, but this water really is something.

From a tall alder tree a shrike flew down among the willows, bobbed about on a flimsy branch, let out a frightened twitter and flew off.

The sun wasn't up yet, but daylight had started to give notice of itself. On the flat land beyond the road, the young verdure of the month of June was starting to shine, darker in the willows and alder groves around the spring and the brook, but almost yellow in the cornfield across the road, and at the foot of the low hills not far away, veiled by a light grey cloud, it had a grey and bluish sheen. The slightly acidic water flowing through a metal spout out of the huge grey concrete block with its metal canopy, swashed and splashed among the stones that had been scoured clean. It was surrounded by an area of greensward, on it some low willows, taller beside the brook where they were intermingled with alders, and not far away, next to the road, stood upright, abandoned and forlorn, a length of tubular yellow metal, bent down and round at its top end, and inside the bent section there shone something blue-and-white and circular with a red sheet-metal oblong beneath it – a bus stop. Apart from old man Bajkovský, there was no one around, the land just stretching away ahead of him, behind him, to his right and left all the way to the nearest forests, hills and mountains, the whole mantled by a pale-blue firmament, which seemed propped aloft on clouds, here grey, there yellowing. The air swelled and billowed with birdsong. The general twittering was interrupted by the low- and high-pitched calls of a golden oriole, which let out the odd squawk as if clearing its throat with a grating sound. Beyond the bus stop two birches gleamed white, crowned by their drooping branches, and beyond them was the green of some aspens.

"Aha!" said Mr Bajkovský under his breath. "It's going to be a nice day. That'll bring an odd mix of folk along. But they all seem so harum-scarum, as if running away from something... They come charging along on their motorbikes and in their cars... And all they ever talk about is goals, football, sport, more sport, cars, motorbikes – technology, inventions... People are doing all right, forever thinking stuff up, dreaming up new ways to come a cropper in the shortest time possible, people have never had it so good –" He looked round at Lysaňa, shook out his legs in their warm green-and-brown trousers, jiggled his matching coat at the shoulders, leaned on his hefty stick and puffed away at his short curly pipe. Grey smoke shot from his mouth. His old face was all astare because on any Sunday morning he liked to gaze at the mineral spring ahead of him, at the wide concrete road that looked down on it, that old face of his, scrawny beneath the cheeks and with scorn written in his eyes and on his lips. "Odd!" he muttered under his breath. "How come no one's showing up today! Overslept I expect. Though it is still a bit on the early side. What would they be doing here?" He watched and waited. On a Sunday morning there were always things to watch. A motorbike might come, old Mr Bajkovský surmised, with a load of demijohns, the young lad will fill them up at the tangy spring and load them onto the bike because it's so much better than beer after a Sunday lunch, it's got such a tang that it brings tears to your eyes, the lad will ask: "Well, Granfer? How are you doing? Still grazing?" – "Aye, that I am, all the time!" he'll reply and ask: "Good water, this, isn't it? People are going to enjoy plenty of it today, right?" – "Right, plenty!" – "And why so much tangy water?" – "Well, Granfer, we've just moved into our new place so we need to celebrate, and water like this is the dead best thing after a lot of home-brewed plum brandy!" – "True, true," he'll agree. Then the lad will go on: "And how come you're still grazing? Hand your cow over to the cooperative like the rest of them and you can stop worrying about it!" He'll leave and another bike will come, a bigger one, for two, a him and a her, they'll dismount, have a drink and drive on, having first turned to call over to him: "'Bye, Granfer! Thanks for the tangy water." – "'Bye, you're welcome!" he'll call after them. Then more bikes will arrive, perhaps as many as ten, big ones, small ones, and they'll all collect some of the water to go with their Sunday lunch. Then suddenly three bikes on a holiday trip might show up together, or, right here, above the spring, a coach will stop. Not your everyday bus, this kind only comes on Sundays, packed with tourists. And all of these are on their way to Teplice. Tour traffic, goodness knows where the people are from, but they'll ask about this and that and tell him things. And a car will stop by, black, grey, blue, green, yellow – and someone might well start going on like the chap last Sunday who insisted that all cars should be red. You can't tell black and grey ones from the road, green ones from the trees and seedling corn, yellow ones from ripe corn and fields of stubble – and that's how accidents happen. In such and such countries such and such a colour is banned, someone will chip in again. You have to keep your eyes open even for colours. These days people fuss about so many things. People will come, have a drink at the spring, have another drink, light up, have a sandwich or something, offer to share one with him, but then our springwater with a tang is good for the appetite, they'll chat about all and sundry, about how this or that happened wherever it was, all sorts of stuff. You learn far more from people than off the radio! The radio just yatters on and on and won't say anything twice even if you ask it to... And sometimes you need it to... Old Mr Bajkovský looked out from his willow carr as if he'd seen it all before, though the road was empty and silent both in this direction and that. He shuffled his feet, his shoulders jiggled the green-and-brown coat made of military fabric that he'd been given by his second son while he was still in the army. Now he's..., hm, I wonder what he's up to...! He never comes back home any more, or if he does, then only in his Spartak. The old girl would be so happy to see him if she were still alive, poor thing! Ondro might have been doing okay as well, our young-est lad, but he, poor chap, was killed by the Germans somewhere or other. Mr Bajkovský leaned on his stick, and let out a puff of grey smoke. They'll be along anytime now, a motorbike, a car, people, there'll be the chance of a chat, time will have passed, Lysaňa will have grazed her fill and we'll both go home. The silence reigning about the Koštice mineral spring, overlying the babbling of the brook, the splashing of the water from the spring, and the birdsong, might have been what turned his old face, still well-knit, slightly red in the cheeks, his chin with its weeks' growth of stubble, towards the pale-grey concrete block and the letters and numbers "AD 1944", which, Ondrkál, the Koštice mason, had etched into the soft, drying concrete with an iron spike. At that moment, the letters and numbers grew sharper, the pale-grey concrete block seemed to be completely flooded in a yellow light, and the letters and numbers turned blue. Old Mr Bajkovský fal-tered at the sight of the inscription, rocked from side to side on his feet, jiggled his coat at the shoulders, rammed his stick into the ground ahead of him and flung his left hand up into the air, because he'd never seen the inscription like this be-fore. It was clear, sharply defined, bluish inside the grooves of the numbers and letters, and yellow as gold round the rough edges of the grooves. "Aha!" he said, ramming his stick into the ground in front of him. "That's *not* when it was!" he said as if he was speaking to the concrete block, from which the water was splashing down, as he if wanted to drive the water away from the lovely glade, all sparkling with the dew on its grass, "No, that's not when they built over you, my dear tangy spring. That year was just the beginning, you hadn't been concreted over yet. They'd only made a start, once all the spring jobs were all done, it took ages for the locals to agree, time just flew by. One lot thought one thing, another favoured something else. As always. Why all the malarkey? Such frippery! But yes. Everywhere else has one. And so they began, but they just couldn't make up their minds and the arguing went on and on. One side didn't mind how much it cost to concrete you in, others wanted to keep it cheap and unassuming, they brought in the sand, started digging, then came harvest time and at harvest time it rained on and off, then came threshing, and then, my tangy spring, they didn't get you concreted in, at that stage it was all jobs half-done, a pile of sand, a huge pile of sand, planks and other bits of timber – and then all sorts happened..." Despite himself, old man Bajkovský tore his eyes away from the inscription and settled them on the shining stream of water gushing from the black metal spout and glinting in the yellow sunlight. Quite still, he stared ahead of him at the yellow glittering water and had a sense that the inscription had never been so clear and so blue. He wanted both to look and not to look at it. It seemed to be shouting at him. Yes, as if it had let out a shout! And they say it doesn't spook people in the daytime. Only those who've got something to be spooked about... "No, that's not when they concreted you over, my dear tangy spring," he said. "Back then there were other things on men's minds, other things for the people of Koštice to worry about. The threshing was all done, autumn arrived, no, it hadn't, but it was on its way – and on that Sunday morning, then as now, I came out here to graze the cow, actually more, three of them, these days there's just the one, just Lysaňa. I'd given my cows to my son, and he – but what of it, all cattle's now on the cooperative farm... I had a few more to graze than just the one, and back then, that very Sunday it was, I'd come like this into the willow carr – and I pricked up my ears because somewhere, over that way it was –" he pointed his big stick, "– there was a sudden burst of gunfire and a lot of noise. I swear to God! The day before, I thought it was, the chaps in the village were chatting and said something was in the offing, that, I mean, partisans or something... But, says I, they've been talking like that for a fortnight or more. Now it's partisans, now the Germans and all sorts of other folk... In next to no time the noise got louder and along the road here, past our tangy spring, hurtled eight large new trucks, I know there were eight, I counted them. They were ours, that much I could tell. Where they'd come from and where they were heading I hadn't the foggiest idea. They were hauling three cannon, a field kitchen and they were full of soldiers. What on earth! I scrambled up to the road there and gazed after them for a time, then when all I could see was that the road had swallowed them up, I came back here to my willow trees somewhat perturbed. Something's astir, something's going on, no doubt about it, there's something. My lad Ondro, poor lad, he's also in the army. I glances at the cows. What the lads were saying last night, I says, it wasn't just hot air. Folk always get to hear things...! Something's broken out nearby, and there's fighting. Who's fighting who? Soldiers here, soldiers there, the front line's in a mess, broken through in places – in a war like this you've no way of knowing which way to lean. Not towards the Germans, I reckon, that much is obvious. They can just clear off home, what do they want here? Why are they still hanging around? They can't hold out much longer anyway. And it's been like this for a fortnight or more, some going this way, some going that... Our men aren't doing anything, just kicking their heels about the village and having not so clever ideas... The front line's in a mess, I'm thinking – when we were on the front line in Russia, don't give an inch was the watchword and the front line held! That was a *Schwarmlinie*, a firing line. But this? Just a mess. Then after about half an hour... What *is* this? Who can make head or tail of it? When even war has no order to it... The soldiers had gone past in their trucks, disappeared from sight, even the noise had subsided – if it hadn't been for our tangy spring!"

The sun was creeping slowly up over the horizon, turning yellow among the yellow clouds, while the alders, willows, the white bark of the birches and the grass were all turning yellow too, as was the concrete block inside which the mineral water gathered before flowing out through the iron spout. It gurgled among the stones below.

In the willow carr behind old Mr Bajkovský the grass parted either side of a black grass snake, the grass snake made a sharp turn, ran off and slithered into the brook.

Silence reigned, overlying the birdsong and the babbling of the brook, nothing moved, not a hint of a breeze even, just two collared doves flew over the mineral spring. Furiously flapping their wings.

Old Mr Bajkovský watched them, thinking back to one autumn Sunday that had been plaguing him on and off for nigh on twelve years. Some trucks loaded with soldiers had passed along the road, leaving silence behind them and all quiet again that morning beside the mineral spring, very early as usual when you came there to graze the cows. He'd stood there in the willow carr, lost in thought, leaning on his hefty stick, with his ancient, heavily patched coat slung across his shoulders and his short curly pipe between his lips – and suddenly he stopped dead. Never had he seen the like before at the spring. Coming down from the road was a tall man with nothing on his head apart from a shock of dishevelled hair, grey about the ears, thin he was, all skin and bone, trudging through the grass. He was supporting himself on a dry stick that he'd picked up somewhere, a twisty, spiky bit of wood, and he was wearing some ragged, lightweight, brown trousers and a flimsy old shirt. His face was lit up behind his spectacles by his large black eyes. Old Mr Bajkovský didn't recognize him, he'd never seen him before – and this stranger, a printer, Robert Freystatt from Vienna, came down the path, spotted the cows and stopped short, paused for a moment, looked all round, and then noticed the pile of sand brought there for crowning the spring in concrete, and the spring itself. He walked down towards it, sat down on the sand, had another good look round and then a wash. A moment later he started drinking and he drank and drank. Old Mr Bajkovský was watching him from the willow carr. Bound to be one o' them, he mused, he's not local, one o' them from those camps – either let out or escaped. They say there are folk like 'im there. He's not local. Dear God, what a wreck, so wasted! Why do people do this to people? They say folk in the camps get starved to death. Old Mr Bajkovský watched him a while then stalled because he realised that the man couldn't get back on his feet. Freystatt had hauled himself up onto his hands and knees, then he slipped down off the pile of sand and remained flat on the ground. Poor fellow! Old Mr Bajkovský came forward out of the carr and ran over to the man as he lay on the ground next to the spring. Freystatt slid a little further across the ground and turned his terrified face towards the man standing there speaking to him. What's wrong? What do you want? He didn't understand. Old Mr Bajkovský, with his stick and pipe in his hand, was seized with a strange fear. "What happened to you? We can't have you giving up the ghost right here! Where d'you come from?" Freystatt twisted round slightly and opened his large black eyes wide. "Deutsch?" he asked. "Sagen Sie mir, bitte..." – "What's that? What are you trying to say?" – "Sprechen Sie deutsch? Wo sind die Partisanen?" – "You're not feeling too good, eh? You hungry, or cold? What do you need most? It was quite cold last night, usually is this time of year. But partisans? Have they been mistreating you? Are they after you? But then why would they be? I can tell you're speaking German, but I don't have a clue what you're saying. I was in Prussia and Austria myself in the dim and distant, but didn't pick up a single word," the old man said. Freystatt looked at him briefly, stretched out on his back, rolled over on one side and sank one elbow into the sand. He rose slightly, then fell back. "You made yourself ill with our tangy lass," said old Bajkovský. "She's not good on an empty stomach. She only makes you even hungrier. She does have quite a tang, there's none like her anywhere... Me too, once..." Old Mr Bajkovský put his pipe in his trouser pocket, placed his stick on top of a pile of old planks, all smirched with concrete and lime, grabbed Freystatt under the armpits, raised him up and laid him back against the pile of sand. From his coat pocket he took a slice of bread, which he handed to Freystatt, and he'd never seen anyone tuck into bread like at that moment.

First, Freystatt broke off a couple of pieces, popped them in his mouth and started chewing, then, using both hands, he crammed the whole slice of bread into his mouth at once. The old man watched as the crust almost reached the stranger's ears. He watched, sat down on the pile of planks intended for use once the mineral spring was being concreted over, and began filling his pipe. "Russian, Hungarian...?" Freystatt carried on chewing as if he hadn't heard. "German, French... God knows what you are, man, you speak German, but – the whole world's fighting... Are you hungry? Are you cold? Where've you been? Is someone after you?" Freystatt stopped eating, with both hands he removed the crust from his mouth and looked at old Mr Bajkovský, who was smiling and still looking surprised. His large eyes were smiling, looking in a way watery. "Danke Ihnen, sehr schön," said Freystatt in a low, exhausted tone. He looked at old Mr Bajkovský. You're a bit surprised, you've no idea who I am, he thought. Thank you for that slice of bread, it tasted good, but... I'm from Vienna, a printer, till now I've been at my brother's in Trnava, then we went into hiding in Hrušov, at least I think that's what the village was called, I'm looking for some partisans... I'm sick, my stomach – I don't know if I'm going to make it... I'm so weak, I'm even finding it hard to speak... "Wo sind die Partisanen?" Freystatt tried to ask. "Is someone after you? Who? The Germans? The partisans?" old Mr Bajkovský asked. Freystatt gave a slight shrug. "You know what?" The old man got to his feet, started pointing in turn at the man, at himself, at Koštice and at the three cows still grazing on the greensward. He helped Freystatt to his feet and led him into the willow carr. "Look, see. You look after my cows, I'll nip home and fetch you something to see you on your way. Dry bread's not up to much. To you it's next to nothing. Like a fly to a dog. And you're as light as a feather!" Then he slipped his coat off his shoulders and handed it to Freystatt as he sat their on the grass inside the willow carr. "I'll be back in no time, and don't you worry about the cows. They're hungry, they're going nowhere. They're so dumb you could light a fire under them! Old Mr Bajkovský left. "Maybe I shouldn't have done that," he mumbled in the willow carr, casting an involuntary glance at the shrieking blue sign, outlined in the yellow light, "AD 1944", and jiggling his army-fabric coat at the shoulders. "I've left, I took a last look at the cows, at him, I was in a hurry to fetch him something to eat... Maybe I shouldn't have done it, probably better to have picked him up, given him a piggy-back, he was a light as a feather, carry him back to Koštice and hide him away somewhere, but my mind was on bringing him something to eat, then he'd have eaten something and left –"

The willow carr and alder carr had a shrike fly over.

Its nest must be round here somewhere, old Mr Bajkovský thought, and once more he was sent whirling back to that Sunday that had been plaguing him on and off for nigh on twelve years. How could it have happened? In such a brief moment? He knew nothing about it. He'd left the spring and Robert Freystatt, the printer from Vienna, who for the previous six years had been in hiding at his brother, a doctor's in Trnava, and later with the brother and his wife and two young sons in Hrušov, and, in flight from Hrušov, had come all the way to the Koštice well, gazed after the old man as he left for the village, in haste, but he understood nothing. Nothing since that moment he'd left the loft after the man who'd let him stay the night had said in terror: "Soldaten, Soldaten!" He'd escaped from Hrušov, they were there now... For four days he's had nothing to eat, until that bread today. He was still gripping the crust in his hand. The man in Hrušov certainly couldn't have brought him anything, all he had was a pitchfork, he was tossing hay down from the loft, there were soldiers knocking about outside the house. They took his brother, and his wife and the two children, but he himself managed to escape, so far he has always landed on two feet, as if the whole thing was a game, a match... It isn't, this isn't a game... Freystatt had yielded to imaginings that had been pursuing him for such a long time. Walking or running, he'd gone in and out among a patchwork of streets and lanes, his flight had gone well, lights shone, red, amber, green, he dashed through the patchwork when the lights were red, when he was outnumbered by countless black rubber wheels, huge, ribbed, hard. Maybe that's why they'd missed him, hadn't spotted him – but where are they, the partisans? And where has the old boy gone? And what was all that that he'd been saying? Will he come back? How can I get him to tell me where the partisans are? Who's he going to bring back with him?... At that moment, Freystatt was as if pressed to the ground by the astonishing realisation that he wasn't afraid, though fear did come, all at once, and it pressed him down even harder. Not being afraid is a very bad sign... Nearly an hour passed and in the course of it the road above the Koštice mineral spring thundered and clattered with the passage of German trucks and motorcycles, a thundering and clattering that were repeated several times before silence was restored. Robert Freystatt was scared stiff in the willow carr, he wasn't looking up towards the road, and just as he thought there was nothing more to come, he caught the sound of a motorbike in the distance. Its voice grew louder, then softer, harsher, spluttered and backfired as it drew ever closer to the spring and Freystatt. The bike went quiet and then gave one last cough, and as Robert Freystatt looked out from the willow carr up to the road, three German soldiers dismounted. They strolled slowly down the path towards the planks, the sand and the spring. All three wearing helmets and new grey-green uniforms. The black and white of their epaulettes shone bright and clear. The last one paused half-way down the path, glanced at the cows and the willow carr, then at the sand and the spring, and on the pile of planks he spotted the hefty stick that old Mr Bajkovský had left there. "Hello there!" he called out in a clear, pleasant voice. "Who's in charge of these cows?" Freystatt remained motionless among the willow trees, hunched down inside the old man's greasy and grimy, patched old coat. The soldier, a strong, tall, broad-shouldered man, stormtrooper Theodor Knopp from Oettingen, called out once

again: "Anyone there? Who's in charge of these cows?" Freystatt remained seated, merely turning his head slightly to see,
through the thin willow foliage, all three soldiers. He took
fright at the man calling, who was still standing on the path,
with his submachine gun levelled and a pistol at his hip, concealed within a black leather holster. "Wait, don't drink that!"
said Knopp to his men. "Who knows what the water's like. It
might not be fit to drink. We should ask the chap who's grazing these cows – except we'd probably get no more sense out
of him than out of his cows." He trotted down to the spring
and his two men and picked up old Bajkovský's hefty stick
from the planks. He looked it over, weighed it his hands and
grinned. "Got scared of us and ran off – but you'd have to be
foolish to be scared of us..." Knopp didn't finish his sentence
because he'd just caught sight a tiny part of a thin white leg
and a brown trouser leg. He grinned, beckoned to his men,
took a step towards the willow carr with the stick in his hand
and said: "Get up! what are you doing here, Mein Herr? And
why don't you answer when I call? Is this your stick? You were
afraid of us, right? You ran off when you saw us coming. How
odd though – you ran off so fast that you forgot your stick, or
dropped it." Freystatt looked back at him, his large black eyes
bright, his spectacles shining, in the dark green of the carr
even his white face shone, in part overgrown with black stubble which was turning grey here and there. Kill me! he said
mentally to the soldiers, as he'd been saying for over five years.
In his mind's eye he could see the letters and rows of type that
he'd set sometime in the past. He couldn't remember what they
were from. "Kill me!" he spoke the lines in his mind to the
soldiers. "You've been pursuing me for so long. Stop pursuing
me, what's happened to me will happen to you! You've been
turning sensible people into madmen and monsters and the
well-intentioned into fiends and savages." Kill me at last! Freystatt told them mentally, I can no longer act the monster and
the savage where you're concerned. I don't have the strength,
I'm sick. "Please stand up." Freystatt tried to rise, fell back into

the grass and tried again. "You can't?" Knopp asked. "Let me give you a hand! Now then. Are you going to tell me you're in charge of these cows? Who are you?" – "I've got a pain in my stomach...," said Freystatt, clamping one very thin, white hand to his belly. "You're not much use to these cows, mein Herr, the cows round here don't speak German," said stormtrooper Knopp. "You could be lying, right? Please stand up!" Freystatt struggled onto all fours, but with his limbs trembling and vainly trying to straighten up from the waist and adopt a kneeling position, stormtrooper Knopp told him to stop being foolish and pointed a finger at him for one of the soldiers to take note. "I'd come rushing back to the spring here and these willows," old Mr Bajkovský mumbled to himself, to the tangy water and the sign that said "AD 1944". He didn't spell out the whole story, just the snatches that thrust their way to his tongue. "If only I could tell it to someone, say how it was! Today people don't speak about such things, they don't listen. Perhaps if some luckless stranger showed up, he might be glad to hear about it... I'd come rushing back to the spring here and these willows with some bread and a bit of bacon... People today don't want to listen to such tales any more, they're cheerful now, carefree. Old Bajkovský lapsed into silence, listening to the twittery matinal background noise coming from the trees and fields and the nearby forests and hills. "I'd come rushing back with a bit of bacon, and I had a lump of curd cheese as well, and suddenly I heard a burst of gunfire. A grating sound, from a submachine gun. I know now what sounds like what. I stopped, petrified – it grated like a rusty nail being got out of a piece of oak! – I took another couple of steps, stopped again and saw, right then I saw, here on the road above the spring, a motorbike and three German soldiers getting onto it, ready to go... I knew that was a bad sign," old Mr Bajkovský went on in a low voice, "and I hurried on, ran as fast as I could. But an old man like me isn't up to much running! I got there with the lump of curd cheese, the bit of bread and the bit of bacon, and my Sunday coat so the chap would have something to wear..."

He fell silent and began to stare at the yellow concrete block, the blue numbers and letters, that nagging inscription. Its rough, lumpy edges were lit up by the early yellow sun, rising out of the yellow aurora.

With its bobbing flight a hoopoe flew over the road.

Everything round the Koštice mineral spring gleamed with the early-morning green of June, the greensward, grass, the willows, alders, birches and aspens, the fields and the nearby woodlands, hills and knolls, gleaming ever brighter, the sun carried on rising behind old Mr Bajkovský, casting his shadow on the willow trees' leaves. The willow carr oppressed him, held him in its grip, as did the silence.

So long ago, that was, so far back, he mused. It'll almost twelve years now. He was angry that it had crossed his mind, angry, then sorrowful. It's like if – it makes you want to say a prayer for the poor fellow. He shook out his legs in their green-and-brown trousers, jiggled his matching coat at the shoulders and turned to see Lysaňa. She was grazing peacefully, her head close to the ground as she picked at the short green grass. He leaned on his stick and listened to the water trickling out of the concrete block and the metal spout and splashing down among the clean, scoured stones. He smiled. They didn't concrete it in until 1947, and then put "AD 1944", because that was what he'd wanted, though he never told anyone why. That was how he'd wanted it, they'd asked him why, kept asking him, why here, why this, but in the end they'd done it as he asked. There were mutterings, why's Old Dry-thorn Jano making such a fuss? Why did it have to be so fancy? But in the end they'd let it happen, Ondrkál the mason, he was the one who'd done the embellishing... Ah, my lovely tangy spring, you deserve a much prettier wellhead! A stone one, like the ones they have at Teplice... Ondrkál doesn't know how to make one, so he just created this concrete monstrosity, and my, how proud of himself he is! Oh, my dear tangy spring! A beggar came, gave some to a little blind girl, got it out of the ground – "Well, well!" Old Mr Bajkovský said to himself after a while. "Well, well! Upon my soul! Still nobody here this morning! But then it really is quite early still. They're having a sleep-in! People can sleep longer these days. Oh, my tangy lass! Whatever the sign says, perhaps this isn't what it should. If feels like it's screaming at you –" He stood there in the willow carr, watching.

Everywhere was quite, like on any Sunday morning first thing, everywhere just the greenish light of early morning and birdsong. Lysaňa, head to the ground, was grazing nicely for old Mr Bajkovský.

For another moment or so everything remained silent, then he caught the sound of a motorbike. "Heigh-ho, off we go, but they're starting very early today," he said in his willow carr. "Any minute now they'll be drawing it off into bottles and demijohns. My tangy lass tastes so good after a fatty lunch and these days people really do indulge themselves! That poor chap, how thin he was, all skin and bone, starving, and light as a feather! He was really done for that time, maybe he was done for becase he couldn't get on his feet and take to his heels – but there's no knowing what did for him. Could have been my tangy lass, or the bread, maybe I shouldn't have brought him into the carr..." The cold of early morning made old Mr Bajkovský shiver, as did the idea of blaming the mineral spring for the death of one unknown, wasted man. "There's no knowing what did for him, no knowing what manner of person he was. He'd got nothing with him, just those glasses..." His thin features wore a brief smile. And sadness, the remorse that now inhered firmly inside his sunken eyes and on his drooping lips. He listened to the motorbike and waited. He enjoyed watching as, every Sunday, people drew the acidy water. In the past it wasn't like that. His tangy lass ran to no purpose, he mused, and if anyone did fancy a drink, they had to come on foot and carry some away by hand or on their backs. Nowadays people have got motorbikes and time to spare, and money, and petrol – and suchlike.

"Aye, aye!"

On the road overlooking the mineral spring a red motor-bike stopped.

A girl, the student Majka Štancl, alighted from the rear seat, while her companion, Ivan Podhájsky, general manager of parks and gardens in the nearby town, stayed put. The engine was pulsating away beneath him like an uneasy, sick heart.

Majka Štancl stepped away from the bike and looked back at Podhájsky as if to summon him.

"Are you going? Do you have to?"

"Yes," said Majka, hanging her head wearily. Then she turned and smiled at Podhájsky. "You come too, Ivo."

"No!"

"Why not?"

Podhájsky dismounted, heaved the bike onto its stand and turned to face Majka. "We don't have the time, we need to get a move on! Be quick, Majka! In Teplice we can meet up with the others, Tibor – and the rest. They're all coming, even Zuz and Mia, Pedro, Jack –"

Majka hung her head again, directing her huge dark glasses towards the ground.

Can she be feeling sick, losing her grip? old Mr Bajkovský wondered, shifting his gaze to the gloomy young man, who had pushed his very wide, brownish-red goggles above his eyes and was striding towards the spring. Smartly dressed... The old man rather liked the brown trousers and shepherd check coat he was wearing. Nice, but hardly the thing for a day out... And so early in the morning!

Majka Štancl looked back as if unsure of herself, hung her head even lower and walked slowly ahead of him.

Can she be feeling sick? Has she got stomach ache? My tangy lass is good for the stomach, and in the past people used the water on their eyes, certain gentlefolk came all the way from Pest because of their eyes, but these days people, whatever ails them, they just trot off to the doctor's. The beggar gave that little girl her sight, but these young people have got those huge spectacles as if they've got really bad eyesight. And old Mr Bajkovský remembered Freystatt, who he'd given that bread to. That poor chap might have been done for by the springwater... But this pair? Young people like them are usually jollier, laughing and larking about, sometimes they even douse one another with the water, oblivious to any other person and not listening.

Majka Štancl, wearing blue pedal pushers that left half her lovely tanned calves exposed, a balloon-silk windcheater and a headscarf with a picture of boats and sun-bronzed people beside some water, approached the spring and then turned to Podhájsky, who was just getting a cigarette out. She watched him for a moment then said: "Wait, Ivo, don't light up!"

"Why not? I don't want any water... If only there was something a bit stronger on tap! Coffee! Or – do get a move on, Majka, we need to get to Teplice!"

"Didn't you have enough last night? Do you want a bite to eat? I've got something left over from yesterday."

"No! Do get a move on!"

Up on the road the motorbike was vibrating, idling with an irregular beat.

What a –, old Mr Bajkovský chafed at Podhájsky. If he let his stomach try the water, it'd make its own demand for more. He must be a gormless oaf!

Majka bent down to the water, washed her hands and stood back up. The lower half of her face bore a smile. Her eyes, too, wore a sardonic, but imploring smile, but Podhájsky couldn't see that from behind his wide, dark goggles, glinting and reflecting the sky, the clouds and the sun. Majka's glasses captured the alders and willows. "Wait, Ivo. Don't light up yet. I'll be done in no time!" She bent back down towards the water, cupped her hands under it and offered it to Podhájsky, as if ready to raise it to his lips.

"Come off it!"

"Have a sip. Do you remember? Last year you..., you know, and it was better that way, but afterwards –"

Podhájsky tossed his head, gave Majka a scornful smile and lit his bent cigarette.

Majka let the water go, shook out her long, thin hands and her entire frame seemed to slump. She bent down, grasped the spout with her left hand, let the water keep filling her right hand and took gulp after huge gulp of the running, splashing, outflowing water. She shook out her hand, stepped back from the water and from Podhájsky and just stared into the ground.

I reckon those two have had a tiff, thought old Mr Bajkovský as he began to fume. He found Podhájsky ridiculous for having come so close to the tangy spring, not giving it a try and just smoking, and he found Majka also ridiculous, just standing there looking crushed and staring down at the ground. Hm! Others at odds have made up over my tangy lass, and not just such young ones. If this is how their morning's shaping up, I can't see their day out being much fun! Suppose I were to shout at Lysaňa, give them a bit of a fright, and any bad feelings between them would vanish like a puff of smoke, smelly smoke... It looks like all she wanted was to make him taste the water to bring back some memory or other... Poor thing... Just shout at Lysaňa! Then they'll be back together. "Hey up!" old Bajkovský nearly shouted. "Hey up, Lysaňa!"

"Ivo," Majka suddenly burst out. "Why did you invite me out last night? I didn't want to go but you talked me into it, and in the end we went nowhere – and why did you then take me round to Tibor's –?"

"I was just thinking. Majka, please, listen –!"

"Thinking," she sneered as she clenched her fists. "Why are you dating that woman, answer me that! And why was she also at Tibor's last night?"

"Who am I dating? Listen, please –!"

"Come off it, stop pretending! Miss Vranovská. The whole school knows you're dating a teacher! Why did you invite her there yesterday? She was there, she saw everything, she knows about everything!"

"Oh, boy!" Old Mr Bajkovský got a firmer hold on his stick. And again he almost shouted "Hey up, hey up, Lysaňa!"

Podhájsky produced a smile filled with disdain. "Are you so utterly clueless? Why such naive questions?"

"I want to know, right?" Majka shrieked. "I've a right to know, don't you think?"

"Look here." Podhájsky paused briefly to gather his thoughts. He didn't know how much else to tell her. He'd picked her up at Tibor's, on his bike, he had to get them to Teplice and wait there, and here she was thumping him in the back with both fists next to a mineral spring. He had to pause. He smiled at Majka, the young creases about his mouth deepening. Do you have some money, Majka? he wondered, and thought: maybe he should have had a sip of the water she'd offered him. Like last year. He might have to tread carefully with her. He looked at her as if she were a total stranger. Suddenly his mind was made up, he'd knock the stuffing out of her! Maybe then you'll go on with me to Teplice, Majka. Maybe you'll admit whether Tibor gave you something. "You mustn't let that bother you," he said. "I have to keep dating her for now, otherwise you could fail your maths. And where would that leave you? They'd all be laughing at you. You wouldn't be able to stay on. You have to be practical. If I didn't date her, you'd fail – and she might even tell on us. And it was you I invited along yesterday, not her. You. After all, I can't take a teacher on a date by motorbike. She'd said no anyway, no, it's out of the question. You have to be practical, Majka," he went on, fully resolved to take the wind out of her sails, disarm her and get her back on the back seat of his bike. She can't stay here on her own, and anyway she can't not go to Teplice! "Vranovská's great. It's best doing it with her in the stock room. Sometimes she even has some drink in there, but not water like this stuff! Be reasonable, please! Be practical and not so naive! I don't want any pointless gossip, people talking. And anyway, you got on fine with Vranovská last night. You weren't in the least bothered that she showed up at Tibor's.

And you were quite happy chatting to Tibor. Listen, Majka, please," he said in a subdued tone, paused briefly, then went on: "Listen, Majka, ignore all that! I'm sorry. You know I was just teasing you. But, Majka, listen –" he continued, almost in a whisper, "did Tibor give you some money, I mean, Majka my dear, money, like a largish sum –?"

"What?"

"Money!"

Majka Štancl spun round, hared up the path from the spring to the motorbike and quickly released her green canvas bag in a grey polythene wrapper from under the rear seat.

Podhájsky ran up after her. "Come here!" He swung his fist at her, but at that very instant he spotted the cow and old Bajkovský lurking in the willow carr. He drew his arm back.

"No!" Majka shrieked. "I'm going nowhere!"

"You can't stay here!" said Podhájsky quietly. "You have to come with me!"

"And why?" she asked, and she burst into a fit of choking laughter, as if someone were trying to strangle her. "I'm staying here – go! I'm not going with you."

Old Mr Bajkovský watched as Podhájsky stiffened somewhat, not knowing what to do next. He tossed his cigarette aside, secured another canvas bag like Majka's that had come loose, and shouted back: "You should remember Vranovská! You should come with me and stop playing up like this! Vranovská ought to matter to you!" before giving Majka one last look, slipping the idling motorbike off its stand and riding off. Old Bajkovský turned to watch Majka as she walked slowly, with the bag slung across her shoulder, towards the yellow metal tube with the blue-and-white circular plate on top. He glanced at Lysaňa. She was grazing peacefully. "Hm!" he grunted and withdrew deeper inside the willow carr. "Hm! Upon my soul! He really is a gormless oaf! He was going to hit her! Do even people like that get violent? Something must have happened between them. He was going to hit her – and – it was like neither one nor the other knew what they were doing. It must have been something bad for them to have come here that early. He was going to hit her, the gormless oaf! And the way she kept buckling at the knees... Ah well, you never can tell with people, they get up to all sorts of things. Even my old girl would blow her top, lashing out with that tongue of hers, any time you gave some other woman's skirt a twitch. She's dead now, poor soul..." He stared for a while at the yellow concrete block. He made to go after Majka and say something, but instead he stayed put in the willow carr and stared very pensively ahead of him. In his eyes he had the bluish letters and numbers, yellow from the sun about their rough edges. He heaved a deep sigh because he seemed to see before him the stranger he'd offered his bread to, and asked himself if the girl up there by the bus stop was miserable enough and if she might be able to hear him out. He shuddered. The stranger is lying face down in the grass, he had three holes in his head, another three in his patched coat, holes in his head, back and chest... Robert Freystatt was lying there, he made no move as old Bajkovský came up to him, on his head, on his coat and in the grass there was red blood... "They killed you, man?" he asked, "They killed you, what on earth for? I've brought you some bread, curd cheese, bacon and this coat, so you've got something to wear when you move on..." He had lifted up his Sunday coat, twill, striped, bent down to remove the stranger's old, patched coat full of holes and cover him with his Sunday coat, but fear had got the better of him, so he marshalled his cows and drove them home, to Koštice. He drove them fast, fearing lest the German soldiers show up. If only he hadn't given the man his bread, if only he hadn't left him here, if only had hadn't forgotten his stick, if only he hadn't gone off home to fetch the coat, bacon, bread and curd cheese... if only he'd picked the chap up and carried him on his shoulders to Koštice and hidden him somewhere, after all, he was as light as a fether, and instead he'd trotted off to fetch him a coat... You do what's right and end up doing something terribly wrong... These are such god-awful times when this is what things come to. Doing good's no good, you have to do better, I reckon... Old Bajkovský stared into the ground as if he could see at his feet the stranger who'd been shot, who'd only come for a sup of springwater. He checked on Majka.

She was standing alone at the tubular metal pole, completely worn out, hurt and on the brink of tears. Money... Does Ivo know about the money? And what is it to him? Why did he want to hit her? Money? A largish sum? A thousand crowns is a largish sum. She'd never laid hands on such a large sum. Ivo wants some of it? Majka, hurt and crushed by grief and self-pity, fought back her tears, she could feel her body tingling and shaking. She leant against the tubular metal pole. On her head the scarf with the picture of water, boats and sun-tanned people, on her trunk a thin red slipover, stretched even thinner over her prominent breasts, with a balloon-silk windcheater on top, her legs in sky-blue pants and her feet in dark blue shoes, a green canvas bag in a polythene wrapper slung from her shoulder, black hair, a white face, smooth cheeks with a hint of suntan, a slim figure, noticeably narrow at the waist, and her right leg sort of hooked round the yellow tubular pole. She was looking at the red, sheet-metal oblong and the patches of white that were all that was left of the torn-off timetable. Gone four o'clock – where to now? She'd left home the day before after a row with her parents and she'd said the day before that she was going on a trip with her girlfriends Zuz and Mia, though she'd been with Ivo – Ivo had casually picked her up, as a casual Sunday item. She suited him well enough for a casual Sunday fling. Ivo was having it off with Vranovská in the store room, it had become quite a habit, but before that he'd been going out with her, with her, Majka – and it had all begun right here, by the mineral spring, the year before, twelve months back... Like it was only yesterday, but how long ago it was... They used to go on daytrips to Teplice, stopping here on more than one occasion, Ivo would drink from her cupped hands, he would call her his blossom and say he was sipping at a flower – and then she'd begged him go and see Vranovská to put in a word for her. He did go and see her and for the next fortnight she never met up with him, he kept avoiding her and Miss Vranovská completely ignored her, avoided even looking at her, as she still was – and then yesterday she'd been at Tibor's... Majka looked at her lovely, slender hands, her white palms. Maybe Ivo now finds them disgusting, finds the whole of her disgusting. She glanced to the right, to the left, the white birch trees glinted on her glasses. The wide, long road, grey except down the middle, where it gleamed black from the streak left by tyres. Where did Ivo go? Really to Teplice? He's to meet up there with all the lads and lasses. If only he were to come back and take her home... Maybe he's right, maybe her exam results do depend on Vranovská. To the right and left, the road drifted away into Sunday's morning green, the green fields, meadows and trees. At that instant it struck Majka Štancl as like in that colour film. A grey, grey-green river is running past, drifting away into some far-distant jungle. It's a long way back to town on foot. Someone might happen along and give her a lift. But what if Ivo came back for her? No, she won't go with him... She rested her weary body and aching head against the yellow tubular pole, stared up into the sky and saw nothing. Her headache seemed to keep draining away, and then it seemed to drain back in again. She'd drunk a lot at Ivo's friend Tibor's – wine, cognac – what did they say it was? Larsen? Yes, Larsen – they'd eaten, smoked, drunk, there was that bikini, at first it had been fabulous... Cognac, wine – where did Tibor get it from? At home, at the Štancls', there was always a bit of a hoo-ha over even the slightest out-of-the-ordinary lunch, her father's nothing, just an honest bank clerk, and he's even studying for a degree in economics – and clothes? Buy more, have some made? Majka shifted the leg she had hooked round the pole. And why did the party break up so suddenly? Someone had appeared on the scene, someone extra, Tibor had an argument with someone, Ivo nudged her awake after she'd dozed off on the sofa. At home there was going to be a row and tears over it. She oughtn't to do it. But she'd been doing it ever since the previous winter. For Ivo's sake. Behind her dark glasses, Majka Štancl's sleep-deprived eyes were hurting with the brightness of the sky, stinging with the tears that were forcing their way up and jabbing at her beneath her eyelids as if there were were some tiny, sharp grains of sand in them. Ugh! She'd accepted some money from Tibor. For the first time. "I'd give you more, Majka," he said. "I'd give you even more, you'd be looking after it for me, just looking after it, dearest Majka, and if you needed some, you'd just help yourself. That okay by you?" She didn't want this. Why was he offering her money? Where does he get it from? She patted the purse inside her trouser pocket, she'd never had it so plump. She'd only taken a thousand from Tibor. How was she going to buy those shoes, that skirt and blouse with it? How would she explain that at home? That she'd earned it working under Tibor? "Under me, you'll make your-self some beautiful clothes, dearest Majka! That okay by you?" he'd said to her. Ugh! The sharp light from the sky was making her eyes sting. She took out her purse, looked at the ten brown banknotes inside it and suddenly whipped them out, screwed them up and tossed them into the rank grass growing round the pole on the raised bank alongside the road. Ugh! Ivo's a beast. Tibor's another one. How come Ivo knows? How could he have asked her if Tibor had already given her some money? Could Tibor have said something? And what else had he told him? How much had he let on to him, him and Vranovská? She'd been asleep, missed things – and they'd had a lark at her expense, maybe poked fun at her, made jokes about her... Majka leaned against the tubular pole, shuddered and sur-rendered to her anguished memories of Ivan Podhájský. He's a beast and she's just like him, accepting money from Tibor... She swung round the pole like a snake winding itself round a slender tree, glanced at the screwed-up thousand crowns. She surprised herself with a sudden ripple of gratification at the cash she'd dumped.

The bright sky was taking on a bluer hue, the yellow clouds were fading, and the sun was adding a yellow sheen to the green of the trees and the silently standing young corn crop. Nothing stirred, not a breeze blew, there was nothing but the silent cool of the morning lingering along the road.

Inside the willow carr, old Mr Bajkovský had been thinking, eventually he walked up to the road, he looked right and left. He looked back at Lysaňa, who was grazing peacefully, and went slowly across to Majka Štancl. "I say, don't stand here –!"

"Sorry?" she asked, startled. "What do you want? What's going on?"

"I mean..."

"Sorry?"

"Don't stand here," he said again, "don't wait here! On Sundays..." He gestured with his broad hand. "No buses come this way on a Sunday, only plenty of tourist coaches, and they hardly ever stop here. If they do it's above my tangy friend. Some do stop for that. Come down there with me, someone might give you a lift in their car. There'll be no shortage of cars and motorbikes – and they'll begin coming by very soon. You're better off without that gorm– –!"

"Where should I go?"

"There, to my tangy friend!"

"Your tangy friend!"

"Yes!"

"And who's that?"

"You don't know?"

"No!"

"Down there, the mineral spring –"

"And who are you? What are you? What are you doing here?"

"Me?" old Bajkovský evinced some surprise. "I – like – I graze a cow there – and this and that." He pointed his stick at Lysaňa. "That one there."

Below her dark glasses Majka's smooth cheeks were quivering as she gazed into old Bajkovský's reproachful face, filled with a sadness that seemed to be giving way to joy.

"Are you coming?"

"You say there's a spring, and tangy?"

"Indeed so!"

"And why do you call it your tangy friend?"

"People have always called it the tangy one."

Majka disengaged her leg and let go off the creaky pole, arched her supple frame and took a closer look at old Bajkovský. Her lips parted slightly as she looked him up and down a second time.

He smiled, raised his hefty stick and gave the solid concrete roadway a tap. He looked round at Majka and set off back down towards the spring. After a few steps he turned, stopped and spoke to her again. "I meant to help you before, both of you, but when I saw –"

Majka tossed her aching head. "How so?" she asked. "What would you have...?"

"Look, that's my cow grazing there," he said. "She grazes so nicely and quietly, she's the kind of calm, lovely cow you could light a fire under, but I wanted to shout at her, like "Hey up, Lysaňa!", that was just as you were squabbling by the spring –"

"You saw us?"

"Saw, heard, didn't get everything. If I had shouted, you might have been startled, then started laughing and all the anger between you would have blown away like a puff of smoke, smelly smoke... Anger is the devil's stench. But then I told myself that because of that gorm-, that gormless oaf I'd better not do it... He doesn't deserve you anyway. So it strikes me that you can't help people these days, even though you'd like to."

"You want to help people?"

"I'd like to."

"Why though?"

Old Bajkovský offered no response, merely looking at Majka. Her face filled with sorrow and reproach looked thin and brownish, like a drying leaf in autumn. It was shining bright in the red-yellow sunlight. The sun had now risen above

(452)

the horizon and out from behind the yellow clouds with their random patches of grey-blue.

"Why would you –?"

"Ah well, I'm off to join my cow by my tangy friend. Though she's not mine, she's my son's. I've got one son at the cooperative farm, another in Bratislava, and I had another one, but he got killed, one of the fallen..." The old man shrugged, turned and walked off down to the spring.

Majka Štancl stood a while longer, leaning against the tubular pole, surprised at his addressing her. What did he want? Was he bored out here? Bored...? She suddenly sensed that she might have offended him, and she was overwhelmed by the loneliness of the road, the green banks leading down from it, the bus stop and the surrounding fields. People like this man probably don't get bored. He could be right, it probably is a waste hanging around here, there are no buses on a Sunday and someone or other will stop by at the mineral spring... Suddenly she felt thirsty again after the previous night's feasting and the wine and cognac. He wants to help people, she hadn't heard that in ages, and no one was going to help her now. Who would help her at home, at school, at Tibor's? Those beasts? Someone had arrived in the night, she can remember a noisy conversation, as if they were having a row, then Ivo woke her up: "Quick, Majka, we're off to Teplice!" She'd left, she'd felt good in the fresh air and wanted to break the journey here, for Ivo to come to his senses and stop being such a beast. She kept thumping him in the back. He stopped. It was on his account that she'd been to Tibor's countless times previously, on his account she'd larked about with him... and taken the money... Majka Štancl was overcome by loneliness and fear of the road. If only Ivo were to come back... What did he ask her about the money? One thousand crowns is a largish, indeed a very large sum. Enough for some very nice new clothes. Suddenly she felt nauseated by the place she was in, the lonely tubular pole, nauseated also because there in the grass lay the thousand crowns she'd taken from Tibor, and she at once became afraid that they would give her away, reveal everything, the night at Tibor's, the night when she'd taken money from him, and she drew away from the pole, meaning to leave. She'd go to the old man, ask him whether a bus or a car might be coming... He'd said something would... She'd ask him anyway. She drew further away, gave a shrug and suddenly thinking that she really was not a practical person and extremely stupid, she bent down into the grass, picked up the thousand crowns, put them in her trouser pocket and walked slowly down the path for about twenty paces to find old Mr Bajkovský, and having reached the grassy area around the spring she found him sitting on one corner of the concrete block. Majka leant against another.

"I've been coming here for a very long time now," he said. "I lease this patch from the council. And you are what?"

"Me? A student."

"A student? And is he also a student, the – that gormless oaf of yours?"

"No."

"No?"

"He's a general manager."

"A general manager? What does he generally manage?"

"The borough parks and gardens."

"Good grief! And what's to become of you?"

"No idea."

"How so?"

"It's all one to me."

"All one?"

"They've got something lined up for me."

"And how do they do that, line something up?"

She didn't reply. She was pleased the old boy had called Podhájsky a gormless oaf, though it sounded a bit odd coming from him. To her, old Bajkovský smacked of countryside and cowshed. She held her face up to the sun, which made it go yellowish and pinkish, and in those wide, dark glasses before her eyes, she saw the sun, the clouds and the azure sky gleam as in tiny mirrors. What is her father going to do? she wondered in a fit of fear such as she hadn't had since the moment, the previous afternoon, a Saturday, when she'd gone to see Podhájsky. Maybe he's done something already. She shrugged. Maybe he's had Tibor's den of vice turned over already. He's forever saying what a strange blighter Tibor Kornel is, that they should check out his flat, he spent half of yesterday blustering, but by morning nothing had come of it. It had been fun, fabulous bikinis, and not for the first time, Tibor fancies her, if only she could be a bit more practical... That would be great! Ugh! She took the money from Tibor and Ivo also knows about it... If only Tibor... Why did Ivo ask her about the money, why did Tibor offer her money? A lot of money, he said he'd give her. If they'd come to check out his flat... if they'd found them all there... She's got some money from him... At her throat, she slowly undid her gaily patterned headscarf, folded it, took off her jacket and put the scarf in one of her jacket pockets. A breeze began to blow. The fresh air passed through her jumper onto her lissom body. She ran both hands through her hair.

Old Mr Bajkovský glanced back at her and saw the breeze causing tufts of her black, close-cropped hair to flutter.

Her hair was catching the glint of the sun. An unpleasant cold washed over her thighs, hips and body with an unpleasant tickling sensation. Tibor's got money, and that's a bit different from a stroll in the park with Ivo, sitting on a bench in the dark with him, listening to him going on about how nice the parks were going to be, there, and over there, and around the new housing estate. A bit different from day trips to Teplice or this tangy natural spring here. She'd got drunk, Tibor had taken photos of her in the nude, she was laughing with her hands over her eyes, one hand over her eyes, the other over her mouth... Spotlights, sit like this, lie down like this – she'd seen photos like these before, some of the boys at college have got entire collections of them. Could be that Tibor produces them in bulk, sells them, they say he deals in all sorts of stuff. Maybe he'll start dealing in photos as well, but she has to be practical. She slipped her green bag from her shoulder, hung it on the metal spout jutting out of the concrete block and stared at the water streaming out of it onto the clean stones below. "... all sorts of people show up here," she suddenly registered that the old man was speaking, "really, all sorts, on a Sunday, like this, though not this early. And how come you were off on a day trip so early in the day? Have you got a watch? What's the time?" Majka raise her slender hand. "Quarter past four."

"That really is early –"

She yawned, covered her mouth with her hand and thought back to the yard filled with the remains of rusty old cars and motorbikes, and to the nice, beautifully furnished flat where her friend Tibor Kornel lived, and to the vast wall, painted yellow. In her mind's eye she could see the overpainted black letters that read MICHAL KORNEL CAR & MOTOR-BIKE SERVICE trying to break through off the yellow wall, and her mind turned to Tibor Kornel. The black moustaches sticking out both ways from under his nose. She recalled her two classmates, Zuz and Mia, brought along to Tibor's by Ivo. They'd disappeared somewhere with her friends, Pedro and Jack, they'd been, then come back, got drunk, she'd got drunk, Tibor took some nude photos of her... He smelled of petrol – and in the next room was Ivo with Vranovská... Could have been that Zuz and Mia were in a third room with Pedro and Jack. You went and got drunk, Majka, on account of Ivo... But, come to think of it, why *had* they had to leave on a day trip so very early? Someone had come, everything sprang into life, came back to life... "Quick, Majka, we have to get cracking, it's already daylight!" Ivo said, and she had to go with him, though she felt so good on the sofa, so good as she sought to repel that obnoxious sleep. Sleep had come, horrible it was, and when, not long after, Ivo came to wake her, it was as bitter as coffee that's gone cold... She took the money, a large, very large sum, a thousand crowns – and Ivo knows about it, maybe he's after it, maybe he'd have hit her if... She yawned again, without covering her mouth this time. "You saw us here?"

"I did," old Mr Bajkovský said, "Why was that gormless oaf going to hit you?"

"We'd had," Majka gave a shrug and yawned, "we'd had a row."

"You really haven't had much sleep," said old Mr Bajkovský in a tone of surprise, and he began packing tobacco into his curly pipe. "Well, it's like I said, we get all sorts coming here – there was one time, autumn it was –"

Majka yawned.

"Goodness, you really haven't had much sleep, getting up so early for a day out – listen, do you mind if I ask...?" She must be unhappy, having split up with that gormless oaf, he thought. "Do you regret it?"

"Why? Regret what?"

"Breaking up."

"Why do you ask?"

"It strikes me that people who come here are on the whole jollier than you. "

"I'm regretting nothing."

"And do you like it here?" old Mr Bajkovský asked after a pause. "Here by my tangy friend?"

"Here? Yes, it's nice, for spending the odd moment. I do come here, now and again, used to come here."

"You?"

"I've never seen you here before."

"Perhaps you just didn't spot me."

"You could be right, it really is a nice spot, lots of people come here – and one autumn, the year that's inscribed here on my tangy friend –"

"Where?"

"Here, written into the concrete," said old Mr Bajkovský, pointing his stick at it, "here's the inscription, our mason did it, Ondrkál from Koštice, he's the one who made this concrete

(457)

surround, but he's a... A case of the work matching the man. It was then that –"

"And what does it say?"

"Just look!"

Majka bent down towards the stream of water, supported herself on the metal spout and began to guzzle. She drank for quite some time. She was thirsty after the cognac, wine, cigarettes, black coffee and a sleepless night, she was thirsty from fatigue, indignity and her raging disgust at Tibor Kornel and Ivan Podhájsky. She took two steps back from the concrete block and looked at the letters and numbers "AD 1944" carved into the concrete. She pushed her dark glasses closer to her eyes and re-read the date. "What's that about?"

"What? What do you mean?"

"Why did you put it there?" Majka Štancl smacked the concrete with her little hand. "Is it when the water began to flow?"

"No."

"Or did something happen here?"

"You've no idea what might have happened here?" Old Bajkovský's reproachful, sunken eyes gleamed in the yellow sunlight. He sat on the concrete block, holding his pipe and tobacco pouch in one hand and dangling his stick from the other. Suddenly he raised his feet in their large boots and struck the concrete with his heels. He was overcome with sorrow for the stranger he'd given his bread to. Ondro, poor lad – he, too, had fallen that same year, the Germans had killed him somewhere in the mountains and he'd never been able to discover the circumstances. Why couldn't the stranger have been his son? Losing a son as if he's just vanished into thin air, that's horrible – this lass here, she's not a happy person, and an unhappy person may be less unhappy if they learn of an even greater misfortune, but it won't be easy to tell her a story about some strange, unknown person who got killed here... Why couldn't the stranger be his son for now at least...? And maybe a person feels better if he can at least see his son dead. Why couldn't the stranger have been his son? Maybe they both met the same end. "You've still no idea what might have happened here?"

"I do now."

"Well –"

"And what exactly did happen here?" Majka Štancl didn't wait to hear what the old man would tell her, she'd suddenly felt hungry, removed her bag from the concrete block, unpacked it to find something to eat, took from it a little packet, a ham sandwich wrapped in a paper serviette, and her hands began to shake. Her thin fingers twitched. She tried to clench them, but they wouldn't stop. Under the sandwich she'd spotted the money, lots of it, lots of smoothed-out, unfolded 100-crown notes. No longer held down by the sandwich, the notes bobbed up. "I say, Granfer," she quietly asked in consternation, "do you fancy a bite?"

"You suddenly feeling peckish?"

"Yes."

"That's my tangy friend here, always whets the appetite – my son as well one time, in the autumn it was – comes here thin as a rake, completely spent. He crawls across the road there, has a piece of wood in his hand, nothing on him except some tattered trousers and a ragged shirt, comes down to my tangy friend here and suddenly starts to drink, and then he got hungry –"

"Don't you want a bite?"

"A bite?"

"Yes," said Majka, stifled by fear and with her mind on Tibor Kornel and Ivan Podhájsky, "a bite to eat. I've got plenty and I shan't be going on any day trip now. We were supposed to be going to Teplice –"

"Aah, I haven't got any teeth."

"Why don't you see a doctor?"

"Where would I find that kind of money?"

The general twittering was interrupted by the low- and high-pitched calls of a golden oriole, which let out two squawks as if clearing its throat. The aspen leaves trembled in the light breeze, and the birches gently waved their dangling branches.

Majka tore open the paper serviette round her sandwich.

"Do you," old Bajkovský began, "do you have a mother, and father?"

"Yes."

"I also had a son, called Ondro –"

Majka heaved a sigh.

Old Bajkovský looked round at her, mystified, and Majka began to remove the paper serviette from her sandwich. She put her hand in her bag and covered the money with it, she got hold of it, couldn't get her hand round it properly and shuddered. Her sore head began to buzz with the sounds of the night before, the voices, one low voice came over clearly, Tibor's, whispering: "I'd give you money, Majka, okay? Take it, hide it, don't mention it to anyone, Majka!" – "I don't want it." – "You don't, don't you need it?" – "No, I don't want it, I don't want it." – "Dear sweet Majka, take it, you can just look after it for me – and if you needed some..." – "You've given me some already! You..." She kept on saying "No, I don't want it, I don't want it!", but, probably after she fell asleep, he'd put it in her bag. Here. Maybe he'd made a mistake, meant to give it to Ivo. Perhaps that's why Ivo asked her. Cars, cars, car parts, they'd gone on and on about them, vast sums of money... Possibly Tibor didn't want to have so much lying about the house. Someone came... Then the party broke up, suddenly, all of a sudden, and they fled. She didn't even say good-bye to Tibor. Ivo had woken her up since she'd fallen asleep on the sofa. That's why he'd asked her whether Tibor had given her some money, a largish sum... During the night, as day was breaking, someone had come – perhaps to tell Tibor something had gone wrong... Could have been the police, as her father had threatened, perhaps Vranovská had spilled the beans, after all, how could she have been happy to see her and Zuz and Mia there, all having a good time...? Tibor certainly wouldn't want to have the money lying about the house... a fat wad she could hardly get her long, thin fingers round, pressed it down the best she could, and as the old man stared into the willows and at his cow and was going on about his son, how he'd been waiting for him in the willow carr and how he'd brought his son some bread, bacon and a lump of curd cheese so he'd have something to eat on his way to join the partisans, and a coat so he'd have something to wear, she took the money from her bag and dropped it on the concrete block. It slipped off the concrete and ended up in the grass next to it. With a sense of relief she took a bite out of her shrivelled ham sandwich, chewed it laboriously and swallowed it down. From her trouser pocket she took the thousand crowns, tossed them down with the other money and listened to what the old man was saying.

" – with this stick," he was saying, and he lifted his hefty stick up a bit so that she could register it, "with this stick they got him round the neck, dragged him by it out of these trees like a sheep onto the open grass and shot him. He was lying here face down on the grass, three holes in his head, three in his back, the grass soaked in blood. And this stick of mine still on his neck. I removed it from him, then didn't know what to do. If only he hadn't stopped by my tangy friend, if only he hadn't drunk from it, if only I hadn't sent him here into the willow carr, what am I talking about, sent, I carried him, he was as light as a feather, if only I hadn't gone off to Koštice to get some bread, bacon and curd cheese and a coat, perhaps nothing would have happened to him... I shouldn't have left him here, I should have taken him, piggy-back if need be, he being as light as a feather, and carried him to Koštice and hidden him away somewhere. Then nothing would have happened to him..." Old Bajkovský fell silent; he looked at Majka.

She was slowly eating her sandwich staring up over the willow carr. Her whole body was trembling with fear, she was only listening to Bajkovský with half an ear, so as to know whether he'd stopped speaking or not. She was trying to control her feelings, but she was glad that he'd rid her of the loneliness, that he'd called to her. If only there wasn't the money... Should she run? But where to? Something must have happened during the night... How come she doesn't know, can't remember a thing? "Do you think someone will come?" she asked.

"Bound to."

"And do you think they'd take me home or –"

"I'm sure they will if they've got room. I've witnessed that on more than one occasion... And who wouldn't be happy to have you in his car? A nice lass like you... Well, that's the way it was and this tangy spring really ought to be streaming out from a nicer top, and there ought to be a proper sign like they have in most places. It bothers me and that's why I'm unhappy, and you... Honestly, all kinds of people come here – see, here we go," he said and lapsed into silence, a car was approaching. "Here we go, they'll be tapping the water into bottles and demijohns."

"Do you think someone will come?"

"Bound to, even now –"

They both looked round.

A blue car passed along the road above them, its brakes squealed and the car stopped.

A moment later, two men got out, both wearing grey, fairly crumpled trousers, one in a brown shirt, one in a green one, Melich and Vavrík, former classmates of Majka's father, construction company engineers who'd recently moved to the town and had been working for over a month on the construction of a factory that was going to produce sections for prefabricated housing units.

Melich trotted down to the mineral spring and Vavrík, having slammed the car door, ran down after him. "Nice, is it, the water?" Melich asked, smiling broadly at Majka and old Mr Bajkovský and thinking: We never thought we'd find you here, Majka lass, we thought we'd find you in Teplice. "Nice, is it? May I? Can I have a sip?"

"It is nice, indeed so," Mr Bajkovský assured Melich. "There's many have said so."

From inside the car, which was parked on the road not far from the spring, gathering warmth from the sun and resonating to the sound of lively morning music coming from the car radio, the conversation going on beside the spring wasn't audible, and Majka's father, Jozef Štancl, was watching Melich, Vavrík, his daughter and the elderly stranger, waiting and on edge. He'd sent them after her, having spotted her down by the mineral spring. He himself hadn't wanted to go down there in case she fled at the sight of him. She doesn't know Melich and Vavrík, maybe she'll let herself be talked into the car. They might invite her into the car, or force her... She'd have fled at the sight of him, given that actually... Štancl thrust his fists into the soft car seat, glanced about the car's interior, then looked back at Majka. As it was, she was already trying to get away from home, from him, whether because he was so strict, or because they were so short of things. He watched Majka as she stared blankly ahead, and would have loved to hear what was being said down there beside the spring. The radio was bombarding him with plinky-plonky music, giving him earache and a headache and being really quite offensive.

"What are you doing out here so early in the day?" Melich asked, running his eyes over the concrete block and back to Majka Štancl, he would have liked to say more to her, but held back. Dear Majka, he thought to himself, your father's in the car, he spotted you here. He thought, we all thought, you'd be in Teplice, and we've already looked for you all over town, couldn't find you, so we set off to look for you in Teplice. Kornel's flat's crawling with police... It's lucky your father spotted you. We can easily nab you and haul you back to the car. They've bagged your gang, my dear Majka. Kornel won't be buying any more cars in other people's names, or building any more houses in other people's names. "How long have you been here?" Melich asked old Mr Bajkovský. "So early in the day! There's not a living soul in sight yet." You, Majka, might not have a clue, he was thinking, I'm pretty sure you don't have a clue what you've got yourself into. Kornel likes messing about with people like you, but his brother's blown the whistle on him. Last night it was, allegedly because he wouldn't lend him the money to buy a car. They had a row. "Not a soul in sight," said Melich, "and you here like this –"

Old Bajkovský stopped filling his pipe.

Majka Štancl rested her ebow on her green canvas bag, where it lay on top of the concrete block, and slowly, with some distaste, chewed at her shrivelled ham sandwich. She was looking at Melich. Her red lips, with white crumbs sticking to them, were quivering. She was overwrought and worried that one of them might spot the money.

"What are you doing here?"

"Me," old Bajkovský replied in a low voice, "I've been here ages, I graze my cow here, Lysaňa." He pointed his stick in her direction. She was grazing calmly, her head to the ground, plucking at the short grass. "I've been here ages, since about three I reckon –"

"How come you get up so early, old man?"

"Oh, you know, I couldn't sleep and my head was full of all sorts, so in the end I got up and decided to bring the cow out to graze. I've had this patch on lease from the council for a long time now."

"And you too?"

"Sorry?" Majka Štancl parted her lipstick-red lips. "What was that?"

"You couldn't sleep either?"

"I'm on a day out."

"A day out? This early? Alone?"

"Yes – not that that's any business of yours."

"All right, all right," said Melich, "I was just making polite conversation. Okay? My apologies!"

"Well, Granfer, it must be nice grazing your cow in such pretty company," said Vavrík, "I get it, the only reason you didn't let the cooperatve farm have her was so you could enjoy the odd chat with pretty girls."

"The cow and the cooperative?"

"That's what I said."

"My last one?" old Bajkovský queried. "Do you suppose my bride would enjoy milking a tractor?"

Melich laughed.

Majka gazed idly at the yellowing green of the alders, the willows and the grass. The clearing round the mineral spring was growing warm in the sun, sparkling with dew that was starting to steam. It left Majka stifled as the air around deteriorated.

Vavrík fished his cigarettes out of his sweat-soaked shirt, lit up and offered one to Melich. They both smoked as they watched the old man and Majka. Old Bajkovský set his short curly pipe between his sunken lips, lit it and blew out three thin clouds of grey smoke, slightly put out by the man in the green shirt, who was making fun of him, and Majka Štancl went back, slowly and with some distaste, to her shrivelled ham sandwich. She was shaking with fatigue, she had an urge to yawn, but stifled it. The bread scratched her gums.

"And where are you going for your day out?"

She made no reply, just went on eating, slowly.

"The young lady came by," old Mr Bajkovský said, "she came by, stayed, she'd been in an argument and I thought –"

"How did you get here?" Vavrík asked Majka. "On foot?"

"Of course not," said old Bajkovský, "have you only just woken up, sir? People like her don't come here on foot, they come on motorbikes or by car, like you. I reckon the last person to visit my tangy friend on foot was my son, Ondro, poor fellow – they were chasing him, caught up with him here and killed him. Since that day I've never known anyone arrive on foot, today I'm the only one who comes on foot, today everyone's in such a tearing hurry, driving past on their bikes and in their cars, and I'd like to ask you, sir, do people know where they're in such a rush to? Where were you in such a rush to, in that car of yours? You didn't half brake hard, what a screech!"

Vavrík said nothing, nor did Melich.

The breeze grew stronger, ruffling Melich's greying hair. It made the loose ribbon on Mr Bajkovský's old grey hat flap.

With difficulty, Majka Štancl swallowed a chunk of only half-chewed bread.

Štancl could see her from the car. His whole body was on edge. He felt he'd been waiting for her for an inordinate length of time. Why didn't they just grab her and bring her back...? He made to get out of the car. He'd leap out, run down there, sieze her by the hair, throw her to the ground and haul her back. He was suddenly overcome by a really odd urge, not to be there, for them to bring her home, but for him not to be anywhere near, for Majka not to see him now. If only he could take care of her, but without ever being seen by her. She hates him – but whose fault is it that Kornel...? How can Kornel still be at it, today, of all times...? He wangles the sale of building plots for people, and building materials, makes a fortune from it, he's said to be making so much money he doesn't know what to do with it... He's got rid of his wife and young son, and lives in what was his father's large flat at the edge of town, invites girls along and has a lot of fun with them... How's it all possible? And there's no one, there's been no one, nowhere, to turn to, but last night they turned Kornel's henhouse upside down – and here was he, having to catch his own offspring in the middle of nowhere. If he steps out and she spots him, Majka will be off like a shot and they'll have to try and catch her. No, he can't do that to her... People would make her a laughing-stock, that's how self-serving they are, no better than Kornel. Štancl seized the door handle, gripped it hard, pressed it down. Once more and the door will open –

"The young lady got into an argument with some gormless oaf," old Mr Bajkovský said, standing next to the spring. He looked at Melich and wanted to ask him to take her in his car, "so I was thinking, like, I'd ask you..." He fell silent.

Melich looked at Majka. Dear Majka, he was thinking, we ought to be off! Your dad must be getting very impatient in the car, and your mum's at home, probably in tears... So let's be going. He opened his mouth wide, smiled at Majka's thin quivering fingers as she held her ham sandwich up to her mouth. "Did you come here by motorbike?" he demanded to know, and following a pause he bellowed at her: "Who with? Alone? You're Majka Štancl, aren't you?"

"Yes," she spluttered, her mouth again full of shrivelled bread. "Yes, and –"

Old Mr Bajkovský removed his pipe.

"And where is the bike?"

"It left."

"And who did you come with?"

"Wait, ehm, just wait a moment, sir," said the old man. "This young lady arrived here with some gormless oaf and they got into a row – and that's how I got to thinking, see, if you might be good enough to give her a lift. What can she do, left to her own devices here? And now you're shouting a her, kicking up a rumpus –"

"Who did you come with?"

"A friend," Majka Štancl replied. "Not that that's any business of yours! Who are you anyway?"

"Me? My name's Melich and this is my colleague, Mr Vavrík, not that that matters. No, it doesn't – but something else does. What's your friend's name? Ivan Podhájsky?"

Majka stopped chewing.

"Where's he gone?"

"That way," said pointing along the road. "I don't know, Teplice, I expect."

"When was that?"

"About fifteen, twenty minutes ago."

"You're coming with us!" he said sharply. "This minute!"

Majka Štancl went rigid, and suddenly she felt doused in a sense of relief at the chance to escape from Kornel's money. She hesitated briefly, then hung the strap of her green canvas bag with its polythene wrapper on her shoulder, looked back fearfully at the concrete block and walking ahead of Melich and Vavrík, she walked slowly towards the car up the path leading from the mineral spring to the road.

Old Mr Bajkovský stepped down from the concrete block and turned slowly to follow them with his gaze.

Majka opened the car door, let out a yelp, almost leapt right back, but got in because her father was pulling her in towards him.

"Come on, Majka," he said as he reached behind her for the door handle. "Don't be afraid, I've got some cash on me, we're heading for Teplice, where we might..." Štancl was at a loss for what else to say.

Majka wiped her cheeks below her mirrored sunglasses.

The car's back doors slammed shut, both front doors slammed shut, the car set off and the breeze blew the grey exhaust fumes off the road.

"Hm!" old Bajkovský grunted. "What weird day tourists they were!" He walked up to the road and briefly gazed after the blue car. It grew smaller and smaller down the grey belt of concrete, passing out of sight until it disappeared for good. The old man turned, went back down to the concrete block and the stream of mineral water and entered the willow carr. He came to a halt, shook his green-and-brown-trousered legs, and leaned on his hefty stick. He stared ahead with his sunken eyes, his drooping lips and his sad, disapproving face. "A shame I told her all that stuff," he said to himself. "And a shame I brought poor Ondro into it, a shame as well about the poor fellow they killed here – and it would have been a shame if I'd shouted at Lysaňa to get them to make up. It's a shame people like that come anywhere near my tangy friend... Ah, my dear tangy friend! I went and told her everything as it was, and wasn't. One should tell these things only to oneself, not that there's any point in it." He stood in the carr, lost in thought, set his short curly pipe between his lips and lit it. He blew out some grey smoke, took another puff and blew out some more. "That poor fellow, whoever he was, was lying here in the grass, covered in blood, holes in his head, holes in his back, and this stick on his neck, dragged him out of here like a sheep, they did, poor chap... Shot through the head, he was, and through one side of his glasses. And this lot! Charging around on their motorbikes and in their cars like madmen – a great way for a madman in a car or on a motorbike to come a cropper." Old Mr Bajkovský remained standing there in the willow carr for quite some time.

The verdant Sunday morning was ablaze with the light of the sun, which had now risen well above the horizon and the clouds, and the fields, trees, forests, hills and knolls were all gleaming green. Vapor was rising from the clearing, the willows and the alders beside the mineral spring, the sparkling dew was drying off, and a shrike flew down among the willows, bobbed about and flew off, two collared doves flew over the mineral spring, a stripy hoopoe flew over the road with its bobbing flight, a black grass snake ran across the grass beyond the carr and slithered into the brook. Midges twinkled in the sunlight. Next to the concrete block, the breeze began to flutter a number of banknotes this way and that, like the pages of a book.

All was peaceful around the Koštice mineral spring, the air was filled with ceaseless birdsong, interrupted from a distance by the cuckooing of a cuckoo and the hoo-hoo-hoo of a hoopoe, the silence overlay the birdsong, the patter of the water among the clean, washed stones and its trickling along the brook, and old Mr Bajkovský, standing there in the willow carr, felt as he if were drowning in memories of his son, Ondro, and of the stranger to whom he'd once given some bread beside the acidy spring. His tangy friend, at least his tangy friend ought on their behalf to be spouting from a much nicer header. Not this thing. People might give more thought to many different things if it was a proper wellhead with a sign over it like they have in other places. Getting oneself killed by Germans, that's no laughing matter – and today people go charging about on motorbikes and in cars. Goodness knows where they're in such a hurry to get to! Once upon a time a poor beggar came along and summoned my tangy friend out of the earth with his stick, and if it had a nice surround to it, who knows how many people's sight it might restore even today. What was the matter with that girl today? It was like her very stomach was shaking with fear! All was peaceful around old Mr Bajkovský and the clear sky overhead shone with the blue tone of June, reaching up high, and the air beneath the silence was all a-twitter with birdsong and babbling with the mineral spring and the brook. Old man Bajkovský stood in the willow carr, swaying on his legs, shuffling from one foot to the other, leaning on his stick until, after quite a while, he started as a red motorcycle stopped above the mineral spring.

A young man in a shepherd check coat and wearing huge brown-and-red goggles got off the bike; it was the general manager of the borough parks and gardens, Ivan Podhájsky. "Hi there!"

"Yes?"

"Granfer!"

Old Mr Bajkovský stood up straight.

"I say, old man!" Podhájsky called down from the road. "I say, have you seen –?"

"What?"

"Did you happen to see a young lady? If so, do you know which way she went?"

The old man came out of the willow carr. "What?"

"Where's the young lady? Where's she gone?"

"Ah, well, sir," he replied. "She got picked up. Two gormless oafs like – they came by car and took her with them... They shouted at her and kicked up quite a rumpus, made this whole place echo. Count yourself lucky you weren't here. They might have grabbed you too. Just get on your bike and be off!"

Podhájsky mounted his bike. He suddenly felt so weary, couldn't stop thinking about the previous night, when Tibor Kornel's brother had come to see him, they'd got into a row about money. Must have been him who blew the gaff, thought Podhajsky, meaning the brother. Did Kornel also give some money to Majka? If so, how much? Will Majka keep her mouth shut? The engine was throbbing away beneath Ivan Podhájsky like an uneasy, sick heart, making the bike and the man shake. Podhájsky engaged the clutch, turned the bike round and left.

Bajkovský watched until he disappeared from sight. It looked as if the gormless oaf had been swallowed up by the road. He glanced at his cow. She was grazing peacefully. He glanced up at the road, high above the babbling mineral spring, and suddenly he froze, startled, when his eyes settled on some banknotes poking out of the grass, next to the concrete block, and being ruffled by the breeze. "What's this?" He came out of the trees, walked slowly over to the concrete block and stood over the money. The pile of brown notes gave him quite a turn. "Good God!" he exclaimed. "Who's gone and lost you lot?"

The sheaves of countless banknotes were flipping this way and that, towards him, away from him.

"So much? Who's gone and lost you then?" He bent down, picked up the bundle of the notes, including a thousand-crown one. Even his broad hands could barely hold them all. He looked about him, could see no one, nothing, only his son's cow. "Who's gone and lost so much of you, I wonder? The young lady...?" He removed his hat, didn't even count the money, stuffed it all inside his hat and set it back on his head. He pulled it down tight back and front, and a hump formed in the middle. "Only those fellows can have lost you, there's no dew on you, and they must know I'm from Koštice, so they'll be back to collect you. All sorts come here to visit my tangy friend. It must be funny money, easy come, easy go, to be left lying here like this."

A golden oriole broke into the general birdsong, uttered a noisy squawk, then in a flash of black and yellow it shot down towards the brook, flew back up and landed in a birch tree beside the road. It let out two more squawks.

A moment later, old Mr Bajkovský suddenly felt as if he'd gone completely deaf. He could now hear neither the morning birdsong, nor the distant, diminishing sound of Podhájsky's motorbike, he turned and, completely crushed with fear because of the money, walked over to his cow, stroked it with his stick and said: "Let's go, eh, Lysaňa, let's go." Lysaňa raised her head from the ground, flicking away some flies. "No, no! Hey-hey!" he told her. She went back to her grazing. No! he thought. Must stay here! That lass may show up, she might come back, the money's probably hers. Poor thing, she has to have it back. A good thing I didn't let that gormless oaf have it... No, no, I must wait here! He stood beside the mineral spring in the willow carr, holding his head erect, afraid that the money was mounting on top of his head, making his hat swell out and threatening to make it fall off. He wondered about the chairman of the local national committee. Perhaps he should pay him a visit and hand the money over to him... "Suppose no one were to show up, like, to ask about the money," he muttered, taking fright at his own quiet words, "suppose they didn't, my that would be something! What it would mean to the lads, one would do his house up posh like, one would build himself a new one, and it would come in quite handy even for the one in Bratislava..." He stayed by the mineral spring, waiting for people, and not in vain, he chatted to many of the arrivals about all manner of things, and his mind was fixed constantly on Ondro, and on the stranger, whom Sturmmann Knopp had dragged out of the willow carr by his stick like a dead sheep and had him shot, and after it got very hot and Lysaňa grew restless, disinclined to graze, and kept flicking the flies away with her tail, head, ears and feet, he went off home, completely at a loss.

* * *

Not a year had passed and now, there by the Koštice mineral spring, the men of Koštice were putting their heads together, and they even had an architect with them. Over the mineral spring there was to be a nice new header of grey stone. Mostly they put their heads together without saying much. They listened to the June birdsong, the sound of all kinds of traffic on the road, and still they hadn't fathomed how "Old Dry-thorn Jano", poor chap, dead by now, had come by so much money that he could leave, on his deathbed, over fifty thousand crowns for the construction of a stone header with a sign as a memorial to an anonymous stranger and Jozef Antal, Andrej Bajkovský and Ján Horečný. The unknown man had perished here, while the other three, no one knew where. But they had all died in the same year. The men mostly put their heads together without saying much, because it was all settled and all that was left was to get the work started. They'd only come for a last look and to consider the matter as a whole and within the context of the site.

"Not like that!"

"Eh?"

"No, I'm telling you chaps, it won't look right."

They all turned towards the short figure in a grey shirt and faded blue trousers, Ondrkál, the Koštice mason who had once boxed the spring in with his massive concrete block.

Ondrkál looked about him and treated them all to the nasty smirk with which his little eyes and wizened mouth were charged. "Not like that!"

"Why not?"

"It won't look right, I tell you, it'll look horrible!"

"So what then?"

Ondrkál gave a shrug, left the men and ambled off towards the spouting mineral water and then took a further fifteen steps towards the carr. "Why should a spring come spouting from among the dead?" he snapped. "Have it your own way, for all I care," he said after a pause, "but I'd have thought that for the sum the late Old Dry-thorn Jano left we should cap the spring in stone – and for the money made available by the council we should erect a nice memorial here, with a plaque on it!" Ondrkál pointed to the spot where people from Koštice had found Freystatt's corpse. "And there can be another plaque there," he said, pointing to a spot above the concrete block, "yes, another one there. And let it say that – let that one be all about the beggar and the blind girl!" Ondrkál gave a shrug and left.

The men of Koštice watched as he strode slowly away, they were smiling, but the one thought that passed from one to the next was that Ondrkál was right. As they put their heads together again, this time they did have things to say, that it really would be best to furnish the spring with a stone cap and to erect a memorial with a plaque.

p. 8: *the Uprising is being joined by deserters* – Shorthand for the Slovak National Uprising against the Nazi German occupation of the nominally independent, fascist Slovak State towards the end of World War II.

p. 36: *"They had an exemption," he said, "from Tiso."* – Jozef Gašpar Tiso (1887–1947), a Slovak Catholic priest, who became the wartime president of the fascist Slovak Republic, a client state of Nazi Germany. After the war, in 1947, he was tried for a range of war crimes committed under his auspices and executed for treason in Bratislava.

p. 106: *the brownish-purple stalks and grey-green foliage of a thing they called 'old maid'* – It has not proved possible to identify what plant is meant, possibly a trailing tradescantia. The Slovak folk name 'old maid' is also applied to certain other plants, including hydrangea, clearly not the case here.

p. 113: *She'd been given her Christian name by a priest who'd christened a number of girls in his parish with the same name, both under the monarchy and later.* – So christened for love of Princess Zita of Bourbon-Parma (1892–1989), wife of Charles I, the last monarch of Austria-Hungary. As such, she was the last Empress of Austria (the 'monarchy' in this sentence) and Queen of Hungary. For much more on this fascinating woman, including the fact that she completed her education at a convent on the Isle of Wight, and had been exiled to Switzerland in 1919 with the help of a detachment of British soldiers following an order from King George V, see https://en.wikipedia.org/wiki/Zita_of_Bourbon-Parma (accessed 05.09.2023).

p. 114: *"Herr Oberleutnant," Staff Sergeant Obmann, commander of the unit* – I have retained, as in the original, the German titles and forms of address of the various German officers in direct speech, but in the narrative I use throughout the established English equivalent ranks, any literal translations being mostly cumbersome in the extreme. The English equivalents are drawn from https://en.wikipedia.org/wiki/Ranks_and_insignia_of_the_Waffen-SS.

p. 115: *Hals was distressed that the Germans were losing the war, for which he blamed the Blockwarts, those snoops* – The job of the Blockleiter, later Blockwart, 'block warden' was exactly as described; the word outlived the war to mean, in today's German, snoop.

p. 119: *"You'll be getting plenty of flour, lard and all that, even bacon!"* – Bacon has much more resonance here than in any normal English context. It had been mostly produced in Denmark and exported to Britain, but after the seizure of Denmark by the Germans, the stocks fell prey to them and they then distributed it in countries under occupation according to their own specific regulations. It was, then, something of a novelty. See, for example, the entry in Karel Tauš: Slovník cizích slov, zkratek, novinářských šifer, pseudonymů a časopisů pro čtenáře novin, Blansko: Nakl. Karel Jelínek, 1946, p.57.

p. 140: *couvée* – A brood of newly hatched chicks.

p. 148: *when they were down to their last seventeen hellers* – Heller = 1/100 of a Czechoslovak crown.

p. 151: Krementchuk – A Ukrainian city 90% destroyed by the Germans during the war. It was liberated on 29 September 1943, which is now celebrated as 'City Day'.

p. 179 : *Stargard* – A town about 25 miles west of Szczecin, Poland, for a large part of its history part of the German empire. It is probably best known as the site of various notorious POW and concentration camps during World War II.

p. 179 : *Vlasovites* – Members of the Russian Liberation Army, which, under General Andrey Andreyevich Vlasov (1901–46), broke from and then opposed the Red Army alongside the Germans.

p. 196: *Katzen-Gebirge* – Today's Trzebnickie Hills in today's Polish Silesia.

p. 196: *Kotelnikovo* – A small town near Volgograd/Stalingrad and a German base during the Battle of Stalingrad. It was liberated by the Soviets on 29 December 1942.

p. 229: *"Davay!"* – The imperative of the verb 'give', having various meanings, here basically something like 'Come on, let's have some!'.

p. 230: *"Zdravstvuy, khazyay!"* – 'Hello, man!'

p. 230: *"Kakiye loshadi?"* – 'What kind of horses?'

p. 230: *"Davay, khazyay, v Rakytovce!"* – 'Let's go to Rakytovce, man!'

p. 230: *"Davay, davaj! Gani, gani!"* – 'Let's go. Drive on!'

p. 233: *"Aaaa! Nichevo neboysya, babushka!"* – 'Nothing to fear, gran!'

p. 238: *"Vychadi!"* one of them said to Beta Mitúch, beckoning. *"Vychodite!"* – Both phrases, one singular, one plural, mean 'Come out!'

p. 239: *"Myortvy, ubit. Davay!"* – 'Dead, killed. Come on!'

p. 244: *Karachev* – A small town in Bryansk oblast, Russia, about 240 km east of the frontier with Belarus.

p. 256: *'Davaj chasy!'* – 'Give me your clock.'

p. 256: *'Job tvoju mať! Ty ubila mashinista!'"* – 'Fuck you [actually, 'your mother']! You've killed the driver!' In various slightly different mutations this joke lasted for at least a couple of decades, bolstered in part by encounters with cloddish Russians, lacking in clocks and watches, during the invasion of Czechoslovakia in 1968.

p. 271: *kultprop* – a Soviet-style neologism denoting an officer whose job it was to propagate, promote, steer along Party lines, anything relating to culture, including education.

p. 287: *Martin* – up to 1951 Turčiansky sv. Martin, 'St Martin on the Turiec', a largish town in northern Slovakia and the scene of some major events during the Slovak National Uprising. It was liberated in April 1945 by the 1st Czechoslovak Armoured corps and the Romanian army. Note the appearance of Romanians elsewhere in this volume.

p. 310: *a "green" from Birkenau* – "Criminal" prisoners (Berufsverbrecher – BV), who had been imprisoned as a direct consequence of having committed a forbidden act, or after release from prison wherever the police regarded the sentence imposed by the court as too lenient, had to wear a green triangle; other categories of prisoners wore triangles of other colours. Prisoners in the green category were mostly Germans. See https://www.auschwitz.org/en/history/prisoner-classification/system -of-triangles/

p. 353: *Labour be praised* – The conventional period greeting used by hard-line members of the Czechoslovak Communist Party.

p. 408: *Labour be praised* – See the footnote on p.353.

p. 429: *Spartak* – The popular name of the Škoda 440, Czechoslovakia's first post-war car, prototype introduced in 1953, mass-produced from late 1955. The sub-text here is that in the circumstance of the time such a perfectly ordinary, simple, but prohibitively expensive car could only be afforded by anyone doing very nicely under the new Communist régime: he might be legitimately thought to be a corrupt official, black-marketeer or an illegal dealer in foreign currency; a fourth option, rich relatives abroad, is clearly inapplicable.

AFTERWORD TO ALFONZ BEDNÁR:
THE HOURS AND THE MINUTES

It is little exaggeration to say that the history of modern Slovak fiction begins with the early stories of Alfonz Bednár (1914–89). *The Hours and The Minutes* was first published in Bratislava in 1956, the year of Nikita Khrushchev's 'secret speech', in which the Soviet leader formally acknowledged Stalin's tyranny and opened the way to destalinization in culture and society throughout the Eastern Bloc. While Prague was slow to respond, in Slovakia, more comparably to neighbouring Hungary and Poland, hints of cultural liberalization had been detectable since 1953, not least with the publication of Bednár's first novel, *The Glass Peak* (*Sklený vrch*), in 1954. It was, however, *The Hours and The Minutes* that allowed the new generation of Slovak writers to assert their independence from nationalist and communist propaganda, and to follow Bednár's example in rejecting the ideologization of life in didactic, schematic literature, co-opted in the period by both the Fascist right and Stalinist left, and find more empathetic ways of exploring human fallibility and the complexity of human experience.

The Hours and The Minutes emerges directly from the violence, upheaval and oppression that swept through east-central Europe in the mid-twentieth century and constitutes the most essential literary insight into the end of the Second World War and the onset of Stalinism in Slovakia. On March 14th 1939 Slovakia had, for the first time in history, become at least nominally an independent state, in practice a Fascist puppet state of Nazi Germany, led by a Roman Catholic priest, Jozef Tiso, and his Slovak People's Party. On August 29th 1944, Germany invaded Slovakia to stop the increasingly disruptive activities of groups of resistance fighters – partisans – supported by the USSR. This invasion triggered an uprising by a coalition of anti-Fascist resistance groups and individuals, including both Communists and liberals, which had been planned by exiled representatives of Czechoslovakia in London and Moscow. For two months, the Uprising established a 'free Slovakia' in central Slovakia, governed from the town of Banská Bystrica until it was taken by German forces on October 27th 1944. As depicted in *The Hours and The Minutes*, with the defeat of the Uprising, those who had participated and evaded capture reverted to partisan warfare to facilitate the Soviet advance, disrupt the German retreat, and avenge German reprisals that included local massacres, summary executions and the destruction of villages deemed to be helping the partisans.

While historians may debate the strategic significance and merits of the Uprising domestically and internationally, it quickly became the defining episode in the formation of modern Slovak national identity. Almost exactly a century after the academic, politician and codifier of standard Slovak, Ľudovít Štúr (1815–56), and his followers had first formulated the political demands of an autonomous Slovak nation and organized a failed revolt against Hungarian rule, thousands of Slovaks had ostensibly taken up arms to fight for a non-Fascist, democratic Slovakia. Before and after the restoration of Czechoslovakia in May 1945, this narrative was eagerly adopted by the Communist Party, which cast itself as the architect and driving force of the Uprising and in Slovakia presented its takeover of Czechoslovakia in February 1948 as the ultimate realization of the Uprising's aims. The takeover, however, ushered in a period of Stalinist authoritarianism marked by show trials, politically motivated executions, mass imprisonments and the forced collectivization of agricultural land, ideological gestures that, as Bednár shows in *The Hours and The Minutes*, at local level masked the ordinary settling of scores or covering of tracks.

In each story, Bednár juxtaposes the time of the Uprising and its aftermath with the time of Stalinism in Slovakia. The five stories in *The Hours and The Minutes* trace in parallel the chronology of the period from the Uprising to liberation and from the early months of the Communist takeover to established Stalinism. 'Neighbours' takes place in September 1944, with the Uprising in progress, with an epilogue set in July 1948, several months after the Communist takeover. The central action of 'The Cradle' takes place in February 1945, after the defeat of the Uprising and before the liberation, framed by a description of the protagonist listening to her husband giving evidence in a radio broadcast of a show trial in July 1952. The title story takes place in April 1945, in the final hours and minutes before a village is liberated, framed by an unexpected encounter between the protagonists seven years later. By contrast, the main action of the last two stories, 'Awaiting Completion' and 'The Stone-Capped Spring', takes place in the communist period – in the autumn of 1953 and in June 1956 (with an epilogue set a year later), respectively – with flashbacks to the war.[1]

This technique of confronting the two periods would later be borrowed by Bednár's contemporary, Ladislav Mňačko (1919–94), in *The Taste of Power* (*Ako chutí moc*, 1968), the only Slovak novel from the post-Stalin cultural liberalization published in English by a commercial publisher until 2007. Here, Mňačko, a disillusioned former Stalinist and senior Party journalist, who had fought with the partisans after the Uprising, uses it to highlight the discrepancy between what he perceives as the bold idealism inherent in the Uprising and the flabby corruption of communist Slovakia.[2] Bednár, however, abandons idealism altogether, focusing instead on the harsh, ambiguous reality of both periods as experienced by individuals on the ground. While the Party sought to characterize 1945 and 1948 as 'revolutions', new beginnings that broke with the past, Bednár by contrast highlights continuity: the continuity of memory and of personal qualities, especially weaknesses, the inability to forget past actions, the tendency to repeat mistakes. His characters lack any sense of an overarching purpose or of participating in a collective effort; generally, they find themselves isolated, no course of action seems right, and their own survival becomes the sole aim.

From 1945, Slovak literature had played a dominant role, alongside cinema, journalism, and political rhetoric, in establishing the myth of the Uprising. *The Hours and The Minutes* reads like a

1   The first Slovak edition from 1956 contained the first four stories. 'Awaiting completion' attracted the fiercest criticism from Party ideologues because of its focus on contemporary communist Slovakia and was omitted from the 1962 second edition, which appeared under the generic title *Novellas*, undermining any sense of the collection of stories as a cycle. This edition included 'The Stone-Capped Spring' and a full-length novel, *Cudzí* (Not one of us), both of which had first been published in 1960. For the third, definitive Slovak edition and the Czech translation, both published in 1964, when cultural liberalization was finally gaining pace, 'Awaiting Completion' was reinstated alongside these two texts and the title *The Hours and The Minutes* restored.

2   Mňačko's experience of the German destruction of an east Moravian village as a partisan formed the subject of his first novel, *Death Is Called Engelchen* (Slovak 1959, published in English by the state publisher Artia in Prague in 1961).

systematic repudiation of the components of that myth. The very first scene of the first story, at the height of the Uprising, is marked by doubt and pessimism; the young working-class partisan leader, Štefan Tesár, who conspicuously fails to become a Socialist Realist hero, constantly asks, together with his band: 'What can anyone do here? [...] It's a lost cause!' At the end of the story, Tesár, now a local Party official building the new society, repeats a similar thought to himself. Bednár signals the possibility of a Socialist Realist romance between Tesár and Marka Bernadičová, the only wholly good and brave character in the story, but the prospect peters out in his failure to stand up for her in the face of unjust discrimination by the Party. Her continued persecution perpetuates a falsehood that keeps the local Party chairman in power; we might even read the illegitimacy of that power as emblematic of the illegitimacy of the power of the Party, founded on a false account of the Uprising.

The character who knows the truth about Marka's father is, significantly, the local parish priest, typically a demonized figure in post-war Slovak Socialist literature because of the Catholic Church's role in the Fascist state. This priest, however, while compromised, is shown not only to use his status with the occupying Germans to intercede for local villagers, but also to take the risk of harbouring Marka and a Jewish family when the Germans are hunting them. While Bednár's female characters can essentially be reduced to the stereotypes of either idealized maternal 'madonna' (Marka, Zita in 'The Cradle', Eva in 'Awaiting Completion') or demonized femme-fatale 'whore' figures (Gizela in the title story, Soňa in 'Awaiting Completion'), his distinctive incorporation of female experiences, which began in *The Glass Peak*, tempers the typical masculinity of representations of the Uprising and intensifies the overall emphasis on weakness, vulnerability and loss of agency, as well as a peculiarly feminine form of resilience and the desire to protect and preserve.

Bednár does not depict any unequivocally heroic actions by the partisans. In 'Neighbours', until the final, futile ambush by remnants of the partisan band near the end of the story, in which Tesár loses his left arm, he focuses on the occupying Germans' efforts to suppress the Uprising and wipe out the partisan resistance. In the title story, in the final 'hours and minutes' before long-awaited liberation, partisans unwittingly kill a 'good' German who had deserted the

Wehrmacht and supplied the partisans with dynamite. Kalkbrenner, a farmer, who accepts the principle of collective German guilt for the atrocities of the war, is the most radical example in the cycle of Bednár's replacement of the conventional collective dehumanization of Germans with a few relatively individuated portrayals. Sadistic Germans are the exception; most appear to have been brutalized by war. They share with the Slovak partisans and villagers a sense of confusion and lack of a clear purpose beyond saving their own lives and are sometimes shown acting, or at least wanting to act, humanely. By contrast, Soviet soldiers, typically idealized in post-war literature, are marginal strangers in Bednár's account. Describing an encounter between them and a positively portrayed Slovak livestock farmer, Adam Mitúch, the narrator of the title story notes: 'although Mitúch had heard long ago, from men who had served during the Great War, that it's easy for another Slav to converse with Russians, he wasn't understanding a word they said.' Bednár thus questions the myth of Slav brotherhood reasserted in the Communist period to strengthen Soviet power in the region.

The Hours and The Minutes is one of the very first texts published in the entire Communist bloc to suggest the equivalence of Nazism and Stalinism, a taboo subject since the Party derived its legitimacy from claiming to be the antithesis of Fascism, which it had helped defeat. In 'Neighbours', the priest says pointedly to a local Communist official: 'I'm assuming you're more fair-minded than the Germans', but it turns out that they are not. To the implied reader in 1956, several remarks made about Nazism would seem inescapably applicable to their own times. Adam Mitúch looks forward to the liberation, believing that: 'The Germans would be gone and with them all ills; liars and cheats would go to blazes, and a person could breathe again. There'd be no more spying on people to check what they're saying or thinking.' A German officer, condemning Nazism, promises himself 'never, never again to believe in an Idea because, once you do believe in it, even killing becomes just grinding drudgery whose sheer monotony you need to relieve'. Most tellingly, at the very centre of the cycle, Adam's brother, Jozef, says to his lover, Gizela, about the Slovak puppet state:

'What we've got today, fascism, Gizzie, it's a boundless unfreedom. You yourself know well enough what it is. The heart filled with apprehension, the head with humiliation, the bowed shoulders, the mendacious words or words obtuse and vacuous to the point of blasphemy, a world smashed to pieces, boxed in with borders, the disregard for human dignity and human worth, people in prisons, prison camps, degraded, humiliated, many by now tortured to death, and more than many killed outright. Informers all round. All that is fascism and unfreedom. Today people lie as they speak, they lie in the papers, courts are no longer courts, they take away people's property at will, the papers are censored, telephones are bugged, people are herded into labour like cattle, people torture people, brutalize them...'

Bednár cements the connection by having Gizela reply with words that she will later repeat identically when describing her attitude to communism: 'these days everyone lives by their instincts. To avoid danger. I've also tried to avoid it, still do, and will continue to do so [...] The only way to live today is to let oneself be denounced – or to denounce others.' The continuity between Nazism and Stalinism is demonstrated by the fact that Gizela and Dugas in 'Awaiting Completion', collaborators with the Germans, are embedded in the new society, one as a secret police informer, the other as a local Party functionary.

After the first publication in 1956, Bednár faced attacks from critics for 'discrediting and disrespecting the Uprising and its achievements' and for giving an unremittingly bleak portrayal of Slovak communist society, especially in 'Awaiting Completion'. Responding in early 1958, he rejected these accusations, arguing that it was, on the contrary, those accounts which failed to acknowledge the hardship and pain, the 'dirt, blood, terror [...] hesitation, doubt and betrayal'[3] involved in the Uprising and in building Socialism, that trivialized these 'great episodes' in recent Slovak history. Bednár's ambivalence in the stories, however, is encapsulated in the title of 'Awaiting Completion'. The literal translation of the Slovak title is 'A half-built house', a metaphor presenting the building of Socialism as a work-in-progress, which reflects the shift in the period from triumphalism to the more sober acknowledgement that much work still needed to be done. In the story, the title, however,

3   A. Bednár, 'O dvojakej kritike', Kultúrny život, 13 (1958), 1, p. 3.

refers to two buildings under construction that are unequivocally negative. Dugas's grotesque villa, which causes the sacrilegious uprooting of the village cross, should not be being built at all, while the housing block where Soňa falls down an empty lift shaft to her death, either in an industrial accident, by suicide or because she is pushed, should at best be being built differently. A camp survivor compares the post-war housing estates to concentration camps.

It would therefore be a mistake to align Bednár too straightforwardly with those Czechoslovak writers who in the 1960s embraced Alexander Dubček's 'Socialism with a human face' with the same enthusiasm with which the same writers had once embraced Stalinism. The portrayal of the housing estate reflects Bednár's fundamental preoccupation in *The Hours and The Minutes* with what he presents as the insensitive, even inhuman, rootless and amoral modernity that the war and then the Communist Party import into traditional Slovak life. The Uprising and its aftermath arrive in manifestly pre-industrial rural communities that are terrorized by alien modern weaponry and warfare. The post-war, Communist-period settings are, by contrast, strikingly urban, signalled by technology like planes and wirelesses, and by unhappy, alienated human beings living alone, in dysfunctional nuclear families or fractious, ideologized workplace collectives. The destruction of the traditional Slovak countryside during the twentieth century through modernization and urbanization, and with it a particular approach to life, forms a central theme of Bednár's subsequent work. That approach to life is represented in these stories by the cross, not so much a symbol of explicitly Christian faith as 'a symbol of love and respect for man, and infinite love and respect at that', by the eponymous cradle in the second story, which has been passed around the village for generations to be used by each new baby, by various older peasants who reject their sons' espousal of communism, especially collectivization, and ideological notions like the collective guilt of Germans, by those nurturing female characters who intuitively recognize and selflessly perform their duty to help others, and by the quiet, self-renewing beauty of nature, especially woodland, fleetingly glimpsed and often destroyed amid the violence.

It has become a commonplace to link the changes in fiction from the Eastern Bloc after the death of Stalin to the influence of fashionable Western writers like the Americans Ernest Hemingway and John Steinbeck and French Existentialists Albert Camus and Jean-Paul Sartre, whose politics made them relatively 'acceptable' to Party ideologues as culture liberalized. We can see their influence, for example, in alienated, disillusioned male intellectuals like Jozef Mitúch, an engineer, or Martin Dubovský, a doctor, representatives of a type that would become prominent in literature throughout the bloc in this period, who through university study have become detached from their farming roots and are beset by debilitating, emasculating doubt and indecision.

Bednár was especially familiar with English and American literature because of his work as a translator. Between 1946 and the publication of *The Hours and The Minutes*, he had published Slovak translations of, among others, Sinclair Lewis, Jerome K. Jerome, Jack London, Mark Twain, and Howard Fast's *Spartacus*, and would go on to translate *Robinson Crusoe*, *A Farewell to Arms* and *For Whom The Bell Tolls*, and all Conan Doyle's Sherlock Holmes stories. In a 1968 interview, he observed:

It is essential to go abroad to learn things, that's what every literature has always done. Modern Slovak literature needs to do that more than Slovak literature of earlier times because with the last world war, Slovakia entered modern world history, life in Slovakia became multifaceted in a wholly modern way, and this can no longer be expressed in fiction in the manner to which we were previously accustomed. At one time Slovakia was firmly on the windless side of history, today it is on the windy side, and literature has work to do to make sure it is not blown off completely by a storm.[4]

Perhaps paradoxically, given his criticism of modernity, Bednár's style reflects a desire to modernize Slovak prose, to adapt it to the new conditions in which the language finds itself. In conversation with his daughter, Katarína Kenížová-Bednárová, in the late 1980s, shortly before his death, Bednár scornfully rejects the perception in Slovak literature that ornate, 'lyricized prose' represents the peak of literary achievement, arguing: 'lyricized prose is static prose, it forgets about movement, it neglects it, it neglects the circulation

---

4 'Juliús Vanovič: Antidialógy so slovenskými spisovateľmi' in A. Bednár, *Sklený vrch a iné*, Bratislava, 2008, pp. 568–9.

of action, the flight of fates, it forgets the canter, the gallop of life, it treads water, it stands on the spot.' Bednár, however, insists that his approach to prose writing was not inspired by Hemingway, but rather by the terse language and focus on action he found in Slovak folk ballads, on which he wrote his university dissertation: 'When working on the ballad I felt for the first time a desire to start putting my language into text, to write something epic, without lyrical or lyricized, lyrical-epic relics, contrivances and acrobatics. No summaries, no descriptions, no depictions, no rhetoric, no metaphors, not even that, nor the clustering of metaphor'. In *The Hours and The Minutes*, we can already see the devotion to plot, establishing tension and building towards dramatic denouements that perhaps inspired Bednár's subsequent move into screenwriting. The language encourages the reader to visualize the stories cinematically.

The Hours and The Minutes is a crucial milestone in the history of Slovak literature. With these stories, Bednár created a political and aesthetic space that the next, remarkable, generation of young Slovak writers in the 1960s would exploit to the full, laying the foundations for the extraordinary blossoming of contemporary Slovak writing after the fall of Communism in 1989. It is also a major artistic achievement in its own right, worthy of comparison with the best works written in the period anywhere about the war and its aftermath, and a genuine Slovak classic.

Rajendra Chitnis, Oxford, March 2025

MODERN CZECH CLASSICS

Published titles

Zdeněk Jirotka: *Saturnin* (2003, 2005, 2009, 2013; pb 2016)
Vladislav Vančura: *Summer of Caprice* (2006; pb 2016)
Karel Poláček: *We Were a Handful* (2007; pb 2016)
Bohumil Hrabal: *Pirouettes on a Postage Stamp* (2008)
Karel Michal: *Everyday Spooks* (2008)
Eduard Bass: *The Chattertooth Eleven* (2009)
Jaroslav Hašek: *Behind the Lines: Bugulma and Other Stories* (2012; pb 2016)
Bohumil Hrabal: *Rambling On* (2014; pb 2016)
Ladislav Fuks: *Of Mice and Mooshaber* (2014)
Josef Jedlička: *Midway upon the Journey of Our Life* (2016)
Jaroslav Durych: *God's Rainbow* (2016)
Ladislav Fuks: *The Cremator* (2016)
Bohuslav Reynek: *The Well at Morning* (2017)
Viktor Dyk: *The Pied Piper* (2017)
Jiří R. Pick: *Society for the Prevention of Cruelty to Animals* (2018)
*Views from the Inside: Czech Underground Literature and Culture
(1948–1989)*, ed. M. Machovec (2018)
Ladislav Grosman: *The Shop on Main Street* (2019)
Bohumil Hrabal: *Why I Write? The Early Prose from 1945 to 1952* (2019)
Jiří Pelán: Bohumil Hrabal: A Full-length Portrait (2019)
Martin Machovec: Writing Underground (2019)
Ludvík Vaculík: *A Czech Dreambook* (2019)
Jaroslav Kvapil: *Rusalka* (2020)
Jiří Weil: *Lamentation for 77,297 Victims* (2021)
Vladislav Vančura: *Ploughshares into Swords* (2021)
Siegfried Kapper: *Tales from the Prague Ghetto* (2022)
Jan Zábrana: *The Lesser Histories* (2022)
Jan Procházka: *Ear* (2022)
A World Apart and Other Stories: Czech Women Writers at the Fin de Siècle,
trans. and ed. by Kathleen Hayes (2022)
Libuše Moníková: *Transfigured Night* (2023)
Beyond the World of Men: Women's Fiction at the Czech Fin de Siècle,
trans. and ed. Geoffrey Chew (2024)

Forthcoming

Jiří Weil: *Moscow – Border*
Ivan M. Jirous: *End of the World. Poetry and Prose*
Jan Čep: *Common Rue*
Egon Bondy: *Unsound Siblings*
Jaroslav Hašek: *The Good Soldier Schweik*

*Scholarship

MODERN SLOVAK CLASSICS

Published titles
Ján Johanides: *But Crime Does Punish* (2022)
Ján Rozner: *Seven Days to the Funeral* (2024)
Leopold Lahola: *The Last Thing* (2025)
Alfonz Bednár: *The Hours and The Minutes* (2025)

Forthcoming
František Švantner: *Nevesta hôľ*
Gejza Vámoš: *Atómy Boha*

Printed and bound by CPI Group (UK) Ltd, Croydon, CR0 4YY

02/10/2025

14745772-0001